# WATCHING
## OVER YOU

# LORI FOSTER

# WATCHING OVER YOU

**HQN**®

Recycling programs
for this product may
not exist in your area.

ISBN-13: 978-1-335-42629-1

Watching Over You

This edition published by arrangement with Harlequin Books S.A.

For questions and comments about the quality of this book, please contact us
at CustomerService@Harlequin.com.

HQN
22 Adelaide St. West, 41st Floor
Toronto, Ontario M5H 4E3, Canada
www.Harlequin.com

**Printed in U.S.A.**

To all the readers on my Facebook page,

What a year it has been! Holy smokes, we were overrun with spam—but you all helped me to combat it, and you stuck with me. I can't tell you how much I appreciate that. So many of you are now familiar to me and I look forward to your comments on the various posts. You made the year easier and I want you to know—to really understand—just how much I appreciate you.

Big, big hugs,

*Lori Foster*

# WATCHING
## OVER YOU

# CHAPTER ONE

When Crosby Albertson frowned, he didn't just show displeasure in his incredibly handsome face. He also showed it in the rigid lines of his big body, in his tightened fists and the angle of his wide shoulders, how his feet braced apart and the way the muscles in his thighs flexed.

Honestly, Madison McKenzie thought he was downright scrumptious top to bottom, though now wasn't the best time to be admiring him.

Using her admittedly incredible digital surveillance skills, she'd been shadowing Crosby online for a while now, ever since she realized that *he* was keeping tabs on *her* family.

Granted, her family had made unique choices to combat injustice, specifically every form of human trafficking and forced labor. She and her brothers, under their father's instruction, had become elite fighters weaponized with skill, knowledge and drive.

As a cop, Crosby had somehow caught on to them, despite how she meticulously covered their tracks.

He'd impressed the heck out of her, which wasn't easy to

do—especially after he worked with them to bring down a truly heinous trafficker who'd gotten far too personal.

But Crosby was still a cop through and through, and she and her family still skirted the edges of illegal activity by pursuing their goals without involving the law.

Didn't stop her infatuation with him.

When he found out that she'd ramped up her surveillance of him, he'd likely be annoyed.

That couldn't be helped, though. No other man had fascinated her like Crosby Albertson did, and in her line of work, as her brothers had often pointed out—the hypocrites—she couldn't be too careful. She knew a lot about Crosby already, but now she wanted to know more.

Physically following him today wasn't exactly necessary, but she'd had a little free time, so why not? Never mind that Ridge Trail, Colorado, was experiencing extremely severe weather, with a huge dumping of snow and freezing temps making the roads slick.

Her thinking was that if Crosby could go out, she could, too. Overall, she figured she could do just about anything a guy could do, with a few notable exceptions. Like, she couldn't pee standing up. Then again, she had no desire to.

She couldn't get a testicular injury, so yay, score one for lady parts.

And honestly, as strong and skilled as she might be, she still took pleasure in her femininity, so knocking out a dude with one punch—something her hulking brothers managed easily— was usually out of her realm. Not that she couldn't effectively disable a guy in other ways. She *could*—hello testicles—and yet, the majority of her contribution to the family business was handled behind a computer screen.

Now, with Crosby, she wanted to be a little more hands-on.

Snuggled into her chic white snowsuit, complete with a faux fur trimmed trapper hat and attached goggles, Madison parked her SUV behind Crosby's car, all the while wondering why he would tool around in this weather in a sedan. At least he had chains on his tires, using some common sense.

She wondered, too, why he would stand there on the sidewalk outside a small mom-and-pop store and do that whole-body frowning thing. Something had angered him, but she didn't yet know what. Since he hadn't looked at her, she figured she wasn't the cause of his irritation this time—a nice change for once.

After staring through the window for a flat ten seconds, Crosby went into the store, leaving her with a tingle of anticipation at seeing him again. The last time she'd been so close to him was well before Christmas, and now it was early February. She'd kissed him then... And he'd *laughed*.

Worse, he thought she'd kissed him for underhanded reasons.

She was still mad at him for that—she really was—but even though their relationship was strained at best, hostile at worst, she'd missed him.

Assuming he wouldn't recognize her bundled up as she was for the weather, Madison trudged through the deep snow and entered the quaint store. A bell jingled above the front door, drawing attention her way.

As was her habit, she immediately did a quick assessment of the small interior. Shelves lined every wall, packed from top to bottom. Besides Crosby, she noted a clerk behind the counter and a youth who'd been stocking the shelves.

Unfortunately, there were also three men in the process of robbing the place.

Well. She supposed that explained Crosby's fierce frown.

She also had the terrible suspicion that he recognized her even under all her winter gear. Had he been onto her following him all along?

His cleverness was just one more appealing trait she admired.

Guns drawn and faces hidden behind thick winter ski masks,

the robbers mostly kept their attention on Crosby and the clerk, but they did repeatedly glance her way.

Aggressively, one of the men gestured with his gun, saying, "What the hell are you people doing out on a day like this?"

Another man said, "I knew we should have locked the door."

Crosby said, "I offered, if you'll recall."

So he'd considered locking her out? Too bad for him.

Dressed as she was, the men couldn't see much of her face or body, but she felt certain they knew she was female. It was there in the way she stood with her hands on her hips, in the long hair trailing out of her hat and probably in the way her lips smiled. "Am I interrupting?"

The man who waved the gun around barked, "Over here, now."

That suited her just fine.

As Madison started forward, her awareness of Crosby sharpened. Today he wore a dark puffer coat, thick wool scarf and padded gloves. Always, no matter the situation, he managed to look like an impeccable male model. Well, except for his sandy-brown hair. He wore it just long enough for it to curl a little at the very ends. It gave him an appealingly messy look in stark contrast with his otherwise immaculate appearance.

Those dark-as-sin eyes of his never left the men standing before him, though he didn't look anxious about the situation.

Annoyed, yes. Alert, certainly. She sensed more than saw that all he needed was an opening, and he'd take on all three of the intruders.

In that, she could certainly assist.

As she strode forward, she asked the stock boy, "Would you mind ducking behind that shelf?"

Startled, the kid said, "Um…"

The robbers all started protesting at the same time, one of them barking, "No one fucking moves!"

Speaking over him, Madison said to the clerk, "If you could possibly duck down very quickly?"

Crosby issued a sound like a snarl and took a quick step to his left, which effectively shielded the clerk. The older man dropped fast behind the counter. That got the kid moving, too, and he jumped behind a shelf of canned goods.

With the two innocents protected, she set about wrapping up the danger.

"Bitch!" one of the robbers snapped, lunging for her and catching her arm in a viselike grip. Madison let him propel her forward. Deliberately crashing into him, she grabbed his wrist to control the weapon. Because the floor was concrete and could cause a ricochet, she forced his arm up and back. The gun discharged, the sound loud in the small store, but the bullet merely hit a wall of beer cases. The yeasty brew sprayed out.

Fluid, even graceful—or so she liked to think—she swung the first man's gun hand around and, since he fired again, caused him to pop the second man in the thigh, making him buckle.

Guy number two cursed a blue streak as he went down.

The dummy who'd grabbed her slipped in the beer and went down, finally releasing the gun. She wrenched it away, turned and shot him in the shoulder. His shout of pain mingled with curse words.

Crosby had already gone after the third man, making quick work of subduing him. She heard the snap of bone and knew it was the man's arm breaking. That one wouldn't be holding a gun for a while.

Furious, guy number two held his bloody thigh with one hand and took aim at her with the other.

Crosby kicked his gun away at the same time she stomped his privates. Her snow boots were heavy, her aim sure.

As if in slow motion, the dude curled in on himself, his groan low and deep.

She had just a moment to admire Crosby's skill, seeing him

finish off the third man with a punch that sent him collapsing back into a display of chips.

Three men, now all wounded, two with gunshot wounds and one with a broken arm. Crosby grabbed the one she'd shot in the shoulder, stopping him from scurrying away.

He used that effective one-punch power she so often admired in her brothers and put the guy to sleep.

"Well done," Madison said, smiling at how seamlessly they'd worked as a team. Leaning over the counter, she said to the clerk, "Could you call 911, please? In this weather, it might take them a bit to respond. They'll need as much notice as possible."

Rigid, Crosby stood there glowering at her among the fallen bodies, spilled beer and scattered chips. Rage still permeated his entire being.

Those clenched fists of his? Impressive.

The rock-solid line of his shoulders under his coat? Very stirring.

"You," he whispered, the sound raw-edged with anger, "are not in charge here."

Smiling, Madison held up her hands. Unlike her brothers, she didn't mind stepping back—just a little.

He then proceeded to secure the men, rolling them one by one to their stomachs and fastening their wrists together with nylon zip ties. Had he brought those along? Obviously he'd known there would be trouble.

She kept watching him, but not once did he look at her.

Okay, the robbers hadn't unsettled her, but Crosby's attitude made her a little uneasy.

Pretending it didn't, she moved to the boy, who continued to cower behind the shelf. He looked fifteen or so, in that awkward stage of long limbs, acne and sparse facial hair on his upper lip, which he wore like a trophy.

She crouched down in front of him. "You okay, bud?"

"They were going to hurt us this time," he whispered, his face still ghostly pale.

*This time?* "Did they say so?" she asked, wondering what in the world she'd walked into. Maybe it hadn't been a simple robbery after all.

"They didn't have to," the boy agonized. "It was their attitudes. If Crosby hadn't showed up—"

A long arm reached past Madison, offering a Coke to the kid. She glanced up to see Crosby's set face.

With his tone sounding mild, Crosby said, "Drink up, Owen." When the boy took the can, Crosby rested his hand on Owen's shoulder. "Why don't you join your dad behind the counter? I've put up the closed sign and locked the door so you can both have a few minutes."

Nodding, Owen shot to his feet, then skirted around the downed men and the beer that now crawled across the uneven floor. When he reached his father, Madison heard the low murmur of their voices, both of them sounding shaken.

Now that Crosby said it, the two did have a similar took. "So father and son were here working together and you—"

His finger pressed against her lips, shocking her silent. When had he removed his gloves, and why hadn't she noticed? She rarely missed a single detail.

"Give me a minute," Crosby rasped, still looking somewhat savage. "Do you think you can do that?"

Madison nodded. She wouldn't mind giving him a week. Maybe a month.

Resisting the urge to lick his finger required more concentration than keeping quiet.

Crosby moved away.

Freed from that strange and overwhelming effect he had on her, she dragged off her hat and unzipped her coat, suddenly feeling far too warm.

Letting Crosby do his thing, she moved to stand before the

counter and held out her hand. Keeping her voice very low, she said, "Hi. I'm Madison."

The older man took her hand in both of his. "Winton Maclean. Thank you for helping us."

Proving he had excellent hearing, Crosby said, "I had it in hand."

Winton smiled at him, his look almost paternal. "I'm sure you did, but a little help didn't hurt."

"Depends on the help," Crosby shot back.

Well, she liked that! Had she, or had she not, taken out one of them and helped with a second? She *had*. So…

Leaning in, Winton confided, "He's angrier when he worries."

Oh, she liked Winton. "Have you known Crosby long?"

Rubbing his forehead, Winton cast a quick glance at Crosby. "Most of his life."

Now on his phone, Crosby pinned her with a warning gaze that pretty much stated: *Don't ask questions about me.*

Fine, she'd save her questions for later. "Mop?" she asked Winton.

He was shaking his head to deny her offer of help, but Owen said, "Through those swinging doors," then caught his dad's exasperated huff. "But you don't need to—"

"Thanks, but I'm not good with idle time." Smiling to reassure them both, she went for the mop and found it with a big bucket. Used to cleaning the sparring mats at her family's at-home gym, she quickly added water and cleaner, then rolled it out. Using the mop, she stopped the beer from spreading farther across the store, but she was careful not to interfere with the "scene." Cops could be prickly about things like that.

Good thing one of the robbers helped stem the flow, too; the beer was currently soaking into his side, all along his waist, hip and thigh. He tried to shift away, but one glare from Crosby and he went still again.

Suddenly police sirens echoed over the snowy streets. Blast, she'd run out of time. Abandoning the mop bucket, she sidled into the back room and quickly called her father. Crosby would be busy for a few minutes at least. Hopefully, everything would be wrapped up before her brothers could barge in. They tended to be overprotective where she was concerned.

Hearing the front door opening and the voices of officers, she quietly explained the situation to her father, giving him the address of the shop and assuring him it was all under control.

Never one to get ruffled, Parrish said, "So you're okay?"

"Of course."

"Are you positive you don't need any help?"

"Absolutely certain."

"I suppose it's too late for you to pretend to be a weak woman?"

She grinned. "Afraid so."

Her father hesitated a moment, then said, "Try not to get too involved, but if you get dragged in, let me know and I'll start covering our bases."

Yes, given their family enterprise, it was never wise to make the law too curious. Except for Crosby. Since they'd come to an understanding of sorts with him, he could be as curious as he wanted—about her.

*Not* the business.

One of the swinging metal doors moved, and then Crosby was there, his dark gaze accusing, assessing and… More. "Calling in reinforcements?"

"Do I appear to need them?"

Instead of answering, his gaze took a slow trip down her body.

Madison struck a pose. "It's a great snowsuit, right? Soon as I saw it, I had to have it."

One side of his mouth barely twitched before settling into a hard line again.

A near smile? She wanted to think so.

"Detective Bard wants to speak to you now."

She affected a pout. "If I have to talk to a cop, I'd rather it just be you."

Without even a blink, he said, "I'm not a cop anymore, so that won't do."

It wasn't every day that he took a McKenzie by surprise, so Crosby enjoyed the rounding of Madison's bright hazel eyes and the slight parting of her lips.

Then all her arrogance rushed back in, and she stated, "Impossible. I'd know if you left the police force."

"Apparently not." He took her arm and urged her from the room, not in the least surprised when her confidence melted into the mien of an untrained person. Somehow she managed to look rattled, unsure and wary all at the same time.

Crosby resisted rolling his eyes—barely.

Not that long ago he'd crossed paths with the McKenzie family. For a while, he'd suspected her father of organizing vigilante justice, with her two brothers employed to see through well-planned rescue missions. Too many times human traffickers had been thwarted, practically dumped on the doorstep of the police precinct with all the necessary info to make a tidy sweep of the scumbag perpetrators, along with their contacts and clientele.

Crosby had appreciated the end results, but not the methods utilized. It had taken a lot of diligence, but he'd finally found his way to the McKenzie clan. No problem.

That is, no problem except for Madison. She was the tech whiz, and he did mean *whiz*. Practically genius level. If she wanted to hack NASA, she probably could. Hell, even the White House might not be safe.

That alone made him uneasy, but then for her to set her sights on him? Talk about unnerving a man.

It didn't help that she was equal parts gorgeous and bold.

Nearly six feet of slender femininity shot through with brilliance and wrapped in wicked skills.

For too many reasons she unsettled him, and that was a new feeling for Crosby. Didn't stop him from wanting her, but he wasn't an idiot. That road led to trouble and he had enough on his plate already.

Standing back, arms crossed, Crosby watched her weave her spell on Detective Bard. The poor guy never stood a chance. He bought her act, every trembling, grateful, soft-spoken second of it.

Hell, even Winton and Owen looked convinced, and they'd watched her easily annihilate a grown man.

Good thing he wasn't a cop anymore, or he'd have to set the record straight. The goons still might, but who would believe them? They each had long records of petty crimes, like trespassing, simple assault, vandalism and public intoxication. Now there was proof that they'd been harassing Winton and other small neighborhood businesses, forcing them to pay for "protection." What a joke.

Luckily, he'd just put an end to that.

Poor Madison. She'd shown off her skills with ease, but now couldn't gloat about it. Too many people were willing to give Crosby the credit for taking down all three men.

It'd be hilarious if he was dealing with anyone other than the McKenzies. Madison might be the only one on the scene right now, and God knew she was enough, but he wouldn't be surprised if the rest of the family had their noses in it before the day was over.

Once the thugs were taken away and the police left, Madison went right back to cleaning, swinging the mop with practiced ease. Swipe, rinse, wring, repeat.

Her family had deep pockets, so he hadn't expected her to even know how to clean.

Was there anything she couldn't do well?

"Whew, it's getting warm." Propping the mop handle against the counter, she dragged the snowsuit zipper down and down and down, all the way to the flare of her hips, then she peeled off the top layer and let it hang over her stellar tush.

Beneath the snowsuit she wore a black turtleneck that hugged her breasts and fit snug to her narrow rib cage. Using both hands, she gathered her long, light brown hair, then asked Winton, "Do you have a rubber band or anything?"

Owen scrambled to a drawer and produced one with a flourish that left his face hot.

Recognizing that infatuated look, Crosby figured the poor kid would be dreaming of Madison for weeks.

She bent forward at the waist, quickly put her hair into a high ponytail and straightened again—still looking like a wet dream.

"I'm going to change this water. Be right back."

All three of them watched her roll the bucket to the back room.

Winton slowly turned to stare at Crosby. Owen grinned.

Shaking his head, Crosby said, "No. It's not like that, so don't get any ideas."

"Too late," Owen said, then he quickly ducked the smack his dad aimed at the back of his head. "I'll, um, go see if she needs any help."

Crosby couldn't help but laugh. Fifteen-year-old boys—almost sixteen, as Owen said anytime his age was mentioned—were made up of testosterone and determination. An uncomfortable combo, from what he remembered, though it'd been twenty years since he'd had to deal with that anatomical and emotional upheaval.

"Quit frowning, Winton. He's a good kid."

"I know." Winton sighed. "And he's currently in love with a cheerleader at his school. But still…"

"Madison will handle it. No worries." Switching gears and

getting down to business, Crosby added, "Thanks for follow-ing my lead."

"You know what you're doing." Bracing a hand on the coun-ter and lifting his brows, Winton asked, "What *are* you doing?"

So much for Winton's patience. "I know her and her family. Trust me, the less she's involved, the better."

"Because?"

Unable to share the reason, he shrugged. "I knew she was fol-lowing me today." She was always following him, usually on-line, but it figured Madison would decide to tail him in person during a snowstorm. "Warning her off wouldn't have done me any good, and I didn't want to take the time to try to reason with her." Lessons in futility weren't really his thing.

"So she wasn't part of your plan?"

Snorting, Crosby said, "Definitely not."

"That put you in a tight spot, since you knew they'd be here today."

Crosby nodded. He had good street informants. Winton's store had been targeted more than once, and Crosby had planned to put an end to the harassment. Things had gone according to plan...

Except that his initial plans hadn't factored in Madison crash-ing the party. Once he'd realized she was following him, he hadn't had time to reconfigure things. Losing her would have been tough, too, with the roads so slick, some of them impass-able. He'd had no opportunity for tricky driving or fast turns.

Delaying his arrival at Winton's store could have put Winton and Owen in danger. He'd been caught in an untenable posi-tion, not the first time when dealing with McKenzies.

Emerging from the back room, Madison returned to mop-ping the floor, now with fresh water. "Might need to go over them one more time, so they won't be sticky."

"We'll take care of it," Winton said. "With the weather wors-ening, there's no point in us being open anyway."

Owen hefted the damaged case of beer and carried it into the back room.

Winton began cleaning up the spilled chip display.

"I'm glad to help," Madison insisted, using the wringer on the bucket. "We'll have it all tidied up in no time."

"You," Crosby said, feeling very divided, "have some explaining to do."

She smiled and, proving she'd been listening, said, "You were right, you know. If you'd told me not to come in, it would have only sharpened my curiosity."

Winton laughed. "I'm sure Crosby could have handled it on his own, but I admit I enjoyed seeing you in action. Are you in law enforcement?"

Her gaze slanted over to Winton. "Have you ever seen a cop fight the way I do?"

"Only Crosby."

Her slim eyebrows climbed high. "Is that so?"

Always ready to sing his praises, Winton paused in his cleanup. "Before he was even Owen's age, Crosby was training. He's always been a fitness buff. Every coach at the high school tried to talk him into playing sports, but he was never interested. Said team sports weren't his thing."

"Dad says he's mostly a loner," Owen added.

"Or at least he was before—"

"Winton," Crosby warned. There weren't many things he could tell Madison that she didn't already know. She'd made no secret of researching him, using methods to open files that even cops couldn't easily access. What she didn't know she'd eventually find out, whether he liked it or not.

Winton shot him a look of apology—one that Madison didn't miss.

What concerned Crosby most at the moment was *how* Winton would tell things, with all the nuances and added affection of a father.

Winton and Owen fell silent.

Madison didn't. Returning the mop to the bucket, she folded her arms on the counter—a pose that had her breasts thrusting forward and her backside sticking out in an impossible-to-ignore way.

Deliberate, he was sure. Everything she did or said had a purpose. He'd never known a woman who was so entirely badass, a research whiz who could uncover anything, a fighter capable of leveling a grown man with ease, who also flaunted her sexiness.

It was an enticing mix, and damn it, he wasn't immune.

"I already knew he was a fitness buff," she said, using a casual tone likely meant to elicit Winton's trust. "I mean, look at him."

"He's rock-solid," Winton agreed.

She turned her head to see Crosby, her glittering hazel eyes far too compelling. "He's into fashion, too. Looks like a cover model, don't you think?"

Hooting, Owen completely relaxed again. "That's exactly what Mrs. Cline says. She always shops on Monday at six so she can time her visits with Crosby's."

"Mrs. Cline?" Madison asked, her interest no longer playful.

Winton patted her hand. "Pam is nearing seventy and just likes to flirt."

"Ah." Grinning again, Madison asked Crosby, "Have to deal with a lot of flirting, do you?"

Since it was none of her business, Crosby declined to answer. "You should get going while you still can. The roads are getting worse by the minute."

Her smile curled even more. "Not without you. In fact, I'm convinced your car won't even make it away from the curb."

Crosby opened his mouth, but again, Owen beat him to it. "He has an SUV, but Silver probably—"

Winton interrupted his son with, "Go bundle up so you can help Madison clear her ride."

Once Owen left the room, Madison took a turn eyeing each one of them before straightening to face forward. With her penetrating gaze locked on Crosby, she folded her arms under her breasts. "Why is everyone trying to get rid of me?"

Crosby didn't hesitate. "We have private things to discuss that don't concern you." He saw one scenario after another flit over her features as she determined how to proceed. So damned tenacious. "Enough, Madison. It's time for you to go before Winton, Owen and I get stranded here."

Concerned, she turned to Winton. "Do you have far to travel in this mess?"

"Um…" Shifting, looking guilty as hell, Winton muttered, "No."

Damn, Winton was bad at lying, even lies of omission.

He knew the second Madison looked up that her quick mind had already put too many things together.

Golden eyes slanted in his direction with accusation. "Let me guess. They live upstairs?"

Winton cleared his throat. "I'll go see what's keeping Owen." He literally fled the shop front.

Knowing he couldn't do the same, Crosby mimicked her stance, arms crossed and expression arrogant. "Contrary to what you believe, *some* of my business is still private." It was a miracle she hadn't uncovered every bit of his life yet—including the things he'd worked so hard to hide.

To his surprise, she retrenched with a sigh, her hands falling to her sides, her expression subdued. "I've been too pushy."

That pretty much described her, always.

Two tentative steps brought her closer to him, and with her height she nearly looked him in the eye. "I'm sorry. It's a bad habit of mine."

Damn it, now he felt like an asshole. "No one is perfect."

"I want to be," she admitted. Then with surprising candor, she added, "I guess I've been competing with my brothers for so long that being anything less than perfect—perfectly informed, prepared and capable—makes me a little nuts."

Incredible insight… That made sense. "Was I wrong in think-ing your brothers would show up here?" His experience had been with assertive men who wanted to take over every situa-tion. That rubbed Crosby the wrong way, so how bad would it have been for a younger sister?

"I called Dad. He's the only one who could hold them back, and *he*," she said with emphasis, "trusts me."

Her father was an imposing figure to be sure. Crosby likened him to Batman because of the way he entered a scene to the awe of all spectators. The man definitely brought a lot of larger-than-life presence everywhere he went. His sons weren't much dif-ferent. And Madison? Overall, she was cut from the same cloth.

The senior McKenzie had probably been a strict taskmaster. After all, he was the one who'd determined that his kids would be the alphas of all alphas, apex predators who would go up against the worst society had to offer. Each of them had incred-ibly honed skills and a drive to be the best.

Crosby could have easily labeled them with the criminal class, except that the more he'd learned, the more he'd…respected them.

He could label them vigilantes, true, and that definitely placed them in the category of illegal activity. The conflict for him was that they fought against human trafficking, and for that, they had his deepest gratitude.

"I see you're not going to agree."

Crosby had no idea what she was talking about.

"Trust?" When he still hesitated, she said, "Never mind. I guess it's too soon for that."

Shaking his head to gather his thoughts, Crosby asked, "Are you ready to go?"

"Guess I might as well." Disgruntled, she began feeding her arms into the sleeves of the white snowsuit. "I'll feel better about this whole cluster if you answer one question for me."

"You need me to confirm something? Seriously?"

"Oh, I'll be on my computer as soon as I get home, but given the weather, that could take a little time and it really wouldn't kill you to share one tiny tidbit."

Deliberately, he exhaled as if impatient. In truth, he had a difficult time keeping his hands at his sides when he really wanted to touch her. Just a small stroke of that long, sun-kissed brown hair. Or a grazing of his knuckles over her downy cheek. Or...

"What is it?"

"You're really not a cop anymore?"

"No."

"Well, why not?"

"That's two questions."

Her eyes narrowed. "I think I feel faint. Maybe I shouldn't drive? I should probably ask Winton if I could hang around for a little while to—"

"No." She didn't even try to look sickly as she said all that, but then the point was for her to prove she'd do anything to get her way. That was something that alarmed him the most.

Madison McKenzie had no idea how to give up.

"I retired," he said.

She snorted. "At thirty-five?"

Easy enough to explain. "I have an old injury that was causing me some difficulty."

Her brows leveled over her eyes. "Someone actually bought that story?"

Jaw tightening, he explained, "I was shot in the leg."

"Five years ago, but it hasn't slowed you down. Heck, I just saw you in action, remember? So try again."

# CHAPTER TWO

Chagrined, Crosby did his own share of staring. "You may be able to pick through files with ease, but you can't pick through my brain, so don't pretend you know what I feel." True, the leg hardly pained him at all anymore, but he'd needed to retire, and so he had.

"So what do you do now? I know you're not just sitting around enjoying a life of leisure."

"You know that, do you?" His leisure time was definitely limited, but likely not for the reasons she suspected.

"Of course." With her so close, he picked up the subtle fragrance of her citrusy shampoo and the more stirring scent of her skin, both distracting. "I know you as well as I know myself. You are not a man content to be idle."

Her persistence was almost comical. Since he knew she'd have the answer within the hour, he saw no reason not to tell her. "I've found a new job." He wasn't about to detail it for her, not if he ever hoped to get her out the door.

She tucked in her chin. "What does that mean?" Then with slightly widened eyes, she asked, "Does it have anything to do with Silver?" And before he could groan, she tacked on, "Is that a person's name? Man or woman?" And more hopefully, "Maybe a pet?"

The questions had come rapid-fire, leaving him no room to answer. As usual, Madison was incorrigible. What she wanted, she went after.

She'd been clear that she wanted him.

Crosby took in her stiffened posture, the suspicion in her eyes and the slight purse of her lips, as if the answer really mattered to her. So why did he suddenly want to kiss her?

He *didn't*. Or rather, he definitely did, but he wouldn't give in to the urge.

To put her off, Crosby said, "Like most of what I do, Silver is none of your business."

"You *do* Silver?" Her mouth tightened. "A woman, then. Is it serious?"

Good God. He would not suffer her inquisition. "You need to stop, Madison." Crosby kept his tone calm but firm, hiding even a hint of emotion. "I mean it. Stop following me, stop digging into my life, stop asking me questions and stop thinking any of it will matter."

The corner of her mouth twitched down and the sparkle in her eyes disappeared. "Because you're not at all interested."

Proving to be a better liar than Winton, he said, "No, I'm not." He couldn't be. The new job mattered a lot. He wouldn't risk losing it by getting involved with her.

Madison's chest expanded on a shaky breath and for once, she broke eye contact. With a small nod, she stepped back and finished pulling up her zipper. "I should apologize."

"Not necessary."

She gave another small nod.

Damn it, he'd never seen her like this. Subdued. Maybe hurt...? That definitely hadn't been his intent. He'd just needed her to—

Turning to the swinging doors, she said with false cheerful-ness, "Goodbye Winton, Owen. Take care."

Both of them peeked out, making it obvious that they'd been there all along, listening in.

"Thank you again," Winton said, his tone solemn.

Owen looked from Crosby to Madison and then back again, this time with a scowl. Stepping out, he asked, "You'll be okay?"

"Of course." She produced a cocky smile.

Crosby knew it was forced. Already he saw the differences in her smiles. Some were snarky, some anticipatory. Some bordered on feral, especially when she was ready to engage physically.

Usually they were sincere, but this one?

It fell flat.

Without a word to Crosby, she stepped around him, unlocked the front door and disappeared into the flurry of blowing snow.

Cursing low, he stalked to the window and watched her trudge through the accumulated snow to the driver's door. With some effort, she got it opened despite the thick coating of ice. After starting the engine, she emerged again with a scraper and began clearing the windows.

He stood there, aware of Winton and Owen crowding in be-hind him so they could see, too. Every instinct he possessed de-manded that he go out and do the chore for her, but he knew Madison well enough to understand she wouldn't want his as-sistance. Especially not now.

So he locked his muscles into a deceptively casual pose and kept an eye on her.

It didn't surprise him when she finished with her own car and strode to his, quickly clearing his windows, as well.

It's what he would have done for someone.

"I'll be damned," Winton murmured.

"Why am I standing here?" Owen asked in a disgusted tone. Already in his coat and boots, he shouldered his way around them and stepped out while tugging on his hat. He slipped on the walkway twice before getting his balance and hurrying over to her.

Crosby saw Madison laugh. He saw Owen try to take the scraper from her.

And he saw Madison give it up!

So maybe it was only grown men who drew out her competitive nature. Or maybe she knew that, like most boys on the verge of being men, her rejection would have wounded Owen.

The two of them spoke for a moment more before Madison lifted her gloved hands in surrender and got into her SUV.

Owen made quick work of finishing, then returned the scraper to her. After a brief hug, she shooed him back inside, waited until he was at the door, then got behind the wheel, pulled out and drove away.

Without once glancing toward Crosby.

Huh. Maybe she'd taken his declaration to heart. He hadn't expected her to give up so easily.

Could that really be the end of her pursuit?

The idea shouldn't bother him, but it did. And what did that make him? Fickle? Well, shit.

Cheeks and nose already red, Owen came back in, stomping his feet to remove the snow. He, too, made a point of not looking at Crosby.

Winton locked the door again. "You think this'll be the end of it?"

"With Madison?" Crosby asked.

After three seconds of silence, Winton shook his head in pity. "Actually, I meant the street punks."

Damn. He'd just given himself away with that gut reaction. To escape Winton's scrutiny, Crosby headed for the back room where a pot of coffee always waited.

Following, Winton clapped him on the shoulder. "Now that they know you're onto them and the cops are involved, do you think they'll bother us again?"

"I plan to have a talk today with the idiots just arrested, and as soon as the weather breaks, I'll visit the rest of their gang." *Gang* was a word he used lightly for the small-time punks with big aspirations. "If any of them come around again before I get the chance, play along with them, be careful and let me know."

Winton hesitated. "And what will you do about Madison?"

Crosby reached the pot and filled a disposable cup, breathing in the scent of strong coffee. "Hopefully, I won't have to do anything since it seems she's finally given up."

Crossing his arms, Winton leaned back against the wall and gave him a long, telling stare.

"What?" Crosby asked, feeling as young and awkward as Owen. It was that stare of Winton's that had gotten him off the wrong track so long ago. Damned if it didn't have the same effect still.

Slowly, Winton smiled. "I've never known you to bullshit yourself before. This ought to be interesting."

Crosby blew out a breath. Yeah, interesting. That was one word that applied to Madison.

Interesting…and sometimes all but irresistible.

Madison stewed for two miserable weeks. Oh, she'd found out all about Winton and Owen, how thugs had been harassing not only them, but other local businesses on a regular basis. They'd extorted money, robbed and vandalized without consequences.

Crosby had easily squashed that nonsense, though, and he didn't need the law on his side to do it. She almost smiled, remembering how remarkable he'd been.

But her smile slipped… Because he hadn't been impressed with her at all. Instead he'd made it clear that her interest wasn't returned, and never would be. That stung as much today as it had then, causing heat to flush her cheeks.

Thank God she had enough pride to brazen her way out of there.

None of it stopped her from wanting him, but never, not in a million years, would she chase him now.

The images on her computer screen blended together and she realized she'd gotten lost in her thoughts again.

Cade, her oldest brother, came into the kitchen of their father's expansive house. It was the general gathering place for them all, and they only used the formal dining room for dinners. As wealthy and influential as her father might be, they were, overall, a casual family.

"What's wrong now?" Cade asked, taking the seat across from her.

"Nothing." She was glad her father hadn't yet joined them, and that Bernard remained busy at the stove.

"Madison."

As a retired army ranger, Cade had a calm, imperturbable way about him that demanded total honesty. With most people, it worked like a charm.

As his sister, she ignored it and hunkered closer to her laptop.

"I bet she's mooning over Detective Crosby Albertson." Reyes, the middle sibling, had the same skill set as Cade, but with an edge of caustic humor that often rubbed people the wrong way.

She shot him a narrow-eyed glare and went back to her PC. Nothing unusual in that. She spent most of her time buried in tech research. Without an active case, much of her focus lately had been on Crosby.

He hadn't lied about leaving the police. She knew that now. What she didn't know was why. There had to be a reason other than the lame one he'd made up.

As Madison had told him, curiosity was an issue for her, so of course she'd uncovered his long-standing relationship with Winton.

It seemed the kindly store owner had been a stand-in father to Crosby when he'd needed someone the most.

Lightly, Madison touched her fingertips to the online image of a much-younger version of Crosby that she'd easily uncovered. At fifteen, his clothing was too small, his body too lanky, his hair messy, and there was no smile on his face.

Totally different from the polished, extra-fine specimen he was now. Well, except for the lack of a smile. Crosby was still pretty stingy with those.

What had happened to make him look so solemn? Yes, she knew his dad had passed away the year before, and that his single mother worked in housekeeping for a local hotel. Those details hadn't been difficult to find.

But weren't kids usually resilient? Didn't they rebound when given enough love?

Her heart squeezed at the idea of him suffering a difficult childhood. In many ways, her own had been challenging, too. Losing her mother, and then her father's single-minded focus on ensuring that she, Reyes and Cade were trained in every manner of defense. Overall, she'd embraced the regimen because it gave her an outlet for her grief and allowed her to spend a portion of each day with her siblings. While it had been a serious undertaking, they'd also shared plenty of laughs.

Maybe because of their upbringing, she and her brothers were uncommonly close. Another benefit was her vast knowledge of weaponry, and as she'd proven in Winton's store, her ability to stay calm and hold her own in physical encounters. Her instincts had been refined for speed and accuracy, which helped make up for what she lacked in bulk strength.

And none of that had impressed Crosby.

Frowning, she clicked to the photo of Crosby one year later. He stood with Winton at the edge of a grassy bank, holding a large bass and grinning with pride. Tethered to a tree behind him, a wood fishing boat floated on the river with a tackle box and rods filling one end.

Winton had obviously worked wonders.

"Definitely Crosby," Cade said, scrutinizing her in that consuming way of his. He had the knack of taking in every detail with a single glance.

"What's that?" Madison asked, forcing her gaze away from the laptop. "Were you speaking to me?" It wasn't unusual for her to be engrossed in her work, so her brothers shouldn't think anything of it.

A slight smile told her Cade wasn't fooled. "What are you working on?"

"Researching Crosby, actually." Going with the truth might help throw him off the scent.

"Still?" Reyes asked. "By now you probably know the color of his toothbrush."

She wasn't *that* bad—was she? Madison shook her head. "After seeing him at that robbery a few weeks ago, I've been curious to know if he resolved the extortion of those small businesses."

Cade kept staring.

Clearing her throat, she added, "And I wondered why he left active duty policing. That's all."

"Uh-huh," Reyes teased. "You have the hots for him."

Keeping her temper in check wasn't easy, but she merely said, "You are so crude."

Brows up, Reyes asked, "What would you call it?"

Ignoring Reyes, Cade's gaze grew more intense. "Knowing you, I assume you've made your interest known?"

Fat lot of good it had done her. "I like to play hard to get."

Reyes barked a laugh. "Is that what you were doing? Cuz it looked like the opposite to me. What I don't get is why Crosby isn't biting."

Cade scowled at him. "Did you *want* him to bite?"

Reyes opened his mouth, then shut it. "Bad choice of words." He shook his head. Hard. "Damn, now I have an image in my brain."

To taunt him, Madison leaned closer and asked, "An image

of Crosby nibbling on me? Nice. Why don't you draw me a picture?"

Reyes tapped a fist to his skull as if to dispel the visual. "Stop that or I'll have to go visit the good detective—"

"Ex-detective."

"—and have a big brother talk with him—using my fists."

"You wouldn't dare," Madison whispered in warning. "I would demolish you."

"It might not be a bad idea," Cade said. "At least if we chatted, we could—"

Alarm ripped into Madison. *"No."* Even her arrogant brothers couldn't be that overprotective. They knew she could handle herself, for crying out loud.

"You're a catch," Reyes assured her. "He should be jumping for joy."

As her father joined them at the table, she complained, *"Dad,"* in the same way she'd been doing since they were toddlers when she wanted him to intervene on her behalf.

"Leave your sister alone," Parrish announced in the equally familiar tone of voice that silenced everyone. He seated himself just in time for Bernard to set out a hearty meal of breakfast meats, scrambled eggs, fried potatoes and various breads.

Down-home cooking was the best, and a breakfast favorite at the McKenzie household.

Patting her shoulder, Bernard promised, "They'll soon have their mouths too full to make you screech."

Oh, God, she *had* screeched.

Bernard sat across from her and gave each of her brothers a look. "Anyone not enjoying my breakfast will immediately lose his plate."

Cade lifted his hands.

Reyes lifted his fork.

After all, her brothers were bossy, and pushy in the extreme, but they weren't fools.

"Thank you, Bernard," Madison said sweetly. "You're too good to us."

With a long-suffering sigh, Bernard said, "Indeed, I am."

At sixty-five, Bernard had been with them for over twenty years. He ran the household, served as her father's assistant and made the very best of chefs, covering everything from fine cuisine to comfort food. Even better than that, he was like family. Yes, quirky family, since Bernard liked to put on lofty airs, especially whenever they had guests. Tall, thin and silver haired, Madison often wondered if he stole that impersonation from Alfred, Batman's butler.

Once everyone was peacefully eating, Parrish regained their attention by saying, "I spoke with Crosby recently."

The statement dropped with the impact of a thunderclap.

She and her brothers started asking questions at the same time.

Lifting a hand, Parrish said, "He applied as a corporate security manager."

*What?* Crosby had applied for a job *with her father?* That sneaky bastard. She specifically remembered asking him what he planned to do now that he wasn't a cop.

"When did this happen?" Madison demanded. "At which business?" Her father had a great many interests, and even more financial investments. "Did you hire him?"

Unfazed by her rushed questions, Parrish said, "He applied a few weeks ago, the position is at Cornerstone Security, and yes, I did."

Slowly, she let out a breath. Did that mean he'd already been hired on before the conflict at Winton's store? At least Cornerstone was one of her father's local businesses, run in conjunction with the task force that helped victims of crime, specifically victims from human trafficking.

Crosby wouldn't be leaving Colorado.

Not that it mattered, since he'd made it clear he wasn't interested.

Gathering herself, she sipped her juice and waited, knowing her brothers would ask the rest of the questions she wanted answered.

Reyes took the first shot. "What exactly will he be doing?"

"He wanted as close to regular hours as he could get, so I've adjusted things to suit him. Big picture, he'll coordinate the security for the business and for the people we're helping, as well as organize and train the staff hired to see to the physical protection. He'll also secure the facility, handle risk assessment and any immediate threats that arise."

Cade whistled. "That's a job for one person?"

Shrugging, Parrish said, "Jones, who had been in charge of staff, recently put in for retirement. I was relieved because his methods were dated anyway. The security system is getting old and I want it updated. That's actually one of his talents. I was overseeing the rest of it before meeting Crosby, but I like him. More than that, I trust him. He'll be able to handle it."

Inwardly, Madison beamed. She was the one who'd declared Crosby trustworthy after a thorough background check. For her family, though, she kept her expression impassive.

"When does he start?" Reyes asked.

"Monday." Parrish checked the time on his phone. "I'm meeting him in thirty minutes to go over everything."

"You're going to the facility?" Cade asked.

Attention on his plate, Parrish shook his head. "Crosby is coming here."

Shock left them all silent. Generally speaking, her father's home was off-limits. That hadn't stopped Cade from bringing Sterling into the mix, or Reyes from bringing Kennedy. But they'd married those women, and both she and her father had known from the onset that they would end up as family. How her brothers had been with them was telling. Love, at least in the case of her brothers, was easy to see.

Crosby, though? If Dad was matchmaking—an unbelievable prospect, for sure—then he was doomed to disappointment.

Her family had been at odds with Crosby for some time and the man didn't even like her. "Maybe I should clarify something."

Bernard stood to start clearing away the empty dishes. Reyes grabbed the last of the potatoes and Cade snatched up another piece of toast.

Her father refilled his coffee cup.

They all waited.

Madison started to shift, but that was such a clichéd reaction to discomfort, she resisted. "If any of you are thinking that Crosby and I...that he might..." Double damn. She wasn't sure what words to use. Blowing out a breath, she admitted, "I chased after him, yes, but his total disinterest was too obvious to miss, so end of story."

"Is it the end?" Cade asked.

"Absolutely. Having him *here* isn't necessary because he won't become a permanent fixture."

"He seriously turned you down?" Reyes asked, as if he couldn't fathom it.

Sibling loyalty was a wonderful thing to have. She couldn't help but smile. "I didn't make an offer, so no. But he's made it very clear that he doesn't return my interest."

Cade shook his head. "You know men can be idiots sometimes, right?"

"Not you."

He flashed a grin. "No, but Reyes did a lot of denying with Kennedy before—"

"Bullshit," Reyes said. "Kennedy was the one doing all the denying."

Parrish gave them quelling looks. Yeah, at least her dad noticed how that made her feel. Her brothers had gone after the women they wanted, which more or less proved that Crosby had no intention of getting involved with her. He'd probably taken the job *despite* the family relationship, certainly not because of it.

Doing her utmost to appear nonchalant, Madison closed her laptop and stood. "I think I'll head back to my house. I have a lot to get done this afternoon."

Watching her, Cade also stood. "Madison—"

Parrish gestured for them both to wait. To Cade, he asked, "How are we proceeding on the nail salon?"

"Star got her nails done there the other day with me at the pawnshop across the street, just in case."

Star, or as everyone else called her, Sterling, was Cade's wife and a legit force in her own right. Madison understood why her brother had stuck close. If Sterling had noticed anyone in immediate need, she would have razed the place without a second thought.

"Did she notice anything?" Madison asked. They'd all had their suspicions about the salon for a month now. Unfortunately, it was such a hole-in-the-wall there was almost nothing in the way of security. Not a camera in sight. And the one computer at the shop had only business records on it.

"Yeah, she did. A back door opened and she saw two girls sleeping on the floor with only a blanket. Another woman raised hell and closed it again."

Madison's heart twisted.

"Maybe it's only forced labor," Reyes growled, but to each of them, there was no *only* to it. Yes, being forced to work tirelessly without pay under grueling conditions was pure hell, especially with no end in sight. But being sold for sex would be undeniably worse.

Both Cade's and Reyes's wives knew the bitter horror of that firsthand. Sterling had joined their enterprise to free victims and dole out retribution, but Kennedy, Reyes's wife, took a different road. She gave informational talks to high schools and colleges, and she had a bestselling book on her experiences that detailed what to look out for and how to hopefully escape—or at least survive.

The pall that had fallen over the room finally infiltrated Madison's inner musings. Forcing a complacent smile, she said, "I'll see you all for dinner." Her small house was on the same property with her father's, farther down the slope of the mountain, toward the entrance. Literally, her home could fit in her father's kitchen, but she liked the compact coziness.

And the privacy.

As she turned to go, Reyes made a clucking sound.

Her back stiffened. *Was he calling her a chicken?*

Molars locking together, she turned to fry him and was met with his enormous grin.

"Do it again," she taunted in a whisper. "I dare you."

"Ah, no. I don't think so. I'd rather you partner with me for some sparring since Cade gets most of his workouts with Sterling now."

Cade and Sterling were still in the honeymoon stage of marital bliss. They used every excuse they could find to spend more time together, including sparring. She had no doubt Cade would return to his regular workouts with Reyes soon.

Cade narrowed his eyes. "Anytime, brother."

"Now?"

Without missing a beat, Cade clarified, "Anytime but now."

Turning back to her, Reyes held out his hands. "That leaves you. C'mon, Madison. Whatever work you have to do can wait a few hours."

Parrish concentrated on his coffee. Bernard began to whistle while loading dishes into the dishwasher. Blast. She didn't want to be here when Crosby showed up.

*Not* because she was chicken, but because… Well, she just didn't want to.

"It's a big house," Reyes reminded her. "Sterling claims it's a lodge. Kennedy swears we could fit all of Ridge Trail in here. Surely you can bear being in the same—"

She took an aggressive step forward, and her father interceded yet again.

"Take it downstairs, both of you." To Madison, he added, "Use your frustration, but don't let it control you."

"I know, I know." A cool head was needed at all times. "I don't know why I bother though because Cade and Reyes both hold back on me."

"Not this time," Parrish decreed, earning a frown from Cade, Reyes and Bernard, all three. "Don't maim her, but she needs to be challenged in order to keep improving."

Now Reyes looked uncomfortable. "I've got a hundred pounds on her."

True enough. She was only four inches shy of her brother's nearly six and a half feet of height, but where he was solid muscle, she was slim. Toned, yes, but she lacked the bulky strength that her siblings had.

"One day, she may run into trouble with a man your size. She needs to know how to handle herself."

Forgetting Crosby for the moment, she grinned at Reyes. "Oh, this is going to be fun."

Grumbling, he headed to the stairs that led to the lower-level gym, among other things.

"Now I wish I had time to stay and watch," Cade said, coming up to press a kiss to her forehead in an uncharacteristic show of affection. "Go easy on him."

She laughed. "Pretty sure you don't have to worry about that."

"I do, because I know bruising you will hurt him a hell of a lot more than it hurts you."

Likely true.

She walked Cade to the front door, then headed downstairs. All three of them had their own suite of rooms on the lower level, though they were usually only used in emergencies. Parrish liked to cover every contingency, and on the off chance they needed a safe place to defend against an attack, the family home on the mountain was a veritable fortress with not only top-of-the-line security, private satellite connection and phone lines, but an armory of weapons and enough ammo to last for months.

They could literally withstand a siege, not that they expected ever to face such a thing.

With half her brain anxious to spar and the other half day-dreaming over Crosby, she entered her suite in a rush. She darted into the bedroom and quickly located formfitting shorts and a snug tank top. In the bathroom, she flipped her head forward, gathered her hair in a ponytail and secured it with a band.

Sitting on the end of the bed, she pulled on lightweight, flexible shoes. Snatching up her laptop again, because it was rarely out of her sight, she went to the gym and found her frustrated brother stripped down to shorts, pacing along the mats. He'd already donned protective gear and had the same set out for her.

She couldn't wait to begin.

Crosby had been impressed with Reyes's log cabin at the base of a mountain that he'd seen once, but this? Holy shit.

At first, he wasn't sure if he'd followed the directions correctly. Surely the massive stone-and-brick structure sprawling against the mountainside couldn't be a single home. And yet, he knew Parrish McKenzie was loaded. His research on the family, though not quite on a par with Madison's ability, had shown numerous linked businesses, incredible wealth and a lot of philanthropic work.

He'd still wanted to dislike them all because, as a cop, he'd known that they had no problem crossing the line. Even more disturbing was that they seemed to do so with impunity.

Parrish was connected—in business, politics and in local law. Apparently, if you did enough favors for the right people, you got massive benefits in return.

Okay, so he'd learned that the favors were the good kind. The same type of things cops did every day when serving the public. The difference was that where a cop sometimes couldn't succeed, the McKenzie family could.

Learning all that had intrigued Crosby enough that he'd wanted to be a part of it.

The complication, of course, was Madison.

She tempted him far more than was wise. Under his circumstances, getting involved with a woman like her—Parrish's only daughter, sister to Cade and Reyes—would be nothing but reckless. And yet, he thought about it far too often.

Would Madison understand the things he'd done? He thought so. Hopefully he'd find out, and soon, because that last image of her as she'd left Winton's shop had been uncomfortably seared into his brain. When she was ballsy and taking charge, she affected him. Appearing hurt by his rejection? Leveled. He'd been positively leveled and he didn't know how to get his feet back under him until he cleared the air with her.

On the drive up and up the mountain, he spotted another, smaller house and slowed even more to stare at it. Quaint instead of ostentatious, it looked perfectly nestled into the base of the mountain with currently barren tall trees around it and a small creek running behind it. In his gut, he knew Madison lived there. Interesting.

Too much so.

Would she be with Parrish today? Or was she in that small house right now?

The thought of being caught staring got him moving again. If she was at her father's house, he'd deal with it. They were both adults and the job with Parrish McKenzie was too good to pass up. With the added pay, excellent benefits and more reasonable hours, he'd be better able to assist Silver.

And Hallie.

Through his troubled thoughts, he counted the numerous se-

curity cameras—twenty that he'd easily noticed—while maneu-
vering up the winding road. Making note of massive boulders,
towering aspens and rugged terrain, he was glad he'd driven
the SUV, and it had absolutely nothing to do with Madison's
criticism of his sedan. Because the weather was still so lousy,
Silver had planned to stay in anyway so she wouldn't need the
sturdier ride.

When he reached high, iron gates, he looked for a way to
alert Parrish to his arrival, a buzzer or something, but the security cameras must have done that because they opened wide,
staying that way until he'd driven through.

Up ahead, colossal stone columns supported a large curved
roof over a second story wraparound deck. Floor-to-ceiling
windows glinted in the sunshine that reflected off the snowy
landscape.

Inside or out, whatever the season, the views of the mountains would be spectacular.

Pulling up to the front of the sweeping entry, Crosby wondered where he should park. There were plenty of choices, and
a few vehicles present—one of them Madison's—but also a ridiculous number of garage bays ahead. As he pulled up beside
Madison's ride, the enormous double front doors opened and
a tall, silver-haired man stood there. He held up a hand in the
universal symbol for *halt*.

Crosby put the SUV in Park and stepped out to speak to the
man over the roof. "Crosby Albertson. Mr. McKenzie is—"

"Yes, we've all been expecting you."

That formal tone of voice took him aback. And what did he
mean by *all*?

# CHAPTER THREE

Wondering if he'd been set up, Crosby asked, "Where do you want me?"

"Where you are is fine, sir."

*Sir?* Crosby studied the man again and wondered if he was some sort of butler. Wouldn't surprise him, not for a house that size. Having never met an actual butler, he couldn't really tell. "Got it, thanks." After turning off the car, he locked it and headed up to the entrance.

The house had looked large from a distance, but up close it was downright enormous. The deck he'd noticed was probably twenty feet overhead, meaning the first floor had to have incredibly high ceilings. All around the property, security lighting would keep it well illuminated at night.

He realized there was no snow on this part of the driveway, the parking spaces, the curb return or the cobbled walkway to the door. Curious, he searched around and spotted the sensors. Huh. A heated driveway.

Talk about luxury.

From the doorway, the man regally stated, "Mr. McKenzie is waiting in the library. If you'll follow me?"

"Sure," Crosby said, more than a little put off by all the stiff formality. Once inside, he tried to subtly look around without actually gawking. He felt like he'd stepped into a museum. It wasn't easy to reconcile Cade and Reyes, who despite their lethal edges were everyday men, to this type of privilege.

And Madison? Had she been a little girl racing through these wide halls, listening to her voice echo from the soaring ceilings? Had she slipped on polished floors? Played hide-and-seek in all the different rooms?

Spent an hour searching for her father?

Finally the man leading him stopped at another set of double doors and announced, "Detective Albertson is here."

"No longer detective," Crosby said, stepping around him.

Parrish stood from behind a desk. "I see you've met Bernard the butler."

"So he is a butler?"

"When he chooses to be." Parrish shot Bernard a mocking glance. "He's also an amazing chef."

"Thank you," Bernard said, his chin elevated.

"An adequate assistant."

"I am the *best* assistant," Bernard insisted.

"Can't forget cat lover."

"Chimera is special. You know that."

Looking back and forth between them, Crosby wasn't sure what to think. "All that?"

Smiling, Parrish said, "He's also a longtime friend, as close as family, and we couldn't get by without him."

Losing his starch, Bernard grinned. "No, you couldn't. But since I'm not going anywhere, it doesn't matter." To Crosby he asked, "You want anything? Coffee, cola, iced tea? I'd offer hot tea, maybe from a little porcelain teapot, but that might be taking my butler gig a bit far."

Slowly, Crosby grinned. "It was all an act?"

With a shrug, Bernard leaned in the doorway. "Have to keep up appearances."

"Except where Chimera is concerned," Parrish added. "Around that cat, he's pure mush."

"Well, the kids turn me inside out a little, too." Bernard came farther into the room. "Cade is so well-ordered, I enjoy treating him to my best aloof impersonation."

Crosby couldn't disagree. With his iron control, Cade was one of the most measured men he'd ever met. The man could face three armed gunmen without a single shred of concern.

"Reyes does everything he can to needle me."

"Like asking for beer with brunch," Parrish mentioned.

Bernard smiled fondly. "He's always been a little devil."

There was nothing *little* about Reyes McKenzie. The men had inherited their incredible height from Parrish, though Crosby thought Cade might top his dad by a bit.

He liked seeing this side of the family, getting a sense of some warmth instead of all the rigid training. He wouldn't be fooled into thinking they were average, not by any stretch of the imagination. But at least it wasn't all workouts and target practice.

When no one mentioned Madison, his smile slipped away. What the hell? Parrish had three children, and Crosby didn't like the idea of one being overlooked just because she was female.

Finally, with his voice softer, Parrish said, "Madison has Bernard wrapped around her little finger."

Crosby didn't mean to, but he grew alert, anxious to hear more about her.

A gentle expression fell over Bernard's features. "She's as cocky as the boys, but with her own unique spin on things."

It amused Crosby to hear men with lethal skill referred to as *boys*.

"Don't misunderstand. My daughter's character and determination is as strong as anyone's, but she has a soft, gentle side, too."

Yeah, Crosby had noticed that right off. Now he doubted

he'd ever forget it. "Cade and Reyes don't?" he asked, just to get his mind off Madison's softness.

"Before meeting their wives, the answer would have been more difficult. Now I can say with confidence that they do—it's just that most don't see it." Parrish gestured for Crosby to have a seat before settling back into his chair behind his desk.

"Drinks," Bernard said. "What will it be?"

"Iced tea would be terrific," Crosby decided. "Thank you."

Looking very much like an omnipotent leader, Parrish folded his hands on the desk. "Have you eaten?"

It was after breakfast and too early for lunch, so Crosby nodded. "I'm fine, thanks."

Bernard left, and Parrish sat back in his seat. "It goes without saying that my home is incredibly private. Anyone who attempts to come here uninvited will be immediately rejected. However, I wanted to show you some of the operation, just so you know exactly what it is I'm protecting."

Curiosity sharpened. "I'd appreciate that."

"If you're going to work for me—with me—then it's important for you to understand the scope of our operation."

"Agreed." For too long, Crosby had resented their intrusion into legal matters.

Until he started adding up their successes.

The number of scumbag traffickers put behind bars. All the women, men and children freed.

He couldn't argue with that success.

Yes, the law was important. He couldn't see himself ever crossing those boundaries. But what mattered most was giving victims a true champion, and that's what the McKenzie family did.

Over the iced tea that Bernard served, they discussed the logistics of the task force's work, including the safe housing supplied to help victims recover. Parrish had purchased and remodeled a nice hotel for that specific purpose.

The range of his philanthropy impressed the hell out of Crosby. He didn't know anyone, or any organization, that did as much as this family.

Thoughtful, his gaze on a place behind Crosby, Parrish said, "I suppose I should explain how I got started on this path."

Months ago, Madison had told him a little about the family history and the loss of her mother in an effort to deflect his suspicions. To protect her family, she'd been judicious with her details, telling him just enough to earn his understanding.

He'd sympathized with all of them, Madison especially, but it had only whetted his curiosity about the family enterprise. Now he had the feeling he was about to learn something monumental. "I'll admit, I've wondered."

"Of course you have. You're a cop."

"No longer a cop," he corrected.

Parrish gave a small shake of his head. "That's like saying you're no longer a take-charge man. You may not be working for the police force now, but you are and always will be a cop at heart."

True enough. Because he still wanted to right the wrongs, protect the innocent and nail the bad guys, he shrugged his concession on the point.

Parrish met his gaze. "Marian was the love of my life. Mother to my children. She didn't birth Cade, but you'd never have known it to see them together."

Whoa. That was news to Crosby. So Cade was a half brother to Reyes and Madison? "You already had Cade when you met Marian?"

He gave a subtle nod. "I won't call him a mistake, but we were young and Cade's mother wasn't ready to take on the responsibility. When she offered me my son, I took him." A smile of pride touched his mouth, there and gone. "I've never regretted that for a single moment. And Marian…she loved him on sight. He's only two years older than Reyes, six years older than Madison."

"You were a family," Crosby said simply. It's how he'd always felt. Blood didn't determine everything. Love did that.

Parrish's voice lowered. "Marian was taken."

He couldn't—*wouldn't*—tell Parrish that Madison had already shared that tragedy, so he simply said, "I'm sorry."

"Money can't buy everything or Marian would be with me still. However, it does allow you to purchase the best. The best investigators, the best trackers and the people who are best at dealing with evil." Pushing back his chair, Parrish drew several even breaths.

Crosby had the feeling that he didn't talk about this often. Maybe never. Had Madison been given a chance to talk if she'd needed to? Didn't seem likely. He was glad she'd confided in him, but he wished he'd realized just how monumental that concession had been. His assumption that she'd told him to sidetrack him could be far off the mark.

"There were no lengths I wouldn't go to find her," Parrish said as he stood. "At times, it was brutal. Other times, even deadly." His gaze sharpened. The muscles in his jaw tensed. "The team I hired uncovered several trafficking organizations before we found Marian. You should understand that I didn't mind breaking bones to get answers."

Uncomfortable with the information, Crosby rubbed the back of his neck. Most of that discomfort came from knowing he would do the same for someone he loved. "You got her back, so your methods worked."

For the longest time, Parrish didn't reply. "One year to the day that I found her and brought her home, she killed herself. The pain of her ordeal was too much for her to bear."

Silence stretched out, the tension tightening. Memories bombarded Crosby, along with thoughts of what might have happened if he hadn't been in the right place at the right time. No one should have to suffer as Marian had. As Parrish did still.

There was really only one thing he could say. "I understand."

"I thought you might." Parrish propped a hip on the corner of the desk. "Marian left a note saying that she loved us, and that she was sorry." He locked his gaze to Crosby's. "She also insisted that I should do everything in my power to ensure that other women didn't go through the same ordeal that she had." Oddly enough, Parrish gave a small smile. "She knew me so well. Motivating me to do something about the atrocities gave me a purpose, a way to cope with my grief. I'd already experienced what was possible, what I could accomplish when I used my fortune and resources combined."

"It's admirable." Crosby meant that. One hundred percent.

"I wanted the same for my children." Parrish paused, shook his head. "I *needed* to know that they could defend themselves, and others, if they needed to. It happened to Marian, so I knew it could happen to anyone. There was no safe social status, no invisible financial barrier that protected her. No amount of love that kept her from being vulnerable."

Crosby found it hard to breathe. He couldn't fathom the torment Parrish must have suffered while searching for Marian. Not knowing if she was dead or alive. How badly she'd been hurt.

He curled his hands into fists. To find her and then lose her anyway...

Yes, he understood. He'd move heaven and hell to protect the people he loved.

"I trained with the best," Parrish said, "and the kids trained with me. Everything I learned, I wanted them to know, as well."

Why did that suddenly seem like the right answer? Until this moment, Crosby had resented Madison's upbringing, seeing it as too disciplined, focused only on retribution instead of living. He'd worried that she'd missed out on being a little girl, but now?

Now he knew she was capable of protecting herself in ways most people couldn't. Maybe he should rethink things with Silver…and Hallie, too. "You created an elite team, made up of you and your kids, and now you do what you can to protect others."

"A nice summary that leaves out all the grisly aspects. And, Crosby? I want you to know, things do get grisly on occasion."

They *do*, not that they *did*, meaning he engaged in those same practices still. "The summary left out the years of hard training, too, but I'm starting to get the big picture." Nothing came without a cost. This family had lost a lot, and in return, they'd given back. How amazing was that?

Parrish straightened. "Thank you for understanding. Now, how about I show you around?"

"Around your home?"

"It's not just a home, you know. I was a well-respected surgeon before I changed my focus. Or had it changed by circumstances." He led Crosby from the room. "I have a fully functioning medical space here, but we also have a gym, an indoor shooting range, two pools, an armory—"

*"Armory?"* Crosby barely noticed the luxury of the gazillion rooms they went through because the conversation was so enlightening.

"Since Reyes and Madison are sparring, we'll save the gym for last."

Well hell. That statement all but guaranteed he'd be distracted throughout the entire, fascinating tour.

Worse, he had a feeling Parrish had planned it that way. Why would he do that? Surely he didn't want Crosby to get involved with Madison.

But if he did? That would eliminate his main reason for resisting her.

The house seemed to go on and on forever. He'd gotten only a cursory peek into the suites set up for Cade, Reyes and Madison, mostly so that he'd understand the layout of the house, but Parrish had explained that each of them had given input on their unique designs.

Madison's suite was classy, but also pretty without a lot of fuss. Like her.

Truthfully, he'd barely noticed Cade's or Reyes's rooms except to note the obvious upscale features.

Now the armory… That astounded him. He couldn't recall ever seeing such a wide array of weaponry, from street ready to military grade and everything in between. It left him in awe.

He and Parrish were strolling a hall, chatting amicably, when he heard a grunt coming from an open room ahead.

"The gym," Parrish explained. "Sounds like Madison and Reyes are still training."

Intrigued, Crosby detoured toward the noise. The air was thicker here, warmer, scented by clean sweat and sanitizer. He was only vaguely aware of Parrish silently keeping stride with him.

"Don't take your frustrations out on me," Reyes complained.

"I'm not frustrated," Madison said, the statement followed by what sounded like a kick against leather.

"Baloney. You want the pretty boy cop and he's not having it so you're trying to demolish me."

Crosby froze. Parrish did not, so he had to take two steps to catch up. *Pretty boy cop?*

There was a distinctly feral and feminine growl, along with a series of loud thwacks.

Then Reyes's laugh. "Way to prove my point."

"Crosby isn't pretty," Madison huffed. "He's *gorgeous*."

They were discussing *him*. Crosby felt his ears go hot. *Damn it, Madison.* A quick glance at Parrish showed her father's barely checked amusement.

See, this was why he shouldn't get involved with her. The woman had no filter, at least not that he'd ever seen. On more than one occasion, she'd taken him by surprise with something unexpected.

With *many* things unexpected.

Parrish said nothing, but he also didn't halt their course to the gym's entrance. In fact, he might have prodded Crosby along.

What did that mean? Encouragement? Or a test?

"I'm betting he's also interested," Reyes said around a few huffs, as if dodging blows.

"You'd lose that bet."

*No, he wouldn't*, Crosby thought with a scowl. Interested wasn't the same as willing, though.

"He's probably just intimidated. You should lighten up a little."

"Do I intimidate you, brother?"

Crosby stepped into the open doorway just as Madison attacked Reyes with several fast left-right punches. It amused Crosby to see Reyes backing up and dodging blows—right up until he tripped her, sending her sprawling to her face. Quickly she transitioned to her back.

"Frustrated *and* distracted," Reyes accused. "Hey, you know Crosby isn't the only game in town. If you're wantin' some, go get it."

"Shut up, Reyes." When her brother made no move to continue the match, she ripped off her headgear and lay there staring at the ceiling.

"Good idea," Crosby said, striding forward and drawing too much attention. "Shut up, Reyes."

Before he got too close, Madison turned her head to glare at him and said in warning, "No hard-soled shoes on the mat."

He stopped at the edge, eyeing the way she stretched out, legs in a straight V and arms limp at her sides. "Are you all right?"

"Ha!"

Reyes snorted. "What my sister means is that I'm the one with the bruises."

Crosby considered braining him... Until he saw his grin.

"Don't act like I'm better than you." Madison sat up, her arms braced behind her, palms flat on the mat. "You still pulled back, treating me like I'm twelve instead of twenty-six. How am I supposed to learn when you won't push me?"

Reyes rolled a shoulder. "Sorry, I can't help it. Sparring with you is not the same as sparring with Cade."

"Because Cade would have knocked you on your ass."

His grin widened. "As I recall, you tried."

Crosby barely heard them. His attention was taken up with the sight of Madison all dewy with sweat, her high ponytail straggling loose, her shirt clinging and her chest lifting with each deep breath.

Annoyance obvious, she turned dagger-eyes on Crosby. "What are you doing here?"

*Ogling you.* Yeah, not something he'd admit, especially in front of her father and brother. "Parrish was showing me around."

"Sure, around pertinent places. The gym is not pertinent— not to you, anyway." She came to her feet in one agile move and, using her teeth, freed the hook and eye fasteners of her fingerless gloves.

His own defensive attitude came to the fore. Folding his arms, Crosby gave her a derisive smile. "If I'd known the two of you were going to gossip about me, I'd have steered clear."

Ambling over to a stack of towels on a shelf, she snagged one. "My idiot brother did all the gossiping."

"Hey," Reyes said. "I was trying to help."

"Giving her *terrible* advice," Crosby pointed out. *And calling me a pretty boy.* That had stung.

Madison gave Reyes a brittle smile. "I'm sure your heart was in the right place." She turned to her father. "Remind him that he has to treat me like an equal, not a sister, if he wants me as well trained as possible."

Parrish agreed. "Reyes, let's have a talk." He started to the far side of the gym.

Reyes groaned, but trailed after him.

Without a glance at Crosby, Madison headed out of the room.

Seeing that Parrish and Reyes were already in close conversation, Crosby gave in to the urge to follow her. "Hey."

Just outside the room, she paused. "Hmm?"

That blasé attitude didn't fool him. He knew Madison well enough to know she was currently running on pride. "Got a second?"

"If you don't mind my sweat."

If that was meant to discourage him, it failed. Actually, she smelled good. Heated and sensual—like a woman who'd just had vigorous sex.

Bad thought.

Having no idea what to say, he stopped in front of her. The conflicting feelings she inspired kept him off-kilter, but he knew he couldn't let things go like this. "Will it be a problem for you, me working for your father?"

"Why would it?"

Okay, so not just pride, but hurt, too. Crosby ran a hand over his face. "I haven't exactly been—"

"What?" Her chin angled up. "Tactful? I don't need that. I've always preferred that people speak their minds. It makes things easier."

"And if your brother was right?" *Shit.* He definitely hadn't meant to say that.

Dabbing the soft terry towel to her throat and upper chest, she held his gaze. "Right about what?"

"My interest?"

The massive chip on her shoulder remained in place. "Ah, so you're interested now?"

He looked back, but Parrish and Reyes had moved and now he couldn't even see them.

"Are you schmoozing up to me to cement your job with Dad?"

"What?" Brows drawing together, Crosby fumed at the ridiculous claim—until he remembered that he'd accused her of something similar months ago when she'd kissed him. Because her father and brothers hadn't trusted him then, he'd thought she was just trying to get info. Wincing, he said, "I guess I had that coming."

"Is that an apology?"

"Yes."

Surprised, it took her a second, then she nodded. "You realize they're matchmaking, right? That's why they're having the long heart-to-heart while we talk." Rolling her eyes, she said, "Hilarious, isn't it?" Then she pivoted and stalked away.

Crosby tried to cement his feet to the floor, to let her leave, but it didn't work. He caught up to her in three long strides. "Where are you off to?"

"My rooms." She never slowed. "Where I plan to get naked and shower."

"Thanks for putting that into my head."

"You're welcome." She shot him a sidelong glance. "Given your reaction to my kiss a few months ago, and then your clear statement at Winton's place, you might want to stop following me."

"Yeah, I probably should." But he didn't.

She stopped abruptly and jerked around to face him. "What the hell, Crosby? You made it clear I should get lost, so I did."

"You've still been tracking me online."

She didn't deny it. With a shrug, she said, "So? At this point it's just a habit. Don't worry about it."

He *had* to worry about it...she didn't know that, though. Another glance back, but he still didn't see Parrish or Reyes.

If Parrish was matchmaking, it'd be like tacit permission, right? He wasn't sure how he felt about that.

"Any reason we're both still standing in the hall?"

Her sarcasm wore on him. "Could we drop the animosity?" He gave her a very long look that must have been effective, given how she shifted. When her shoulders relaxed marginally, he took a step closer. Voice low, he said, "There really is something we need to talk about."

Her gaze searched his, and he saw the moment she relented.

"Fine. Finish up whatever you and Dad have to do while I shower and change. I'll meet you out back."

"Out back?"

"Yeah, outside. You're not afraid of a little Colorado winter, are you? I've already been down to the lake a few times, so there's a nice trail through the snow. It's the only privacy we're likely to get."

Luckily he had boots in his SUV. "All right."

"Twenty minutes."

"What do I tell Parrish?"

That slow smile curved her lips. "It doesn't matter what you tell him, he'll still know exactly what we're doing. Nothing gets by Dad."

If Crosby didn't know Parrish himself, he'd think her faith in the man's intuition was misplaced.

Instead, he agreed. "I'll tell him you're going to show me the lake."

"There you go." Patting his shoulder, Madison again walked away.

And this time he let her.

Yup, she was going to look anxious, but she didn't care. Again in her snowsuit, Madison leaned against the outside wall beneath the back deck. Cold wind stung her cheeks and nose, but the rest of her was cozy enough. She waited a full five minutes before she heard the crunch of boots on snow. Crosby came trudging around the side of the house, a knit hat pulled down to cover his ears, his puffy coat zipped high around a muffler and dark snow boots that fit him to midshins. He had his hands tucked into his pockets, but she assumed he also wore gloves.

Just before he reached her, she said, "This way," and started off.

It was either that or continue gazing at him like a lovesick sap, noticing silly things like the way the ends of his sand-colored hair curled from under the hat or how his shoulders filled out that coat.

Silently, he fell into step beside her.

"Cold?" she asked.

"Not too bad. You?"

"Toasty warm."

"Your nose is red."

She heard the smile in his tone and had to resist moving closer to him. "The lake is ahead. It's frozen right now, but still pretty." Idle chitchat made her feel better, and at the moment she didn't care what he thought of it.

"All of this is incredible," he agreed. "The mountains, the trees, the skies… It's beautiful land."

"Right?" Glad that he was seeing it as she did, appreciating the incredible scenery, she said, "I love it, too."

"The smaller house I passed on the way up is yours?"

"Yup." The cold and snow muffled all sound so that their voices seemed to float around them. "You've been to Reyes's house." That's where she'd first met him in person, when he'd come looking for her brother in the hopes that Reyes could give him information on a scumbag trafficker. Even before that she'd been keeping tabs on him—and was already infatuated. Seeing him face-to-face? She'd fallen hard.

Too bad he hadn't.

"Cade has his own house, too. Neither of them are on Dad's property, though. I understand their need for some distance, but I like it here too much. And of course, I have my own privacy."

"Plus it's all damned secure."

She grinned. "There is that."

"Madison?"

Oh, she loved the sound of her name leaving his lips. "Hmm?"

"Why are we going to the lake?"

Rolling a shoulder, she said, "I felt like a walk. You wanted to talk. It seemed like a good compromise." She absolutely was *not* getting him away from her brother and father so she could kiss him again. Nope. Definitely not. One big rejection was enough for her. "Here. Climb up on this boulder and check out the view."

Appearing dubious, Crosby eyed the rock. Patches of ice covered it. "I can see the view just fine."

She laughed at his expression. "Wuss." With practiced ease, she scrabbled up, braced her feet apart, stood tall and opened her arms. "If Bernard was here, he'd claim himself king of the mountain."

Tense, as if he expected to catch her at any minute, Crosby shook his head. "Bernard does *not* climb on boulders."

"Wanna bet?" Looking down at him, she tipped her head. "I guess you met Alfred?"

"Who?"

Was it crazy that she enjoyed this so much? Being out in the snow, alone with Crosby, chatting as if they were friends? "Don't you think Bernard is a lot like Bruce Wayne's butler, Alfred?"

He grinned. "Since your father presents himself like Batman, I suppose that would fit."

Words of automatic defense tripped off her tongue. "My dad is amazing."

"Agreed." Then with a shrug, he added, "Bernard is an Alfred for sure, but he's also a regular guy."

Madison snorted. "Not even."

"So he climbs boulders, but remains a stuffy butler?"

"Well, not with me. With you, though? Probably." Now that she was up so high, she realized getting down would be far more difficult with the ice coating the rock. "Other than when he melted for Chimera, Bernard likes to be very proper."

"Maybe I've gotten to see a side of the man that many others don't."

Surprised, she asked, "Bernard was himself with you?"

"He was both, actually. He started out all proper, but while your dad and I chatted, he was just like every other guy I know."

"Wow." That, more than anything else, made her feel as if her family had really accepted Crosby. So now what? "Guess that means you'll be around for a while?"

"I hope so." He scowled at her, but not for the reason she assumed. "You can't get down, can you?"

"'Course I can." She just needed to figure out the best way.

Deciding for her, Crosby experimentally stationed one booted foot in a niche on the boulder, then extended his hands up to her. "Come on. I'll help."

They were both so bundled up, she wouldn't be able to feel his gloved hands, and still a wave of heat coursed through her, flushing her cheeks and even warming her nose. "I don't know if that's a good idea." She peered over the side. "I could just jump." But she was at least five feet up and she couldn't see what might be beneath the snow. What if she landed on a sharp rock and twisted her ankle?

Would Crosby carry her back to the house like a white knight?

If he did, Reyes would never let her hear the end of it.

Mind made up, she carefully lowered herself to a sitting position. *Whew, talk about cold.* Her tush felt the sting even through the snowsuit. Reaching down, her hands came close to Crosby's shoulders. His hands were almost to her waist.

And disaster struck.

Her feet slipped, and she felt herself dropping back. Eyes wide, she wondered if she'd humiliate herself by bashing her head on the boulder. She really would have to be carried back!

But Crosby caught her forearms and pulled her toward him and they both landed in the hard-packed snow.

With her partially on top. *Of him.* Hmm…

Her chin cracked his nose. She heard him groan.

Sharp rocks! Sitting up in a rush beside him, she cupped his face. "Are you all right?"

He opened those sexy bedroom eyes and grinned at her. "The frozen snow broke my fall, but I could do without having it inside the collar of my coat." Gingerly, he sat up, took off his gloves and rubbed the back of his neck.

"Here, let me." Scurrying around behind him, she stripped off her gloves, too, dropped them, then removed chunks of snow from his neck and around his ears. "You lost your hat."

"Lost my sanity, as well." Twisting to face her, he caught her hands. "Are you okay?"

"You're even harder than the snow, but you did break my fall, so thank you."

Shaking his head, he said, "No more climbing icy boulders, show-off."

Since she'd only shown how awkwardly she could fall, she had no problem agreeing with that. At least he wasn't razzing her like her brothers would. She appreciated that. "Want to head back up to the house where it's warm?"

"And miss the view of the lake?" he teased, as he shoved to his feet. "I'm okay if you are." He bent to retrieve his hat, shook snow out of it, then tugged it onto his head again before pulling on his gloves.

Damn. So she'd have to be the one to call it quits? Like hell she would. She got her own gloves back on, then said, "This way."

# CHAPTER FOUR

"Mind if we talk while we walk?" Crosby asked.

Here she'd been thinking of other, more sexual pursuits, and he had talking on his mind. "Shoot."

"First…" He hesitated, silent, and finally said, "I'm sorry I was a dick."

Another apology? She didn't know what to think. "We already covered this, right? You were honest, which is good. If you're worried that I'll bother you again, I won't."

"You bother me all the time, Madison." Before she could remark on that, he added, "But what I mean is that I need you to stop searching my background."

"Why? What do you have to hide?" She waited for his denial, but to her surprise, his jaw clenched. So he *was* hiding something. "It can't be anything big or I'd have already found it."

"Maybe I'm really good at covering my tracks." He caught her arm, drawing her to a halt. "Seriously, Madison. It's important that you stop digging before you draw someone else's attention."

The wind carried a dusting of snow past their faces. She tucked in her chin to block the worst of it while her mind churned with possibilities.

Casually, as if it meant nothing at all—and maybe to him it didn't—Crosby put his arm over her shoulders, tucking her closer to shield her. Warm breath teased her cheek when he asked, "Can you do that? Can you please let it go?"

She'd just harped on honesty, so it wouldn't be fair to mislead him. Snuggling closer, one hand gripping the front of his coat, she breathed in his rich scent and whispered with much regret, "I don't think I can."

Instead of exploding, he huffed a resigned laugh.

"I'm sorry," she said in a rush. "It's just so easy for me, and you know curiosity is my worst vice. Will it help if I swear that no one else will see my tracks?"

"No, because as good as you are, others are good, too."

"You, for example?"

"Good enough that I knew you were poking around."

By silent agreement they continued on, now with his arm around her. Probably a ploy to keep her from climbing any more boulders, but hey, she'd stay out in the cold all night to enjoy the familiarity.

After walking a bit more, they stopped. Stretched out before them, the frozen lake glistened like frosted glass. Every so often, a swirling drift of snow would tumble over the surface, driven by the wind.

She turned to see Crosby taking it in, a small smile on his mouth. Her heart beat faster. "Was it worth the walk and the cold?"

"Even worth being tackled in the snow." He gazed at her. "Do you ice-skate?"

"I haven't in a very long time. Dad worries the ice will break and I'll fall in. Mostly I just come here because it's pretty." Did he like it as much as she did? He seemed to. "My brothers used to swim in the summer when they were younger. Even then, the water stays frigid so I wasn't a fan."

"I think I'd much rather look at it than get in it." He held silent for a full minute, then sharpened with resolve. "Where I live, there's a park nearby."

He said that like a concession, as if he was giving her new info. She didn't point out that she already knew everything about him. "Within walking distance, right?"

Nodding, he said, "I go there sometimes." He turned his face up to the bright afternoon sunshine. "There's a pond there. Much smaller than this, of course, but in the spring you can see some noisy geese, koi carp and frogs along the shoreline. Right now, it's frozen, too."

"You know that because you've been there to see it?" She'd like it if they had a love of nature in common. "Or are you just assuming?"

"I go there often." His gaze met hers. In this light, the hair curling out from under his hat looked more golden than sandy brown, but his eyes appeared darker. "Can I trust you, Madison?"

*Whoa.* "Yes," she breathed quickly, so he wouldn't change his mind. "You absolutely can."

He took a few seconds more to study her, then stated, "I have a daughter."

Even with her snow boots planted apart, she felt ready to topple. Talk about bombshells! *"Impossible."*

"Apparently not."

"I'd have known if you did!"

"I told you, I'm good at covering my tracks—which is one reason your father hired me."

Hurt vied with anger. Her lips were suddenly too cold and stiff to work correctly. "Are you married?"

"Ah, no."

Suspicion remained. "Divorced, then?"

"Never married, actually."

Her brain tried to catch up with her heart, but both seemed to be fumbling. "Involved? In a relationship?"

"Why don't you hold on to your questions for a few minutes and let me explain?"

She didn't want to, but she gave a brisk nod.

Studying her, he warned, "It's not a pretty story."

Her heart stuttered. With her line of work, she knew all about tragic stories. "Should we go back inside?"

Shaking his head, he took her arm and led her to a line of tall evergreens that would, he hoped, act as a buffer to the wind. Standing close to her, he spoke in a low, gruff voice. "I met Hallie, my daughter, while closing down a cult. We'd tracked traffickers there, and we knew there was a lot of abuse, drugs and prostitution going on. I specifically wanted Rob Golly, because he was known to buy girls from there, but we somehow missed him."

She'd met Crosby in person because of Golly. In the end, she and her brothers had helped to bring the man down. Actually, with assistance from Reyes, Golly had blown himself up with a homemade bomb he'd intended to use on others.

This story explained why Crosby had been so keen on getting him. "How old was Hallie?"

"Two."

Her breath shuddered in. "A baby."

Nodding, he said, "We'd rounded up everyone we could find, including traffickers, victims and some in-between. We were going through all the rooms." He struggled for words, his jaw working.

Seeing that it was a difficult memory for him to share, Madison reacted on instinct. Putting her arms around him, she hugged him tight. It took him a second, then his strong arms came around her, too. He spoke in a hush against her temple.

"I heard a noise, not much louder than a mouse, but thank God I'm cautious enough that I investigate everything. It took me a minute to realize the sound came from under the bed. I didn't see anyone hiding so I shoved the frame over a few feet."

Madison felt the heavy beat of his heart. Pressing her face to his throat, she tried to lend him her strength even as she shored up her own courage to hear what he'd found.

"There was an old ratty rug. I pulled it away…and found a locked trapdoor." His hand cupped the back of her head, pressing her closer. "Jesus, I was conflicted. I wanted to rip it open to see if there was another victim or a trafficker hiding. But in my guts, I knew it would be horrendous and I dreaded it so fucking much."

She swallowed heavily against the sadness squeezing her throat. "It was the baby?"

Pure torture sounded in his tone. "Two years old, hurt, locked in a fucking hole in the floor."

"Please tell me you killed them all."

He gave a gruff laugh, a release of pent-up emotional pain. "There were twenty people involved, men and women. Believe me, I was tempted, but it would have been a massacre, and we were still sorting out who was who."

She nodded. Sometimes it was difficult to distinguish a victim from a victimizer. When people were treated cruelly long enough, they did what they were told, no questions asked, whether they wanted to or not. "I understand."

"She came right to me, Madison." His hand drifted up and down her back. "Poor little thing was filthy and afraid, hungry and hurt, but she clung to me and… I knew I couldn't ever let her go."

Right there, in that moment, he stole a huge chunk of her heart. "Of course you couldn't," she said, trying to sound brisk and self-assured, and instead she sounded soft and deeply affected.

"While we waited for an ambulance, one of the officers brought her peanut butter crackers he'd included in his lunch. Another found a bottle of water in his car." Breath left him in a broken sigh. "Hallie wouldn't take anything from them. She just kept hiding against me. But I got her to eat and drink a little."

There were no words in that moment, so she merely nodded.

"We were all leveled," he admitted.

As cops, Madison knew they sometimes witnessed the worst of the worst in society. Pain, hunger, neglect as well as violent crime. "Abuse is never easy to see," she agreed. "With a child? It's soul crushing."

His chest expanded on a deep inhale. "She didn't have a diaper, but we found a big towel and I wrapped her in that."

Already knowing the answer, she asked, "You went with her to the hospital?"

"Yeah. They kept her three days, but she recovered. Physically, anyway. I visited her every single day, staying as long as I could, bringing her gifts and just trying to make her feel better. Safer."

Madison smiled against his shoulder despite the twisting of her heart. "You bonded."

"When children's services couldn't find immediate placement for her, I knew I wanted her."

Because he was a good man, and good men could never tolerate seeing a child hurt or afraid. Smiling past the heartache, Madison tipped back to see his face. "That's wonderful, Crosby."

"I scrambled to find clothes for her, the right food, diapers." He paused. "The perfect sitter—because I knew it would take someone special. Someone with an enormous heart and plenty of patience. Someone who knew what it meant to suffer abuse."

Tears started to blur her vision, but she blinked them away. She was not a woman who gave in to crying.

"Remember at the store when Owen mentioned Silver?" She nodded. "Yes."

"Silver Galloway, who escaped her own abuse, has been Hallie's sitter for two years now. It was tight financially, but I found two small houses side by side, away from established neighborhoods. Hallie loves her, and she loves Hallie."

He spoke of Silver with so much affection and admiration, a kernel of jealousy tried to wiggle free. Madison ruthlessly stomped it into submission. No matter how Crosby might feel about Silver, she was glad the baby had someone wonderful.

As if he'd read her thoughts, Crosby looked into her eyes and smiled at her. "Hallie thinks of Silver as a grandma."

Oh, well, that was nice. "How old is Silver?"

"Only forty-five, but she could pass for younger. Hallie also considers Owen a big brother and Winton a grandpa."

"Winton and Silver…?"

"No. Winton lost his wife six years ago and he's never looked at another woman that way."

"Like my dad, I guess." It made her even more melancholy to think about how much Parrish still missed her mother, so she moved on. "You adopted Hallie?"

"It was final only a few weeks ago. All that time, I kept thinking something might happen. Amy, Hallie's mother, was there the day we found her. The poor woman was young, confused, drugged out of her mind. Later, Amy said she'd tried to escape with Hallie, but the drugs kept her compliant, and even once we freed her, she couldn't seem to get it together. She'd been through too much trauma, too much suffering."

Yes, Madison understood that, as well. Her mother had taken her own life for that very reason.

"Christ, I lived in fear of what would happen. I wanted Hallie's mother to get well—hell, I wanted all of them to recover, to be able to reclaim their lives."

"Of course you did," Madison said. From the beginning she'd understood Crosby was a man determined to make a difference in the world, a man who wanted to correct wrongs and protect those who couldn't protect themselves.

He gave her a brief, easy hug, like a silent thank-you for believing in him. Voice lower, rough with guilt, he added, "But then I'd think of Amy getting custody of Hallie…" He went silent for a few seconds. "Talk about conflicted feelings."

"You didn't want to lose your daughter."

Another squeeze and a small, grateful smile. "That's it exactly. Unfortunately, Amy blew off every program. I kept trying to arrange rehab, and she couldn't…" His jaw flexed. "She's gone now. Dead, I mean."

"How?"

As if he didn't quite believe it, he gave an abrupt shake of his head. "It appears she OD'd in a gas station restroom."

His wording and his expression told Madison that Crosby wasn't buying it. So what had really happened to her?

"Hallie never knew her," he continued. "Even as a baby at the compound, Amy was mostly absent from her life—though that might not have been by choice. I've told her some about her mother, what I could, anyway."

"I assume you painted a prettier picture?"

"No four-year-old should have that harsh reality dropped on her."

"I agree." Madison made herself suck it up, blinking away the sadness and giving up Crosby's heat to stand on her own two, very strong legs. "Why are you keeping things quiet still?"

He seemed both disappointed that she'd stepped away from him and more relaxed because of it. "Golly wasn't the only one who got away the day we raided the cult's compound. We're fairly certain two other men slipped out of our net. Golly is gone now, blown to bits, so he's no longer a threat."

"Yay."

He cracked a half smile. "The thing is, three of the people we recovered from that ordeal have now died. All OD'd in very public places where someone was sure to find them."

Madison whistled. "That's a little too much of a pattern."

"Hallie's mother was the most recent, a few months ago. I'd already gone through the training and the home study, so finally the courts made her officially mine. But I'm still worried."

With good reason, if what she suspected was true.

"Until I can figure out what's happening, I don't want anyone to know about Hallie."

"That seems like a tall order. I mean, if people see you with a kid…" She shrugged. "It would all be easy enough to figure out."

"You didn't," he reminded her.

Feeling defensive, she countered, "I didn't know to look for a *baby*."

"That's the thing, Madison. No one does. Hallie is four now, and she spends her weekdays with Silver. Once I'm home from work, we make the exchange, but we're always careful."

"Careful how?"

"No close neighbors, no community cameras aimed my way. We go places that aren't monitored—like the park."

She took that one on the chin, since he knew she excelled at hacking into Wi-Fi–enabled camera feeds. Most security systems had them, making it easy for owners to check on homes or businesses via their smartphones.

The setup also allowed her to see what happened in urban areas. With a clear picture, she could pick up faces, license plate numbers and any number of other relevant details.

In more rural neighborhoods? Yup, those could be challenging.

Leaning against the trunk of a barren tree, Crosby watched her. "Most people assume Silver is her mother. Because of Hallie's circumstances, the adoption was kept private. The thing is, I can't rule out someone coming after me and using Hallie to do it. It's one reason I left police work."

That would certainly be a worry. Pacing away and back again, she listened to the crunch of her boots on ice-covered snow.

Crosby said, "I also wanted steadier hours to be with Hallie, so Silver could have more time to herself. And the pay will go a long way to making their lives easier."

Their lives, but not his? "And when Hallie starts school?"

"Time is ticking away on that. Kindergarten isn't far off. It's a problem."

"If my family had known about this, we could have—"

"Killed them all?" he asked with a frown, throwing her words back at her.

Madison gave him an exasperated frown. "Contrary to any impressions you've gotten, we don't indiscriminately murder people. Whenever possible, we bring them to justice, usually with success."

"And when that doesn't work?"

She wouldn't admit anything to him, so instead she said, "You know my father has extensive resources. I admire him so much because he could have used his money to corrupt, to expand his own accounts or his power, but that's not who he is." Parrish McKenzie had a streak of honor a mile wide that was made of granite. Nothing weakened it. Nothing weakened *him*.

He would always do what was right, using any means necessary. To Madison, he was a true hero.

"Dad uses his assets to help others. If we told him about this, he might have been able to help with Hallie's mother, too."

Crosby's gaze never wavered—except that it did veer from her eyes to her mouth a few times. "I'll admit, his task force is incredible. Unfortunately, I didn't know much about your family, and what I was able to find out only made me uneasy."

Madison waved that off. "Together, we probably would have figured out a way to find the men who escaped capture. Surely there was evidence."

"None that would hold up in court."

Because the police were held to such a high standard of proof. "My father could have—"

"Planted something solid?" He shook his head. "Remember, until very recently I was a cop. Besides, I tracked the men as much as I could, but only found Golly. The other two seem to have disappeared."

Again, she moved past the question without answering. "There are ways to ensure protection for those who need it, as your daughter does." Picturing the little girl brought on a smile. "I'd love to meet her."

It was Crosby's turn to ignore what he didn't want to address. Namely *her*.

"We should be getting back," he said.

Why had it felt like they were connecting? Clearly nothing had changed, not really, and she had to be a dolt to think it would. "You want me to stop snooping on you."

"It'd be better, safer, for Hallie and Silver."

It wasn't easy, but Madison managed to look indifferent when she said, "All right. Consider it done." Still too emotional, and feeling like a fool for repeatedly expecting too much, she started away.

Frowning, Crosby caught her arm. "Just like that?"

"What did you expect?" Before Crosby, she'd never had a quick temper, at least not with anyone other than Reyes. Around Crosby, though, she teetered on the edge of annoyance at all times, as if he fractured her control. "Ah, I get it. You thought I'd push ahead with my own agenda, even knowing I might endanger a baby."

His gaze searched hers. "No. I figured you'd understand."

"So was it that you thought I'd insist on meeting her, even though you're so obviously opposed to spending more time with me?"

"We've been out here alone for thirty minutes, which shoots your theory to hell." He took a step closer.

Her heartbeat tripped into double time. "It's not my theory. It's what you've said."

"I apologized for that."

"I accepted. So?"

His brows drew together, not in anger but with concentration. "Things are different now."

Should she go down this road again? Wavering, she whispered, "How?" And then, "What exactly do you want?"

Closing his teeth on the finger of one glove, he tugged it off. Gently, his warm fingers dusted snow away from her cheek. "Actually, I thought..." His mouth quirked to the side and his fingers slid over her cheek.

With her heart lodging high in her throat, she asked breathlessly, "What?"

"Since we've covered new ground, I was hoping I might get a second chance for a kiss."

Her eyes flared wide. *He wanted to kiss her.* Madison didn't need more of an invitation than that.

Giving in loosened all the tension in Crosby's shoulders and neck. It felt like he'd been fighting his attraction for Madison over a decade instead of a few months. But that's how she was. All-consuming.

When she was around, she was *there*, impossible to ignore, too present to dismiss.

Bold and sensual, smart and quick.

What man wouldn't want her?

Her mouth landed on his with the same take-charge firmness she'd used the first time she'd kissed him.

And just like that time, it made him smile.

Madison would always want to lead. She'd always want to be the one in control. He was the same, so at least in this, he understood her.

Against his lips, she growled, "If you dare laugh at me again, I'll—"

"Hold that thought." Cupping her head in his hands, he took his turn, and yes, he had a little more finesse, easing into things instead of treating it like an assault-kiss.

His mouth brushed over hers until she relaxed against him.

"Tease," she murmured, but she didn't take over.

"I want to savor this," he replied, taking her top lip between his and tracing it with his tongue.

She made an excited sound of anticipation, her gloved hands gripping the front of his coat.

Kissing his way to the corner of her mouth, his nose drifted over her cheek and he breathed in the clean, crisp scent of chilled skin, warm woman and scented shampoo. Intoxicating.

Madison tipped her head, managing to expose a small portion of her neck.

Accepting the invitation, he put a few biting kisses along the sensitive skin beneath her jaw, then higher, where he nuzzled aside her hair to tease the lobe of her ear.

"FYI, my toes are curling in my snow boots."

He liked that breathless quality in her normally self-assured voice.

"FYI," he whispered back, "I'd love to kiss you all over."

She went perfectly still, her breath held, her hands tightening in his coat. Then she nodded and said in a rush, "Yeah, okay."

Crosby couldn't help but grin. *Not* fighting Madison was a hell of a lot more pleasurable. This time he took her mouth with deliberate intent, urging her lips apart and licking in to taste her.

Her arms squeezed around his neck as she crushed closer, her tongue as bold as his. They moved together perfectly; when he shifted, so did she. He tilted his head one way; she went the other. Breaths mingled and heat rose between them.

Her damned plush snowsuit kept him from being able to really feel her, her curves and the heat of her body. He wanted his hands on that perfect ass he'd admired so many times. He wanted her breasts firm against his chest.

In that moment, he wanted it all.

Freezing wind blew around him, snow constantly drifting off tree branches overhead—and he felt himself getting hard. *From a kiss.*

But then, that pretty much summed up his relationship with Madison so far. Turbulent, unpredictable, and most definitely scorching hot.

It wasn't easy, but he forced himself to ease up. They were both breathing hard. Madison had her eyes closed, her body limp against him.

"That was—" she drew two more long breaths "—inspiring."

"Somehow, I always knew it'd be like that with you." It was yet another reason he'd resisted so hard.

Daughter to his boss, check. Savvy enough to reveal his most closely held secrets, check. So scorching hot that she made him forget all his priorities, check and check.

Her heavy eyes opened, the hazel gilded by the sunshine. "I had a hunch, as well. Why else would I have chased you like that?"

Kissing her again became a necessity, but he kept it light, touching his lips to the tip of her nose, her forehead, her cheek. "We're standing in a foot of snow, in the freezing cold, in front of your father's home."

An impish grin appeared. "What do you want to bet, Dad is fighting the urge to use his binoculars?"

That gave Crosby pause. "Would he do that?"

"He loves me, but he also respects me. More importantly, he trusts you. So no." Her grin widened. "But I'm sure he'll be waiting for us as soon as we go in."

Crosby hated to disappoint her, but he had to. "I wasn't planning to go back in. Silver wasn't going out today, but I don't like leaving her with just the car in this weather." Would Parrish think he was dodging him if Crosby *didn't* go in?

Patting his shoulder, Madison said, "Put your glove back on," and then started toward the house. "I'll explain to Dad. He won't think anything of it."

Falling into step beside her, he said, "Thanks."

"Now, about you kissing me all over." She shot him a sideways look. "How, when and where?"

He couldn't help but laugh. "Let me give it some thought, okay?" More and more, he considered the idea of Madison meeting Hallie and Silver. If she could be discreet—and he was leaning toward trusting her on that—it wouldn't hurt to have her as an ally. He'd feel better if Silver had yet another reliable, capable person to call in case of a problem.

As to that, it might not be a bad idea to introduce his family to all of the McKenzies. If, God forbid, anything did happen, they'd know what to do.

"Madison?"

She said, "Hmm?" as they reached the back of the house.

One trip to the lake, in a freaking snowstorm, and somehow everything was now different. If he didn't have other responsibilities, sincere concerns, he'd be full steam ahead.

He wanted Madison that much. But he had to put Hallie first. He knew it, and that meant slowing down and thinking through all the possible complications and consequences. "Hate to say it, but this is a big shift and I'm moving too fast—"

"In some ways," she interrupted in agreement, and then added, "But you're dragging your feet with others."

Since he *had* dragged his feet, denying what he really wanted, he couldn't argue that point.

She sighed. "Don't worry. I can be patient when it's something important. Now go on before Dad spots us and insists we both come in. I don't want to make you late."

He hesitated, wanting to kiss her again because kissing her felt right while everything else felt up in the air.

"You'll be around," she said softly. "Guarantee it."

He nodded. Now that Parrish had brought him on board, he was sure to see her again soon, if not in private, then while on the job. They had plenty of time to work out the details. "Be safe."

"You, too." Right before she stepped through the wide French doors that opened into the lower level, she added, "Give Hallie a kiss from me, and tell Silver she already has my respect."

Smiling, Crosby thought about that on the way around the house to the driveway. It was a trek that took a bit of time, and yet his thoughts remained on Madison. That is, until he got to the front and found Bernard waiting for him.

Going still on the snow-free driveway, Crosby waited while Bernard approached.

"Parrish has a schedule for you that he forgot to give you earlier." He handed over a paper, then reinforced that it was unnecessary by adding, "He also emailed it to you."

"All right." Crosby glanced at the list. Tomorrow, 9:00 a.m., he needed to meet a man named Jones, who would introduce him to the staff before his retirement. Jones would be on for another week, to help the transition.

"You'll make the appointment tomorrow morning?" Bernard asked.

"Of course." He'd planned to visit there anyway, to see firsthand what would be needed to update the security system. He'd have gone in the early afternoon, but with what Parrish paid and the benefits he supplied, Crosby could be flexible.

With a barely perceptible relaxing of his shoulders, Bernard nodded. "I'll let Parrish know. It was nice meeting you, Crosby."

"You, too." Eyes narrowing, Crosby watched Bernard retreat back to the house, appearing impervious to the weather. Thoughtful, he started the SUV so it could warm up, then switched out the snow-covered boots for his regular shoes and shed the heavier coat.

As he drove down the winding road away from Parrish's private property, he had the niggling sense that he'd just been set up. Parrish was planning something—he'd bet on it.

And that meant he had to prepare.

# CHAPTER FIVE

Knowing Madison would come up the stairs any minute, Parrish waited, keeping watch on the door, and then the hallway.

Bernard presented himself first. "It's arranged," he said quietly.

"Perfect," Parrish murmured. He needed several pieces to fall into place so that he could further his understanding of Crosby—and decide what to do next. "Now to work on Cade and Reyes." He couldn't make a move without one or both of them knowing it. Madison, in her pursuit of Crosby, had given him the perfect excuse to keep his boys busy for a while.

Bernard shrugged that off. "Once they know, they'll be all over it, I'm sure. Should I contact them for you?"

He shook his head. "No, I should be the one to tell them about Winton, and Madison's involvement with a robbery." He needed to really sell it to make it all work. It wasn't easy to get around his children. Parrish checked the stairs again. What was she doing? "They'll be annoyed that I didn't tell them right away."

"How will you explain the two-week wait?"

"I don't explain myself to anyone. I'll instruct them on what they should do, then let it play out."

Bernard fought a smile. "That should keep them otherwise occupied, at least."

"Long enough for me to do what must be done." Parrish heard footsteps, knew it was Madison and sent Bernard on his way.

He pretended to just be coming down the hall when Madison opened the door.

By deliberate design, they almost collided.

"Dad!" She laughed, stepping back. "Sorry, I wasn't paying attention."

A common occurrence, usually because she had her nose in a laptop. This time, with her laptop closed and tucked under her arm, he knew it was for very different reasons.

Ignoring her secret little smile, Parrish said, "I hope you didn't take advantage of Crosby by the lake. Remember, he'll be an employee."

The secret smile turned into a grin. "If I could take advantage of him, you wouldn't have hired him." She hooked her left arm around his elbow and urged him toward the kitchen. "Why did you hire him anyway? You know I can cover whatever digital security is needed."

His daughter—*his baby*—looked frozen through, not that she'd say so. Though she'd changed out of her heavy winter wear, her nose remained red, her cheeks pink, her lips a little chapped. He shook his head. "You can't be everywhere at once."

She half lifted the laptop. "I can with this."

"You have other responsibilities." To keep her from objecting, he said, "Bernard made you hot chocolate."

"So, um, Bernard knew I was outside with Crosby, too?"

Silly question, because she already knew the answer. Bernard had been with them forever, and beyond that, he was Parrish's closest friend and ally. "Does anything get by Bernard?"

"No?"

Parrish kept his smile hidden until they'd reached the table. For so many years, he and the kids had congregated here to discuss plans, to finalize strategies…and just to talk. Sometimes, when they didn't think he was paying attention, Parrish enjoyed listening to them, the banter, the arguments and the utter normalcy of being siblings.

He hadn't started out with the idea of raising them as elite fighting machines, but that's what he'd done.

Only he'd done so much more, too. At times, it leveled him to realize how remarkable they were.

And he'd had a hand in that.

There were times when he had so many regrets, when he felt the weight of his failures, especially as a father. Yet somehow, through all his pain and his jaded perception of the world, his kids were not only okay, they were exceptional adults.

Unlike him, they'd never lost their humanity. They could pass as living, breathing weapons, but their compassion, their love and his love for them, had made an immeasurable difference.

As Madison took her seat, Parrish glanced at Bernard and knew his friend would ensure she stayed put long enough for him to contact Cade and Reyes. "I'll leave you to your chocolate."

"You don't want to join me?" Madison asked.

Gently, Parrish stroked her hair, amused to see her opening her laptop. "I have calls to make."

Since her attention was already on the screen, Parrish stepped away. Right before he left the kitchen, the words came out. "I love you, Madison."

Her head jerked up, her expression concerned. "Love you, too, Dad." She studied him. "Is everything okay?"

Not precisely, but he'd make it so. "Everything is fine." It was his fault that the words caused such an impact. Clearly he didn't share them often enough.

He'd remedy that, though. As soon as possible.

To Bernard, he added, "No disturbances for the next thirty minutes." Then he made his escape before he acted even more out of character.

Once in his office with the door closed, he paced to the wall of windows and looked out at the pristine white landscape while recent events played out in his head.

Someone had shot at his car.

At first, he'd wanted to write it off as happenstance. A hunter's stray bullet, maybe. But three stray bullets? All hitting the driver's door?

Not likely.

The urge to gather his children and warn them to safety had been nearly overwhelming. And absurd.

Cade, Reyes and Madison had been raised to stay cautious, to always use care. For them, being alert to danger was as automatic as breathing. Unlike him, they wouldn't have been taken off guard.

In recent years, Parrish knew he'd lost his edge. At fifty-three, he'd become an administrator instead of an active participant. He still worked out, still trained both in physical combat and with weaponry, but training wasn't the same as doing.

With a wry smile, he acknowledged that his kids would lose their collective minds if he tried to join them on the next mission. Cade, especially, would nix the idea. In all ways, his eldest son was the leader, the one that the others looked to when in need. Even before his time in the military, Cade had that quiet authority that demanded respect. Maybe that was why they'd butted heads so often. Cade's wife, Sterling, was fond of saying they were too much alike.

Parrish took that as a compliment, but he wasn't sure how Cade felt about it.

For sport, Reyes enjoyed challenging Cade on a regular basis. His middle son was very much the quintessential hell-raiser. Always had been, always would be, and even his wife couldn't change that about him, though Parrish doubted Kennedy wanted to change anything at all. She obviously adored Reyes just as he was.

It was Madison who would worry the most. She had killer instincts coupled with a nurturing streak that made her a most unique woman. At first, Parrish had disliked the idea of his daughter falling for Crosby. But now, seeing how marriage had suited his sons, he wanted that for her. If something should ever happen to him, he needed to know that Madison had found the one person who would fulfill her in ways some people never understood.

Just as Marian had fulfilled him.

Shutting down that line of thought, Parrish went to his desk, sat on the corner and put through a conference call to his sons.

"I wanted to speak to you together," he explained, once he had them both on the line. "There's nothing seriously wrong, just a small worry."

The statement prompted Cade to surmise, "It must involve Madison, since she's not on this call. What did Crosby do?"

Followed by Reyes calmly asking, "Do I need to dismember him?"

Parrish grinned, but made sure to keep the humor out of his tone. "Not Crosby directly. Actually, it was more about your sister overstepping." He went on to explain what had happened at Winton's family-run business. "Crosby got the three present arrested, and with their records, I don't think they'll be a problem. But they're part of a small-time street gang. Not a brain in the bunch of them, however, I'll feel better if you ferret out what information you can. It's not likely that your sister, once on the scene, will be forgotten."

Just as Parrish had predicted, both of his boys were immediately on guard.

"Usually," Cade said, "Madison is levelheaded enough to cover her tracks, but where Crosby is concerned?"

Reyes agreed. "She's so hung up on him she can't see straight."

"Perhaps," Parrish said, "she's in love. All the more reason to look out for her."

Reyes snorted. "She doesn't know him well enough for that."

"*We* don't know him well enough for that," Cade added.

Parrish realized he'd completely lost control of the conversation. Time to rein it in. "Crosby will be otherwise occupied tomorrow. If you're both free in the morning, you could go by Winton's place just to get a feel for things. Winton is a close friend of Crosby's, so try to blend in."

"You can't be talking to Cade," Reyes said as a dig. "Big brother, with his military vibe, blend in with the little people? Can't be done."

"He blends in nightly at his bar," Parrish reminded his most provoking offspring. To facilitate a never-ending stream of criminal gossip off the street, he'd set Cade up in a bar and Reyes in a gym, both on opposite sides of town, each in equally run-down neighborhoods—perfect places for troublemakers to hang out.

So many traffickers relied on low-life scum to keep their schemes going. Word of mouth passed from one willing fool to another—and often into the ears of his sons while they worked.

It used to amaze Parrish how many people would turn a deliberately blind eye to evidence of abuse. Men preferred to believe a woman was willingly selling sex while not seeing the bruises on her body, or the hulking bastard who kept watch from nearby to ensure she couldn't get away. Women got their nails done in salons where skinny immigrants labored endlessly, without adequate sleeping quarters, food or care, and they never thought a thing of it. Underage servers, children sometimes, cleaned floors in dive restaurants and bars, and yet the customers barely paid notice.

The more Parrish had dug around, the more disgusted he'd become with a society that didn't seem to care unless it affected them directly.

He would never be that person who ignored gut instincts, and neither would his children.

"Instead of cautioning me," Cade said, "you better warn baby brother not to go in guns blazing."

"When was the last time I shot up a place?" Reyes asked, indignant because it really wasn't his style.

Deadpan, Cade said, "I wasn't talking about an actual weapon."

"Oh, you mean my arms?" Reyes taunted. "Let me tell you, they *are* weapons."

"Children," Parrish said with a long sigh. Lately, they'd taken to heckling each other even more than usual. "Are you both finished?"

"Yeah," Cade said. "So now it's your turn, Dad. What are you up to?"

Closing his eyes, Parrish wished his eldest wasn't quite so astute all the damn time. "I'm concerned for your sister."

With his voice suddenly alert, Reyes asked, "Since when? You're always telling us how Madison can handle herself."

"Because she can." Using her infatuation with Crosby as an excuse, Parrish added, "But not while she's thinking with her heart instead of her head." Hell, if Madison knew he'd just said that, she'd be infuriated for a month. And hurt. "So that we're clear, understand that I'll disown you both if you ever tell her I said so. I won't have her thinking I don't trust her."

Silence stretched out, then Cade must have accepted his excuse because he said, "I understand. With Star, I wasn't always thinking clearly either."

Reyes chimed in on the defense of his sister. "Same for me with Kennedy. Love dicks up your perspective, big-time."

God love them, they were so loyal to each other that Parrish felt his heart swell with pride. "Visit Winton, see what you can find out about trouble in his area, then update me. But keep it all from your sister unless, or until, we have reason to include her."

Luckily, they agreed. With the plans in motion, Parrish disconnected the call, then sat down behind his desk to attend to other business.

Tomorrow he'd gain his own, far more personal insight on Crosby, beyond what his daughter had supplied. After that, he'd make more important decisions.

Like how to protect himself so he could continue enjoying his family now that it had started to expand.

The next morning, an uneasy feeling nagged Crosby the minute he stretched awake. While thinking about Madison, he prepared the coffee maker and then headed into the bathroom for a shower and shave.

Standing in front of the fogged-up mirror, he combed back his unruly hair. He needed a haircut, he decided, but it wasn't high on his list of priorities, not with so many other things plaguing his brain.

After consuming a cup of strong coffee, he dressed for work, then went to Hallie's room to wake her.

Partially under the quilt, her small body sprawled out across the twin bed. A tiny foot and skinny arm stuck out.

As happened so many times, Crosby paused just to look at her, his chest tight with the memory of their first meeting. Why she'd chosen to trust him that day, he couldn't say—except that desperation and survival were instincts, and Hallie had wanted to survive. From that day on, he knew he'd do anything within his power, move heaven and hell if necessary, to ensure she had a better, *safer* life filled with comfort and love.

Trusting Madison with the facts hadn't been as difficult as he'd imagined. Did he believe she'd let it go now? No. It wasn't in her nature to leave questions unanswered. But because he'd told her, he believed she'd use additional precautions, and that helped ease his worry.

Knowing he'd have to leave soon, he came farther into the room. "Hallie? Time to wake up, honey."

She made a small sound, like a kitten mewling, and stretched, her adorable little face scrunched into a comical expression. Her fair hair, forever tangled, stuck out around her face in pale golden hanks. It'd take him a good ten minutes to gently brush it.

"Come on, sleepyhead." He sat on the side of the bed and patted her thigh under the quilt. "Rise and shine."

Sleepy blue eyes opened. "I don't wanna."

Smiling, he cupped her cheek, then frowned. She felt a little too warm. "Hey. You okay?"

"Mmm-hmm." She snuggled back into her pillow.

"Baby, do you feel sick?"

"No," she breathed, already falling back to sleep.

Hallie was a world-class sleeper. From the very first time he'd put her into a soft bed with a colorful quilt and plush pillow, she'd relished her time to sleep.

Warm and comfortable. Secure.

Without fear.

His heart clenched again.

"Does your head hurt? Your tummy?"

"I'm just sleepy."

Suspecting it might be more than that, Crosby asked, "How about I carry you over to Silver's, and then you can go back to sleep?"

"Okay." She stretched again, then sat up, always an agreeable, easy child.

In the two years he'd had her, his experience was that colds and random stomachaches passed quickly for an otherwise healthy kiddo. At Silver's, she'd likely sleep a little longer, then curl up on the couch with one of her dolls and a cartoon while Silver pampered her. As soon as Hallie felt better, she'd be up and on the go again.

"How about I help get you dressed?" It was far too cold to take her out in her nightgown, even if he bundled her up first.

Nodding, she headed into the bathroom. He heard the toilet flush, then the running of water while she brushed her teeth. He usually supervised that to make sure she did a good job, but today he let it go and instead got out a small white T-shirt, warm purple sweatshirt decorated with a unicorn, pink sweatpants and thick white socks.

Eyes half-closed, carrying her hairbrush, Hallie came back to him.

He didn't know a lot about kids, but she seemed pretty self-sufficient for one so young.

Still drowsy, she pulled off her nightgown and put up her arms so he could tug the T-shirt and sweatshirt over her head. Her panties were now crooked so he straightened those, then helped her into her pants and socks before lifting her onto the bed so he could start on her hair. "Ponytail?"

She shook her head, her eyes closing. Crosby left her hair loose and again put a hand to her forehead. She felt sleep-warm but not really feverish.

Leaning against his shoulder, Hallie smiled up at him. "Will you bring me home a present?"

Poor baby. He could tell she was under the weather—and was willing to use it against him. "I don't know if I'll have time to go to the store today."

"Oh." She stared at him with sincere blue eyes.

The grin tugged at his mouth. *Such a little manipulator.* "I have a new coloring book for you that you haven't used yet and a new box of sparkly crayons."

Her eyes flared with interest. "Can I have them?"

"Sure." Standing, he found her snow boots and coat, and got her moving. When they were ready to step out, he lifted her into his arms and crossed the backyard. She held the coloring book and crayons and tucked her face against his neck.

Silver met them at the kitchen door. "What's this? Is someone being a slug today?"

Doing a one-eighty, Hallie whined, "I'm sick, Grandma," and reached for Silver.

"Ah, baby, it's okay." Silver gathered her up, giving Crosby a questioning look.

He lifted his hands. "To me, she denied being sick. Said she was just sleepy." He watched the maternal way Silver rocked her, how she kissed her forehead.

Used to be, it bothered him how Hallie favored Silver in some situations, but Silver swore it was natural, saying kids always behaved differently with their mom or dad than they did with a grandma. That was proven true every time Hallie wanted to roughhouse with him or have him carry her on his shoulders, something she didn't do with Silver, and how she preferred for him to read to her each night.

Silver's thick, dark hair hung loose to just below her shoulder blades, the streak of white tucked behind her ear. Wearing an oversize sweatshirt and skinny jeans, her gray eyes free of makeup, she didn't look like anyone's version of a grandma.

"I told her you'd let her go back to sleep." Crosby followed them to the couch, and because he knew Silver's house as well as his own, he got a quilt and pillow from the bedroom Hallie used and carried them to the couch.

He helped his daughter get comfortable, and when he started to kiss her forehead, she wrapped her arms around him and squeezed him tight.

Her innocent love was a comfort against the ugliness in the world. Smoothing her hair, he crouched down and said, "Silver will call me if you start feeling worse, okay?"

"Will you color with me when you get home? I'll save you the best picture."

That was always her lure—the *best picture*. Coming from Hallie, it was a generous offer. "You bet I will." She yawned, closed her eyes and snuggled down.

Silver walked with him to the front door this time. "She'll be fine, Dad. Don't worry."

So often, Silver seemed to read his thoughts with uncanny accuracy. "Let me know if she runs a fever."

"Of course I will." She shooed him on his way. "I'll make her favorite soup and we'll spend the day chilling. Now go on before you're late."

He was incredibly lucky to have someone like Silver. "What would I do without you?"

"You?" She snorted. "You'd have found a way. But what would I have done?"

"How about we just say we're lucky to have each other?"

"Works for me." She glanced out at the snowy yard. "Now go, before my heating bill doubles."

Laughing, Crosby stepped outside, waited until he heard the locks click into place behind him, then cut across the yard to his own garage. He noticed that the walk needed to be cleared again. He'd take care of that as soon as he got home. Pressing in the code, he opened his garage door and... A niggling of disquiet skated up his spine.

Turning, he scanned the area around him but saw nothing and no one, only snow-topped trees, the occasional flutter of a bird and the bright sun breaking through gray clouds.

He stared toward the park, but didn't detect any vehicles.

Knowing Silver would keep the house locked, and that she planned to stay in today, he didn't share his uneasiness with her. No reason to alarm her unnecessarily.

But the concern was there, an itch under his skin.

Something wasn't right.

Hopefully it was only Madison and her surveillance setting off his alarm bells. With the thought of her now front and center in his brain, he chose the SUV to drive.

As he traveled along the street, he kept up his vigilance, his gaze searching everywhere. All was quiet. Wasn't that why he'd chosen the two homes here for him and Silver? Being the only two houses on the short cul-de-sac, they were remote enough to be private, with only empty lots, woods and a park nearby. Yet within a ten-minute drive, he could shop, visit a restaurant or get on the highway. Convenient.

Now that he was away from the houses, he used hands-free calling to ring Madison. He'd find out if she was still snooping around… And maybe invite her to lunch, too. One way or another, they would come to an understanding.

And somehow he'd eventually get her alone. Preferably naked, with all her enthusiasm still in play.

But unfortunately, it wasn't going to be today.

Stepping out from behind the tree and lowering the binoculars, Parrish considered what he'd just seen. Crosby with a woman. A stunningly beautiful woman.

He realized he was still staring at the door and frowned at himself.

Leaving his car a mile back and traveling stealthily through the park, he was sure he hadn't been detected. And yet, there had been a moment when Crosby obviously sensed him. Parrish had watched him search the area. Crosby had good instincts, he decided, but then he'd already known that or he never would have hired him.

Soon, he'd have a talk with the younger man about always trusting those instincts. Just not today.

If he wasn't determined to keep his kids out of this for now, he would contact Madison. She'd have the name of the neighbor in minutes, along with a background history that would tell Parrish if he should be worried about the woman or not.

Oddly enough, he half hoped she would prove problematic, just so he could investigate further.

The problem, naturally, was that Madison might be hurt. She didn't pay attention to men often, and he'd never seen her as interested as she was with Crosby. If there was something going on here, something intimate, Madison would be crushed.

And that felt like incentive enough for Parrish to look into things more.

Watching the woman's wide front window partially concealed by gauzy sheers, he held back for another twenty minutes. He wanted to make sure no one else was around, and that the woman wasn't onto him.

When it all stayed quiet, he stealthily circled around to Crosby's house, using the cover of mature trees whenever possible. The walkway and driveway were covered with fresh snow, making his tracks visible. No way would Crosby miss that, so it was likely they'd have to have their talk sooner rather than later. He didn't want Crosby alarmed about intruders.

Luckily, there was no one around, not even the neighbor, to see him peering in windows, testing locks and looking for an easy way to enter. Truth, he could get in no matter the challenge, but he'd rather not break anything.

The back door, even with secure double locks, seemed to be his best bet, and yet just as he finished picking open the second lock, he heard the unmistakable sound of someone racking the slide of a gun to load a round into the firing chamber.

Adrenaline surged through his bloodstream but didn't disturb his outward calm. With his profile to the intruder, one hand on the doorknob, he slowly withdrew his own handgun from the back holster, then swiftly stepped behind the door and took aim.

*It was the woman.*

Their eyes met and held, neither of them blinking.

Astounded, Parrish made note of frosty irises the color of a winter sky, lips set in a firm line, long hair blowing loose in the chill air and a mature but still shapely body not adequately dressed for the Colorado winter.

She didn't lower her gun, so he didn't either, but he did choose to speak first. "There's no need for that."

"Oh, honey, I think there's every need. In fact, my only decision now is whether I should shoot first and then ask questions, or vice versa."

"What if I shoot you first?"

She lifted one delicate shoulder. "I'll get off a shot anyway." Lowering the barrel of the handgun, she redirected her aim. "And if I blow off your balls, I don't think you'll be crawling out of here."

His balls, as she'd put it, were mostly behind the door, but at her threat he tucked his hips farther back. "I know Crosby," he calmly explained.

"Mmm, so do I. I guarantee you he doesn't want you poking around his house."

"Admittedly, I was overstepping." And if Cade, Reyes or Madison found out he'd been so easily busted, he'd never hear the end of it. They'd probably want to retire him right off.

"Is that what you call breaking in? *Overstepping?*"

"Nothing is broken. I merely opened the locks." It occurred to Parrish that the woman had to be freezing. She stood in fuzzy pink slippers, for God's sake, which didn't look even remotely waterproof. Without a coat, hat and gloves, the cold air would slice right through her sweatshirt and body-hugging jeans.

For her sake—or so he told himself—he decided to wrap up this mistake in the making. Stepping out from behind the door, his hands raised as if in surrender, he explained, "I'm Crosby's new boss, and with the line of work he'll be doing for me, I wanted a better look around his home. I wouldn't have stolen anything or done any damage."

Slowly, her very lush mouth curved. "Baby, I know who you are. None other than Parrish McKenzie. See, Crosby doesn't leave me in the dark. Soon as he decided to work for you, he made sure I'd recognize you and all three of your kids. Said he didn't know what any of you might do, so I should be aware." Sooty lashes lowered over those icy eyes. "Now we know you'd do plenty, don't we?"

Well. That was certainly smart of Crosby, which reinforced that it had been a good decision to hire him. "I see." After tucking the gun in the holster at the small of his back, Parrish took two steps forward, wondering how she planned to proceed.

Defiant, she came forward as well, her slippers kicking up snow and leaving heavy tracks behind, shoulders straight, chin elevated. She seemed oblivious to the cold wind that played with her long ebony hair.

"And you are?" he asked, still gradually advancing.

"I'm the woman who will shoot you if you don't stop creeping up."

But he didn't stop, he just made the moves more subtle. "We can't stand out here forever. You're freezing."

She pretended not to care.

To throw her off, he said, "I can see your nipples even through your sweatshirt."

Shock wiped the smug expression off her face real fast. Pressing his advantage, Parrish glanced behind her as if seeing someone, and when she quickly did the same, he was on her. Their bodies collided, his big and strong, muscled from years of staying in shape, hers slender and soft, decidedly feminine.

He couldn't help but take notice, even as his training took over.

Snatching the gun from her proved easy enough. One-handed, he shoved it into his coat pocket, but then he also had to dodge a knee aimed for his crotch. To retaliate, he caught the knee and lifted it higher, throwing her off-balance. She fell back in the snow—with her hands gripping his coat, meaning he went with her. To keep from landing full force upon her, he turned and fell more on his side. He didn't stay there.

Before she could move, he shifted over her, bracing himself on his forearms and trapping her long legs with one of his.

The calm, in-control woman vanished, replaced by a hellcat. She fought hard, wildly, trying to claw his face.

The very last thing he wanted to do was hurt her, so he used care as he subdued her hands and gave her more of his weight. "Easy, now. I swear I won't hurt you."

Breathing hard, she stared up at him, fear fighting against pride in her pale eyes. "Get. Off."

It leveled him, making him feel like the biggest bastard alive. "I just didn't want to get shot," he explained softly. "If I let you up, will you settle down?"

*"Settle down?"* she hissed.

He winced. Yeah, he knew better than to say something so stupid. "Just give me a chance to explain. Can you do that?"

A small voice intruded, filled with tears. *"Grandma!"*

They both looked toward the doorway to her house, and Parrish positively melted. A tiny girl, her blond hair in disarray and her clothes wrinkled as if she'd slept in them, clutched a stuffed unicorn and wailed, the sound echoing around the snowy landscape.

"Jesus," he muttered. "I'm sorry." Parrish sprang back to his feet, taking a step farther away for safety.

Breathing hard, the woman reached up a hand. "I have snow on my bare back." She shivered. "My neck, my feet. I feel like a block of ice."

Trusting her, Parrish pulled her up, and when she staggered, losing a slipper in the process, he decided *why not?* Lifting her into his arms and grabbing the fallen slipper in the process, he said to the little girl, "Your grandma is fine, honey, I promise." He carried her toward the open doorway where the child stood. "We just slipped in the snow."

She continued to sob until the woman crooned, "Baby girl, hush now. This is a friend of Daddy's, okay?"

On a shuddering breath, the girl stared at him wide-eyed.

"Daddy?" Parrish croaked as he stepped into her kitchen.

"Crosby," she clarified, almost taking out his knees. When she saw his shock, she curled her lips. "Yeah, wasn't something he wanted you to know, and when he finds out that you do, he's going to be fightin' mad."

Parrish pushed the door shut behind him, his thoughts leaping ahead. "I knew he was hiding something."

"Did you, now?" She wiggled to get free, and when he set her feet on the floor, she shivered and brushed snow off herself. "Bet you never guessed the truth, did you? Shows you're not such a hotshot after all."

How the hell had Crosby kept such a thing quiet?

"I'm Silver, by the way." Kneeling in front of the girl, she said, "It's okay now, Hallie. Daddy will be back soon."

"Is that so?" Automatically, Parrish went to the counter and pulled off several paper towels to clean up the snow they'd just tracked in.

Her gentle hands smoothed back the girl's hair. "Oh, baby, you seem to have a fever now."

Parrish said, "Or your hands are just frozen." He pulled off a glove and slowly, carefully, touched the backs of his fingers to the little girl's head. "No fever."

Silver shot him a cross look.

He liked her name. Silver suited her, especially with that streak of white in her hair.

He liked the look of her too, all sexy but comfortable lines, enhanced with attitude and a sharp tongue… "I raised three kids," he said, just to rein himself in. "I do have some experience."

Rather than argue the point, she stated, "I have to change before I freeze to death."

With silent agreement, Parrish handed the slipper to her.

Pointing to a kitchen chair, she said, "Sit, don't touch anything, and I'll be back in a minute." She took Hallie's hand, still talking softly to her, and led her away. Although the little girl kept glancing back, her gaze was now fascinated instead of afraid.

Ignoring Silver's order to sit, Parrish peeled off his gloves and coat, then filled the teakettle with water and set it on the stove.

*Crosby has a daughter.* Why the hell hadn't he said something?

In no time, Silver returned and found him making hot chocolate. She stalled in the doorway, her eyes flaring. "You dare to make yourself at home?"

Now she wore a black sweater with some type of shawl thing over it, another pair of jeans and thick white socks. "Warmer?"

Refusing to answer, she helped Hallie get settled at the table, tucking a small blanket around her and giving the unicorn a seat of its own right beside her. "How do you feel, honey? Better after your nap?"

Hallie absently nodded, her gaze glued to Parrish.

How could he not smile? The girl was adorable, all big blue eyes, fine messy hair and ripe suspicion. "I'm sorry I frightened you, Hallie."

She folded her arms and stated as a fact, "Daddy says no one is allowed here."

"Your daddy is a smart guy. And you know what? That makes me a smart guy, too, because I hired him."

Silver snorted. "Crosby will be here shortly, and then we'll see how smart you are."

"He's working," Parrish corrected, knowing Crosby would be going over staff and doing an assessment of the task force offices for hours yet.

Putting a hand on Hallie's shoulder, Silver said, "The second you showed up, I texted him that you were here." She gave him a superior smile. "Before you ever noticed me, he was already on his way."

Interesting. "You contacted him before coming out to confront me?"

"Of course."

Parrish thought of how she'd taunted him with that gun, threatening to shoot important things—like his testicles. He also thought of how she'd felt under him for that very brief moment when they'd been sprawled out in the snow. Cold as it had been, it hadn't obliterated his awareness.

Years, that's how long it had been since he'd gotten horizontal with a woman. Years since he'd felt the soft cushion of breasts. Since he'd breathed in the uniquely sweet scent of female skin. Too many years since he'd felt that particular stirring in his blood.

He also remembered how she'd stiffened, breathless and fearful, despite her bravado. "I assume you told him it was me?"

"Sure." Again taunting him, she said, "Also told him not to worry."

Exasperating woman. Bold, brave, yet also somehow wounded. "If you knew I wasn't a threat, then why did you—"

"Oh, sugar. A girl's gotta have her fun, right?"

# CHAPTER SIX

Luckily, the roads were mostly clear with only a dusting of fresh snow on Crosby's drive to work. Unable to shake the feeling that something might be wrong, he'd stayed extra vigilant, yet saw nothing of concern, just the usual morning traffic.

He'd just gotten into the building when the text arrived from Silver. Forestalling the two men who'd come out to greet him, he lifted his phone in a rush and read:

Boss man is here snooping around. All fine. Not worried. Just FYI.

Boss man. *No.* Parrish wouldn't dare... Ha! Who was he kidding? Every one of the fucking McKenzies dared to do whatever they pleased. To be sure, he replied: McKenzie?

Yup. Was peeking in ur windows. U didn't tell me hes a hottie.

*Son of a bitch.* Crosby now saw the task today for what it was—a diversion. And that must have been Parrish he'd sensed when driving away. He should have trusted his gut, should have come up with an excuse to stay home, should have... Crosby blew out a breath.

He should have known that something was up.

He texted Silver back with: On my way.

I figured. See U soon.

He turned to leave and damn near plowed headlong into Madison. The laptop, which she carried more often than a purse, nearly fell from her hands. "Whoa." She juggled it, then stared at him, her slim brows arching high. "You going somewhere?"

Of course she had come early. *McKenzie*, he reminded himself, the family who lived by their own rules, their own timetable. They never did the expected and weren't polite enough to stick to agreed plans. "I mentioned lunch," he growled with growing ire. "What are you doing here now?"

Discounting his dark mood and tone, she bobbed her eyebrows and said low, "I figured I could show you some of the empty rooms upstairs."

No fucking way. She actually thought, in the middle of his workday at his new *job*, for her *father*, surrounded by *employees*, he'd sneak off to grab a quickie in an unused room?

His jaw clenched so hard, his temple ached.

Sidestepping her, he said over his shoulder to the confused, waiting men, "I'm sorry, but Mr. McKenzie needs me elsewhere." That would keep them from asking questions. "I'll try to make it back later." It still felt rude as hell to leave like this.

Not a good way to make a first impression.

"Hey, what's wrong?" Madison hurried to keep pace with him.

"Your father." There'd be no keeping secrets now. Here he'd gotten Madison's agreement to respect his privacy, and her father blew past any and all boundaries.

Practically jumping in front of him, Madison asked in a breathless rush, "Dad? Is he hurt? What's happened?"

Because he'd never seen her alarmed before, Crosby allowed her to stop him. Today she'd skipped her white snowsuit and wore only a black parka jacket with the faux-fur-trimmed hood back. Black leggings showed off the length of her shapely thighs, and her knee-high snow boots looked both stylish and practical.

"All in black today?" It suited his mood.

"Crosby," she warned.

He didn't want her to worry, so he gave up and explained. "Your father sent me here today to get me out of his way, so he could show up at my house." Frustration got the better of him again, and he stressed, "My *house*, Madison."

Worry, and maybe guilt, settled in her expression. She hugged the laptop to her chest. "How do you know?"

"Silver texted me." He walked off again. His current priority was to get home so he could salvage whatever privacy hadn't yet been breached. Not that he expected to keep much from the McKenzies.

Hell, hadn't he known all along that it would be like this? That taking a job with the McKenzies would be a trade-off— better pay and benefits for less privacy? Yes, he had. Just as he also knew it was for the best. Silver and Hallie would be safer with the McKenzies looking out for them. An undeniable truth.

But he'd wanted to do things in his own time, not like this. Not with Madison's family forcing the issue.

Matching him step for step, Madison kept silent while sorting that out. "Silver and Hallie are both there?"

"Yes." He reached his SUV and unlocked the door.

Touching his arm, Madison asked quietly, "What are you going to do?"

"Quitting seems like a good idea, and then I might punch Parrish in the nose." The idea had merit, though he knew he wouldn't do it. It made sense to have the McKenzies as allies, not enemies. Attacking the patriarch would be the same as a battle cry. He'd have all the McKenzies breathing down his neck, Madison included.

Her mouth twitched. "You can't quit because it's the perfect job for you. Also, I wouldn't recommend punching Dad." Leaning in, she teasingly confided, "He punches back. Hard. Don't let his age fool you."

Her ever-optimistic and upbeat attitude never failed to steal some of his anger. Rolling his eyes, he said, "Parrish is fifty-three, Madison. Not ninety."

"Right. Still fast and strong."

"At the moment, I don't give a shit." As he opened the door, another text came in. Groaning, he freed his phone from his pocket, glanced at the screen, then had to resist cursing a blue streak.

Concerned, she crowded closer, trying to see the text. "What is it now?"

"More McKenzies." He was just put out enough to say, "Meeting the lot of you has been a damned curse."

She flinched, then rallied. "We can be a little overwhelming, I admit." Going for pragmatism, she asked, "Cade or Reyes?"

"Both." He honestly couldn't believe it all. "They're at Winton's shop, apparently trying to blend in and terrorizing all the locals instead."

This time she grinned, but quickly apologized. "I'm sorry," she said, her tone absurdly soothing given her humor. "Want me to go to Winton's to sort that out so you can get home?"

What he'd wanted was sex, with Madison—and damn it, he'd been willing to settle for lunch. But now?

Now he wouldn't even get that because he had to deal with her whole damned family. "You shouldn't even be here, at least not until noon as we agreed."

Issuing a dramatic sigh, she nodded. "I know, but once you called, I couldn't stop thinking about you, and knowing there were empty rooms here, I just…" Giving him a small shrug, she said, "Couldn't resist."

Crosby squeezed the bridge of his nose. "You may as well ride along. We'll greet your dad together, and I can call Winton on the way."

She looked as if she'd just won the lottery. Or maybe, considering her family was already loaded, the lottery wouldn't make her shine like that. It humbled him to be wanted so much. After becoming Hallie's father, there hadn't been a lot of room in his life, or even interest really, for women.

Never, not even in his imagination, had there been a woman like Madison.

She didn't give him a chance to open her door for her. No, she practically ran to the passenger side and got in, as if she thought he might change his mind. Before he could get behind the wheel, she'd already stowed her laptop beside her and fastened her seat belt.

"This is almost like a date, right?" She glanced around his SUV with interest, taking note of his insulated coffee cup, the blanket and first aid kit in the back seat, and the hat and gloves on the console. "I mean, we can talk and I can tell you all the wicked things I want to do to you when we finally have time."

The insanity of it made him laugh as he drove out of the lot.

"Keep it up," she said in good humor. "You're going to owe me for all those insults, and I'm relentless when it comes to paybacks."

Reaching over, Crosby clasped her thigh. "That wasn't a mocking laugh, I swear. It's just that I never know what to expect from you."

Staring down at his hand, she breathed a little deeper, then covered it with her own. "Expect my full cooperation." Her gaze tipped his way. "I'm not shy about what I want."

"I noticed." He pulled away from her hold to hand her his

phone, with Winton's text still visible. "Call him for me, will you? Then put it on speaker."

"Oh, um, sure."

For once, she seemed uncertain. Because he showed a modicum of trust? Likely. So far he'd been equal parts unyielding, irritated and cynical. If he could get her family to chill a little and stop crowding him, he'd like to change his relationship—at least with her.

On the first ring, Owen answered. "Crosby, hey," he whispered. "Are you on your way?"

Madison bit her lip. Anyone could hear that Owen was spooked, but then, Cade and Reyes could have that effect on grown men, much less an impressionable kid.

"It's okay, Owen. They won't cause any trouble. You have my word."

Madison smiled in approval. "Owen? It's me, Madison."

Shocked silence met her greeting.

Didn't slow Madison down, though. "I'm with Crosby right now. Do me a favor and give your phone to the tallest guy, okay? That's Cade, my brother."

"Yeah, sure. Um, just a sec. Dad wanted me to wait in back for Crosby's call. They're still out front." There was some rustling, then they heard Owen clear his throat. "Hey, um, excuse me."

Cade's deep voice murmured something.

"It's your sister. She wants to talk to you."

They both heard Cade's groan, followed by his voice directly into the phone, saying, "Madison, where are you?"

"I'm with Crosby, and get this—Dad is at Crosby's house, though no one knew of his planned visit. He sent Crosby off on a job, and apparently sent you and Reyes on a fool's errand so no one would know he was playing sleuth."

"Son of a bitch." Then more softly, probably to Winton, Cade said, "Sorry." To Madison, he complained, "Nothing about this felt right. From what I can tell, Crosby's already taken care of the problem here."

"Of course he did. Winton and Owen are family to him. He wouldn't leave them at risk."

"Got it." With a sigh, Cade asked, "We're meeting at Crosby's?"

"Might as well."

Crosby squeezed the steering wheel. "I didn't agree to that."

Giving him a cautious look, Madison belatedly said, "Let me ask Crosby first, though." Switching the phone off speaker, she laid it against her thigh. "Taking charge is a very bad habit of mine."

"Not just yours. It's a McKenzie trait."

"Yeah, we're pretty much all-in once we know about something." She smoothed a hand over his shoulder. "Dad is up to something. I'm concerned that he's in trouble, otherwise he would have told us his plans. Not to jump the gun, but I have a feeling he was going to bypass his own kids to dump his problems on you, once he'd cleared you—up close and personal."

Crosby had the same suspicion.

Softly, she said, "You know us now. None of us will abide that."

Yeah, he did know it. "Fine, we can meet at the house. I need to warn Silver, though."

"Warning her will also be warning Dad, and he might not wait around for us. Couldn't it just be a happy surprise?"

Another laugh escaped him. "You think it'll be happy?"

A smile played over her lips. "I think you're already agreeing, otherwise you'd be doing that intimidating, mean scowling thing you do where your whole body looks angry."

He had a mean scowl? *His whole body looked angry?* Well... good. When it came to dealing with the McKenzies, he needed every advantage he could get, even if it was only an intimidating look. "Fine. We'll all meet there. Now how about getting Winton on the phone so I can talk to him, too?"

Madison waited until Crosby finished assuring Winton that all was well, claiming it had been a misunderstanding. Oddly enough, Winton was now more interested in asking why she was with Crosby. He sounded encouraging, as if he might be in her corner, rooting for her.

At the first red light, Crosby promptly took the phone off speaker so she could no longer hear the conversation, but his replies to Winton were curt, with *"No"* and *"Yes, I'm sure"* and *"You're going to have to trust me on this."*

Hmm. Trust him with what? Was he promising Winton that they weren't involved? The thought irked; she realized *she* was scowling now.

Once he disconnected the call and drove forward again, she demanded, "Are we involved or not?"

"We are," he stated, casting an eye over the immediate area. Apparently finding nothing amiss, he added, "At least as far as I'm concerned."

Well, that was good to know. "So what were you denying to Winton?"

One side of his mouth kicked up in a quirky show of amusement. "Winton wanted to know if I was at odds with your family. I *am*," he claimed, "especially at the moment, but I didn't want him to worry so I denied it."

Wow, okay first things first. "Why would he think such a thing?"

"Have you looked at your brothers lately? They ooze menace."

"They do not," she scoffed. "They're both kind, considerate men." She felt certain that they'd been on their best behavior with Winton and Owen. But then, she supposed Cade and Reyes could only smooth down so many sharp edges. No matter what, their lethal capability would always be there, sparking the instincts of anyone with a sense of self-preservation.

Crosby shot her a quick look. "When they choose to be, maybe. Not sure they showed that side of themselves to Winton." His frown returned. "I'm guessing your dad made them think they needed to be there?"

Probably. "Dad has a lot to answer for," she agreed, before circling right back to her second question. "What makes you think you're at odds with my family? I did hear that correctly, right? You lied to Winton instead of telling him the truth?"

Rolling one shoulder, Crosby said, "I fudged the truth, yes. But you're not obtuse, Madison. You know your brothers—"

"Have a general distrust of everyone," she finished for him, rather than hear a possible insult. For herself, she could take it. Against her brothers? Not so much. "They're protective of me, that's all, just as I'm protective of them." She gave that quick thought, then added, "Just as they'll be protective of Silver and Hallie once they meet them."

"I hope that's true. It's the one upside of having my whole life turned around by the McKenzie hoard."

*Hoard?* Her eyes narrowed. "Am I not an upside?"

After another sweeping glance at the exit they passed, he grinned. "You're an enormous distraction, an interrupter of sleep and a possible complication."

All in all, that didn't sound too awful. "You're a distraction, too, you know. I've had to listen to my brothers razz me endlessly whenever my mind goes wandering. I usually have laser focus, but now that I know we'll eventually get together, it's all I can think about."

After a beat of surprised silence, he growled, "Guess we'll have to do something to get ourselves back on track."

Oh, the low, suggestive way he said that... His sensual teasing was something new, but she liked it. "I'd planned to do something, remember? Early arrival, empty room? You nixed the idea before I could even finish explaining it."

With the sun suddenly in his eyes, he lowered the visor and pulled on sunglasses. "You didn't really expect me to fool around while on the job, did you? Basically the *first day* of the job."

He sounded so appalled she withheld honest comment.

"To be clear," he continued, "I have a rock-solid work ethic. As pissed as I am at your dad right now, when I'm on the clock, he'll get one hundred percent."

Okay, so maybe she was too used to doing what she wanted, when she wanted. She got his point. They'd have to figure out another way to get together.

Bypassing the part about him being pissed, she asked, "Will you tell me about Winton? About your relationship with him?" She'd found some of it, of course, but she wanted to hear his take on it, his personal perspective that went beyond dates, random facts and the occasional photo.

"What do you want to know?"

"How did you meet him?"

His mouth flattened. "I tried stealing from him. He busted me. Instead of calling the cops, he held me accountable."

"That's a shortened version with all the juicy stuff cut out."

Crosby shook his head, and the sternness left his mouth. "No, those are the facts. If you want the nuances, then understand that my dad had died and Mom worked all the time, taking as many hours as she could get to make ends meet. Every day she came home tired. She tried, but one grieving woman can only do so much." He rolled a shoulder. "So I rebelled. Guess it was my way of dealing with shit, or so Winton later said. After I tried swiping a candy bar, he got hold of my mom and they had a long talk while I was banished to my room. Once I was allowed in on the conversation, I found that Mom had agreed for me to take a job with Winton."

"He put you to work?"

Crosby relaxed in the seat, still watchful of the surrounding area, but less tense. "He gave me direction. Importance. Pride."

"I knew I liked him," Madison murmured, wanting Crosby to continue.

"I'd have to sweep the floor twice because Winton would point out stuff I missed, then he'd give me a pat on the back and tell me what a great job I did. We'd share a Coke and just talk. His wife was terrific, really kind and understanding. Sometimes I'd eat dinner with them, and then she'd send a plate home for Mom." He grew quiet, lost in thought, before he added, "They never made it feel like charity."

"Because it wasn't," Madison said with confidence. "It was good people lending a helping hand."

"My time with Winton was important to me, but it also helped me to realize what more I could do to help Mom, too. The first time she got home and I'd cleaned the house, she actually cried, she was so pleased. Talk about a leveling experience. I realized what a shithead I'd been, and then, because of Winton, I knew I could do better. So I did."

Trying to be subtle about it, Madison drew a steadying breath and forced a smile. Though she already knew, she asked anyway. "Your mom passed away, too?"

He nodded. "She'd long since retired and was enjoying life with her friends before she was diagnosed with congestive heart failure. Less than two years later, following a night out with dinner and bingo at her church, she died in her sleep."

"I'm so sorry."

"After the diagnosis, she said often that she'd had a happy life, and that she was proud of me. According to her, she'd had a wonderful husband and had the best son in the world, so even though she'd been through some hard times, she wouldn't trade a minute."

"Damn, Crosby. I like your mother, too." She tried to wipe her eyes without making a big deal of it.

"I loved her so much, but I also liked her. And I respected her, not only for how hard she'd always worked, but for pushing through and staying a terrific mom. Like she said, we had a rough year there, but with Winton's help, we got through it and things were really good after that." Quietly, he added, "I miss her still. Mostly I wish Hallie could have met her."

He was breaking her heart—again. She sniffled, wiped her eyes and smiled. "Thank you for sharing with me."

"I figure you and I will do a lot of sharing in the coming weeks."

Weeks? Oh, she hoped that meant he wanted a longer term relationship, and not just a quick thing that ended after satisfying their sexual chemistry. "Will you promise me something?"

"Depends."

She laughed. Crosby wasn't a fool, so of course he'd want the details first. "Will you resist punching my dad? It really would make things awkward."

He laughed, too. "Sure, I think I can manage that—*if* he swears never to pull another stunt like this."

Ouch. Her dad would always do what he thought was right, so odds were he'd refuse to make such a promise. "Let's just see how it plays out, then." She'd hope for the best, and by God, her brothers better be on their best behavior, or they'd answer to her.

Crosby did his utmost to tamp down his temper. A cool head was needed to deal with Parrish. Madison hadn't been wrong—this job was perfect for him, and even better, it was perfect for him as a father, allowing him to do more for Hallie, to better secure her future. He had to keep his priorities straight, for Hallie and Silver both.

And now, damned if Madison didn't feel like a priority, too.

She, however, could take care of herself. Hallie couldn't. Even Silver, who liked to think of herself as hardened by the trials of her earlier life, needed him.

Madison made no secret of wanting him. But needing him? No, she'd get by just fine without his assistance.

It struck him that there was a certain freedom in that. Never would he shirk his responsibilities; he wasn't that selfish kid from long ago anymore. With Winton's help, he'd turned the corner and become the son his mother deserved, and a man she could be proud of.

But now it felt good to think about spending time with Madison, just because he wanted to, for fun and companionship, with no obligations at all.

He loved being Hallie's daddy, and he was eternally grateful to have Silver in their lives. But his growing relationship with Madison was something altogether different.

Something fresh and new.

So he sucked up his ire—for the most part—and parked in his garage as usual.

Madison appeared keenly curious about his house. It was smaller than hers, older, and missing the top-notch interior design she was used to.

"I'd show you around, but I want to get next door."

With her laptop hugged close, she waited for his cue while looking around at the typical garage storage of lawn mower, Weed eater and gas in one corner, a snow shovel and bag of salt in the other. Various tools hung on pegboard, and he had a large rolling tool cabinet against the far wall.

"I'm picturing you living here," she said, "all domestic and stuff." She flashed him a smile. "It's a really nice image."

That was the thing about Madison. She saw everything in her own unique, upbeat way. Holding out his hand, Crosby said, "Come on. We'll go out this door and around back to the kitchen."

He'd already closed the garage door, and after taking her out back, he relocked that door, too. Immediately he saw the tracks in the snow that led to his kitchen door. Visually following them back toward Silver's house led him to the disturbance in the snow. It looked as if grown bodies had rolled on the ground. He scowled, seeing that the tracks led to Silver's door.

Renewed irritation surged. "Parrish had probably planned to break into my house."

She kept her eyes down, but her hand tightened on his when she murmured, "Mmm, probably."

Poor Madison. She knew exactly what her dad had dared, but she wanted to keep the peace.

Silver's door opened right before they reached it. She stood there, arms around herself to ward off the cold, her expression comical. "'Bout time." She eyed Madison. "My, my, aren't you a beauty. And Crosby's already latched onto you. Whatever am I to make of that?"

As usual, Madison didn't miss a beat. "Talk about beautiful! My God, Crosby said you were, but he didn't say you were stunning. You have such unusual eyes. Showstoppers, that's what they are. And I love your hair." She pulled free of Crosby and trudged ahead of him. "On behalf of all the McKenzies, I hope you'll accept my apologies for the intrusion."

Blown away, Silver looked past where Madison stood on the step just below her—which, given Madison's height, made her eye level to Silver—and met Crosby's gaze.

Usually Silver's snarky comments offended people, but instead of being put off, Madison had effusively praised her and then apologized.

Slowly, Silver's smile cracked. "My, oh my. The surprises are runnin' fast and loose today."

"Where is Dad, by the way?" Madison asked. "Through here? Never mind. I'll find him." And in her typical high-handed way, she edged past Silver and into the kitchen.

Silver actually laughed. "Come on in, Crosby, and join the party."

Disgruntled, Crosby followed Madison's act of kicking the

snow from her boots before he stepped in beside her on the kitchen entry rug. She hadn't gotten any farther than that because the sight of Parrish sitting at the table, drinking hot chocolate and coloring with Hallie kept her riveted.

Had a similar effect on Crosby, too, stealing what wits he had left.

"I'm making cookies," Silver said, nudging him forward so she could close and lock the door.

"Cookies?" Crosby asked.

"Seemed the thing to do." Going back to the counter, Silver dumped chocolate chips into dough and began stirring with a vengeance.

Madison stood there, her attention fixed on Hallie.

Beside her, Crosby tried to take it all in.

Parrish, the dick, ignored them, as if invading his life in such an overblown way was an everyday occurrence. He was *coloring*, for God's sake.

It was Hallie smiling up at Crosby that finally got his feet moving. He knelt down just in time for Hallie to launch against him, her little arms squeezing around his neck, her baby-fine hair tickling his cheek. Pressing back, she held his face and stated, "Daddy, I'm coloring with Mr. Kenzie."

"McKenzie," Crosby corrected with a smile, hugging her close again and kissing her temple, relieved to see that she seemed to feel better.

"Kenzie is fine," Parrish said, concentrating on the horn of a unicorn that he colored a garish shade of pink. "She's a little listless, by the way. Sniffles, too. Likely coming down with a cold, but no fever that I could detect."

At that calmly stated diagnosis, Crosby slowly turned to look at Silver.

She immediately rolled her eyes. "You see what I've been dealing with? Man is a total know-it-all."

"I'm a retired doctor," Parrish said. "When it comes to colds, I know enough."

Silver narrowed her frosty gray gaze on Madison. "What about you, honey? You a know-it-all like your pops?"

"Pops?" Madison grinned and, after placing her laptop on the table, peeled off her gloves and coat. "If you ask Crosby, he'll probably say I am. Though I like to think of myself as well-informed." She draped her coat on the back of a chair, took a seat and looked at the selection of coloring books.

Hallie, unused to so much company, continued to watch Madison with unblinking eyes.

He'd be willing to bet Madison didn't interact with kids often. The proof of that was in how she stared back at Hallie, equally fascinated.

It amused him. Armed assailants didn't fluster her, but his four-year-old, very petite daughter did. "Madison?"

She shook her head, as if realizing what she'd done, and said to Hallie, "Hi there."

Hallie's eyes narrowed and she scooted over closer to Parrish. "Who is she?"

"My daughter," Parrish said, "and a nice person. Can you give her a smile?"

"No."

Parrish laughed, glanced at Crosby and said, "She reminds me of you, at least in disposition."

Crosby shared a ghost of a smile. "Madison *is* nice, I promise. Do you want to color with her?"

"Oh, I would love to color," Madison enthused—and damned if she didn't look as if she meant it. "You have so many nice books to choose from. Would you share one with me?"

Immediately, Hallie scampered over to join her. "This is the bestest one. It has mermaids." Sotto voce, she added, "Kenzie wanted the unicorns, and I only have one of those."

Appearing charmed, Madison held out a hand. "I'm so pleased to meet you, Hallie."

Hallie stared at her hand a moment, then accepted it. "Kenzie is smart, huh? He hired my daddy."

"Yes, that makes him very smart."

"He said it did." She crowded closer to Madison. "Which mermaid do you want to color?"

"Since you know the 'bestest' ones, why don't you pick a page for me?"

While Hallie happily complied, Crosby assessed the scene before him, determining how to proceed. He had two McKenzies sitting at Silver's small round kitchen table, *coloring*—as if that was the most natural thing in the world for a dangerous family with elite training.

Ground rules, that's what he needed. He'd start by making himself clear. "Parrish," Crosby said, trying to take the bite out of his tone, "we have some things to discuss."

"Might as well wait for Cade and Reyes." Parrish looked at Madison. "Since you're here, I assume they'll shortly follow?"

"Yup." She frowned at her dad. "Whatever you're up to, you should have told us."

Parrish waved that off. "Hindsight. At the time, I felt I was doing what's best."

Hunkering over the open coloring book and beginning to shade the hair of a mermaid, Madison asked, "Was Bernard in on this?"

As if he hadn't plotted against Crosby, Parrish said matter-of-factly, "In case something went wrong, I needed someone to know my plans."

Silver glared over her shoulder at him. "You don't consider this going *wrong*?"

Parrish smiled at her—smiled!—and said, "Meeting Crosby's family? Enjoying an afternoon of hot chocolate, coloring books and—" his gaze skipped over her "—pleasant company?

Of course that's not wrong. In fact, it's been both enlightening and enjoyable."

Color rushed into Silver's cheeks and she jerked around to work on her cookies with single-minded focus.

After looking her over once more, Parrish stabbed Crosby with his critical gaze. "It would have been nice if we'd been properly introduced."

Oh, hell no. Parrish was *not* going to turn this on him. With teeth-clenching clarity, Crosby stated, "If I'd wanted you to meet my family, that's what I would have done. Since I didn't, you have no damn business being here."

Madison looked from one man to the other, then cleared her throat. "Dad, you should apologize."

Inclining his head, Parrish said, "My sincere apologies. Trust is a commodity I have in very short supply."

"What does trust have to do with you snooping around my home?" Crosby wanted to let it go, he really did. He understood the McKenzies, and even approved on occasion, but this? This crossed too many lines for him to easily dismiss it.

Parrish glanced at Hallie as a reminder that he couldn't yet speak freely, then, with measured words, he explained, "In many situations, emotion adds a dangerous distraction. I had hoped to bypass my children with a certain concern, and whether you wanted it or not, you were going to be my confidant. Of course now, I'll have to come clean to all of you."

Parrish's calm, sincere admission took the tension from Crosby's shoulders. "You're in trouble?"

Just then a knock sounded on the front door.

Since he wasn't about to budge, Crosby planted his feet and waited.

Madison glanced at Silver.

Silver snorted, then lifted her big bowl of cookie dough. "Occupied. Someone else will have to get it."

Parrish and Crosby stared at each other, so finally Madison

pushed back her chair with a huff. Pointing at each of them, she said, "No chitchat until I've returned."

Parrish just smiled.

Crosby wouldn't make any promises.

To Silver, Madison said, "Men, am I right?"

Silver cracked a smile.

Holding out a hand, Madison asked Hallie, "Want to meet my brothers? I'm sure that's them at the door, and if we don't hurry, they'll be picking the lock."

Scurrying out of her seat, Hallie rushed to her.

The second they were out of the room, Parrish turned to Crosby. "My kids will insist on involvement, but I'll want you to be in charge. Are you okay with that?"

Him in charge over the unpredictable, autocratic McKenzies? What a novel idea. This hadn't been in the job description, whatever *this* might be, but how could he say no? Whatever endangered Parrish would also endanger Madison, and that made it personal for Crosby. "You honestly think they'll go along with that?"

"If they want info, yes, because I'll be reporting to you. It'll be up to you how much you share."

Damn. Parrish wasn't kidding about this. Instinctively, Crosby knew the siblings would blow a gasket. Only half under this breath, he said, "For that, I'd need a raise."

"Consider it done." Parrish stood just as Cade, followed by Reyes, stepped into the kitchen.

Negligently, Silver glanced back and away, then slowly, jaw loose, pivoted for a longer, wide-eyed stare.

Yeah, Crosby got it. The brothers had an impact on anyone who met them. Actually, Madison did, too.

Crowding in around them, still holding Hallie's hand, Madison took over introductions, and in the process, she stressed his relationship with Silver, making it clear that they were family.

Cade and Reyes nodded at Silver, then turned their focus on Parrish.

It would have been an identical stare except that Cade's eyes were blue, while Reyes's and Madison's were hazel.

Without many choices left to him, Crosby decided it was up to him to sort it all out. "We're out of chairs in here." Silver's table only had four seats. She'd never needed more than that since it was only the three of them and whichever of Hallie's dolls she included.

Crosby scooped up his daughter. "Honey, I want you stay in here with Silver while I talk to our company for a minute, okay?"

Hallie peeked past him to Cade and Reyes. "They're all giants," she whispered.

"But they're nice giants," Crosby promised. He kissed her nose and set her in her chair. Turning to Silver, he asked, "Do you mind?"

She didn't look as if she'd blinked yet, but she managed to say in her usual sassy way, "Not as long as you catch me up later."

"You have my word." He didn't keep anything from Silver, because she needed to be informed on all fronts. How else could she be on guard against all threats? Gesturing at the doorway they'd just come through, Crosby said, "Let's go to the living room." Anything they said could be heard, but it was as close to privacy as they were likely to get here without invading a bedroom.

Madison went out first, followed by Cade, then Reyes.

Parrish went to Silver instead. "When will the cookies be done?"

Even though he hadn't gotten too close, Silver stiffened. "I'm putting them in the oven now, so ten minutes."

Parrish smiled. "Then I'll ensure we're done by then."

"Who says I'll give you any?" Silver asked.

In a husky tone Crosby had never before heard from him, Parrish murmured, "I can be persuasive when I put my mind to it."

Good Lord.

Why would Parrish, who'd spent more than seventeen years alone, decide *now* that he was interested? And why pick a member of Crosby's family?

Annoying, yet the interest was there in how Parrish looked at Silver, the expression in his eyes and the tone of his voice.

Even more confounding was that Silver didn't seem entirely disinterested. Over the last few years, Crosby had reminded her that she had a right to her own life, too. If she'd wanted to date, he'd have worked it out. But she'd repeatedly said that she'd taken dating off her list. Understandable, given her past. It had always bothered him, though, because Silver was a smart, warm, caring woman—moments of sarcasm aside—and she deserved to have someone special in her life.

He'd never had reason to have "the talk" on her behalf, but he felt one coming on now. Parrish needed to understand that if he toyed with Silver, all bets were off. Crosby liked the security of the job, and the higher pay would make a big difference in their lives, but the people he loved came first. Silver was family, had been for years now.

The sooner Parrish understood that, the better.

# CHAPTER SEVEN

Parrish could have easily guessed what was going through Crosby's mind. It was the younger man's honesty and his lack of subterfuge that had first drawn his notice. Crosby didn't play games. He could be as cold-blooded, or as compassionate, as a situation warranted. But you didn't have to guess which way he was going. He was no-nonsense, up-front and capable.

All admirable qualities.

As they reached the living room, Parrish went to the big front window and casually noted the attached alarm. If anyone broke the glass, it would not only sound off, but, given the looks of it, would send an alert to authorities.

Same with the doors and the window in the kitchen. He assumed the bedrooms were equally protected.

If he'd gotten into Crosby's house next door, would the police have shown up? Likely. Of course, he'd have noticed the alarm and avoided that mess if Silver hadn't confronted him.

He smiled, remembering.

"What are we doing?" Cade asked, resting his shoulder against the wall.

Overall, it appeared Crosby had secured the house as much as possible with his limited means. In short order, Parrish would see that everything was brought up to the highest standard.

Turning, he faced various expressions of concern and anger from his kids, while Crosby stood off to the side, no doubt waiting for the fireworks to start.

"First," Parrish said to Crosby, "I do apologize for overrunning your home like this."

Crosby shrugged. An angry shrug, yes, but also an acknowledgment of necessity. At least, that's how Parrish chose to interpret the lift of his bunched shoulder.

Because Cade had asked the question, Parrish looked at him next. "A few weeks ago, as I was driving west of I-25, a shot hit my car. Three shots, actually."

Madison sucked in a hard breath. "What?"

"Driver's side door."

"What the fuck, Dad!" Reyes said, rising from the seat he'd taken.

Cade merely stared, a wealth of volatile emotion in his eyes.

"Language," Parrish said to Reyes, earning disbelieving glares from the others and a nod of appreciation from Crosby. "There are a woman and a child nearby."

"And we can both hear just fine," Silver sang out. "Whoever said the bad word just lost a cookie."

Running a hand over his face, Reyes glanced back toward the kitchen. "Sorry."

"Accepted—but you're still a cookie short."

Reyes *almost* smiled. "Yes, ma'am." The humor vanished the second he faced off with Parrish. "How come we didn't know about this immediately?"

"I didn't call it in because I had hoped it was a stray bullet from a hunter's rifle. I didn't want to alarm anyone." When they all started to speak at once, he held up his hand, silently requesting patience. "Of course, I realized I was wrong when I saw there were three shots close together—all sniper rounds." Hands behind his back, he began to prowl the room. It was a cozy space with a gray sectional decorated in a multitude of brightly colored throw pillows and sitting partially atop a thick rug. "Because the shots missed the window—" and him "—I assume the shooter either has lousy aim, or he meant it as a warning."

Cade seemed to grow bigger, Reyes angrier. Madison fisted her hands.

"I'd still been hoping to write it off as a fluke, maybe mistaken identity, until I received a message at Cornerstone Security."

"Where you just hired Crosby to work." Reyes said it as an accusation, not a question.

Without looking at Crosby, Parrish nodded. "I need someone there who's above reproach. Someone I can trust one hundred percent."

"What kind of message?" Cade calmly asked.

"Voice message on the landline."

"Directed to you?" Madison asked. "Or left for whomever answered?"

"To me, on my personal line."

Crosby shifted. "What was the message?" he asked, getting to the heart of the matter.

Parrish met and held his gaze. "A male voice stated my name, I assume so I'd know without doubt that the message was for me, and then he said that I shouldn't have interfered."

"With *what*?" Reyes demanded.

"That was the entirety of the message." Parrish resumed pacing, going around a plush leather stool used as a coffee table, matching end tables, a rocking chair with a cushion on the seat... "Understand that when I went after your mother, I didn't hide my identity. I doled out punishment while giving them my name. I wanted them to know who I was, so they'd understand who had destroyed them." Those memories were not pleasant. He'd been wild then, insensate with grief. Brutal. Quietly, he admitted, "I was driven by rage and the need for revenge."

A movement in the kitchen doorway drew his attention. He glanced over and found Silver standing there, her face pale, her eyes sympathetic.

If he didn't blink and look away, his kids would immediately become aware of the chemistry arcing between them, and Parrish didn't want that. He had enough explaining to do without adding the sudden strong, undeniable attraction he felt.

Right before he would have shifted his attention, Silver turned away, disappearing back into the kitchen.

Because Reyes currently looked the most explosive, Parrish concentrated on him. His hotheaded son. An extraordinary sniper.

And an exceptionally good man.

"Of course," Parrish said by way of a reminder, "I've learned that cooler heads have better odds of succeeding, and for years now, I've stayed in the background."

"Rob Golly," Crosby said, already taking a mental leap ahead. "The day he blew himself up, you were there."

"After the fact, but yes. I thought you would arrest Reyes, so I'd already alerted our legal team. I wanted Reyes to know I had things covered." This memory, at least, was a better one. "But you surprised me, Crosby." He hadn't arrested Reyes. In fact, Crosby had seemed to comprehend the entire scenario, grasping the ramifications in a nanosecond. "I knew then that I'd eventually hire you." He shrugged. "The threats just expedited things."

At that, Crosby scowled. "Who else might have been involved?"

"No one," Cade said. "We scoured that entire operation. Madison followed every lead, no matter how small. We left it wrapped up tight."

Madison hadn't said much, but that was her way. His daughter was notorious for calculating outcomes. She and Crosby had that in common—among other things.

"It might not have anything to do with Golly." She stood, then moved to stand by Crosby. "We've had dozens and dozens of cases. I'll need to start going over all of them again."

"No," Crosby said. "We'll start with the most recent and backtrack. Since this just happened, we can assume it's related to a more recent event."

"Those within the last year?" she asked.

"Maybe last three years." He frowned in thought. "Actually, now that I'm saying it out loud, something else occurs to me. It's possible someone just got out of prison, right? So it could be from a case longer ago."

"If it's even related to that," Madison mused. "Could be someone Dad fired. Or involved with his legit businesses."

"There are all kinds of disgruntled people in the world." Crosby had an intense frown. "I don't know. My gut tells me we should backtrack no more than two years, and at the same time we need to set up some extra precautions so another call, a letter, a sniper will be easier to track down."

Satisfaction seeped into Parrish's every pore. Hadn't he known Crosby would be like this? No, he wasn't like Cade and Reyes, but he offered a good counterbalance, which would keep things on track. As he'd predicted, Crosby, being unrelated, was the most coolheaded.

Even better, Madison automatically aligned with him, and they were already working together.

Sweeping his gaze over each of his sons, Parrish said, "There will be no arguments."

Automatically defiant, Cade's shoulders squared up. That had always been his way. Quiet rebellion was as much a part of his character as leadership. Cade would want to take over, but he was also smart enough to see that having someone outside the family made sense.

Reyes, always battle ready, and with a short fuse, put his fisted hands on his hips. "Arguments about *what*?"

Madison's eyes widened. "Dad?"

"Crosby is in charge," Parrish stated. "You'll take your directions from him."

Way to drop a spotlight on him, Crosby thought. Fortunately, no one seemed overly hostile about the idea.

Then again, it could be that they all planned to ignore the edict.

Crosby glanced at Cade first, then Reyes. Because of the singular way she disturbed his thought process, he avoided looking at Madison. "We should probably take the rest of this discussion to Parrish's house."

"Cookies first," Silver called out, proving she was still listening. "And I put on a pot of fresh coffee."

Damn. Knowing Hallie would expect it, Crosby agreed. "Cookies first." He would always do his best not to disappoint his daughter.

"Dad will ride with me," Cade announced.

Reyes nodded. "I'll drive his car."

"Absolutely not." Parrish looked appalled by that suggestion, not that his sons were listening.

Actually, Madison wasn't listening either. "Good idea, since Dad's already been shot at."

"He's obviously the target," Cade reasoned.

"He'll have to lay low for a while," Reyes warned.

Everyone started talking at once. Or more like debating, as they began working out plans.

Parrish glared at Crosby.

Crosby barely refrained from growling out his frustration. *"Enough."* Silence descended.

Incredulous, they each slowly turned to stare at him.

Yeah, now he actually wanted to laugh. He, a retired cop, had dared to shut down the elite McKenzie family.

"As a father," Crosby calmly stated, "I can guarantee you that Parrish isn't going to let one of his sons drive his car if he thinks there might be a risk."

"Exactly," Parrish said, as if exonerated.

Ignoring the interruption, Crosby continued. "I think it'd be better for me to lead, Parrish can ride behind me with Cade and Reyes following. If we're all keeping watch, it'll be safe enough." To Parrish, he said, "I assume you can pick up a different vehicle for any other travel? Something new that no one will recognize as yours?"

"Easily enough. Actually, Bernard is working on that today."

Everyone erupted again.

"No one," Parrish said, his tone inflexible, "will give Bernard a difficult time about this. Is that understood?"

All three siblings agreed, but then, they had massive respect for Bernard—and they knew it was their father who'd kept them in the dark. Bernard only followed Parrish's instructions.

Cade folded his arms. "I'm fine with Crosby's plan, except that I don't see your car out front, meaning you parked somewhere else and walked here."

"A good distance away, actually," Parrish agreed. "But you can get that look off your face because I was careful. I would never bring trouble to Crosby's door, especially now that I know someone is…" He hesitated.

"After you?" Reyes supplied. "Good of you to outright admit it, Dad."

Parrish's gaze slanted over to Crosby. "Of course, when I decided to check out your home, I didn't know there was a woman and child here."

"We've been over that," Crosby said, refusing to be put on the spot. "It was none of your damn business."

"And that," Silver said from the doorway, "is that. Now come get your cookies while they're hot."

It pleased Madison a lot that Hallie wanted to sit between her and Crosby. The little girl even scooted her chair closer, and then stared up at Madison with big curious eyes.

Did she never see women besides Silver? That idea appealed in many ways because it meant Crosby didn't get around. He had that in common with Cade, who'd been superselective about female company until Sterling blew the door off his world.

Reyes, on the other hand, got around far too much, or at least he had until he fell hard for Kennedy.

Was *she* falling hard? Sure felt like it. How could she have resisted? Crosby was not only incredible eye candy, strong and capable and honorable to the core, he was also a wonderful dad.

The man was the whole blasted package so she'd never stood a chance.

Hallie pursed her mouth while watching Madison choose a crayon.

It was a struggle not to think of all the girl had been through. A struggle, but necessary, because when Madison's brain wandered in that direction, her heart clenched so painfully that she was sure it showed in her eyes. She seriously wanted to hold the little innocent close and somehow remove all the pain from her past.

How much worse must it be for Crosby? Several times, Madison had caught him glancing at his daughter with love in his expression. She knew that, in the dark of night when he slept alone, memories had to rip into him. He'd been there, seeing it all, experiencing it…suffering through it alone.

What incredible restraint he must have, allowing the law to handle things that, to him, were so very personal.

She wasn't sure she'd be that strong. Or that moral. For this little girl she'd literally just met, she'd gladly go all Godzilla on anyone who didn't treat her right.

"What's wrong?" Hallie whispered, leaning around to see her face.

Point proven—her upset *did* show in her eyes—Madison smiled. "Nothing at all. In fact, I'm having a great time. Silver makes amazing cookies, and you're pretty darned cute."

"And you like my dad, huh?"

"Oh, yeah. I definitely like your dad."

"So how come you looked mad?"

Aware of everyone glancing her way, Madison brazened it out, saying, "I was thinking of Godzilla." Since a four-year-old probably wouldn't know anything about the prehistoric monster, she explained, "He's a great big dinosaur-looking dude who levels whole cities, but usually for a good reason."

Cade gave her *the* look, the one that said he was onto her. Big brother had the uncanny knack of reading her moods with shocking accuracy. "What city are you thinking of leveling?"

"None, now. Just that I would, if necessary."

Cade's gaze shifted to Hallie, then softened. "Yeah, I'd be there with you."

Reyes leaned across the table toward Crosby to rib him in a loud voice. "They're talking about you, man."

"My family, actually," Crosby replied, unfazed by the taunt as he washed down a bite of cookie with a sip of his coffee. "I can take care of myself."

"But not those you care about?"

"Them too, but I'm not so arrogant that I don't realize how extra protection would be helpful."

"Cease and desist," Parrish said, his obvious displeasure directed at Reyes, and sharp enough to wound. "A smart man always accepts backup from the right people."

Half smiling, Crosby said, "Not sure Reyes would qualify for *right* people."

"What's backup?" Hallie asked.

Unable to resist, Madison scooped the girl out of her seat and onto her lap. She'd been practically in it anyway, as she'd scrunched closer and closer to her side. Madison had been forced to reach around her to color. This was more comfortable. "Backup is when someone is there to help you when you need it. Like you were my backup when I couldn't decide what color to use for my mermaid's tail."

"Purple," Hallie assured her.

"Yes, purple is perfect."

Crosby watched them together, his expression so probing and somehow insightful that Madison felt a little too warm. Few men had ever dared to put her under the microscope, and never because she held a child.

Flashing an impish grin, Hallie stole the half-eaten cookie off Madison's plate and leaned back against her to eat it. As if she often sat with Madison, Hallie shifted around to get comfortable, which involved elbowing Madison in the boob and clunking her head into Madison's chin.

But seriously, she didn't mind. Hallie smelled sweet and her hair was so soft that Madison just naturally nuzzled her nose against her crown.

Crosby gave a small smile over that, making Madison wonder how many times he'd caught an elbow in an inconvenient place. An image of Crosby holding Hallie when she'd needed him most seared into her thoughts, then wouldn't go away. She squeezed Hallie in an emotional hug, but Hallie didn't complain.

With Crosby as her daddy, she must be used to lots of affection.

"Instincts going a little crazy there, Madison?" Reyes asked, grinning at how cozy Hallie had gotten in her lap.

To which Silver asked the table, "Is that one always so annoying?"

Reyes laughed, while Cade confirmed, "Yes, he is." As he pushed back his chair, Cade thanked Silver for the snack, then said to Crosby, "Mind if I look around to assess the security? From what I can tell, you've done a nice job, but—"

"It can be better?" Crosby stood, too. "Share any thoughts you have, just keep in mind that some of us live on a budget."

Parrish waved that off. "We're in this together now."

Madison almost choked. Sure, she'd expected her family to step up now that they'd accepted Crosby, but they were laying it on a bit thick. Heck, she'd only kissed Crosby a few times. It wasn't like he wanted to marry her. He had a nice life already set up…without a wife.

And why the heck did that give her such a pang of desire? Not just physical desire either, but something softer and far more intense. Something that felt too much like longing.

Crosby looked like he'd refuse the offer, but he was a reasonable man who loved Silver and Hallie, so he gave a short nod. "Thank you."

Reyes joined Crosby and Cade. "It'd be smart if we set up the system so that any breach here alerted all of us."

"As well as the cops," Crosby insisted.

Madison knew that wasn't their favored option. Old habits died hard, and more often than not, they steered clear of involving the law.

Before anyone could confirm or deny Crosby's edict, Hallie went limp against her, the cookie almost falling from her hand.

"Oh." Tightening her hold, Madison peered down at her small face and saw that the girl had fallen asleep.

"Nap time," Silver said quietly, setting aside her drink and standing. "Since she'd already taken a nap earlier, I didn't think she'd be out again so soon."

"She's under the weather, though," Parrish said, stepping close to Silver's back to glance down at Hallie with a fond smile.

Madison knew she wasn't the only one seeing her dad's move as a pretense. Sure, it was obvious he liked Hallie, but it was just as obvious that he was drawn to Silver and wanted an excuse to get closer to her. Madison didn't know what to think about *that*.

"I can take her," Silver said. Then she tipped her head, taking in the easy way Madison held Hallie. "Unless you'd like to carry her to bed?"

Before Madison could answer, Cade said, "I'll do it."

At almost the same time, Reyes said, "I got her."

Silver glanced at both of them, then gave a husky laugh. "Looks to me like Madison isn't the only one with some instincts kicking." Hand on her hip, she asked, "You boys thinking about offspring of your own?"

Cade shrugged. "Whenever Star is ready."

"His wife," Parrish explained. "Though the rest of us call her Sterling."

Reyes rubbed his hands together. "I figure I could handle the whole father gig, but Kennedy's career is going strong right now. Maybe in another couple of years."

Settling the matter, Crosby said, "I'll carry her to bed," and easily scooped Hallie from Madison's arms. Sighing, Hallie snuggled against his chest, her head on his shoulder, and continued sleeping. "The rest of you can peek in her room while I get her settled, then scope out the rest of the house after. Just keep it down, so you don't wake her."

"My room last," Silver stated, and she took off in a hurried walk ahead of everyone else.

With her arms now feeling empty, Madison followed the procession from the kitchen. Somewhere down the hall, a door quietly closed. No doubt Silver wanted to put away a few things before they all tromped through her space.

Clearly, Crosby was as comfortable here as he must be at his own house. The arrangement he had with Silver could easily be misconstrued, except that there wasn't a single spark between them, only respect and affection.

That came as a surprise, because Silver was undeniably beautiful. One day soon, Madison would love to hear the backstory on how Crosby and Silver met. Whatever the woman's past might be, she didn't flaunt her beauty. It was there, regardless, but first and foremost, Silver seemed casual and comfortable, secure with her position as Hallie's "grandma." She also had a warm way about her, and a sometimes-biting wit that Madison had seen right through.

She'd liked her instantly. So did Parrish—and he wasn't even being subtle about it. She wondered how Cade and Reyes felt about that. For Madison's part, it made her a little uncomfortable, just because she wasn't used to it.

And now *she* was jumping the gun. Good grief, her dad had literally only met Silver a few hours ago.

Cade and Reyes were in and out of Hallie's bedroom before Crosby finished tucking a light quilt around his daughter. He smoothed Hallie's hair, kissed her brow and stepped back to glance at Madison.

She smiled as she looked around the room. Since Hallie didn't officially live with Silver, Madison had expected more of a guest room, but this had clearly been decorated for Hallie.

Done in soft gray and pale blush, it was girlie but in a sweetly sophisticated way. A cork strip ran along one wall, and heart-shaped pushpins held various pieces of artwork in place. The twin bed was white wrought iron, with a white bookcase as a bedside table. At the foot of the bed was a white wicker toy chest. Hallie had left the lid open and numerous stuffed animals spilled out.

Both the hanging overhead light and the lamp on the bookcase had feathered shades. Hallie had her own small rocking chair and a drawing table with a stool.

Madison thought back on her own childhood, but she couldn't recall ever being that into dolls or toys of any kind. Electronics, that's what she'd always wanted.

"Silver decorated here."

Madison trailed her hand over the ornate edge of the kid-sized rocker. "Wow, she has great taste."

"Hallie's room at home is similar," Crosby said softly, as if he'd known her thoughts. "More of a light purple and gray, and with different toys. Her quilt has her name on it, and she has more clothes there, so a big dresser, too."

Keeping her voice down, Madison replied, "It's like she has two homes." She lifted a worn bunny, liking the softness of it, then returned it to the wicker chest beside a sloth and a baby doll.

"Hallie spends nearly every day here." Crosby's gaze never left Madison, his dark eyes tracking her slow movements around the room. "I wanted her comfortable in both places."

Because he was awesome like that. "She has a lot of toys." And a lot of books. She lifted one from the bookshelf and smiled at the image of a pancake talking to a mouse. "Everything is so tidy."

"Not always. Today she didn't feel well, so Silver let her rest on the couch and watch cartoons. Usually she'd have been in here playing and there'd be papers and toys everywhere." He smiled. "She and I tidy things up before we head home each night."

Funny that Crosby-the-attentive-dad was somehow even more appealing than Crosby-the-tough-cop. "When I was a few years older than Hallie, I felt superior to the boys because I already had my own computer. There were parental controls in place, of course." Smug, she confided, "But I could always get around them."

He gave a short laugh. "Hallie's screen time is limited, but she'd only be playing preschool games or watching something animated anyway. Instead, we encourage her to color, do crafts, bake with Silver or, when the weather cooperates, play outside."

"And you go to the park."

"Yes, when there isn't so much snow." Putting an arm around Madison's waist, Crosby urged her from the room. "Not everyone is a child prodigy as you were."

"I wasn't either," she objected, but she liked the affectionate way he'd said it. "It's just that I wasn't interested in much else."

"Except competing with the boys?"

She leaned her head against him. "That was later, after Mom

died. Gearing up in protective equipment and going hard against my brothers was the only thing that could pull me away from the PC. I loved the physical aspects of sparring as much as breaking code or hacking systems." One memory struck her and she snickered. "I hacked Reyes's computer once. Lord, the things he'd been looking at. I was fourteen, so he must've been eighteen. I couldn't make eye contact with him for a month."

Crosby laughed, stopping her right outside Hallie's room. "So breaking into computers and stomping your brothers were your main pastimes. What about toys? You didn't have any?"

"I probably did." She frowned, trying to think back. "I'm sure Mom and Dad added a few dolls and games in with my other gifts. That's expected, right?"

Crosby leaned against the wall, looking past her to where her brothers went back up the hall toward Silver's room. "Somehow, I don't see the McKenzie family ever doing the expected."

True. Her father had always had his own way of seeing the world. He'd expected excellence, from himself, his employees and his children. Individuality was, to him, a major plus. In every way, he'd encouraged Madison's interest in computers, indulging her with all the latest tech.

And her mom… Her mom had been the soft one, the one who liked to coddle. "No, my family rarely does the expected. Is that a problem?"

His dark gaze settled on her, first looking into her eyes, then lowering to her mouth. "Not with you."

*Not with you.* Why did that feel like a promise?

Being here today, meeting Silver and holding Hallie, made her feel that much closer to him. Like she was getting to know the real him, not just the person he showed to the world.

Drawn to his warmth, the scent that always stirred her and his undeniable strength, she stepped into his space. It wasn't close enough, but from the day she'd first met him, she'd felt that way. Always, with Crosby, she wanted more.

She settled her hands on his shoulders, and of course, that made her wonder how much nicer it would be if his clothes weren't in the way, if she could touch his bare skin, feel the heat of him on her palms.

"Madison," he said, his voice low and husky. "What are you thinking?"

"Probably things I shouldn't, at least not right now." She tried to relax, to shake off the swelling sexual tension. Wasn't easy, not with the way he affected her. "Is Dad forgiven?"

"Do I have a choice?" He rested his hands on her hips and changed the subject. "You were great with Hallie."

"Really?" The praise felt like the best of compliments. "She doesn't weigh any more than my kitten."

"You have a kitten?"

Why did that surprise him? "It's a funny story, actually. See, Reyes brought home this big cat that had been living in the alley near the gym. She was pretty rough, poor thing, obviously homeless, and she'd had cute little kittens. Naturally, Reyes rescued them."

Other than one brow lifting, Crosby said nothing.

"I guess Kennedy, who wasn't real friendly back then, actually found the cat. But she couldn't take it home, so Reyes did. He was supposed to share the cat with her—"

"How do you share a cat?"

"Good question." She grinned. "I think he was going to use it as a way to get closer to her. You know, visits with the cat, joint trips to the vet and stuff. But Bernard took one look at the cat and he went bonkers for her. It was the craziest thing. Stuffy Bernard stretched out on the floor with fur all over him, cooing to a cat with mismatched eyes and a bent tail." Remembering still made her chuckle. "He laid claim and refused to give Chimera—that's what Bernard named her—back to Reyes."

"When your dad was describing Bernard's role within your

family, he mentioned 'cat lover,' but I didn't know he meant literally."

"Thought it was a euphemism, huh?" She laughed. "Because there were four cats total, Chimera and three kittens, each of us got a kitten. Whenever I'm at Dad's for very long, I usually bring Bob with me."

"Bob?"

"Yeah, you know. As in Bobcat." She could hear her brothers talking behind her, their low murmurs pertaining to security. She really should join them, she supposed. "Bob is supersweet, unless he's hunting a bug. Then he's totally ferocious."

"Bob travels well?"

"To Dad's and back, yes." Sudden inspiration hit. "You and Hallie could come visit sometime. She'd probably like meeting all the cats."

Something a little more serious replaced his humor, but Madison didn't get a chance to ask him about it because Silver shooed everyone out of the hallway.

"All done?" Crosby asked.

"They're thorough," Silver said, but it didn't really sound like a complaint. "Now they want to see your place. I'll pick up the kitchen while Hallie finishes her nap."

"Thanks. We won't be long." Crosby stepped away from Madison to lead the pack.

Finally, she'd see his house. She could hardly wait.

Burgess Crow wallowed in his satisfaction. It had taken a lot of planning, but he'd found a way to make Parrish McKenzie pay. He was being cautious, because hey, Parrish wasn't a fool. The man had a nose for trouble—specifically for sticking that nose where it didn't belong. He planned to chip away at Parrish's peace of mind until the man got reckless.

Then he'd end him for good.

A few years back, Crow had been a rising star in the circuit before Parrish swept in with his money and influence, destroying people left and right—with Crow as collateral damage.

McKenzie hadn't even been after Crow, he hadn't known him or the thriving business he'd built with runaways. Girls who felt neglected at home made easy pickings for a guy with Crow's good looks and sympathetic ear.

Pausing in front of a mirror over the dresser in the hotel room where he was currently staying, Crow checked out his messy blond hair—boyish, some called it—and the innocence reflected in his baby blue eyes. He'd been told many times that he looked like a twenty-two-year-old surfer, not a thirty-year-old flesh-peddling entrepreneur who used emotional leverage, and often drugs, to manipulate the girls under his care.

That was his secret, though. If his face hid his intent, all the better.

The room wasn't up to his standard, but he'd easily blackmailed the owner with photos from a few months ago, when the dude had paid one of Crow's girls for sexual favors.

That's where Crow differed from other businessmen. He always collected evidence that he could use in the future.

Now, in his time of need, that business practice came in handy.

If it hadn't been for Parrish's interference, Crow would have joined forces now with two other traffickers, and he'd have been the manager of it all. Combined, they would have had a huge swath of prime real estate wrapped up for business. Several nearby truck stops along I-25 would have been for their exclusive use. Their circuit would have expanded greatly.

Instead, he'd been forced to reassess everything.

Once Parrish busted his cohorts, he'd grown fiercely guarded—and good thing or he'd have been in the roundup when a fucking cop and his crew had stormed the compound. Crow and one guerilla had gotten away by the skin of their teeth, but they'd been stranded, with no way to collect their personal things from the property, no way to retrieve the drugs and money hidden there.

And thanks to Parrish and his rampage against all traffickers, there'd been no one to call to lend them a hand.

What had once been a bright, lucrative future had turned into nothing more than dust.

After losing the compound, Crow had laid low, waiting for the winds to change, but Parrish McKenzie never let up. His task force continued to hammer every outfit, large and small. After two fucking wasted years, Crow was done waiting. He needed backers. He needed clientele. And damn it, he needed to operate openly, as he once had. That's how contacts were made and money earned.

Cops he could get around. But McKenzie? That self-righteous prick seemed to be everywhere at once. He knew things before they even happened. He ruthlessly destroyed start-ups before they could get any traction.

And that left Crow twiddling his thumbs and occasionally working retail so he wouldn't starve, which he fucking hated.

They were *businesses*. Crow didn't kidnap any girls. Hell, most would be considered women. Seventeen, eighteen, hungry to get out on their own, discontented with the restrictions of their families.

All he did was sympathize with them, offer them safety, food, housing… He *listened* to them, when no one else really did, and then they repaid his kindness by earning their keep.

On their backs or their knees, but so what?

At least he gave them worth.

That is, he gave worth to the loyal girls. But the ones who accepted help from the cops? He owed them nothing. They were loose ends who could blab about his habits, his haunts, his friends. They could lead the cops—or worse, McKenzie—right to him. So they'd had to go. He didn't feel bad about that. Actually, he felt righteous, a businessman taking care of business. Done and done.

Arranging for them to overdose while conveniently alone had been so damned easy. A deadly fentanyl-heroin mix left the twits unaware of their own peril. They gleefully shot up, searching for that perfect high that would make their troubles disappear for a little while. And just like that, they were no longer a problem.

Crow remembered that a kid had been rescued from the cult compound, too. He didn't know much about it, except that the brat's mama had shown the good sense to keep her out of his way. He'd never heard anything about a kid dying so she'd probably gotten lost in the system. Good riddance, far as he was concerned.

Shame his current girls were playing in a rustic mountain cabin and communing with nature right now. He needed them earning, but more than that, he needed his revenge against McKenzie. That came first.

Moving aside a curtain, he stared out a dirty window. Thanks to McKenzie and his unwanted meddling, *Crow* was the real victim. But McKenzie wouldn't be a problem forever.

Until then... He grinned. It was time to send Parrish another message. This time he'd be close enough to watch the fun.

Crosby let the McKenzies do their thing, which included checking every window, every lock, every camera and especially every door. Madison consulted with her brothers once or twice, but mostly she just looked around his house.

He wondered what she thought of it. By her standards, his and Silver's homes were miniscule, with both having the same basic layout. Three bedrooms, though one room was too small to really count. Silver used the third room as a sewing room, and Crosby used it as an office, having just enough space for a desk, chair and bookshelf. Each home had one bathroom, an eat-in kitchen, living room and a one-car garage.

He and Hallie didn't need more space than that, and with the house so small, it was easier to secure. He couldn't begin to imagine what it cost to run a home like Parrish's.

Madison's home was moderate, but still probably twice the size of his own.

She peeked into Hallie's room, then asked, "Did Silver decorate this one, as well?"

"Mostly, yeah." He pushed away from the wall where he'd been waiting for them all to finish and joined her just inside his daughter's room. "Purple, but not a garish purple, at least I don't think so." The furniture was all rehabbed, with different pieces that he'd painted white, like the curved wooden headboard and the small round side table. The bedspread, done in a checker pattern of gray and pale purple, had a giant *H* embroidered in the middle, with fluffy white pillows everywhere.

"I bet Hallie loves this room."

"She does, but she enjoys changing things up every so often. Like a few weeks ago, she wanted her bed moved to a different wall because we made these paper flowers and she decided they needed to go above her headboard. Before, the window was behind her bed, so we spent a Saturday morning rearranging everything."

Madison moved closer to see the flowers. Each one was the size of a dinner plate, four in all, tacked to the wall. "These are pretty."

"I should be embarrassed to admit that you can't tell mine from hers, but mostly I'm just proud of her artistic nature."

"I love that you do stuff like this with her." Her mouth twisted. "I'd hate to see how bad my efforts would look."

Taking that as a possible hint, Crosby hesitated, but he knew what he wanted, and really, there was no reason to continue keeping distance between them.

If she could handle the pressure and teasing from her family, he could, too. "Earlier, you asked if Hallie would like to meet your cat."

She turned to face him, her expression expectant. "And?"

Always so enthusiastic. Madison's reactions could go to his head, but instead, they seemed to go to his heart. "I'm sure she'd love it."

"Awesome!" As usual, she jumped right into making plans. "We'll do dinner—Bernard would love to meet her, too, I'm sure—and after she can visit with Chimera and Bob. If the weather lets up a little, we'll even sled outside. Dad has some perfect hills for it."

Pressing a finger to her mouth quieted her, but enthusiasm continued to dance in those golden eyes framed by dark lashes.

So pretty. So *sexy*.

And she wanted him.

Not only that, she'd been terrific with Hallie. A little uncertain, which made sense, but her every move had been genuine. Natural. Guided by care.

Much as he'd been the day he'd rescued Hallie. Good instincts carried across the board, and they both had them.

"That all sounds nice," Crosby said, easing his finger away from her soft lips. "And maybe on a Saturday you could come here. Our dinner would be a lot more informal, but both Silver and I are good cooks. Plus Hallie is always ready for arts and crafts."

Pleasure brightened her face. "Count me in."

Parrish rounded the corner, and in contrast, his expression was stony. "We have to go."

Immediately, Crosby asked, "What's happened?"

"A bomb threat was called into my hotel."

*Son of a—* Already moving, Crosby asked, "Your local hotel?" Parrish had many properties, but Crosby was focused only on those in the vicinity.

"Yes." With his sons right behind him, Parrish headed for the door. "It's where we temporarily house some women removed from trafficking situations, at least until we can find them more permanent housing."

Trafficked victims—and now someone was threatening them again? Fury put Crosby on autopilot. Luckily they'd already worked out the travel arrangements, leaving him time to jog next door to explain things to Silver. Cade would drive his brother and father to wherever Parrish had left his ride, and Madison would stick with him.

Parrish definitely had trouble breathing down his neck. Figured that Crosby would sign on at the absolute worst time.

# CHAPTER EIGHT

"Thank God, there was no bomb."

Taking in Parrish's stark relief, as well as his frustration, Crosby agreed. Keeping his voice low, he said, "Has to be the same person." At first, they'd wondered if it might be a diversion, a way to keep Parrish busy while an attack happened elsewhere. Luckily, it hadn't taken Parrish long to confirm his other local properties were still secure.

That left a different possibility: pure harassment.

"He's trying to wear me down." Parrish gave a harsh smile. "Instead, I'm more determined to crush him."

Because Crosby felt the same, he nodded his understanding.

After a thorough search of the hotel and surrounding grounds, Lieutenant Denzer, a member of the interagency bomb squad, had determined there was no bomb. Parrish hadn't liked giving access to the private garage since no one used that area except family, but he had complied. *"Better safe than sorry,"* he'd said.

Seeing the guests returning to the parking lot, Crosby gave thanks that at least it wasn't snowing.

"Denzer advised me to educate the staff," he said to Parrish, who had introduced him as his head of security. "He made it clear that having armed guards around was fine and dandy—his words, not mine—but the staff shouldn't have called the guest rooms—"

"One by one," Parrish interjected with disgust.

"—to evacuate everyone." Many of them had been standing out in the open for hours now, though most had headed to nearby restaurants. Parrish said the hotel would cover the costs of their meals. It'd be a financial hit for most people, but Parrish only shrugged it off. "The lieutenant also explained that your receptionist shouldn't have hung up, even though the caller did, and that using a cell phone was a no-go because, in the case of an actual bomb, the signals could have detonated the device."

Without his expression changing, Parrish murmured, "Thank God it wasn't real." His gaze went up to the top floor of the hotel.

Two women who'd recently been rescued from a forced prostitution situation were current "guests" on that floor.

They weren't up there now, though.

Crosby had kept a close watch on them until Parrish got them settled at the nearby café, with an off-duty guard to watch over them.

Unknown to the other guests, the extra-secure upper floor of the hotel was reserved for transitional use by the task force when they needed safe placement for recovered victims. It was an aspect of Parrish's operation that Crosby hadn't yet had a chance to explore. Now he'd make it a priority.

To other guests, the guards made sense, given the five-star rating of the hotel. The top-notch security was a draw for many… though it didn't do them much good with a crank call.

"Did the bastard know about the women?" Crosby mused softly. "Did he target this specific property of yours for that very reason?"

"I hope not, but until I have hands on him, we can't know for sure."

If the man's goal was to infuriate Parrish, he'd succeeded. Not that Parrish showed his rage, but Crosby knew it was there.

He felt equally enraged. "Will this stunt negatively impact the hotel's success?"

Parrish shrugged. "It's not my most pressing concern at the moment." Casually, as if it didn't matter, he said, "I don't like unknowns. A direct threat I can handle. I expect it. But endangering all these people?" He gave a small shake of his head. "Someone will pay."

Crosby again scanned the surrounding area. Damn it, he *knew* the prick was out there somewhere, gleeful over the uproar he'd caused.

He shifted his gaze to where Madison sat in his SUV, using her computer to do her magic. How much she could accomplish on a laptop and without her private server, Crosby didn't know, but she appeared wholly invested in the effort.

Cade and Reyes, who were searching the perimeter, checked in. Since they hadn't yet found anything or anyone suspicious, they would broaden their search. Cade said his wife wondered if the bomb threat might be related to their investigation into a nail salon. Crosby wouldn't discount any possibilities, but he didn't see an obvious connection there.

Besides, this could be personal to him, as well. As he'd thought about it, it occurred to him that he'd gotten to know the McKenzies right before the threats against Parrish started.

Coincidence? Not something Crosby believed in.

Parrish shifted position beside him. "If there's anyone skulking around, Cade or Reyes will find them. Madison is accessing the various camera feeds in case they picked up images of anyone a little too interested in the hotel." With certainty, he added, "We'll get him."

"Any chance he called from a traceable line?"

"I doubt it. Most likely he used a burner phone." Parrish put his hands in his pockets as he looked around at the guests anxious to return to their rooms. "He was here," Parrish stated. "I sense it, and so do you."

"Yeah." Crosby was past being surprised by Parrish's insight. "Did Lieutenant Denzer wonder why the McKenzies are all wearing bulletproof vests and packing semiautomatic weapons?"

Parrish shrugged. "Did he wonder? I'm sure. Did he question me on it? No."

So much clout. "Didn't even ask to see your permit, huh?" That didn't sound like any cop Crosby knew.

"I explained up front that the hotel was mine, and that I was armed. A few of the other officers know me well and likely had already clued him in. Denzer didn't have any reason to question Cade or Reyes, because they spread out right away. Madison's barely been out of your car."

Again, Crosby's gaze went to her. She wore the heavy vest with ease, as if it was no more cumbersome than her bra. Such an amazing woman on so many levels.

And he was just…himself. A retired cop. An adoptive dad. A man of many flaws who nonetheless held high standards.

Parrish cast him a dark glance. "I'm confident that the added burden of immediate threats won't dissuade you from keeping the job?"

Distracted by the way Madison leaned forward, excitement on her face, Crosby murmured, "No." He didn't scare easily.

Except when it came to the people he loved.

"Good to know."

"She's found something." Crosby started toward his SUV just as Madison opened the door and stepped out.

Parrish followed. "Don't rush or you'll draw Denzer's attention."

Right. God forbid they keep the cops informed.

Seeing them approach, Madison waited by the open passenger door. "The way you frown." As soon as he was close enough, she reached out and smoothed her bare fingers over his brow.

"It's intimidating, in a dark and sexy way. Makes you look really formidable."

Crosby didn't know if he wanted to growl, laugh or kiss her for being so outrageous. Probably kiss, but not here and not now. "Did you find something?"

She showed her screen. "I've got him."

Crosby felt every muscle tense. The image was from the earlier crowd around the hotel, a crowd that had long since been dispersed. The fine hairs on his neck tingled.

"Burgess Crow," Parrish bit out, before Crosby could say the name. "I know him."

"I recall doing several searches on him," Madison said. "But it's been a while."

Parrish nodded. "We never apprehended him, but he was known as an up-and-comer in trafficking. A slick manipulator, who preyed on younger women, sometimes girls." Parrish's jaw tightened. "He dropped off the radar a few years back so I never had the pleasure of making his acquaintance."

This was exactly why he never, ever, believed in coincidence. "That might be my fault, since I raided his compound. He's likely been in hiding ever since." Though Crosby knew it wouldn't do any good, he immediately turned, searching the area.

"He's nowhere close," Madison assured him, "but I already sent the image to Cade and Reyes. If he's near enough to watch us with binoculars, they'll spot him."

Crosby had to remember that this was Madison, and she could do unfathomable things on a laptop. "Anything else? Did you see how he arrived or left? Maybe get an image of his plates?"

"I'll scour through things more tonight when I'm on my secure server, maybe see if I can find any other feeds. This one," she explained, "is from the restaurant over there. It gave me a whole new angle."

"You're incredible." If anyone could find the details they needed, it'd be Madison.

A warm, intimate smile curved her mouth. "I only picked up on him because I realized he was watching Dad more than anything else. And see his expression? Pretty sure that recognition goes both ways."

"He probably knew I'd been looking for him," Parrish said. "Or he assumed I would eventually, since we took out all his cronies."

"But then there was also this." Madison scrolled forward. "Here. Look."

The feed was far from clear, the image sometimes grainy as it advanced, but they could see Burgess Crow standing with other spectators a good distance away. His gaze remained locked on Parrish with an intensity that had probably felt tactile, which explained why Parrish had sensed he was near.

Then, as if something caught Crow's eye, he looked elsewhere, and froze. Gone was the satisfaction in his expression. Surprise, then anger, took over.

"What did he see?" Crosby asked, concerned that it would be one of the female victims staying at the hotel.

Madison touched his arm. "Pretty sure he saw you, Crosby. You said you know him, right?"

"I do, yeah." Well, hell. So it hadn't been personal, but was now? "He moves out of frame after that."

"Yes, and I haven't yet found him on any other cameras." She hooked her free arm through his. "I will, though. I promise. Only I doubt all of them will have such clear images. Ours at the hotel are great—I saw to that. But the other businesses? Who knows? Plus there's a terrific ornamental lake on the property that offers walking trails for the guests. We have cameras near the hotel, but nothing that covers the entire trail. If he left that way, I won't be able to pinpoint much."

She'd already done more in a day than the police might have

accomplished in a week. He looked at her, really looked at her, seeing her vitality and intelligence, and yes, her incredible sex appeal. In a dozen different ways, it felt like his life was completely spiraling out of his control.

Things he'd once believed with crystal clarity were now hazy with new possibilities. His plans for the future, his priorities, all shuffled like a deck of cards.

"What?" she asked. "What's wrong?"

Crosby ran a hand over his face. "Remember I told you Hallie's mother OD'd?"

"And two other women, all from the same cult. I remember."

"Crow is one of the two guys who should have been at the compound that day."

Madison's eyes widened. "But he got away."

Nodding, Crosby said, "And if he recognized me, I have to wonder if he knows I have Hallie." Suddenly he was more aligned with the McKenzie family than ever before—because he wanted Crow gone, long gone… Before the bastard could threaten his daughter.

Son of a bitch. Crow couldn't believe he'd stumbled onto something this big. The very cop who'd raided them was all cozy and shit with none other than Parrish McKenzie. They'd stood together, talking with familiarity.

Tall and taller. Arrogant and more arrogant. They were a pair all right. A pair of total dicks.

What a small, fucked-up world!

And who was the woman in the SUV? Repeatedly, Parrish and the cop had glanced at her. She had to be someone important. Seeing her clearly through the windshield she sat behind wasn't easy, but he'd gotten the impression of long dark hair.

He'd find out. If she was related to McKenzie or the cop, she might be an easy way to get to them, a way to twist the knife. From what he knew, both were suckers for the weaker sex.

Crow grinned, thinking about it, about how he might use her. It would make his success even sweeter. He could double the big payback, take care of two problems at once and enjoy himself in the bargain.

Maybe he'd even add her to his stable once he got the business up and running again. That'd be poetic justice for the two men who had ruined his life.

Parrish had shut down his biggest business opportunity, a chance to be a fucking king in the traffic industry.

Then the cop had raided the one and only place where Crow had still been able to operate. He'd had a cushy deal, all the luxuries he needed with his best chance to get back on track. Gone, just like that.

*Fuck them both.*

He didn't yet know the cop's name, but he'd find out. Hell yeah, he would. For now, though, it would be best if he didn't stick around. Good thing he'd had two years to work on being invisible.

Over the next few days, Crosby's and Silver's houses got wired with the best high-tech security available. Both she and Crosby had been so busy she hadn't seen him since the bomb threat, but he would be over tonight for dinner and she could hardly wait. She had plenty to tell him. It was figuring out how to tell him that posed the conundrum.

She knew Crosby. Overall she figured she knew him well. But this? How would he react?

Telling Cade and Reyes was out for now. They'd go ballistic. And her dad had enough on his mind already. The McKenzie men had put their collective brains together to install state-of-the-art security systems for Crosby's and Silver's houses, using methods that were largely invisible to the untrained eye.

Cade had shared their progress, so she knew the locks—front and back on each house—had been changed out for top-of-the-line biometrics. Each lock not only stored fingerprints for

Crosby, Silver and even Hallie, but it had a rotating access code, too, so no one could detect it.

As Madison had instructed, extrasensitive cameras were added to the houses and surrounding area so that anyone approaching would be visible. Better still, there were devices added that picked up on sound with the push of a button. They were so sophisticated and so new, they weren't even on the market yet.

Everything could be seen on the monitors—one each in the kitchens, living rooms and master bedrooms of both houses. If anyone came onto the property, a beep sounded to alert the homeowner. Sure, the occasional animal would also activate the beep, but it shouldn't be a problem too often.

With so many cameras, each view on the monitor was necessarily small. No one wanted an enormous monitor taking up space in every room. That problem was solved with highlighting that framed individual shot of the triggered camera. If Crosby or Silver wanted to also hear the intruder, they could push the button.

The camera feeds, as well as the sound options, were also networked to send to Madison and Parrish. Cade and Reyes had access through an app, but for the sake of privacy, they would only access it if one of the others alerted them to trouble.

Thanks to the added security, Madison immediately felt better about things, but she was far from comfortable. A niggling unease disturbed her peace of mind.

Now that she'd found Crosby and Hallie, she couldn't bear the thought of losing them.

She'd tried, oh-so-casually, suggesting that Crosby, Silver and Hallie move in with her. After all, she had three bedrooms, and if she and Crosby shared...

He made it clear that wasn't going to happen, so she hadn't pressed. It'd be tough to expect a man to uproot his family like that. Hallie had the perfect setup and while it could be worked out, it wouldn't be the same.

Plus she suspected Silver would never go for it.

And lastly, at least in her order of importance, Crosby had his pride. He probably wouldn't like depending on her. She understood that, because she felt the same.

Her phone buzzed. She checked the screen, saw it was Crosby and was already smiling before she answered. "Hey, you. I was just thinking about you." *About us. About you living with me, maybe sleeping with me every night.* She rolled her eyes. How had she gone from worrying about a possible threat to imagining the perfect life together? "What's up?"

"Just finished some work at the hotel. The staff is now fully aware of how to deal with bomb threats, plus I added extra guards until the task force is able to relocate the two women they have set up there."

"Go you." She sat back in her chair, enjoying the new casual vibe to their relationship. "Heading home now?"

"Yeah. Hate to say it, but we might be running a half hour late for dinner."

"I'll let Bernard know."

"Give him my apology."

"I will, but it's not necessary." With the way her family worked, it was understood that unavoidable things sometimes came up.

"What have you been up to?"

Madison loved how they chatted just like a longtime couple, asking after each other's day. It was uncommonly nice, something she'd never had before.

Seeing that as an opening, and knowing she had to tell someone soon, she sat forward again. "I have some news."

"On Crow?"

"Actually, yes." Madison was currently very proud of herself. It had been meticulous work that left her eyes strained, but she'd finally uncovered a few new details. "He drives a red Durango, probably five or six years old. He turned left onto the main road, but I lost him after that. Didn't even show up on traffic cams."

"That means he's either staying somewhere nearby, or he ducked into a garage or something."

No praise, no gratitude for her hard work? Disgruntled, she said, "I can show you the feed when you're over tonight."

"No, I don't want to chance Hallie hearing anything about it, and I don't want to leave her alone with anyone while we go off together for business."

Brows climbing, Madison wondered how to take that. Because she wasn't any good at tiptoeing around, she asked, "You're worried about Hallie with my family?"

"Not at all. In fact, it eases my mind knowing they'll look out for her."

Well. That was good. Hearing him say it did a lot to relieve the lack of acknowledgment she'd felt. "Then why—"

With a smile in his voice, he explained, "You might not see it, but your dad's place can be intimidating. Hallie's never seen anything like it. Plus, she's already been asking a lot of questions about the security cameras and why we're getting them. I don't want to scare her."

No, she didn't want that either. "I understand."

"This is after-work hours, my quality time with her where we can talk, play together or just kick back. Unless she chooses to leave my side, I want to stick close to her."

*Awwww.* The image of Crosby with his little angel brought out a sigh. "Is she a snuggly kind of kid?"

He laughed. "Her moods vary, believe me. Some days she doesn't want me to put her down, and other days she wants to play-wrestle nonstop. But the point is that I try not to let work intrude when I can help it."

"I'm glad. You both deserve that special time together." The rest of her tension waned, leaving her just a little…envious? Yep. Funny that she'd never thought about being in a long-term relationship with a guy, much less a guy and his daughter, but now it seemed like the most wonderful thing ever.

The problem was that she had things to tell him, important things about Crow that weren't suited for the phone. Personal things that she didn't want shared—not yet, anyway—with her family.

If she couldn't get him alone, how could she talk with him about it?

"Hey, did I lose you?" he asked.

"No, I was just thinking." Feeling thwarted, she decided she'd just wait and see if they found a moment alone. "I'm really looking forward to having you here."

His voice dropped when he murmured, "I'm looking forward to a lot of things. Eventually."

Oh, hey. Count her in on that, too. Except now she didn't know how that might work. If Crosby had a strict separation of work and home, then where did sex fit in? She was about to ask him, but he didn't give her the chance.

"I gotta run, but first, if the opportunity arises and we have a free minute together, I'd rather taste you again than look at footage, especially since I'm pretty sure I won't notice anything on the feed that you haven't already caught."

There was the compliment she'd wanted, and a sexy promise, as well. "I am rather thorough—at both things." Tonight they could just enjoy the time together, and tomorrow she'd figure out a way to meet with him. That'd be soon enough.

After making a kissing sound into the phone, she said, "See ya soon." She heard his chuckle right before she disconnected.

Smiling, Madison headed to the kitchen to let Bernard know that Crosby would be running a little behind. Of course, Bernard, being such an adaptable chef, promised it wouldn't be a problem.

"Whatever you're making," she said, sniffing the air, "it smells heavenly."

He glanced at her while chopping vegetables. "If I might make a suggestion?"

Bernard at his most lofty was a delight. She waved her hand in a grand gesture. "By all means."

"You mentioned sledding."

"Right." They had perfect hills for it. "I know it's cold and all, but—"

"Perhaps a child would also like to swim? I did a few laps myself this morning, and the water is perfect."

"Bernard! That's an awesome idea." She pulled out her phone. "I'll text Crosby now so he knows to bring swimsuits."

"Excellent. I placed a few beach towels on the lounge chairs. Pity we don't have any floats for children."

True. Anytime one of them used the pool, it was for laps, not really relaxing. "Hmm, yeah." She sent the text, and a few seconds later, her phone dinged.

U—in a bikini?

Grinning, she replied: Will be.

Might be on time after all

Laughing, Madison returned a smiley face, then stuck the phone in her pocket. "He likes the idea of a swim. Thanks for thinking of it."

Bernard dropped all the vegetables into a salad bowl. "If your young man continues to visit, I'll see about picking up pool toys."

Madison paused. "You know you're the greatest, right?" On impulse, she stepped up against him and wrapped her arms around his lean waist. Because his hands were wet, he couldn't return her embrace.

That didn't stop him from pressing his cheek to hers and hugging her with his elbows. "Be careful now. My apron is messy."

"You are never messy, Bernard." As she stepped back, she needlessly smoothed his shirt and apron. "Except for when you play with Chimera, of course. Where is she, by the way?" She hadn't seen the cat all day.

"Planning to use my cat to charm Crosby's daughter and thereby hook him? Clever, Madison. Very clever."

In so many ways, Bernard had been like a gentler version of a dad, with the warm nature of a mom, a careful caretaker and, when she'd needed it most, a friend. She loved him very much. Bernard was the best kind of family. "Don't spread it around, but at this point, I'd try just about anything to *hook* him, as you put it."

He looked surprised for only a moment, then said gently, "I know. I see it in your eyes when you speak of him."

"Oh, jeez. Dad would have a cow to know I was so transparent."

Behind her, her father said, "Have a cow? That doesn't sound like me."

She turned to see him carrying Chimera, while Bob, with his fuzzy tail in the air, trailed behind them. Madison burst out laughing. Chimera now wore a big two-toned bow collar, one side pale blue, the other side yellow-green, mimicking her mismatched eyes. "What is this? You've got her all decked out?"

Bernard melted. "Oh, she looks beautiful, Parrish." Hastily he dried his hands and took the cat to cradle her in his arms. Chimera, all long limbs and bent tail, rested in his arms like a baby, her rumbling purr loud enough to fill the large kitchen. "Obviously she *loves* the bow," he stated, and then to the cat, "Don't you, sweet girl? Yes, you do. Yes, you do."

Madison almost choked. She still couldn't get used to Bernard baby-talking to the cat.

Parrish rolled his eyes, but he smiled.

"Dad," Madison said, trying to look and sound stern, though her amusement kept threatening to break through. "Are you trying to help me hook Crosby?"

"You don't need my help, but yes, I like him," Parrish said. "I also respect him, even more so now that he's explained about Hallie. My only daughter could certainly do worse. *But*," he said with emphasis, "what is most important to me is that you're happy."

Wow, he rarely went this route in their conversations. For a second there, it threw her, then she rallied. "I would never let my happiness depend on a man, so rest easy, Dad."

"I'm glad." In one of his rare displays of affection, he drew her in for a hug—one that lasted a little longer and felt a little tighter than anything in her recent past.

"Dad?"

"I didn't raise you to rely on others." He levered her back, his gaze penetrating. "That doesn't mean you can't enjoy life even more with someone truly special at your side."

The way he had with her mom. "I know," Madison whispered, unaccountably touched by his advice. "Let's not rush things with Crosby, though." She did enough of that on her own. If her whole family got involved, they'd run Crosby off in no time. "He currently has a full plate, right? And you know, we McKenzies are a lot to take in."

Parrish's smile went crooked. "Indeed." He really surprised her when he cupped her cheek. "Only the right man will realize just how fortunate he is to have your attention." When he turned to go, Bob ran to keep up with him. Parrish paused to lift the kitten to his shoulder, then continued on.

Dumbfounded, Madison turned to face Bernard. "He, um, likes Bob, too?"

"Your father has warmed up to all the cats. Since you're here more often than the boys, he and Bob are naturally closer."

The *boys*. It cracked her up when Bernard or her dad referred to Cade and Reyes that way.

After putting a quick peck on Chimera's head, Bernard set the cat down and went to the sink to wash his hands. "By the by, he didn't decorate Chimera strictly for you."

"No?" Madison didn't know what to think.

"Just as you assume my beautiful baby will be a lure, so does Parrish." He glanced at her over his shoulder. "He hasn't said anything, and probably won't, given his reserved nature, but Parrish is obviously interested in Silver."

"Who told you about her?" Madison came closer to lean on the counter, then swiped a carrot curl from the salad.

"I always know what's happening. You should realize that by now."

"Oh, I do. But I doubt you divined it. Seriously, Bernard, I know you have magical powers, but telepathy?"

"Cade and Reyes mentioned her," he said in an offhand way. "She sounds like a charming woman."

The word *charming* might be old-fashioned, but it did sum up Silver. "She's funny, quick with a comeback and is *so* gorgeous, too. Dad is definitely intrigued." Her father had changed so much since Cade brought Sterling around. Now he pretty much rolled with every family situation—an alley cat with kittens, Bernard's total turnaround from stuffy butler to cooing pet daddy, and even when Reyes introduced them to Kennedy, Parrish had barely blinked.

All his razor-sharp edges had rounded out a bit, to the point that he now indulged an affectionate heart-to-heart with her, then sauntered off carrying her cat.

Maybe her brothers' romances had influenced her father, driving home everything he missed by closing off his heart to new love. That would explain why he was so accepting of a romance between her and Crosby.

"Go on," Bernard said. "You have a lot to think about, and I have preparations to make."

Madison nodded. "Thanks again." Now that she knew Crosby anticipated seeing her in a bikini, she was determined to look her absolute best. Pushing her worries about Crow to the side for tonight, she headed down to her suite of rooms with a smile on her face.

Once he got home, Crosby took a few minutes to inspect all the cameras, then to familiarize himself with the feeds. Amazing that something so complicated and detailed could be set up to be so user-friendly.

He quickly showered, shaved again, dressed in casual clothes, then packed his and Hallie's swimsuits, her arm floats and two rolled-up towels in a waterproof bag, and then headed over to Silver's. Before they left, he wanted to make sure that she knew what to expect.

She greeted him at the door, but Hallie wasn't around. Answering his unasked question, Silver said, "She's in her room, getting a few things for her trip. She's excited."

That made him feel guilty for keeping her so isolated. He wanted his daughter to be comfortable in any situation, much like Madison was. Now, with the McKenzie family around, he'd have an opportunity to widen Hallie's social circle and still keep her safe.

Setting the bag aside and shrugging off his coat, he nodded at the monitor. "What do you think? You understand how it all works?"

"Cade is a patient teacher," she said. "Nice young man. I like him."

Seeing the glint in her eyes, Crosby asked, "And Reyes?"

She sniffed. "He's been on his best behavior. Said now he feels challenged to win me over." A smile edged through her stern expression. "You know he's a sweetheart."

Crosby snorted. "Uh, no, I don't."

"Well, he is, it's just that we're both sarcastic and it's not a good mix. He finally said I was better at it than him, all while grinning like a rascal. How could I not like him?"

Smiling, Crosby nodded at the cameras. "They cover the entire area."

She studied them anew. "Gotta admit, I like having all this extra security. Not that I was worried before, so don't go frowning. It's just that with everything..."

"I understand." Before she'd turned her life around, Silver had been in an abusive relationship with an asshole who passed her around like free candy. She'd tried to escape a few times over the two years she'd been with him, but each beating was worse than the last. After he'd damn near killed her, she hadn't tried again for a long time.

Then one day, she saw an opening—Crosby—and she took it.

It was one of the bravest things he'd ever seen, and he often gave thanks that he was there when she needed him. Even before he adopted Hallie, he'd grown close to Silver. There were few people in this world he trusted as much as he trusted her.

He suddenly realized that she was still dressed in a messy sweatshirt, torn jeans and mismatched socks. Hmm... "Is that what you're wearing?"

Mouth twitching, she struck a pose. "What? You don't like it?"

Unsure what to say, he rubbed the back of his neck. Her husky laughter finally clued him in. "Ah, you're joking?"

"Sort of." She turned away to wipe down an already-clean sink. "See, I'm stayin' here. I've got an appointment with a hot bath and then an old movie."

This was news to him. "You're not going?"

"It's your date, sugar, not mine."

"You were invited, too." Uncertainty from Silver was a rare thing these days, but then, they pretty much kept to themselves.

Like his daughter, Silver wasn't used to dinner parties. "They're expecting you, you know."

She shook her head, avoided eye contact and asked, "Have you told them anything about me?"

So that was it? Had she been torturing herself over that? Damn it, he should have realized sooner. He stepped closer and said with convincing sincerity, "I've only told them that you're wonderful, that I've relied heavily on you, and that Hallie thinks of you as her grandma. The rest of your business is your own."

She studied a fingernail. "Parrish hasn't asked?"

Clearly that attraction went both ways. "I get the feeling Parrish McKenzie prefers to find out things in his own time, in his own way." Leaning against the counter, Crosby added, "Madison's shown some curiosity. She hasn't come right out and asked, but she doesn't miss much." Neither did Parrish. "She knows we have special circumstances." It was rare for a man and woman to be so close with nothing intimate between them, but for him and Silver, that had never been an issue. For too long she'd been hurt and suspicious, and he'd been desperate to not only help her in some substantial way, but to win her trust in the bargain. There'd been no room for anything other than compassion, but that had grown into friendship and then a strong platonic love.

"You can tell her." Silver glanced at him. "I wouldn't mind if she knows."

He gave her a gentle smile. "*You* can tell her—once you get to know her better."

Her gaze shot up to his, and understanding sparked in her eyes, giving her a grin. "Ah, it's like that, is it?"

"I think so." He planned to take it slow with Madison—or as slow as she'd let him. As slow as his lust would allow. "I like her."

"I like her plenty, too. You've dealt with so many of us broken souls, you need a thriving gal with some backbone."

"Silver," he chided. Yes, she might have been broken once, but that was in the past. He rested a hand on her narrow shoulder. "You know you're family, right? No matter what I do, now or in the future, that won't ever change. Hallie and I love you. You're important to us and you'll always be a part of us."

She looked so vulnerable it almost broke Crosby's heart. "I feel the same." She braced herself with a breath. "I still think it'd be easier if she hears it from you."

"If you're sure that's what you want, I'll talk to her."

"It'd be best. Thanks."

Crosby would have said more, but Hallie came around the corner in a rush, no less than four dolls in her arms.

Stepping away from him and pasting on an automatic smile, Silver lifted the variety of dolls, one by one, onto the table. "You plannin' to take all these, sweetness?"

Hallie poked out her bottom lip in a pout. "*They* want to visit."

Ah, apparently Silver and Hallie had already had this conversation. He tamped back his humor and said, "Silver can join us another time."

"She's gonna take a long bath," Hallie said in a grumble. "Lots of bubbles."

Crosby figured it was more than a leisurely bath that kept Silver at home.

"I forgot Barbie!" Already racing off for another doll, Hallie said, "She wants to go, too."

Once little ears were out of hearing range, Crosby moved to stand in front of Silver. "Are you maybe skipping dinner because you want to avoid someone?"

"No maybe to it."

That was the thing about Silver. She was usually pretty upfront with him, which made things easier. "So is Parrish going to be a problem for you?"

"No, he's not the problem. I am."

"Silver…"

Ensuring he'd drop the topic, she called for Hallie. "Come

on, honey, or you'll be late." She turned back to Crosby and handed him his coat. "Go, have fun and don't worry about me. I'll have the app opened on my phone while I soak so I'll still be able to see the feeds. A long bath and a favorite movie will make it a perfect night."

No, it wouldn't, but as always, Silver would work through things and then make good decisions. If she needed quiet time alone to do that, then he'd give her his support. "If you need anything at all, give me a call. I'll keep my phone close."

"Tomorrow, plan to give me a full report on how it went. I'll want every juicy detail."

"What Parrish wore? Every word he says? Especially if he says anything about you?"

Laughing, Silver swatted at him. "I meant between you and Madison." Expression softening, she smiled up at him. "It won't be easy to impress someone like her."

That didn't exactly sound like criticism, but to be sure, Crosby asked, "Meaning what?"

"Tall, beautiful, capable, confident—I could go on and on, but the point is, you should *try*. I have a feeling she's the one for you. Don't mess it up."

Wondering if Silver was right, Crosby nodded. "I'll give it my best shot."

# CHAPTER NINE

Madison answered the door before Bernard could, much to his displeasure. He wore a "how *dare* you?" expression as he stood stiffly to the side, putting on his most haughty performance.

"You're here!" She gestured Crosby and Hallie inside. "Come in and warm up."

"Thanks." Crosby held Hallie's hand as the little girl stared, eyes wide and mouth open. She looked everywhere, even tipping her head way back to see the ceiling.

Madison had never thought much about the ceiling, so she looked, too. Huh. It really was way up there, and the chandeliers were huge, which made them impressive.

As he peeled off his coat, Crosby said, "Hopefully we're not too late."

Today he'd dressed casually in well-worn jeans, sturdy lace-up boots and a thermal Henley with a flannel shirt over it. He looked rugged and too damn sexy.

Hallie had a similar look in her own skinny jeans, a white thermal shirt and a pink flannel shirt. Her boots were pink without laces.

"Not late at all." Bernard nodded to Crosby, smiled down

at Hallie, and then frowned when no one else entered. Jerking the door wider, he searched outside and, finding no one there, scowled at Crosby. "Only two guests tonight?"

"Afraid so." Crosby set aside a large bag with dolls on top and helped Hallie remove her boots, which were caked with snow. "Silver decided to stay home."

"She's takin' a bath." While sticking close to Crosby's side, she eyed Bernard. "Lots of bubbles."

Parrish, who'd just come down the hall, faltered.

Madison took in the unguarded disappointment on his face a split second before it was gone.

"Welcome," Parrish said, continuing on as if the moment hadn't happened.

"Kenzie!" Hallie pulled away from Crosby and raced toward Parrish. Unfortunately, her sock-covered feet caused her to slip on the marble foyer. If Parrish hadn't been so quick in catching her arms, she'd have wiped out.

"Ohmigod," Madison said, her hand over her thudding heart. "I thought for sure you were going to clunk your head on the hard floor." That wouldn't have been a promising start to the evening.

Still in that stuffy voice, Bernard added, "Head clunking on these smooth floors is something Madison perfected in her youth."

Lifting Hallie up in front of him, Parrish said, "No running, young lady, or you'll be crashing into every wall."

"The floors are slippery," Hallie said with a grin.

He glanced at Crosby. "She could leave on her boots."

Crosby shook his head. *"Someone,"* he said, giving his daughter a look, "decided to jump in the snow. Her boots are wet, which would just make things slicker."

Quick to change the subject, Hallie put a hand to Parrish's cheek. "Daddy told me your house was big." She looked up the high, winding stairway to the second floor. "It's like a palace, huh?"

"Especially now with a princess in it." He tucked her close, holding her with one arm, and strode over to Crosby, hand extended. "Thank you for joining us."

Madison shifted from one foot to the other, churning with eagerness for the evening. She wanted to get past all the niceties and show Hallie around, then race through dinner so they could swim. She really hoped her swimsuit pleased Crosby.

Too bad Silver wasn't here. She would have immediately distracted her father and Bernard. Both men had obviously anticipated Silver's arrival. Bernard, likely because he hadn't yet met her. And Parrish…well, Madison suspected her dad was beyond infatuated.

While Parrish and Hallie spoke to Bernard, Madison elbowed Crosby. "What gives?" she asked in a whisper.

Catching her arm so she couldn't gouge him again, he stared into her eyes… And then at her mouth.

Mmm, *nice*. Much more of that and she'd kiss him right here, right now. "Crosby?" She smiled. "How come Silver bailed on us?"

"This is all new for her," he said quietly. "She's used to it just being us. Guess she needs some time."

Madison wrinkled her nose. Now she felt like an interloper. "I tried to make a good impression on her."

Crosby lifted a hand to cup her cheek. "You don't have to try because you're always impressive." His thumb drifted over her cheek, then to the corner of her mouth, before he dropped his hand. "It's not about you. In fact, Silver said she likes you."

"Really?" That would certainly make things easier.

"She ordered *me* to impress *you*, if that tells you anything."

Wow, that really did sound like she had Silver in her corner. First Bernard, then her dad, and now Silver, too. Dare she hope it was meant to be? "You impressed me even before we met in person." She leaned closer, thoughts of kissing him clamoring in her head. "Maybe I could show you—"

"Ahem."

They both turned to see Bernard and Parrish standing together, Hallie still held by Parrish. The various expressions were priceless. Bernard managed to look miffed, Parrish appeared indulgent and Hallie grinned like an imp.

"We have a little time before dinner," Parrish announced. "I'm going to show Hallie around."

"I was going to do that," Madison complained.

Bernard snorted. "You may continue playing doorman since you obviously like it so much. Your brothers are due soon."

She didn't want to stand around in the foyer waiting on Cade and Reyes! "What will you be doing?"

"Finishing dinner." Nose in the air, Bernard walked away.

Hallie cracked up. "He's funny."

"He," Bernard called back, "made you something special for dinner. I hope you're hungry."

In a loud whisper, Hallie asked Parrish, "What is it? Will I like it?"

"Do you like spaghetti and meatballs?"

"Yum!" She bounced in Parrish's arms.

"There's also ziti, and I believe lasagna." Parrish shrugged. "My children all have their favorites and Bernard likes to spoil them, especially when he can show off in front of company."

With a smile, Crosby mimicked Hallie's, "Yum," but without her enthusiasm.

"Now, where would you like to start our tour?" Parrish asked Hallie. "Upstairs or down? Or I know, the balcony. You can see the mountains." He started away.

Remembering Crosby's concern, Madison complained, "*Dad.* You didn't even ask. Crosby worked all day. Maybe he wants to spend the time with his daughter."

Parrish paused, as if the idea that he might be overstepping had never occurred to him. "We won't be long."

"Can I, Dad? *Please?*" Hallie pleaded. "I wanna see the palace."

Crosby grinned. "Sure. Stay right with Mr. McKenzie, though. No wandering off."

Setting her on her feet, Parrish took her hand, and this time when they turned to leave the room, no one stopped them.

They were literally alone when Madison didn't think that would happen so soon. Her heart tripped into a faster rhythm and a warm flush spread across her skin.

Bernard was now in the kitchen a good distance away, and Parrish and Hallie had disappeared around a corner.

Crosby continued to stare after them, so Madison cleared her throat. "If you want," she offered, "we can go with them."

His intent gaze landed on her, and that's when she saw it. All the heat, all the need that she experienced were reflected in those dark bedroom eyes. Without a word he backed her up to the double front doors, braced his hands flat at either side of her head and put his mouth to hers.

This wasn't an easy "let's get to know each other" kiss, or a kiss shared during troubling memories. Nope, this was a "damn, I want you *bad*" kind of consuming kiss that she felt clean down to the soles of her feet, where it sizzled like a lightning strike before shooting upward again, exploding low in her stomach, then her breasts and lastly her heart.

Holy smokes.

Pretty sure she did the equivalent of a human-melt. That is, her legs and spine went weak, but her hands had no problem clutching his shoulders, and her mouth happily accepted the sinuous thrust of his tongue.

When was the last time she'd been kissed like this? Oh, yeah. Never. Maybe because no other man had set her on fire this way.

He leaned into her, breasts to chest, pelvis to pelvis. *Whoa.* Tipping her mouth away, she panted. "God, you're hot."

He dropped his forehead to hers with a gruff laugh. "You took the words right out of my mouth."

"Took your tongue, too." She kissed his jaw, then the hot skin of his throat. The rich scent of him, clean musk and heat, really did it for her. Man, she could just eat him up. "It's a very clever tongue, Crosby. My imagination is now in hyperdrive."

For a reply, he took her mouth again. She knew they'd have to stop soon. Pretty sure Crosby knew it, too, since he carefully kept his hands planted flat against the door. She wanted him to touch her, but considering their incendiary reactions to each other, that might be a bad plan. His was better: devouring kiss, full body contact, tense restraint so things didn't get too far out of hand.

His hard shoulders flexed under her hands, muscles bunching and rolling as he adjusted to make the kiss hotter, deeper. Her breath labored, his hips pressed closer—and suddenly someone tried to push their way in.

She got shoved forward against Crosby, their feet tangled and he almost fell. Didn't help that she also lost her footing.

Reaching around the door, Cade grabbed her upper arm with a grumble. "What the hell, Madison?" While stepping in the rest of the way, he made sure she was upright. Then he frowned at Crosby. "What's going on here?"

Crosby frowned right back. "Nothing now."

Sterling pushed in past her husband, took in the situation and gave an ear-to-ear grin. "All right, girl." She offered Madison a high five.

Trying to regain her composure while fighting her own grin, Madison happily smacked her palm.

"Were they making out in the foyer?" Reyes crowded in next, pulling Kennedy along with him. To Crosby, he said, "Dude, there are rooms everywhere. Madison has her own suite downstairs. No reason to put on a show."

"Or block a door," Cade added. "You didn't hear us knock?"

"Er, no." She'd been far too busy falling heavily in lust.

To Madison's surprise, Crosby put his arm around her waist and offered them a smile. "Your dad just absconded with my daughter. We had a moment alone." He shrugged. "Your sister is irresistible."

Kennedy said, "Aww," and stuck out her hand. "Remember me?"

"Of course I do." Crosby accepted her hand. "How are you?"

The first time they'd met hadn't been under the best of circumstances, not with people after Kennedy and Reyes in protective caveman mode. None of them had known Crosby that well then, so her brothers hadn't entirely trusted him, but Madison had wanted him from the start.

Now here he was, and her brothers had better play nice or they'd be dealing with her.

"I'm Reyes's wife now," Kennedy explained, "but I'm still very nice, I promise."

"Hey," Reyes said, pretending affront.

"You're nice, too," she promised. "Sometimes."

Crosby laughed. "Silver said the same thing about him earlier today."

"Oh, yes, Silver." Kennedy glanced around. "Reyes told me all about her. I'm anxious to meet her."

Madison sighed. "She stayed home to enjoy a long bath."

"With bubbles," Crosby said with a grin. "She doesn't get a lot of time to kick back alone."

Cade steered everyone toward the kitchen. "I thought you took Hallie home with you every night."

"I do, but we usually share dinner with Silver."

"I call bullshit on the bath story," Reyes said. "Dad is throwing it out there and she's dodging it, that's all. Where is Dad, anyway?"

Kennedy grabbed his arm. "You will not tease your father about this, Reyes McKenzie. I mean it."

Sterling said, "Well, I might. I still owe him some payback."

Cade gave her a stern frown. "No, you won't. If you start on Dad, he'll dish it right back, and Crosby's visit will be ruined."

"Sucks for Crosby, but I want my due."

Madison took in Crosby's harassed expression and laughed. "Seriously, when Sterling first came around, it was one hell of a show. Dad tried being all autocratic and she just kept cutting him off at the knees."

"Parrish was easy enough to take," Sterling said. "It was this one—" she gave Reyes a playful shove that made him stumble since it took him off guard "—who really irked me."

"But we've made peace since then," Reyes reminded her... while trying to trip her.

Sterling dodged him with a laugh. "Maybe."

Cade moved her to his other side, away from his brother. "You two are seriously giving Crosby a bad impression of us."

"More like an accurate impression," Kennedy said. "But I'm sure Crosby can feel the love."

Though Crosby choked over that, he didn't really seem bothered by their antics. If anything, he seemed amused. Things were off to a great start.

She wouldn't mind sharing many more evenings like this, all of them together, joking around and having fun.

Their small family circle had expanded in the best of ways, and she wanted to be a part of that—but only with Crosby.

Eventually, she'd get some one-on-one time with him. Until then, she'd enjoy every minute of their growing familiarity.

And that reminded her... Keeping her voice low so the others wouldn't overhear, she asked him, "Are you free for lunch tomorrow?"

"If you actually mean lunch, then yes." That ebony gaze drifted over her face. "If you mean anything else, I don't want to be tempted at work."

"I mean lunch." Then she added with hope, "We can plan on more soon?"

"Count on it." His hand slid from her waist to her hip and he leaned close to say against her temple, "I'm not sure I'll survive otherwise."

"Big brothers in the room," Reyes reminded them as they entered the kitchen. Seeing the table wasn't set, he glanced at Bernard. "Guess we're going all hoity-toity in the dining room tonight?"

Stirring a big pot on the stove, Bernard said without turning, "Naturally."

*Naturally*, Reyes silently mimicked with a roll of his eyes. He turned to Crosby and held out his arms. "Since Madison is hankering for some alone time, I'm offering myself up as a babysitter."

Cade choked. "You realize what you're suggesting?"

"I don't mean right now," Reyes said defensively. "But hey, unlike you, I realize that being my sister doesn't mean she can't—"

Kennedy put her hand over his mouth. "That's enough out of you."

"Amen," Sterling stated with feeling.

Bernard turned to face them all. "Please remove yourselves to the dining room. And someone needs to locate Parrish and our other guest. Dinner is ready to be served."

As he waded into the pool with Hallie, Crosby again wished Silver had joined them. He was certain she would have enjoyed dinner—the food and the company—as much as he had. Hallie had been thrilled with the way Bernard had fashioned her homemade roll to look like a snowman. And he'd placed extrasmall meatballs on her spaghetti like a smiley face.

Hallie now considered Bernard almost as special as "Kenzie."

Yes, Silver would be having fun, and Crosby wanted that, but she would also make a nice buffer right about now.

For the tenth time, he glanced at the double glass doors of the pool room.

A freaking pool room. It boggled his mind, but hey, he had to admit the warm water felt great, especially after they'd spent an hour outside sledding.

Hallie was mellow with exhaustion, but that didn't stop her from leaping forward into the water with a splash. "It's like a big bathtub."

*Minus the bubbles*, Crosby thought. He watched his daughter pump her legs while the inflatable arm floats kept her buoyant in the water. "You're having fun, honey?"

"So much fun! I like it here. Can we come again?"

The doors quietly closed, drawing his attention.

"I'm sure that can be arranged," Madison said as she strode in with a towel over her arm and her phone in her hand.

His eyes burned. His lungs stalled. Every male molecule of his being went on the alert.

Christ, she looked amazing.

Barefoot, she stopped at the edge of the pool and smiled down at them. His gaze took a thorough, leisurely trip up her long toned legs to her gently rounded hips, a flat stomach, small waist, modest breasts and proud shoulders. She epitomized lithe feminine strength and well-earned confidence.

Devastatingly sexy, that's what she was.

No other woman could be more so.

Her lips quirked, and she shifted her attention to Hallie. "Pink? Seriously?" She put her hand on a cocked-out hip. "You have a pretty pink bathing suit and all I have is black? Now I'm jealous."

Hallie giggled. "I have a purple one, too."

"Hopefully I can see it next time." She put her phone and towel on one of the chairs.

Seeing her bend like that, his heart punched into his chest. *That stellar ass...*

Smiling, she came down the steps.

Crosby watched the water cover her smooth calves, her taut thighs, up and up until it lapped at her breasts. Breasts he really wanted to cup in his hands. Eyes burning, he said low, "Hi."

"No," she whispered in an aside. "Don't talk to me all sexy like that. I'm hanging on by a thread."

Her honesty helped to ease his sexual tension. "Saying *hi* is sexy?"

"The way you say it, it is." She went under the water, then popped up a few feet away and swam toward Hallie.

She still didn't have her laptop with her, and Crosby wondered if he'd managed to take her from her work. It was a rare thing to see Madison without that laptop close at hand. She'd even had it nearby at dinner.

When they'd gone outside to play in the snow, she'd switched it up for her phone and apparently still had the laptop tucked away somewhere.

For the next hour they had races from one end of the pool to the other where they let Hallie win, cannonball contests where he won with the biggest splash, and Madison showed Hallie how to float on her back. Side by side, they practiced, Hallie's fair hair floating around her head like a halo, Madison's golden brown hair snaking out in long tendrils.

Her body was the thing of dreams, and he couldn't stop looking at her, especially at moments like this where she and Hallie paid no attention to him.

Everything Madison did, even how she did it, drew him closer. When he'd first met her, he never would have guessed that she'd so easily bond with his daughter. It meant a lot that she did, freeing him from many of his self-imposed dating restrictions.

But then, Madison freed him from a lot of things—like secrets he'd kept and feelings he'd suppressed.

When her phone dinged, he realized she hadn't heard it, not

with her ears underwater. Curling a hand around her slender foot, he gave her a gentle tug.

She curled forward, then straightened those mile-long legs. One look at her face and he knew she was happy. Madison didn't have a deceptive bone in her body. All the attention she'd given to Hallie wasn't for his benefit, but rather because she actually enjoyed interacting with her.

She was a natural, and wasn't that a scary thought? A woman like her, lethal and beautiful, bold and sweet, and somehow she was also...nurturing?

Crosby didn't approve of the way her father had raised her, but he definitely liked the final result. He couldn't deny that her upbringing had helped to make her a most incredible woman.

With him staring at her so long, she lifted her brows. "What?"

Crosby rubbed a hand over his mouth. Would he ever get used to her? He hoped not. "You got a message or something." He gestured toward the towels. "On your phone."

"Ah, thanks. I didn't hear it." She waded over to the side, then performed the graceful feat of hoisting herself out using only her arms.

She looked deceptively delicate with her small bones and willowy stature, but he knew she was strong. She literally made the most of what nature had given her. Physically, emotionally and intellectually. Hell, in *all* ways, she exceeded the norm.

As water sluiced down her body, she headed to the chair, did a quick dry off with a towel, and then lifted her phone.

Crosby divided his time between watching his daughter, who looked ready to doze off in the water, and taking in Madison's enigmatic expression as she listened to a voice mail. Her gaze never once came his way and that, more than anything else, told him something was up.

Could it be another guy? Pretty sure they had an understanding and, Madison being so up-front, he discounted that possibility. If she'd wanted variety, she'd have told him so.

Still, it gave him pause because so often his time wasn't his own. He was going quietly nuts wanting her, and she made no bones about feeling the same, yet he couldn't say when they'd finally be able to get together.

After closing out the screen, she put the phone back on the chair and returned to the edge of the pool. She still didn't look at Crosby but smiled at Hallie. In a soft voice, she said, "Looks like someone has run out of gas." She wiggled her fingers at him. "Hand her up to me. I'll wrap her in a towel."

Hallie, who'd been truly zoning in that way of hers that signaled she'd nod off any second, came around with complaint. "I want to swim some more."

"You weren't swimming, honey." Wondering if Madison had any intention of telling him about the call, he scooped up his daughter and started for the edge of the pool.

"I was floatin' like Madison said," she whined. "I'll swim now."

"You're tired," Crosby insisted, knowing she was about to show her not-so-pleasant side. Like most four-year-olds, Hallie's moods could turn on a dime, most especially when exhausted. She'd had a very full day, and it was time to get her home to her own bed.

"I wanna swim!"

"Well, I'm completely whipped," Madison said around a fake yawn.

"I'm not." Hallie's face took on that obstinate look that was all too familiar when she didn't get her way.

"Hallie," Crosby said, his voice firm.

Madison spoke over him. "Seriously, you aren't tired? Wow. How can that be? I'm definitely bigger, so probably stronger, right? But man, I need to chill."

"I don't need to chill." Crossing her arms over her chest and leaning away from Crosby's hold, Hallie said again, "I want to *swim*."

"Well, you're tougher than me, girl. Come on, let me help you out so I see your muscles. I bet they're as big as your dad's."

Humor threatened, but Hallie ruthlessly suppressed it. "They are not."

"I bet they're so huge, they might make your dad cry."

"Daddy is strong," she said in his defense, losing some of her attitude. "I just like swimmin'."

"Yeah, but if you don't quit when it's time, your dad might not want to come back when I invite you again. That'd suck, right? Especially since I wanted to invite you back soon." Again, she wiggled her fingers, and this time, Hallie willingly went to her.

She made a big show of feeling Hallie's arms and measuring her muscles, until they both ended up in ridiculous muscle-flexing poses.

Thanks to Madison's teasing, they were wrapping up the day with laughter.

He got out of the water much as Madison had, and as he dried off he kept looking at the dark screen of her phone. Why had she hidden her thoughts from him while listening to the message?

"It was nothing," she said, eyeing him while drying Hallie's hair. "In fact, I'll tell you all about it tomorrow. What time are we doing lunch?"

Marginally reassured, Crosby glanced at his daughter. She leaned against Madison, looking ready to nod off again. Draping the towel around his neck, he lifted Hallie into his arms and headed for the connected changing room that also had a bathroom and full shower. Honestly, he'd lost track of the number of bathrooms in this house. "Let me get her changed before she topples."

"I'm not sleepy," Hallie murmured, even as she put her head on his shoulder.

"I know." He kissed her temple and said to Madison, "Be right back."

When he returned fifteen minutes later, Madison was dressed

and using the towels to remove puddles of water from the floor where they'd stood.

Quietly, Crosby said, "I can help with that."

She smiled at him. "You've got your hands full."

True. Hallie was out, sprawled boneless in his arms. "It's getting late for her."

"It's not a big deal anyway. With the room so warm it'll dry quickly." She spread the towels out over the chairs. "Bernard has it cleaned twice a week." Turning to him, she asked, "You want to talk now or tomorrow? Either is fine. I promise it's nothing that can't wait."

Much as he would prefer now, he knew it was getting late. If Hallie woke after only an hour of sleep, she'd be up the rest of the night. "Just tell me who it was."

"Ted, from the task force desk."

"Is there a problem?" His thoughts immediately went to the bomb threat at the hotel.

"Nope. Just a message to me about an upgrade to the computer system there. I'll talk to him tomorrow before we do lunch."

Crosby realized he knew her well enough to know she wasn't telling him everything. Her gaze was direct enough, and she'd answered without hesitation. Still...

Crossing her arms and huffing a laugh, she said, "Crosby. You either want to talk now or you don't. Which is it?"

"I'm rethinking my decision to wait." He stepped closer. Luckily, Hallie slept on. "Give it to me in a nutshell."

Shrugging, she said, "Fine. I was going to tell you at lunch anyway, and we can still discuss it more then, but the bare bones are that as I watched all that footage on Crow, I realized that he was looking at me a few times. That is, on the scene, he stared toward me, too. It was like he followed your and Dad's gazes. I doubt he could actually see me, though. Just something to be aware of."

Damn. She rattled all that off seamlessly, too, and still he felt like she was omitting something. "What does that have to do with the call at the task force?"

"Well…" She sighed. "If Crow *could* see me, he likely saw the laptop, too. There's a chance—a very slim chance—that he might have been the caller, fishing for info on me. I won't know until I actually talk to Ted to hear exactly what was said."

"You don't let anyone upgrade the software, do you?"

"Nope. I handle it myself." She brushed the back of one finger over Hallie's cheek. "It's probably nothing, though, so don't worry about it."

He'd damn well worry if he wanted to. "You plan to go out tonight?"

"That's a joke, right? I know I have mad stamina, but it's been a long day. I wasn't lying when I told Hallie I was tired. My plan is to head to my house and crash."

He worked his jaw. "I assume your dad's property is secure all the way down to your house."

"Naturally. If anyone came anywhere near the property, we'd know. And before you say it, I have the same instincts that you do, so yes, I'll be careful on my drive to meet you tomorrow. By the way, you still haven't told me where we're meeting and what time."

A quick topic switch? If he continued to question her, she might take it as an insult, so for now he let it go. "If you're going to the task force anyway, we can meet there. Say eleven? That way we can ride over to the restaurant together." Maybe he'd show up early and hear firsthand what Ted had to say.

"Eleven it is." She stepped around him, anxious—for the first time that he could remember—to wrap up their time together.

"Madison?"

She paused.

"You're going to tell Parrish, right?"

"I'd prefer not to say anything until I talk to Ted."

"I work for him. I can't keep secrets."

"No secret." She turned to him with a dim smile. "That's not how we do things. We always share because that's the safest way to handle any threat. The thing is, this might be nothing at all. What will one day hurt?"

"I guess it won't." But he didn't like it.

"Thanks." She left the pool room, holding the door for him as he carried Hallie out.

He followed her down the long hall, up the wide stairs and into the now-silent main floor.

As they passed the library, the door opened and Parrish stepped out. He saw Hallie and smiled. "Out for the night?"

"With any luck," Crosby said. "I'm hoping she doesn't get a second wind when she brushes her teeth and changes into a nightgown."

"Let it go one night," Parrish suggested, reaching out to smooth a curl over her temple. He nodded at Madison. "When she was this age and fell asleep, which was rare, it was either put her straight to bed without her usual routine, or she'd be wide-awake again."

"I sort of remember that," Madison said. "One time Mom got tired of trying to get me to settle down, so you came in and we talked tech for over an hour."

"Until you started to yawn," Parrish confirmed. "By then it was midnight."

"You've convinced me." Crosby kissed his daughter's forehead. There were still times when he worried about screwing up in his role as Dad. He'd been determined that her teeth would always be brushed twice a day, that she'd spend equal amounts of time learning and playing. That her clothes would always fit and be clean.

And that he would never, ever pigeonhole her into a role based on her gender. He'd already met too many women with a lack of viable options. He wanted more for Hallie. He wanted her to know that she could do anything and he'd be there encouraging her.

How to accomplish that was the question. Many things that, for some parents, came naturally, required more effort from him.

Not loving her. That he did fiercely, from the moment he'd first held her in his arms. But the rest? He didn't mind a few pointers.

"You're a good father," Parrish said, and he sounded like he meant it.

If trying counted, he should be doing all right. "Silver says I worry too much. Personally, I think that's because she worries *all* the time, so she recognizes the signs."

Parrish gave a small smile. "Worrying about your children never ends."

"Dad," Madison complained, "you don't have to worry about me. Now maybe Reyes…"

They all laughed softly.

Parrish confessed, "In some ways, I worry about you the most." Before Madison could get offended, he explained, "You're my only daughter and my youngest. Grant me the right to my feelings."

"Fine," she grumbled. "But it's unnecessary."

Crosby said, "As I tell Silver, fathers have the right to worry if they want to."

Hesitating only a moment, Parrish asked, "Silver is feeling all right? She didn't catch a cold from Hallie?"

"She's fine, and as you can see, so is Hallie now." He wouldn't betray Silver in any way, but he felt comfortable admitting, "I think she just wanted some quiet time alone with her thoughts."

Madison leaned into him. "Have we overwhelmed her?"

Parrish shared a look with Crosby. "I'd say at least one of us has." Forestalling any further discussion of it, he added with a nod at Hallie, "You've been holding that little bundle for a while now."

He looked at his daughter, then brushed a kiss over her forehead. "She doesn't weigh much."

Madison smiled. "Want me to warm up your car?"

"You don't need to—"

"I want to. In fact, I'll probably follow you down in my ride since I'm heading home now, too. Bobcat prefers a warm car so I'll start them both. Where's your key fob?"

Unsure if he wanted her digging in his pocket with her dad right there, Crosby shook his head.

Then Parrish settled it for him. "Here, I'll hold Hallie and you can both walk out. Bernard hung your coats on the tree beside the door, and Hallie's boots are on the rug." He took her away from Crosby with the ease of long practice, proof that he'd held his own children many times when they were younger.

That might have surprised him a few weeks ago. Back then, he'd figured Parrish was a wealthy, influential, uninvolved father. Now he knew better.

Hallie stirred, then snuggled against Parrish and sighed.

"She is so precious," Madison said. "And so tiny."

"You were once, too," Parrish whispered. "Though by four, you were probably twice Hallie's size."

"I was tall," she said to Crosby. "We all were."

"And still are." No child could have too much love, and Hallie more than many deserved nothing but happier times in her future. Crosby couldn't put into words how much it meant to him to have the McKenzies' open-arm acceptance of his daughter, so he merely nodded. "Thank you." With a hand to Madison's back, they started for the door.

They pulled on their coats, then stepped out to the heated drive. He'd never get used to that, though he wouldn't mind trying. He went to his black SUV and she went to her white one. They probably had two parking spots separating them.

Crosby started the engine, adjusted the heat and even rearranged the seat belts in Hallie's car seat before walking over to where Madison now waited by her front bumper.

"More shadows here," she whispered, and pulled him in. "The security lights reach everywhere, but no one can see us behind my SUV if you want to give me a kiss good-night."

"I want," he said, and cupped his hands to her face. After their swim, she'd partially dried her hair but it still felt damp. "Are you cold?"

"Burning up." She leaned in and took the initiative, licking over his bottom lip, tugging with her teeth, and then pressing her plump, damp lips to his.

God, she tasted good, felt good, and her scent hit him like pure temptation.

She hadn't zipped her coat so he was able to slide his hands inside, over her slim back... Then under her top to feel the warm silk of her skin. "Seeing you in that bikini has me strung tight," he whispered against her throat. He wanted to touch her all over.

"I don't mean to press—"

Lowering a hand to her behind, he *pressed* her into sizzling contact. They both groaned. "Press away, babe."

She went still, then wiggled free to see his face. "You called me *babe*."

Her expression was so comically surprised, he almost laughed. He didn't want to hurt her feelings though, or have her misunderstand, so instead he smoothed a hand over her damp hair. "Is that a problem?"

"No one's ever called me that before."

Most guys were probably too intimidated to use endearments. Not for the first time, Crosby wondered how much dating a dynamic, take-charge woman like Madison had done. He had no doubt guys would be more than willing, even with the imposing males of her family keeping watch and with Madison's larger-than-life personality.

But there was still something about her that made him think few men had measured up to her standards.

For one thing, Madison was so damn tall, she topped many men in height. He couldn't see her looking down to a guy, especially when her father and brothers were so big. She was so clever that it'd be difficult for her to accept anyone, even for a casual date, who wasn't on par with her intelligence. And all that stunning ability…would she be able to accept a man without her skill set?

Somehow he didn't think so.

Many of those same qualities were important to him—minus the issue of height. In so many ways, Madison fulfilled everything he could ever want, when he'd never even thought to look for someone like her.

Trying to be as serious as she appeared, he gently brushed his lips over hers. That warranted a second taste, and then a third, before he remembered he had a point to make.

"I care about you, Madison."

With a huge smile, she said, "Yay, me."

Did she mean that? Did she want to get involved beyond a casual relationship? He hoped so, since he knew he'd already left "casual" in the dust. "Endearments are just part of that, but if you don't like them, I'll try to omit them from my vocabulary."

"I don't mind," she rushed to tell him. "I'm just not used to them." She tipped her head, studying him. "What else might you call me?"

Now the smile really threatened. "Sweetheart? Honey?"

"Not *honey*. That's what you call Hallie."

"Okay." He wouldn't mind just calling her *his*, but it was definitely too soon for a big commitment.

With a groan, she asked, "Will we ever get together? Like, naked and horizontal together? Because seriously, Crosby, I *need* it."

He'd rather she had said she needed *him*, not just sex, but someone of Madison's caliber would never need anyone. Wanting was the most he could hope for.

At least for now.

"Let me talk to Silver, see what I can arrange, and then you and I can get caught up on all those expectations."

"Sexual expectations?"

Always so plainspoken. "Those are the best kind, right?"

She hugged him tight. "Oh, I don't know. With you, all of this has been awesome."

Teasing her, he said, "Then you don't——?"

"Heck yeah, I do." She leaned back again to look him over with blatant hunger. "I want the big payoff."

"Not that I should feel pressured or anything."

With extreme earnestness, she said, "You'll be perfect, Crosby. I'm sure of it."

Not grinning was impossible. "How about we shoot for being perfect together?" As she brought her delicious body in full contact with his for a final hug, he thought it was a good thing that he didn't have performance anxiety. With Madison, he believed sex *would* be perfect—perfectly explosive.

He could hardly wait.

# CHAPTER TEN

Disgusted that he'd taken a risk with no results, Crow paced the hotel room. Calling the task force, even from another burner phone, had been a huge mistake. Ted-somebody, likely a desk clerk or answering service, had claimed he couldn't put the call through at the moment.

Crow had casually tried asking if he could leave a voice message, hoping he'd be able to glean a name for someone. Ted politely refused, so Crow had asked if someone in Mr. McKenzie's family could take the call, thinking the familiarity might assist him. Ted, the tight-lipped fucker, hadn't shown any recognition of the McKenzie name, saying only that he'd take down a name and number and have "someone" call him back.

*Not likely, asshole.*

No matter what he'd tried, Ted hadn't budged, but Crow would bet his left nut that Ted would inform Parrish about the call anyway. That'd put him even more on guard.

Crow had lamely said he'd call back in the morning. He'd disconnected, trashed the phone and driven back to his hotel room.

That's where he got a bit of promising news.

Using the plates on the black SUV he'd seen at the hotel, the one where the chick had waited with her laptop, he'd contacted a computer whiz buddy.

It was dicey, choosing who to trust. Even the best bud would turn on you for the right incentive. Another reason why Crow kept blackmail material on so many people. This particular "friend," known on the street as Brick, had used one of Crow's women so badly, she'd needed a week to recoup.

Crow had video evidence of it, which ensured the sick fuck kept his loyalties straight.

Brick had done his thing without complaint, and now Crow knew the SUV belonged to Detective Crosby Albertson. Brick went one further and found a few images of Albertson. Bingo.

He had a name, a face, and the make and model of his SUV. Eventually he'd find out where he lived. *And then you'll be mine.*

Having contacts on the street also came in handy. He'd instructed Brick to put the word out and got some quick hits.

Seemed Albertson wasn't a cop any longer. From what Crow had seen, the prick worked for McKenzie now.

If he could get the two of them in the same building at the same time, it'd be easier to off them both.

Luckily, his informants knew even more, like the fact ex-cop Crosby kept watch over a certain small business owner. Some very disgruntled fellows complained that Crosby had broken up their embezzling scheme and landed a few of the guys in jail. That stunt ensured a host of people didn't like the overreaching ex-cop. *Making enemies left and right. Dumb move, asshole.*

He already knew how to get to Parrish, and now he had the means to fuck with Crosby, too. He'd make them both nuts with threats—and *then* he'd strike. The end result would be very satisfying.

Especially if he got the dark haired woman, too.

Bernard set down the coffee cup hard enough to cause a clatter.

Lowering the paper he'd been reading, Parrish lifted his brows. "Problem, Bernard?"

Scowling, an unfamiliar look for someone so affable, Bernard sloshed coffee into the cup.

Wow. Parrish put his work aside and scowled back. "What the hell is this? Did someone say something rude to Chimera?"

Startled by the question, Bernard's angry expression lightened. "Of course not. Everyone loves her. She's a beautiful, sweet cat."

Parrish barely resisted rolling his eyes. "Then what has you storming around, throwing coffee cups and splashing coffee?"

"I didn't *throw* the cup—fine." He propped a hip on Parrish's desk and gave him an extended, direct stare. "We've known each other far too long for you to think I wouldn't notice."

"Wouldn't notice what, for God's sake?"

Bernard's gaze turned calculating. "You're disappointed that the woman wasn't here last night." He lifted an imperious hand, as if he assumed Parrish had something to say to that. "Don't deny it."

"Wasn't going to." Sitting back, Parrish braced his elbows on the arms of the chair and put his fingertips together. "There's a reason she stayed away."

"Likely she's as interested as you are, but you're both unfamiliar with chemistry. Yes, Madison told me that Silver had trouble in her background, but she didn't know the details."

"Nor do I," Parrish said absently. "But it's more likely she *isn't* interested, and that's why she opted to stay home."

"Don't be an ass." Bernard straightened, then stated firmly, "You're handsome enough."

Getting compliments on his appearance from Bernard was beyond strange. Pretty damned humorous, too. "Why, thank you, Bernard."

Shooting him a dirty look, Bernard added, "You're well-mannered, though of course, far too autocratic."

"Of course." Parrish had started to wonder about that. Had he come on too strong? Holding back wasn't his way. Besides, a woman like Silver would have seen right through his reserve.

"You think my...*autocratic* manner would scare someone who didn't know me?"

Nodding, Bernard said, "As well as people who do know you, yes. But you wouldn't be fascinated by a woman who scared easily, so that's not an issue."

What a relief. At least he had Bernard's stamp of approval. Biting back his grin, Parrish asked, "Other suggestions, then?"

"You know I'm always up-front with women."

"I see." No, he didn't. What did Bernard's approach with women have to do with anything? "If there's a point—"

"I've been lucky enough to live here for much of my mature life. I've watched your kids grow as if they were my own. I've been able to indulge my love of cooking, with every luxury imaginable around me. I'm not the least bit interested in changing my circumstances."

What had brought that on? Parrish cleared his throat. "I've told you many times, Bernard, if you did want to settle down, we could make it work." It wouldn't be easy because they were all very dependent on Bernard—but they were not selfish, and they all cared enough to want his happiness. "You have a right to a life outside of this household. I wouldn't mind—"

Full of affront, he snapped, "I just said I didn't. Aren't you listening?"

"Er...yes?"

"You're different," Bernard continued, as if the interruption hadn't happened. "I've always thought you should—"

"What?" Tension gathered in the base of Parrish's neck. Tension spurred by guilt. "Put Marian from my mind? Forget how much I love her?"

Pausing, Bernard stared down at his feet a moment. "Loved, Parrish. You *loved* her. But she's gone and your life must go on."

"I've been living a full life." One where he'd been unable to think of another woman in any intimate way.

"No, you've been enacting nonstop vengeance. I commend

you for it—you know that. I'm proud of you and I know Marian would be, too. Just as I know she'd want you to be as happy as humanly possible."

That's what he'd been—with Marian. Now? He felt like he'd lost a dimension of himself, as if one-third of him had been buried with Marian and the other two-thirds didn't know how to function properly without the missing piece. He was, overall, incomplete.

"Parrish." Bernard came to stand by his side. "What you've built is amazing. You've helped so many people, and you'll continue to do so in one way or another."

"In multiple ways," he corrected, because the need was great. Not just physical retaliation, but there were monetary necessities, legal assistance and emotional support required to truly make a difference.

Bernard gave a small nod. "Now that they're grown, forces in their own rights, the kids will continue, too, and that means there's room for you to think of yourself."

Though he suspected, Parrish asked, "What exactly is it you want me to do?"

Bernard put back his shoulders. "I want you to *attack* this problem with as much determination as you do every other!"

So effusive. "Attack?" He scoffed. "Problem? I'm not sure Silver Galloway would like your wording."

"Oh, for crying out loud." Bernard grabbed his arm and urged him to his feet, then started pushing him to the door. "Get your coat. Take the new car I procured for you. Go and see if you have a chance with this woman, or so help me, *I'll* go after her, and you know what a success I am with women."

Parrish sputtered a laugh. "Hold up, Bernard. You've made your point."

"So you'll go?"

"Do I have a choice?"

"Not unless you want to rough me up. I mean, I'd do my best

to kick your ass, but unlike the McKenzies, I haven't trained other than to stay in shape, so you'd probably make mincemeat of me right off."

*Probably?* "I appreciate you're holding back," Parrish deadpanned. He truly was blessed to have a friend like Bernard. He'd always known it, but lately, as Bernard had pointed out, Parrish did feel different and he saw things with a new perspective. Maybe that, more than anything else, explained his newfound interest in romance. "I'll go," he promised.

"You should have gone after her last night."

"I considered it," Parrish admitted. God, the urge had been so strong, he'd had one hell of a time fighting it.

"It's not like you to hesitate."

No, it wasn't. Parrish shrugged. "The lady wanted an evening alone to indulge a long bath. I remember when Marian used to do that. She'd insist that I was on sole-parent duty and that she was not to be disturbed. She relished those quiet moments alone. Silver watches Hallie all week long, so I'm sure it's the same for her."

"Fine," Bernard said, not in the least gracious about it. "I forgive you for not going last night. When *will* you see her?"

"Is noon soon enough for you? I'd prefer to go while Crosby is away."

"Perfect. I'll accept the change in my plans."

"Your plans being that I had to leave this instant?"

"Something like that."

Laughing, Parrish asked, "May I get back to my work now?"

"You may, and if you need anything, let me know. I'll be in the entire day and night."

No kidding? Bernard often went out in the evenings. As he'd said, he enjoyed the bachelor life. "No plans tonight?"

"I cleared my calendar in case you needed persuasion to see things the right way." Bernard shared the grin that few ever saw. "Besides, I have a date tomorrow evening."

So much dedication—all for Parrish's sake. Far too often, Bernard focused on others. They'd have never gotten by without him, and all the McKenzies knew it. "Thank you."

"You're very welcome."

"Bernard…you know you're like a brother to me. I mean it when I say we would make any adjustments necessary to accommodate whatever you want in life."

"I'm happy as I am."

"This will always be your home," Parrish continued. "Or if you ever do get involved, we could build another house on the property. You know there's enough room for privacy. Hell, you can retire tomorrow if you want, and I would ensure that you have everything you need for the rest of your life."

"Parrish." His attempt at a frown didn't quite cut it. "Thank you, but you've always been too generous. I can carry my own weight."

"You carry enough for five men. I'm just saying, you're due some leisure time."

"One, I love my life, including what I contribute. I'd be bored in minutes if I tried to retire. Two, you would never be able to replace me, so forget it. And three, I have the best of all possible situations already. I do as much work as I want, and kick back whenever it suits me, surrounded by family." He clasped Parrish's shoulder. "The brother thing goes both ways, you know."

Humbled by his sincerity, Parrish nodded. "You're a good man, Bernard."

As usual, Bernard had a quick reply. "One of the best." As he turned to go, he said, "I won't ever let you forget it."

Crosby was already there when Madison arrived. She recognized his car in the lot and parked beside him. He was early, and that made her suspicious. Why was he here?

At the entry doors she greeted the guards. She knew them well enough to ask after their families, to compliment one on a new beard, to laugh with the other about the antics of his dog. Every employee was vetted by her and her dad, and given thorough background checks before being hired. She knew these people, inside and out.

They were not only sharp, on-point employees, but they were compassionate, too. For the task force, both traits were needed.

As soon as she stepped inside, she unzipped her coat and headed toward the welcome desk. She didn't see Ted, but he might be in back.

Glancing around, she didn't see Crosby either, and those silent alarms prickled. "Hey, Gail. Is Ted in?"

At sixty, Gail was older than most of the people here, but as an office supervisor, she was extremely sharp and could cover most positions.

Madison liked her, not only for her business savvy but because she had a very gentle way about her.

"Madison, it's nice to see you." She looked up with a sincere smile. "I didn't know you were coming by today. Do you want something to drink? Coffee or tea?"

"I'm fine, thanks. Ted left a message for me last night, so I figured I'd just stop by."

"Odd, he didn't mention it to me."

"I'm sure it's nothing." Impatience hummed in her veins. "Where did you say he is?"

"Ted and Mr. Albertson are in the office."

Her molars clicked together, but she kept her smile in place. "Really? What time did Crosby arrive here?"

"Maybe half an hour ago. He and Ted immediately went off to talk." Gail started to leave the desk. "I'll walk you back."

"No, you don't have to bother." She didn't want extra witnesses when she set Crosby straight about overstepping. "It'll be a quick visit."

"All right. I'll just finish sorting through these files, then." She turned back to her computer.

"Thanks." Madison peeled off her gloves and stuffed them in her coat pockets. The heels of her boots clicked along the tile floor as she went down the hall, past the conference room and into the glass-enclosed office where she found Ted with a hip propped on the desk and Crosby leaning a shoulder against the wall.

They appeared to be in amicable conversation.

Doing a quick assessment, Madison decided they looked innocent enough. Not that she ever judged a situation by appearances alone. The fact remained that Crosby was here far too early, and he'd commandeered the same front desk clerk she needed to speak to.

"Ms. McKenzie," Ted said, quickly straightening and holding out a hand. "I was just telling Mr. Albertson about the person who called here last evening."

Crosby watched Madison closely. "I asked him to wait and share it with both of us."

Did he now? She matched his stare. "You're a little early, Crosby."

"So are you, Madison." His mouth curled in a crooked smile. "But then, I figured you might be."

Uh-oh. So…he'd figured she might cut him out? Not really her intent, but yeah, she'd wanted all the info before she started sharing. Not that she'd feel guilty about it. After all, it was *her* business.

As if he felt the sudden tension, Ted looked back and forth between them. He was a slender man, young but astute, and clearly nervous at the moment. "Yes, so…" He adjusted his glasses. "I was here late yesterday, just wrapping up a few things, otherwise I'd have missed the call."

And whoever answered might not have been as shrewd as Ted. "You say it was a man?"

"Yes, and it really seemed to me that he was fishing for something, but of course I can't confirm that. It's my policy to never give out information. That's something Mr. McKenzie stressed when he first hired me."

Ted had worked with them now for four years. "What exactly did he ask?"

"At first he said he had some software updates to share, like he thought I'd just put him through to you. I told him if he'd like to leave a name and number, I'd have someone get back to him. It's odd, but I could practically hear his frustration. He said he could leave a voice message, but if I'd put him through, he'd have gotten Mr. McKenzie's greeting, or yours, and that would have identified one of you to him. I explained again that I couldn't do that, and he said he could just talk to someone in Mr. McKenzie's family. Very strange, don't you think?"

"Yes," Madison said, her thoughts racing as she pieced things together. "Very strange."

"So he obviously already knows Parrish," Crosby said. He quickly corrected, "Mr. McKenzie."

"It seemed so." Ted elevated his chin proudly. "Though I certainly didn't confirm anything for him. It's just my opinion, but I think he was trying to gather names of other employees." He turned to Madison. "And perhaps about you, Ms. McKenzie."

"Why do you say that?"

"When I didn't give him what he wanted, he specifically said that he'd spoken with you, or rather, a woman with long dark hair—though he claimed he'd forgotten your name. He laughed and asked me not to tell you. *Who could forget a looker like that, am I right?* That's what he said."

Crosby didn't move, didn't blink, but Madison felt his expanding anger.

"And you said?"

With a flush staining his cheeks, Ted admitted, "I knew he meant you, but I only repeated the same thing. That if he left a name and number, I'd have someone return his call." He cleared his throat. "He did mean you, don't you think?"

"It does seem possible," she said noncommittally. "Anything else?"

"I'm afraid not, ma'am. The number came through as unknown. I recall asking about the policy that allows those numbers through, only because it's often spam, but Mr. McKenzie explained that people who need assistance seldom want to be identified right off."

"That's right," Madison agreed. "Trust is slow to come and people who've been hurt are naturally wary."

Ted nodded. "Do you think we should talk to the other employees, just to reiterate the protocol for answering calls like this?"

"Excellent idea," Crosby said. "I know you have a full workload, Ted, but could I ask you to talk with everyone working with you today, and tomorrow I'll have an instruction sheet that we can share more broadly."

Right before her eyes, Ted's chest seemed to expand. "I'd be happy to handle it, sir. Consider it done."

"Thank you." Crosby held out his hand. "I appreciate knowing you're on it."

Madison felt a sense of pride as she watched them clasp hands. Crosby was really good with people, not at all the intense, scary, angry cop she'd first met. Well, he hadn't scared *her*; she'd had a very different reaction to him. And granted, he was still pretty intense at times.

"Is that all, Ms. McKenzie?" Crosby asked her with the formality of hired personnel. "Or did you need to check on anything else?"

"Actually, yes. I'd like a few minutes to check the camera feeds. You should probably stay, Mr. Albertson, but Ted, you can get back to work. Thank you for your help."

"My pleasure. If there's anything else you need, just let me know."

Once the door closed behind him, Madison smiled. "Nice

job, Mr. Albertson. Ted looked as if you'd just pinned a medal on him."

"He's a good kid, and even better, I can trust him to handle instructing the others."

"Yes." Now that they were alone, she had a terrible time not kissing him. Unfortunately, the glass wall in the office meant anyone walking by could see them. "Ted is very reliable. I'm impressed with how he handled that caller."

Folding his arms and leaning back against the wall, Crosby waited. For what, she wasn't sure—except that he seemed to know her extremely well, so he probably already knew where her mind had gone.

And now she felt defensive when she asked, "What?"

"You know what."

Was she supposed to apologize for arriving early, when he'd done the same? Fat chance. "How would you like it if I butted into your business?"

Something in his gaze changed, went a little cooler, a bit more distant. "Your father tried to break into my house. If I'm remembering right, I was pretty damned gracious about the whole thing."

Yeah, he was. "This is different." Though she didn't know how. Oh, yeah, her family. "I just wanted a chance to sort things out before Dad and my brothers took over."

"What does that have to do with me?" He pushed away from the wall, his gaze still too probing, seeing too much.

A smile seemed the way to go, but hers felt strained. "You've pointed out a few times now that you're an employee and that you don't want to withhold things from Dad."

He frowned. "One thing has nothing to do with the other. No, I wouldn't keep business secrets from your father."

"This pertains to business."

"This pertains to *you*, and you're his daughter. He has a right to know. Hell, your brothers do, too."

"You've just made my point for me." Unsettled, she moved behind the desk to sit in the big leather chair. "I wanted time to gauge the seriousness of the call."

"And?"

"And I'll tell the others about it tonight. You can rest easy, *Mr. Albertson*." With a few quick commands, she pulled up the recent feeds…and then she tried to pretend to see them.

Crosby wasn't sure what to make of her attitude. Was she so independent that he shouldn't even show concern? No curiosity? No caring?

He knew Madison had something to prove to the rest of her family.

She needed to understand that she had nothing to prove to him. "Seems like it'll be a nice day today."

Glancing up, she asked absently, "What?"

"The sun is out. No more snow predicted." He watched confusion flicker in her pretty hazel eyes. "The roads should be fairly clear. Want to come over for dinner tomorrow night? Sort of a payback—minus the heated indoor pool."

He would have made it tonight, but he couldn't do that to Silver. His raging lust was not a reason to be inconsiderate to her. Silver deserved his respect, and that included a fair warning for a dinner guest.

"Seriously?" In a quick turnabout, Madison's entire demeanor warmed. "I'd *love* that. What time should I get there?"

"How about six thirty?" Actually… "I'd be happy to pick you up."

She shook her head. "Then you'd have to drive me back, and that might mess with Hallie's bedtime. I'm a big girl. I can get from one place to another."

*Big* was a misnomer. Tall, yes. But physically, Madison almost seemed delicate. It wasn't until you got to know her that you realized how wickedly she could utilize every ounce of her strength for power. Coupled with her speed and that keen intellect, she was a force of nature.

"Why are you looking at me like that?" Smiling, she pushed back her chair. "Did you think I'd refuse?"

"No." He'd assumed she'd want to visit. He knew there was something potent growing between them, something beyond the physical. She was the one who didn't seem to understand the depth of it. He nodded at the camera feeds. "What are you looking for?"

She turned back to the screen. "I'm not sure, but I have a feeling."

"So do I."

Her gaze met his with surprise. "I wonder if we're aligned."

He'd like to be aligned. Horizontally. With any luck, he'd make it happen tomorrow. "Crow is trying to target you."

"Yes, that's it!" She seemed pleased that they agreed. "Though, so far it's just a hunch."

"No, it's an instinct," he corrected. Coming around the desk to stand beside her brought him close enough to stroke a hand over her hair. He went down the silky length, briefly cupped her shoulder, and then trailed his fingertips to her chin so he could tip up her face. "Let's not ignore it, okay?"

She licked her lips. "Is it nuts that I'm a teensy bit worried about this?"

"I'm afraid not, babe. I feel it, too. The bastard is up to something."

"What better way to hurt Dad than to hurt one of his children."

Of course she'd immediately grasped the situation. Her instincts were as strong as his own. "When you talk to your family, don't omit even the tiniest detail that might help to bring the whole thing together. Look at it this way. If it was one of them and they had a feeling but didn't share, it'd piss you off, right?"

She snorted. "You know them all now. They're stubborn, pigheaded tough guys, who always think they can handle anything."

Damn, she'd just described herself—except for the guy part. He grinned.

Luckily she was frowning at the screen and didn't see it. "They cut me out all the time."

"So start a precedent. Point out that you're sharing and from now on you expect the same. Hell, you can even threaten not to share anymore if they don't promise to share everything."

After only a second of thought, Madison nodded. "That's genius. You know what? I actually like having your input."

Unheard of. Like the rest of her family, Madison liked to plow ahead with her own agenda. And damn it, he liked that about her, too. In so many ways, they were alike.

He glanced around the office. "I think I recall a big utility room in here?" He opened the wrong door and found a private bathroom instead. "Actually, this will do."

Her brows went up. "Do for what?"

Taking her hand securely in his, he tugged her from her seat and drew her into the room.

"*Ooooh,*" she whispered, catching on. "Are we doing something good? I hope so."

God love the girl, she kept things interesting. "I get an hour for lunch. We're down to forty-five minutes now. I'm happy to spend *five* of those kissing you, then we really do need to grab some food." If they didn't, he might get carried away and break one of his own cardinal rules—the one about having sex on business properties.

"Only kissing?" she asked with a pout.

Crosby pressed her to the wall, his hands cupping both sides of her face to keep her right where he wanted her. She was tall enough that their bodies met in all the key places—thighs, pelvises, chest to breasts. Lips to lips.

Yes, *this.* He felt starved for her, already addicted to her taste, her scent and the quick, wholehearted way she responded. He gave her his tongue, and she sucked on it. He growled, and she gave a soft, needy moan.

He couldn't wait to kiss her like this when they could take things to the next level. Naked, ready, him hard and her wet…

Damn. He was half-hard already—so was she wet, too?

Wanting to possess her, to tie her to him somehow, he tilted his head and deepened the kiss even more. Their tongues tangled, breaths heated, and together their bodies moved in a demonstration of what they both wanted.

His dick sure as hell was ready. It didn't help that she snuggled against him, grinding her body to his in a way guaranteed to push him over the edge.

"God." He eased up before he totally lost control. "I can't wait to have you, Madison McKenzie."

"Mmm," she murmured against his throat. "Same, Crosby Albertson."

Before he knew his own intent, his fingers cupped around her left breast. She went still, then her head dropped back against the wall and she closed her eyes.

Yes, he liked seeing her like this. "You are so soft." He rasped his thumb over her nipple, torturing himself, teasing her, wishing like hell he had her somewhere, anywhere that guaranteed real privacy.

God, he never should have started this. *Who are you kidding? You couldn't keep your hands off her.*

"Well…" Madison lifted heavy eyelids and seared him a look. "It's a boob, so…"

That nonsense comment was just what he needed to pull himself together. With a smile, he pressed a tender kiss to her mouth. "It's perfect. You're perfect."

"Really?"

Stepping back from her wasn't easy, especially when she clung to him. He covered her hands with his and peeled them away from his shoulders. "How much time do you need to look at those feeds?"

"It was diabolical for you to get me in here, get me all hot and bothered, and then play responsible employee. You sure I can't tempt you into a quickie?"

Tempt him? Hell yes, he was tempted. "And if Ted busted us? You think he'd tell Parrish?"

Her mouth twisted to the side. "I don't know. He's awfully conscientious."

Crosby touched her cheek. "Keeping my hands off you wasn't possible, so don't expect me to apologize."

"I liked it, so..." She gave a small shrug. "No apology needed."

"If it's any consolation, I'm in worse shape than you because things are a little more obvious on me."

Her gaze took a nosedive to his dick, then lingered.

"That's not going to help, babe."

"I..." She paused, her hand extended as if to touch him.

And honest to God, Crosby wasn't sure if he held his breath wanting her to, or hoping she wouldn't.

Madison bit her lip, then raised her hands as if in surrender. "Okay, this is me also being responsible." She blew out a breath. "I should get extra points for being good."

"Soon," he promised in a hushed whisper. "Then we'll both do all the touching we want."

They heard voices as two people strode past the office. Thankfully, no one entered the room. It'd be tough to explain why they were in the bathroom together.

"Five minutes," Madison whispered. "I can skim through the feed by then. Will that give you enough time to eat lunch?"

He'd need every minute of that time to get his erection under control. Didn't help when he thought, *I'd rather eat you*, but he couldn't hold back the truth.

He wanted her, every part of her, in every way he could have her.

"We'll make it work." He opened the door, turned her toward it, and then gave her a light swat on her very sweet behind.

Typical of Madison, she laughed.

It hit Crosby hard, the thought of Burgess Crow planning to hurt her. She was a woman unlike any other, with a heart as big as her bold nature. Unique, special, and though she seldom needed protection, he knew he'd do whatever it took to eliminate the threat against her.

And that meant Crosby had to get to him first.

# CHAPTER ELEVEN

Knowing Silver would have seen his approach through the monitor, Parrish knocked on the door again.

Still no answer.

Because he'd peered through the garage door window, he knew her car was here. He lifted his fist to knock once more—and the door jerked open.

There she stood, a storm of irritation in her eyes, her long hair in a braid that rested over the left side of her breasts, shoulders squared as if for a confrontation.

"Don't do that," she snapped.

Slowly, surprised at his own reaction—again—Parrish lowered his hand to his side. "Knock?"

"Show up unannounced. You know darned well you shouldn't." That said, she pivoted on her sock-covered feet and stalked away.

Taking that as an invitation, Parrish stepped in and secured the door behind him, all without taking his gaze from her. She wore skinny jeans again, fuzzy pink socks and another oversize sweatshirt.

He knew she had to be in her forties, but dressed down like this, she looked like a college kid.

"Mr. Kenzie!" Hallie charged forward, her arms raised.

At least *she* was happy to see him.

"How are you, sweetheart?" He lifted her for a gentle hug, enjoying the feel of her thin arms squeezing him tight, and even the wet kiss she pressed to his jaw. What was it about a child's embrace that healed the soul?

Not that his soul needed healing. In all the ways that mattered most, he was perfectly...okay.

What a lame endorsement.

"We're playing Barbies," Hallie announced. "Want to play with us?"

Silver looked up from her seat on the floor beside a big plastic house, a dozen dolls and a hideous pink car. "Join us, Mr. McKenzie," Silver taunted. "You can have the prettiest Barbie."

He almost laughed. Did she really want to discourage him that badly? "None of them could be as pretty as you and Hallie." After toeing off his boots by the door, still carrying Hallie, he came to stand over Silver. When she avoided his gaze, he decided, why not?

He put Hallie back on her feet, stripped off his gloves and coat and tossed them to a chair, then sat yoga-style. "That's quite the plastic house Barbie has."

Still irate, Silver immediately got up to put his outer garments on a coat tree. While on her feet, she asked, "Coffee?"

"Don't go to any trouble."

"Already have a pot made."

It seemed to him that she consumed an awful lot of coffee. "Then thank you, yes—that is, if I may drink it in here?" Already Hallie handed him a naked Barbie with very ratty hair and a stack of tiny clothes. Apparently, he was to dress her.

Mocking his formal tone, she replied, "You may," and sashayed away.

He felt a pang over the way he noticed her figure. Not just as a casual observer admiring beauty, but with the warm awareness he hadn't felt since losing his Marian.

Hallie crowded closer. "You can use these shoes."

The shoes, which appeared no bigger than a damned staple, would be a challenge to get on the doll's oddly arched feet. "Let me see if I can manage this." He chose a dress only because it looked easiest, and then had to figure out how to get it over the doll's impressively molded breasts.

Every so often, he glanced at the doorway, but Silver hadn't returned yet. How long did it take to pour a cup of coffee? Did his visit make her that uneasy?

Had this been a truly terrible idea? Maybe he'd kick Bernard's ass after all. But damn it, he was not an insecure youth who reacted like this. He'd made a decision, and by God, he'd stick to it.

In the middle of that self-encouragement, Silver returned with a tray that she put on the soft stool. "Black, right?"

He gazed at her a few seconds too long. "Thank you, yes."

"You'll need to keep it on the tray. Without it, the stool is too soft and it might fall. I used to have a regular coffee table until this one—" she reached out to tug on a curling lock of Hallie's hair "—kept hurting herself on it."

"Pow!" Hallie said, smacking her forehead with a palm and pretending to be dizzy. "Dad said I need a football helmet because I'm always running into things and falling."

"Thinking about important stuff can distract you from where you're going." Parrish continued to wrestle with the plastic shoes. *Why was the doll so absurdly shaped?* "Madison was the same way. She usually had a laptop in her hands. Still does, in fact, though she's learned to maneuver without banging into things, at least around my house and her own."

"I like Mad'son."

Parrish wondered if Silver felt the same, or if she considered

Madison a threat to her current arrangement. "I'm fond of her, as well." Finally, he got all the clothes on the doll. "There. All done." He felt absurdly proud of himself.

"Now these," Hallie said, handing him a whole new outfit.

Boggled, he stared at her. "I hope you're joking, young lady."

Silver snickered. "That's how we play, you know. Gotta keep changing the clothes."

Lord. "Why don't I just put these on another doll? Look, this brunette is only half-dressed." He got started on that to ensure he didn't have to disrobe and re-dress the blonde.

For another ninety minutes, they "played," until all of the dolls were dressed to Hallie's standard. After doing it so many times, Parrish finally got the hang of it, but it was obvious Hallie and Silver had an advantage with their much smaller hands.

"Didn't you ever play Barbies with Madison?" Silver asked.

Choosing very trendy yellow boots to go with the current outfit, he said, "I can't recall my daughter ever playing with a doll." One thought followed another, and Parrish wondered if that was his fault. He'd faced a lot of hard truths lately. "She was always interested in other things."

"Like learnin' to maim?" Silver asked.

Hallie leaned into him. Parrish could see that she was starting to fade, so he kept his voice low and even. "That, yes. She's as skilled as her brothers, though she could well be faster than them."

"That's an unusual upbringing."

Interest? That would be a start. "We had an unusual life." He felt Hallie go limp and adjusted his arm around her so she wouldn't topple. The little angel's eyes were closed, her lips parted and her head lolled to the side. He couldn't imagine being that comfortable around anyone. "What now?" he whispered to Silver.

A loving smile curved her mouth, leveling him in the process. "I always thought she'd outgrow her ability to just nod off, but so far, the girl remains a world-class napper." She set aside the dolls and, on hands and knees, came closer to arrange Hallie on the floor. "Get me a pillow off her bed, will you?"

For just a second more, Parrish took advantage of her nearness, studying the length of the dark lashes that framed her smoky-hued eyes, the way her hair curled at her temple, how pretty her small ears were—ears!—and the light, flowery fragrance of her skin and hair.

Around her, he didn't recognize himself. He was a different man...or more aware of being a man, perhaps.

Determined to maintain control, Parrish rose to his feet. In Hallie's room, he took not only a pillow but a light quilt off the bottom of the bed.

When he returned, Silver reached out for them, but he ignored the gesture. Going to one knee, he gently tucked the pillow under Hallie's head, then spread the quilt over her.

After giving him a disgruntled frown, Silver gathered up the toys and moved them out of the way.

He'd already noticed that she was tidy but not a neat freak. Her house was like her, attractive but comfortable.

When she headed into the kitchen, Parrish picked up the tray and followed. Without a word, he poured himself more coffee, then joined her at the table. Silence stretched out while Silver stared toward the window over the sink—and he stared at her.

Her hair fascinated him, being so dark with that one long streak of white. "How'd this happen?" he asked, nodding at her hair.

"Comes with getting older, I guess." She shrugged. "At least for women with really dark hair."

"It's lovely." There were so many other things he wanted to add, but she didn't exactly look receptive to compliments.

"Again," she finally said, "you shouldn't have come here."

"I had no choice." He sipped his coffee. "Bernard insisted."

"Bernard?"

He especially admired her eyes. They were the lightest gray, like an overcast summer day, but they darkened when she was annoyed. "It's always difficult to explain Bernard."

Dark lashes lifted, her eyes a little more rounded now.

"He's serves as a butler of sorts."

"A butler," she repeated.

"He's an amazing chef."

She blinked.

"He lives with me—"

"Are you two, you know?" She leaned forward, one arm bent on the tabletop, and asked, "Is he your boyfriend?"

It took a second for the words to register, then Parrish grinned. "Bernard is like a brother to me. Neither of us is gay, though Bernard most definitely gets around a lot more than I do."

Her fingers tapped the table. "How often do you get around?"

He really wanted to take her hand in his, feel her warmth, the softness of her skin, but he could tell it was too soon for that. "I haven't, not since my wife died."

A shuddering breath sounded before she whispered, "Not at all?"

"Not at all," he confirmed. "You?"

Her snarky attitude returned, crowding out the glimpse of uncertainty. "I'm as sexless as sexless can be, honey. Not into women, and long done with men. If you're hangin' around because you heard of my past and you think I'll—"

Screw it. Parrish enfolded her hand in his. *Electric.* The sensation, the *connection* was incredibly strong. It would take a little getting used to. "I don't know your past, but I saw pain in your eyes. I've seen that pain before, so I can guess."

She stayed perfectly still, not even breathing, her gaze steady on his.

He brushed his thumb over her knuckles. Such small hands, but he knew this woman had inner strength. Whatever demons had tormented her in years past, she'd been strong enough to fight them. *Unlike Marian.* He shook his head, banishing that awful, disloyal thought, sending his grief with it. "I'm not here to take advantage of you."

Her chin firmed. "I wouldn't let you."

No, she wouldn't, and he admired that about her. "I'm here," he admitted, "because I couldn't stay away."

"Fair warning, sugar, you're wastin' your time."

That attitude had probably caused other men, *lesser* men, to scurry away with their egos dented. Parrish wasn't one of those men. "Today wasn't a waste, not to me. I've had a wonderful time."

"Dressin' dolls?" She snorted—but she didn't pull her hand away.

He chose to see that as encouragement. "With you and Hallie," he clarified. "I have so much respect for Crosby, more so now that I see how he's fashioned his life."

"What does that mean?"

"He's done his utmost to care for his daughter, including ensuring she had someone with a beautiful heart to be with her when he couldn't."

Her lip curled. "My heart ain't that beautiful, bud. Not for everyone."

"For those who matter, then." One day, maybe that'd be him.

She drew another shaky inhale. Since she didn't mention it, Parrish didn't either.

A few seconds passed, then she stated, "Crosby's falling for your daughter."

Parrish hoped that was true, because he felt certain that Madison was already in love. "Is that a problem for you?"

Her lips did that enticing curl again, a small teasing smile that he somehow felt against his own lips. "No problem for me at all. Crosby and I are only friends."

"That's not true. You're family to him, and to Hallie. I don't think that will ever change."

"No, it won't," she said, as if she 100 percent believed it.

Which was good, and another reason to respect Crosby. He'd ensured Silver had reliability and security in her life. "I'd like your permission to come by every so often." She started to speak, but hesitated, so he added, "I also want you to join us at my house the next time we all get together."

She pursed her lips. "Was I too obvious staying away?"

"You were to Bernard." A strange, disturbing emotion filled his chest. "So it was because of me?"

Staring at their clasped hands, she whispered, "You confuse me, Parrish."

"I'm glad, because you confuse me, too."

"How? I've been up-front with you."

"Yes, but you say one thing while looking as if you mean something else entirely." When she started to object, he added, "I will always respect what you say, whether I think it's truthful or not. You need to know that."

After a slight pause, she nodded.

"Good. So can we agree? We'll visit, get to know each other and see where things go?"

"They'll go nowhere."

"I will never pressure you," he promised, ignoring her assurances that he wasted his time. "But I'd like a chance to see if there's something between us. Will you give me that chance? I promise to make it worthwhile."

Surprising him, she shifted her hand so that they shared a handshake. "Deal. But anytime I call it quits, that's it."

Unable to imagine that scenario, he nodded. "You have my word." After lifting her hand to kiss her knuckles, he settled back in his seat. "I have no doubt that Madison knows I came here, and she's likely told Crosby. Just an FYI, in case he asks you about it."

"Okay." Going to a drawer, she got out a pen and paper, and

wrote something, then handed it to him before taking her seat again. "My number. Next time, call first."

The grin came on slowly, then spread out until it felt like there was no room for old, painful memories, just the promise of something new. He got out his phone. "I'll text you my number, and if you ever decide you'd like company, or if you just want to talk, call me."

"I won't."

"You might," he countered. Her phone dinged with the text he sent. Next, he saved her number, then put his phone back in his pocket. "Thank you for sharing."

Silver shifted, crossed her arms, uncrossed them and finally gave him a look of challenge. "Hallie went on and on about your place. Said it was a freaking palace and that you own a whole mountain. She said you have a pool in your basement."

He stared at her a moment, but something about her drew confessions from him. "I was looking forward to showing you around my property. It's private and, to me, very calming."

"So it's true?"

"I don't own the entire mountain, no." His smile slipped free. "Just a good portion of it. Yes, there's a pool in the lower level, as well as one outside, and a large, beautiful lake that I added. The house is rather...sprawling, but comfortable. I think—hope—that you'll like it."

She fought it, but ended up grinning. "So you're loaded, huh?"

"Very much so."

Giving his arm a playful shove, she asked, "Then what are you doin' sniffing around me?"

Sniffing? Parrish dared to cup a hand to her cheek. "I could say it's because you're beautiful. You are, you know."

She didn't blink, didn't show any reaction at all.

"Or I could say it's all that sizzling attitude you project." Leaning closer, he whispered, "It's incredibly sexy."

This time she snorted.

"Or…" He drew his own uneven breath. "I could be honest and say that something about you calls to parts of me I thought had died with Marian." Just saying his wife's name felt like a betrayal, but he thought of what Bernard had insisted—that he'd been solely focused on vengeance long enough.

Silver's hand covered his against her cheek, drawing him from those painful thoughts. His hand was twice the size of hers, hardened from training, capable of crushing a full-grown man.

And yet, he felt wonderfully trapped beneath her gentle palm.

"You loved her a lot, didn't you?"

Explanations seemed impossible so he gave a simple "Yes."

Those incredible eyes of hers searched his. "You been lonely, Parrish?" she asked.

"Hard to imagine, isn't it? To many, it appears I have everything." Yet important aspects had been missing from his life.

"I didn't mean that."

He brushed his thumb over the downy softness of her skin. "You're not someone who disdains people of means and influence, assuming they're eternally happy being evil and selfish?"

"I wasn't mocking you." Her smile held a touch of sadness. "Crosby wouldn't work for someone like that."

"I believe you're right. Crosby is a very down-to-earth, honest man."

"Damn right he is." She pulled his hand away from her face, but surprised him by lacing her fingers with his. Their hands rested together on the tabletop. "When do you want to visit again?"

His pulse leaped. Whatever had changed her mind, he was glad. "When would be convenient for you?"

"If you don't mind coming by in the afternoons, Hallie and I are usually here, especially when the weather's so icky."

"Playing Barbies?" he guessed, trying not to grimace.

"And sometimes finger painting." She winked.

"I would enjoy that." He had the disconcerting thought that he'd enjoy anything with her. She was refreshingly impudent when most in his world treated him with utmost respect.

"I might, too, except that you don't really know me, and when you do, you might not be that keen on visiting." She wrinkled her nose, making light of it. "I have a sordid past."

Not keen on seeing her?

Just as she knew Crosby wouldn't work for him if he was an unkind, manipulative person, he knew Crosby wouldn't leave Hallie with Silver if she was anything less than wonderful. "If you're comfortable telling me about it, you'll see that my interest remains the same. What do you say?"

At his request, Silver pulled away, crossed her arms on the table and affected a "who cares anyway" expression that dredged up both sympathy and admiration in Parrish. Sympathy because she obviously felt her past still affected her today, and admiration because she was willing to face it.

Combined, they created an odd contrast of emotions that left him unsettled.

"Am I already pressuring you?" he asked. He missed the warmth of her touch, the connection. "If you don't want to tell me, it's fine. I understand and I'm sorry I—"

She shook her head. "Are you sure you want to hear it?"

"I want to prove to you that it doesn't matter," he clarified. "Not to me." With that, he shook his head, a new reality striking him. Hell, who was he to judge anyone else? "You realize, you're more likely to reject me. Since Marian's death… I've done many things that others might not understand."

She listened, interested, sympathetic.

Knowing she deserved total honesty, he admitted, "I didn't regret them, Silver. Given a chance, I'd do them again."

He had no remorse for removing vicious abusers.

His life choices were unconventional, to say the least. Not everyone would be accepting of those choices.

"You had good reason," she said, almost as if defending him.

He would defend her, too, if she'd let him. "Yes, I did."

That seemed to decide her. With pride elevating her chin, she held his gaze. "When I was younger and a whole lot dumber, I went from one relationship to another. It was all fun and games, you know? I drank too much, partied too often, and when things didn't go right, I blamed my family for being poor, my dad for taking off, my mom for never working."

"Rough childhood," he murmured.

"Pfft. Lots of people have worse and they don't screw up like I did. You want something different, you gotta do something different. Me? I just continued with the same old bad habits, over and over again."

"Obviously something changed." If not her outlook, then what?

"You ever hear of rock bottom?" She shared a wry smile. "I ended up with this abusive bastard who…" She fell silent and her mouth pinched.

A slow burn started in his guts. Anger, sympathy and so much more. Barely resisting the urge to touch her, Parrish waited.

"He was okay at first. Willing to party, totally into me."

What man wouldn't be? Trying not to let his fury show, he repeated, "At first."

"Yeah, see things started going downhill, but I stayed because I didn't have anywhere else to go, no job of my own, no way to take care of myself."

"So you relied on him." Which made the bastard's abuse that much worse, in Parrish's opinion.

"Yeah, that is, until he started passing me around to his sleazy friends."

*Passing me around…* Not by so much as a flinch did Parrish

show his reaction, but in his heart and head, he was already eviscerating the man who'd dared to hurt and humiliate her.

"My unwillingness didn't matter." Her fingertips traced invisible circles on the tabletop as she grew lost in thought. "He didn't care what I felt, and neither did his friends."

Rage burned behind Parrish's eyes, but he did his utmost to keep his expression composed.

"I tried runnin' off once." She gave a humorless laugh. "I figured even if I slept in a shelter, or outside in the cold, it'd be better, you know?"

"Yes, I know." In desperate times, people were sometimes forced to make impossible choices.

"He caught me, slapped me around—scared the bejesus out of me, really, ranting and raving about how I should be grateful and how I owed him. He figured that'd be that."

"But it wasn't." Already he knew that Silver would have tried again and again. She was a fighter, and thank God for it.

With a twitch of her shoulders, she said, "I ran off a few more times, but every time the beatings got worse. There were a few times I thought he'd kill me." She rushed on from that, as if the retelling brought back the pain. After a few seconds, her mood lightened again, her voice going softer. "Then one day, Crosby was outside the apartment building talking to bystanders about a store that had been robbed. I saw an opening and I took it." Her smile now looked more like satisfaction. "I went real casual-like to the door, then jerked it open and ran like hell. Down the hall, down the stairs so fast I almost fell, and I hit the street like a crazy woman. Cosby looked up and I charged right over to him."

*Thank God Crosby had been there.*

Her smile widened into a grin. "Poor guy looked so startled when I told him I had to get away, that he could even arrest me if he wanted, but what he couldn't do was send me back inside."

"Of course he didn't."

"Nope. You should have seen him, Parrish. Man, he impressed me that day. He went above and beyond, because that's who Crosby is. It was like he got bigger right before my eyes. He had another cop with him, a guy in a uniform, and he left me in that guy's car while he went inside the building and arrested the bastard. I knew that wouldn't do it, that they wouldn't put him away, not for long. I was afraid if Crosby just dumped me at a shelter, I'd be found, so instead…" She bit her lip, blinking fast as if fending off an overload of emotion. "He got me a room at a long-stay hotel. I couldn't believe it. He even got me into a work program, helped get me set up in a permanent place, helped me get a full-time job—and he became my friend. There were so many times he checked on me, took me out to eat, just talked to me. *Listened* to me. Like I mattered."

Parrish felt his own breathing thicken. "Because you do."

"I never had before. Don't misunderstand. Most of it was my own fault. I know that. I never took responsibility for my life. But man, you get a taste of real value and you want more. Least, I did. And in all that time, never, not once, did Crosby hit on me. I don't mean with his fists," she was quick to say. "I mean that he didn't flirt, didn't make any moves or anything. He was truly a *friend*, and I realized I'd never had one before. Not like him."

In his own way, with his limited means, Crosby had done the same as Parrish. He'd provided an alternative, safety. Choices.

For people who'd never had them, those were incredibly valuable. No wonder he'd liked Crosby so much from the start.

"It's clear that your friendship means just as much to him." Parrish wondered about the man who'd dared to hurt her. How difficult could it be to find him if Silver gave him a name? Or perhaps he could get that info from Crosby. He didn't have a single doubt that Crosby would have kept track of the bastard.

"The guy who'd beat on me?" Silver said, as if she'd read his mind. "He's dead now. Dumbass tried cheating the wrong guy. They found his body in an alley."

"Good riddance."

"You can bet I didn't mourn him." She stared off at nothing. "Crosby and I stayed friends. He'd tell me all the time how proud he was of me. Must have been true because once he got Hallie, he…" She paused, her bottom lip trembling for only a second. "He trusted me. *Me.* A damaged nobody who wouldn't have gotten her own life in order if it hadn't been for all his help."

"I don't think that's true."

"Crosby never thought so either, but I know the truth. If it wasn't for him, I'd be living on the street, maybe doing awful things, maybe turning as bad as the worst of them. Instead, Crosby gave me the most amazing opportunity ever." She looked at Parrish with a smile that reflected all the gratitude she felt. "It's not a palace like your place, but it's a home of my own, which is more than I ever thought I'd have. And Crosby's friendship means the world to me. My job is easy—all I need to do is love Hallie, and that happened as soon as I met her. That little baby reached right into my chest and stole my heart. She owns it now, her and her daddy." Silver swallowed heavily and her voice deepened with emotion. "I went from being a person with a screwed-up life, to being a grandma. That was the best gift ever."

Parrish felt his own eyes grow glassy. "I bet if you asked Crosby, he'd feel the same about you. Together, the three of you have made it work."

"We've made a family." She heaved a contented sigh. "I want the best for him."

"He wants the best for you, too."

She shook off the remnants of the sad story, and her grin twitched into place. "Parrish McKenzie, you tellin' me you're the best?"

He wasn't, not even close. But he liked it when she shortened her words and added a little twang to her teasing. "I imagine you could do worse, not that I'm on one knee proposing or anything."

"Ha!" She shook a finger at him. "I just told you how nice my life is now. Bended knee or not, I wouldn't give it up. But hey, if you're not appalled and ready to run from my excess baggage, then let's plan to visit again. It's the truth—I've actually had a pretty good time today."

Something that for too long had been cold and clenched inside his chest—maybe his damned heart—suddenly loosened and thawed. It was an astonishing sensation, one he wanted to hold on to. One he *would* hold on to.

But for now, he figured he should go while he was still invited back. Quietly, he pushed away from the table and stood. "Tell Hallie I'll see her again soon." He briefly cupped Silver's cheek. "I'm already looking forward to it."

# CHAPTER TWELVE

When Madison returned home from lunch, Bob met her at the door. After hanging her coat on a hook by the door and removing her boots, she scooped him up. Without fail, she always took the time to hold him, stroke him, make sure he felt loved…and usually he tired of the excess affection before she did.

She had so much love to give, but both Crosby and her cat kept their affections contained. Buttheads.

"Fine," she said, setting Bob back on the floor. "I suppose you want food?"

Bob meowed in reply and did his funny kitty-trot, tail in the air, in a beeline for the kitchen. After she refreshed his water and put a small scoop of dry food in his bowl, she went to her desk to check her feeds.

It took her only seconds to realize that Parrish had been to see Silver. Huh. Surely he knew that she'd notice. She was rather observant, after all. Sometimes obsessively so.

Since she needed to talk to her dad anyway, she figured she should finish studying everything she could find on Crow, first. She even glanced through all the traffic cams in the area where he'd disappeared.

Wonder of wonders, she picked him up again! Making quick notes on his location and the direction he headed, she visually followed his trail until she lost him again, somewhere on I-25 headed south.

Excited, she called Cade.

He answered on the first ring. "What up?"

"I found Crow. Not found-found him, but I know the general area he was in." She quickly shared what she knew. "There's a lot of lodging available around there. I wonder if any of the places are shady enough to be tied to Crow."

"Or he could just be renting a room and they'd have no reason to suspect him."

"I'll look into it later. I'd do it right now, but I'm heading up to talk to Dad."

"Fine, but listen up, sis." His voice firmed in that "big brother" way of his. "You will not do anything on your own."

Making a face, Madison grumbled, "Did I not just call you? I'm still at my desk, PC still on and I called *you*, Cade. Give me a little credit, please." Damn it, she'd earned it.

He surprised her by saying, "You're right, sorry. If it's any consolation, I'd have said the same to Reyes."

"Really?"

"You know our brother. He runs off half-cocked all the time."

Madison laughed. "That's not true. He pretends to be a hothead still, but he's actually very calm and methodical."

"You think so?"

"I know so. Just as I know that you've loosened up some since marrying Sterling. You're both different now." And by God, she was different, too. "While I have you…" She explained about Crow looking at her during the bomb scare, and the recent call at the task force offices.

"He's targeting you." The quietness of Cade's voice made it all the more lethal.

Though her brother couldn't see her, Madison shrugged. "I

think he's aware of me, but Ted said it mostly seemed like he was fishing, and I agree. He saw me on-site at the hotel during the bomb threat, but he doesn't yet know who I am or how I'm connected to Dad or Crosby."

"Thankfully, Ted handled it well."

"I agree. Crosby praised him for it."

After a slight pause, Cade asked, "So Crosby knew about all this before your family?"

She rolled her eyes. "The point is, I'm on guard. That's why I'm heading up to see Dad, to let him know what I found on the feeds. You want to clue in Reyes for me?"

"I'll handle it as soon as we disconnect."

"We're a team, right?" With her phone on speaker, Madison closed down her PC, stepped back into her boots and snagged her coat.

"We're a team," Cade agreed.

Bob wound around her legs once, allowed her a single stroke along his back, then jumped up to the back of the couch so he could look out the window.

Remembering her conversation with Crosby, she added, "You'll keep me updated on anything you find, and I'll do the same. Right?"

Cade being so intuitive, he read more into her words than what she'd said. He was top-notch like that. "You think I don't do that already?"

"You don't check in with me," she complained. "Neither does Reyes. But I'm expected to—"

"Damn, Madison, that's a joke, right? We *rely* on you. Heavily. Do you not realize what an important role you play in keeping things safe every time we head out? You're our research guru, our eyes for places no one else can see. You're always there, watching over us so we don't feel cut off from backup."

Pausing with one hand reaching for the doorknob, she breathed a little faster—and smiled. "All that, huh?"

"That and more. No way any of this would work without you." His voice turned gentle. "Hon, you're the heart and soul of the whole damn thing."

She dropped her head against the door, giddy with happiness. "Thank you, Cade."

"Don't thank me. I'm considering coming over there to spar with you until you see reason."

Laughing, she opened the door and stepped out into the brisk cool air. "You know I'd love it."

"You probably would."

As she crunched over frozen snow to her car, which she'd left just outside the garage, she said, "Oh, hey, did you know Dad went to see Silver, today? Looks like he visited for a while, too."

"Spying on him, Madison?"

She heard his grin. "There's no way Dad thought I wouldn't notice."

"I agree, so apparently he's okay with all of us knowing. Pretty sure he's making some big decisions on that score."

"You noticed how he is with her, right?"

Instead of answering that, Cade said, "I noticed how *you* are with Crosby. Tell me he's not still being a dope."

"He's being wonderful," she promised. With any luck, he'd be wonderful in bed very soon. "Gotta go. Let me know the second you find out anything."

"You can rush me off the phone for now, but we're going to have another, longer discussion on Crosby very soon. Count on it."

"Why?" she asked. "I don't need your dating counsel."

"Agreed. But you could probably use a sounding board on love."

*Love.* Did Cade now consider himself an expert? So far, Crosby hadn't given any indications of love, and no way in hell would she be the first to proclaim her feelings. She'd done enough of that already. Plus they hadn't even had sex yet. People couldn't declare love unless they were compatible in the sack, right?

"Did that word stun you silent, sis?"

Despite her current boggled emotions, Madison wasn't about to confirm or deny anything to her most perceptive sibling. "Bye, Cade."

"Love you, Madison."

She halted, took a breath and whispered, "Love you, too, brother." Once they disconnected, she smiled. She seriously had the best, most awesome family ever. Not perfect, no. Who was? But she knew she'd hit the jackpot when it came to family bonds.

It took her only a few minutes to get up to her dad's house. She found her father in his office, on the phone with someone.

He waved her in, finished his conversation, and then disconnected.

"Did I interrupt?" she asked, as she set her laptop on his desk.

"Just financial business." He studied her. "I can tell by your expression you have something to say. But let me preempt that. Yes, I'll be seeing Silver."

Madison lifted her brows, unsure why he'd just announced the obvious like that.

Leaving his chair, Parrish circled his desk and stopped before her. "Of course you know that I visited her today."

"Of course," she agreed, trying to match his attitude of grave seriousness, but not entirely successful.

"I hope you don't have any objections."

Madison grinned. "None at all. Why would I?"

He straightened a little more, until he looked down his nose at her in that "I'm your father" way of his. "There is no reason, except that it's not something you're used to—"

"And you think I can't handle it? I mean, I'm so emotionally fragile and everything."

"Don't be absurd."

Tickled over the way he frowned, she put the back of her hand to her forehead and whispered dramatically, "Oh, the trauma. My own father, *dating*. How will I survive?"

The corner of his mouth edged up. "Brat. I take it you're not surprised?"

"Nope." Using two fingers, she pointed at her eyes. "See these peepers?" She wiggled the fingers in the air and said with mystery, "They see things."

"Is that so? Such as?"

"Such as the way you go alert whenever Silver speaks. The way you track her every movement. Especially how you try to cover those two things." She slid her arms around his waist and gave him a hearty squeeze. "I'm happy for you, Dad."

He laughed, but just as he began to return her embrace, she pressed back.

"She better be good to you, though," Madison warned. "I won't like it otherwise."

Parrish kissed her forehead. "So fierce. I appreciate it, but like you, I can take care of myself."

"And like you, I'll worry anyway." They shared a smile over that. "Speaking of worry…" Madison moved away, pulled a chair closer to the front of her father's desk, and then opened the problematic feed that she'd saved to her desktop. "Take a look at this, will you?"

Rather than go back behind his desk, Parrish used the other guest chair. Silently, he watched the entire length of feed she wanted him to see.

When it ended, Madison took in the deadly way he stared at the frozen shot of Burgess Cross.

"There's more," she said quietly, then detailed the call at the task force. "Ted did an amazing job. Whatever you're paying him, he deserves a raise and more responsibility."

"I'll look into it." Without another word, Parrish stood to pace.

Madison didn't interrupt his thought process. Each of them had their own way of doing things. Usually information was related to her father and he formulated a plan, but this was personal, and she could tell by his expression that it had a different effect.

"Who else knows about this?"

"I told Crosby today. He met me at the task force offices and then we went to lunch. I called Cade right before coming up here because I found Crow on a traffic cam. Cade will get hold of Reyes. Between the three of us, we'll locate every possible place where Crow might have been sleeping. Hotels, motels, B and Bs. If all goes according to plan, we'll have him within reach in two days or less."

Parrish surprised her by saying, "I want to be there to confront him. I want to know *why*. Why target me? Why target you? It feels like there's something we're not seeing."

"Remember, Crow was the man who got away when Crosby's team raided that cult compound a few years back." A new spear of apprehension cut through her. "The same compound where he found Hallie."

Parrish McKenzie was not a man who had outbursts. He didn't lose his temper or lash out. What he did instead was get coldly furious. "From now on, we each stay in closer touch with the others. No one goes off alone until we have Crow."

"Dad," Madison said softly, "Silver's house is as secure as we can make it. She and Hallie are safe."

"No one is truly safe and you know it."

Sadly, true. They'd learned that lesson the hard way through her mom's death. "Crosby invited me to dinner tomorrow. I plan to go, but I can certainly check in before I leave and once I'm there."

"And before you head back."

"All right," she conceded, as if it didn't matter. But his worry became her own. She closed her laptop. "I'm going to head home now. I want to round up as many possible locations for Crow as I can find."

"I'll get hold of your brothers. Before you go to dinner to-morrow, we'll scour the area where Crow was last seen. If we don't find him, maybe we'll at least uncover a clue."

"What about Crosby?"

He shook his head. "Not yet."

"What do you mean, not yet? He's working this with us."

"He was, but this is family business now, and we haven't yet had a chance to see Crosby in a situation like this, to know how he'd react and how far he'll go."

Madison understood her father's take on things, just as she knew Crosby wouldn't like it. "You're concerned that if we do find Crow, Crosby will hark back to being a cop." He'd want to do things the legal way, and far too often, that way wasn't final.

"Of course he would. It's in his blood." He frowned thoughtfully. "Understand, Madison, that isn't a criticism. I think very highly of Crosby and I respect that he's so ethical. It's served him well, both as a cop and as a father. For that reason, if we can gather enough evidence to ensure Crow's conviction, we'll do things Crosby's way."

"Meaning?"

"If we can bring Crow in with the confidence that he'll never again be a problem, then we will."

"Seriously?" A spark of hope ignited.

His leveled brows stole it away. "You know that's not likely. Those of Crow's ilk rarely surrender, and far too often they manage to slip through the cracks."

She needed a solid way to convince her father. "You brought Crosby in for this specifically. You trusted him then, so trust him now."

"This isn't about trust."

No, it wasn't. They all trusted Crosby to be competent, capable, and when necessary, discreet. She needed to remind her father of that. "You put him in charge of investigating—"

"Who was after *me*." Proving the difference mattered to him, her father said, "Not with my children as targets."

"We're often targets," she softly reminded him. With the work they did, it couldn't be avoided.

"And when you are, you retaliate in kind, with equal measure. That's something you can't do with a cop involved."

Damn. Was that still true with Crosby? Would he balk at their lethal methods? "For his family, he'd—"

"Probably be as deadly as we would," her dad agreed. "But we're talking about my family, not his, and if it comes down to Crow hurting one of my children, or possibly getting away so he can remain a damned threat, I won't take chances."

Madison knew he was right about one thing. Men like Crow always tried to fight or flee. If he got away, he'd only be back later, maybe when they weren't so prepared.

Understanding that put her in something of a predicament. Should she confide all to Crosby, or respect her father's wishes... And live with the consequences?

She wanted Crosby's trust, yet how trusting would he be if he found out she'd kept details from him?

Monumental conflicts arose in her mind, and she knew only one way to counter them—she'd get to work, find Crow, gather all the evidence needed to bury the bastard, and then there'd be no reason to keep anything from Crosby.

Crow's demise would be a done deal.

Yesterday's move might have been deliberate on Crosby's part, bypassing all the nicer restaurants to take Madison to a small family-run diner, but he hadn't been disappointed with her reaction.

That is, she hadn't reacted. There'd been no glancing around at the old black-and-white photos on the wall, no disdainful noticing of a booth that had seen better days, or the cracked plastic on a barstool seat. The handwritten "special of the day" chalkboard drew her attention, but only for her to say, "Mmm, meat loaf," as if it was a treat.

Maybe it was because he'd started thinking long term that he wondered how Madison would fit in his life. She came from uncommon luxury, and that just wasn't him. He could deal with it, but live it? Day in and day out?

No. It wasn't the life he wanted for Hallie, and he worried that Silver might reject it.

So he'd taken her to the most humble restaurant around, and she'd fit in with ease. The conversation over meat loaf—which turned out to be pretty darned good—was light and fun but with undertones of sensuality. No wonder, considering they were both primed.

When they'd parted ways, him to get back to work, her to head back to her house to go through more details on her PC, he'd reminded her to talk to her family about Crow.

She'd agreed, and he trusted her, but he'd feel better once he spoke with them, too. He planned to do that as soon as he finished chatting with Silver.

After parking the SUV, he exited the garage and headed across the backyard. There were two snowmen off to the side, and two different sized snow angels as well, telling him that Silver and Hallie had played outside today.

*This* was what he wanted for his daughter. A normal upbringing with days of fun, learned responsibility, love and security.

A voice in his head whispered that his time with Madison had been fun, too. Yes, she had a fancy indoor heated pool, but she'd treated it as nothing and had spent her time playing games with Hallie.

Yes, the family home was on a private mountain, but Hallie had only noticed the fun she had sledding.

Yes, the family came from astounding wealth…but the dinner he'd shared with them had been relaxed, filled with conversation and laughter. No one put on airs, except for Bernard, and on him, the affectation was amusing.

Lost in his thoughts, Crosby tapped at the back door and only a few moments later Silver opened it. He stepped into the kitchen, noticed all the lights were low and looked through the doorway to the living room. There on the couch, surrounded by stuffed animals, tucked under a throw blanket, was his daughter. The glow of the television reflected on her rapt expression.

*"Jungle Book,"* Silver said, which explained it since that was one of Hallie's favorites. "After Parrish's visit, then playing outside so long, crashing for a cartoon movie seemed like a good plan."

Crosby frowned. "Parrish was here?"

"Yup." She leaned back on the counter and folded her arms. "S'that a problem?"

"Not if you're okay with it." He peeled off his coat while watching her. "Are you?"

"He and I had a nice long chat once Hallie took her nap."

"And?" Something in her expression alerted him. "You told him, didn't you?"

"Pretty much everything," she confirmed.

"I take it by that small smile, he surprised you?"

"You know, I'd already suspected how he'd react or I'd never have shared." The smile widened. "He didn't disappoint me."

"Meaning he only had good things to say, all of them true, by the way."

"Hearing that from you and hearing it from him are two different things." She ran a hand over her braid. "With you, I've grown to expect it."

"I would hope so." He told her that she was phenomenal every chance he had.

"You've always seen me as a good person. I figured that made you a saint or something, you know?" She didn't wait for a reply to that nonsense. "But Parrish seemed to feel the same."

"All the saints have died and gone to heaven," Crosby pointed out. "What's left is normal human beings doing the best they can under their individual circumstances. Sometimes failing, sometimes succeeding."

"You and Parrish have the same outlook."

Did they? Interesting. "Not sure if I should take that as a compliment or an insult. No, hold that thought," he said, when she laughed. "I'll talk to Hallie a minute, then there's something I want to discuss with you."

"Somethin' serious?"

"Nothing for you to worry about," he promised. "I'll be right back." When he stepped into the living room, Hallie finally became aware of him. She rose to her knees and started chattering a mile a minute about how funny Baloo was and she liked the way King Louie danced.

He picked up the remote and paused the cartoon, then sat on the couch beside her.

She immediately crawled into his lap for a hug and a kiss. "Can I finish my movie before we eat?"

So much for missing him. Crosby laughed. "Let's ask Silver."

From the kitchen, Silver said, "It's soup, so not a problem."

That'd give them a chance to talk privately. "How much longer does it have to go?"

"Not long," Hallie hurried to assure him.

He checked, saw she had twenty minutes or so and agreed. "Give me another kiss and I'll go talk to Silver while you finish up here."

She squeezed her arms around his neck, put a loud smacking kiss to his cheek and scurried back under the blanket.

Smiling, Crosby hit Play on the remote and left her to it.

In the kitchen, Silver had already dished up two bowls of soup and put a few slices of baked bread on the table with butter.

Crosby poured them each a glass of tea. He wanted to broach the topic of inviting Madison over, but it was awkward since he specifically wanted time for sex. He'd need to figure out a way to say it, without disrespecting either woman.

For a few minutes they ate in silence, then they spoke about the meal, the weather and his new job.

Before he could decide on the right words to use, Silver said, "So you and Madison. Why don't you two grab some alone time?"

Wow, the lady was a mind reader. "Alone time?" he repeated, stalling until he could segue into what he wanted.

"Yeah, you know. Privacy for a little somethin'-somethin'. I'm guessing you need it." Only half under her breath, she muttered, "I know I do."

"Whoa, what is this?" Grinning, he leaned forward to see her averted face. "Say that again?"

Chin up, she met his gaze. "You need to get laid. The signs are all there."

"What signs?" Maybe he could spot them on Silver.

"Look, you want time and opportunity or not?"

He laughed. Here he was, trying to tiptoe around the topic, and Silver just tossed it out there. She and Madison shared that forthright, oftentimes bold way of speaking. "I want to know what you meant with that second part—and Silver, if it's what I think it is, I'm happy for you. Seriously." So damn happy. There had been times when he'd thought Silver would never let another man close in that way. For years, she hadn't.

She eyed him, cracked a smile and let out a happy sigh. "Okay, so yeah, I'm human. It's a shock to me, too. Parrish…he's gotten under my skin or something. I want to see if he can deliver, or if he's all talk."

Ha! Parrish, the cocky know-it-all, would make a believer of her. Crosby felt sure of it. "How can I help?"

"Take Hallie out for a movie one evening so she doesn't accidentally see his car here. But *first*," she said, poking one finger dead center on his chest, "it's gotta be you and Madison. I'm still thinking things over, you know? You're just suffering."

He laughed. True, it did feel a bit like suffering. "You already do so much."

"The squirt and I will have a sleepover. Won't be the first time."

There had been times when he was still a cop that a call had kept him out late into the night. "That doesn't mean you need to—"

"Need, want. I adore that child, and you know it. Heck, I'm already looking forward to it. We'll watch another cartoon movie, eat popcorn...maybe I'll do her nails. It'll be great."

"Thank you."

"Hey, it's the least I can do now that you've fallen in love."

*Love?* Uncomfortable with the idea of something that monumental, he said honestly, "That's a massive leap, don't you think?" Though he wasn't sure *what* he felt. He just knew it was consuming and very unfamiliar. Easing into the topic, he pointed out, "We haven't even...been alone together yet."

"Ha! That's a roundabout way of saying you haven't slept together, right? Well, take it from someone who knows. Sex is not the deciding factor on something as important as love."

Crosby easily interpreted her meaning. Silver had once admitted that she'd initially hooked up with her abuser because the sex was so good. She'd mistakenly thought it meant more than physical pleasure, for both of them, and by the time she'd realized the truth—that great sex didn't make up for everything the creep lacked in the way of humanity—she'd already been stuck in an awful situation.

"You know," he said, trying to sound casual, "it's possible to have both. Love and great sex." He knew he wouldn't settle for anything less, and he suspected Madison wouldn't either. That should have made him feel pressured to perform, but instead it just made him hungrier for her.

"An ideal situation, but I don't believe in unicorns anymore."
She flashed him a bold grin meant to reflect her sarcastic wit, but
her eyes told a different story. "I'm wishin' that for you, though,"
she quickly assured him. "You deserve it. You deserve *her*, so
count me in. I'll do whatever I can to aid the cause."

Crosby smiled. "Thank you." Then he detailed his plan—and
he had Silver's wholehearted cooperation.

Worry woke Madison far too early, when she hadn't slept for
much of the night. This was not the way to start her exciting
relationship with Crosby. Keeping things from him...how could
her dad ask her to do that?

Of course she knew. When he just thought someone was after
him, her dad wasn't all that worried. Now that he knew what
Crow was capable of, that he'd maybe set his sights on her, it
became far more personal. He didn't want Crosby's conscience
getting in the way if things got messy, as they so often did when
dealing with the scum of the earth.

She already had a feeling that they would get very messy, indeed.

So then what would happen? How furious would Crosby
be, or would he understand? Cade and Reyes didn't have to go
through this. Cade's wife, Sterling, was usually in on the action, and her attitude was as ruthless as the rest of theirs. Reyes's
wife, Kennedy, rarely involved herself with their investigations,
except to warn them all to be careful and to worry whenever
they were dealing with dangerous situations.

In some ways, she felt like Crosby brought a nice balance. His
contribution would help keep them from becoming too jaded.
At least, that's how she saw it. Clearly, her dad had other ideas.

She felt Bob land on the mattress before he walked up her
legs and curled on her chest. He touched his furry nose to hers
and started purring.

"Hey, baby." Rubbing under his chin, she asked, "Are you hungry?"

He immediately jumped down and headed out of the room. It was the truth, Bob could eat all day long if she'd let him.

Knowing she wouldn't get back to sleep, she dragged herself out of bed and made a beeline to the bathroom.

A few minutes later, wearing her fuzzy housecoat and slippers, an already-fed kitty watched as she made a cup of hot tea. He followed her as she went to her desk and opened her laptop.

Bob made an agile leap up and attempted to walk on her keyboard. "We've been over this, Bob." She hugged him once, then placed him in her lap and pulled up the feeds showing the area where Burgess Crow was last seen. She'd already identified three hotels and one motel where she thought they should start the search.

Each of the hotels had security cameras aimed at the parking lots, but she hadn't spotted Crow's truck. The motel, so far, proved more elusive. For that reason, she wanted to check there first.

Her eyes flared when she saw that a crew of workers were setting up right along that strip of road. Judging by the trucks and equipment, they planned to make repairs to the pavement.

Well, hallelujah. Their investigative work today would be postponed. It was too risky with the complication of additional eyes around, including the crews, the backed-up drivers and local police who would help to direct traffic.

She felt like she'd just been given a reprieve, but she would have to figure something out soon. The problem hadn't gone away. It was only delayed.

For now, she'd remotely uncover as much as she could. Her gut told her to start with the motel, so she'd begin by hacking their system—if they even had one. With any luck, she'd find what she needed to nail Crow.

Then she'd have to decide how much to share with Crosby.

Crosby was just stretching awake when a call came in. A sense of foreboding speared into him. Swinging his legs over the side of the bed, he flipped on a lamp and grabbed his phone.

He saw Owen's name on the screen. What the hell?

Swiping to answer, he put the phone to his ear and stood. "Owen? What's wrong?"

"It's Dad," Owen said in a shaky rush. "He's hurt, Crosby. I know it's early, but we're at the hospital and I didn't know who to call—"

"I'm glad you called me," he said soothingly, switching the phone to speaker and striding quickly to his dresser. "Tell me what happened."

"Dad was up early for some deliveries. God, I wasn't even out of bed yet!"

"Take a breath, okay?" He stepped into slacks while praying Winton wasn't hurt too badly. "I can be on my way in ten minutes, but I need to know what happened." *And how bad it is.*

"I guess the delivery guy left and…someone else was there. Two guys, Dad said. Crosby…they hurt him. I found him on the ground in the back alley."

Where deliveries were made. Crosby knew the spot, and he knew it was secluded from passersby.

"He couldn't get up on his own and there was a lot of blood and…and the doctor said he'll be okay but I—"

"It scared you. I get it, Owen. I haven't seen him yet, but I'm scared, too. I'm glad the doctor said he'll be all right." Crosby couldn't imagine how shocking that must have been for Owen. "Where was the blood coming from?"

"He has a bad cut on his head, but his nose and lip were bleeding, too. And there are a lot of bruises. I panicked and called 911."

"You did the right thing." Crosby wrestled his arms into a shirt and rapidly buttoned it. "I need to get Hallie next door to Silver, but I promise I'll hurry. Which hospital are you at?"

Owen shared the name and then whispered, "Dad might not have wanted me to call you. He said you were working your new job."

Crosby scoffed. "You two come first. I'd have kicked your butt if you hadn't called me. Okay?"

For the first time since Owen called, Crosby heard relief in his voice. "Okay. Thanks. I'm going to get back in there with Dad now."

"Call me if anything changes." *Or if things get worse.* "I'll be there in thirty." Once Crosby disconnected, he raced to Hallie's room to wake her so she could start getting ready, then called Silver and spoke with her on his way to the bathroom.

Naturally, Silver was a huge help. He was rushing around when she knocked on the kitchen door. Still looking half asleep, she came in and headed for the coffee carafe to make a pot. "Go," she said. "Finish getting ready. I've got this."

Thanks to her, Crosby was ready to head out five minutes later. He hadn't taken the time to shower or shave. Hallie was at the table, half asleep, while Silver poured her a bowl of cereal.

Crosby hugged his daughter, kissed her cheek and told her he loved her. With Silver, he clasped her shoulder and thanked her.

She gave him a tired smile. Mindful of Hallie only a few feet away, she said softly, "I hope everything is okay. Call me when you can to let me know."

"Will do." Luckily he had two hours before he had to be on the job. Once he saw Winton, he'd know if he needed to shuffle things around a little.

On his way to the hospital he tried calling Madison, but only got her voice mail. It was still so early the sun hadn't peeked out yet. Thinking she might be in the shower, he left a brief message, but his instincts were rioting. Winton hurt, and now Madison didn't answer?

How telling was it that even with Winton hurt, his thoughts were on Madison?

He had plenty of other things to think about, like Winton's store. Hopefully Owen had remembered to lock it up, but he was only fifteen and he'd had a shock… Damn. This was one of those times when he was glad to have the McKenzies as allies. He didn't even try to talk himself out of it as he opened the screen on his phone, pressed his thumb to Cade's name and heard the phone ringing.

Unlike Madison, Cade answered on the first ring with, "McKenzie."

"Hey, it's Crosby. Sorry to call so early but I have a situation."

"My sister?"

"No. Actually, I tried calling her but she didn't answer, so I left a message. I wouldn't want her involved anyway."

"Got it. How can I help?"

As succinctly as possible, Crosby relayed what had happened. "I'll be at the hospital shortly, and then I'll know better what I'm dealing with."

"Hmm," Cade said. "When I checked, it seemed you had that trouble settled. Odd that something would flare up again now."

Yeah, Crosby thought so, too. "I pissed off several people when I broke up their little gang."

"I like how you say 'gang' with so much disdain."

Crosby might have grinned if he wasn't so worried for Winton. "That group of twits doesn't concern me as much as Burgess Crow. If he figured out who I am, it wouldn't take a lot for him to make connections to Winton, especially with the way word spreads on the street."

"And low-level punks are pretty easily swayed," Cade murmured. "Fifty in cash can convince them to do almost anything."

"Exactly." Though Crosby thought some of the troublemakers disliked him enough that they'd share what they could for free.

Another concern was the idea that Crow might also discover his address. Anyone good enough on the computer could work it out. Did Crow have those skills? Did he know another scumbag who might?

Crosby knew he'd rip the man apart with his bare hands before he'd let him hurt Hallie or Silver.

"Tell you what," Cade said, drawing him from those dark thoughts. "I'll head over to his store and see what I can find out. Maybe I'll notice something the cops overlooked."

Crosby worked his jaw and did his utmost not to take offense. "Thanks. Just don't dick up any evidence."

Cade laughed as if he recognized that as a return insult. "I'll do my best."

"Can you make sure Owen locked up, too? The last thing Winton needs is to return to a bigger mess or to find himself robbed blind."

"Agreed. I'll keep you posted."

Just like that, Cade took a huge weight off Crosby's shoulders. Now to see how bad things were with Winton.


Burgess listened to the update. He didn't smile. Not yet. There was no satisfaction in having an old man bludgeoned; it was a necessary tactic to draw out Crosby Albertson, nothing more. "What hospital did they take the old guy to?"

"No idea," the punk said. "Not like I'd follow an ambulance. 'Sides, you wanted me to hang out here and follow the cop, right?"

Ex-cop, not that he'd correct the idiot. "It stands to reason if you hurt the guy enough that they had to take him to the hospital, that's where Albertson will go, right?"

After a few beats of silence, the goon said, "Uh…maybe."

Crow bit back a growl of frustration. "Never mind. Stay there in case he shows up. I'll figure out the rest another way."

"How long am I supposed to hang around here, anyway?"

Glancing at the clock, Crow said, "At least noon. Maybe until one. Depends on what happens at the hospital."

"One! Are you shittin' me? I'll need an extra C-note, then. My time ain't free."

Greedy bastard. "Done. Just make sure I know what's happening at all times." After disconnecting, Crow started researching hospitals in the area to find the closest one. With that accomplished, he put in another call. Feeling certain Albertson would head to the hospital to be with the store owner, Crow rounded up two other acquaintances. He described the SUV, told them to find it and then follow it when he left.

Once he knew where Crosby lived, the game would be over. He'd have the cop and every fucking thing Albertson had ever valued.

And then he'd destroy it all.

# CHAPTER THIRTEEN

Crosby tried to ignore the anxious pounding of his heart while he followed the nurse's directions to the exam room. As he neared, he heard Owen's voice through the open door.

"I'm not leaving here without you."

"You need to eat, to relax."

Damn, Winton's voice sounded weak. Saying, "Knock, knock," Crosby stepped in. The all-white room was crowded with Winton resting back on the bed in a thin hospital gown, Owen standing anxiously at his side, an officer at the foot of the bed and a doctor at a desk-type rolling table.

Crosby glanced at each of them, then focused on Winton. Mentally he winced at the sight of his battered face, but he kept his expression stoic. Knowing Winton's first concern would be his son, Crosby embraced Owen in a bear hug. "Hey, kiddo. How are you holding up?" Looking over Owen's shoulder, he saw Winton's slight nod of appreciation.

Owen gripped him, *hard*, with a touch of desperation, then he stepped back and flung a hand toward Winton. "Look at him, Crosby! The bastard hurt him bad."

"Owen," Winton said softly, then to Crosby, "I'm going to be fine. The doctor just said so."

The doctor turned, leaned a hip on a cabinet and folded his arms. "You're family?" he asked Crosby.

Before he could reply, Winton and Owen both said, "Yes."

The circumstances sucked, but the sentiment would always be valued. "How bad is it?"

"Fifteen stitches in his scalp. Multiple contusions on his ribs, one on his right hip and another on his right thigh. We just got back the X-rays, but thankfully I'm not seeing any breaks."

"Concussion?" Crosby asked, seeing the blood staining Winton's hair.

With a shake of his head, the doctor said, "No blurred vision, slurred speech, nausea or memory loss. He's as sharp as ever, but with a headache, which is to be expected. I gave him a prescription for pain meds." The doctor picked up a clipboard and straightened, then asked Winton, "Any questions?"

"How soon can I get out of here?"

*"Dad,"* Owen complained, appearing frazzled by the idea of his father leaving the hospital.

"He's okay," the doctor said, laying a hand on Owen's shoulder. "What he mostly needs now is rest, and he'll be more comfortable at home."

"But he wants me to leave him."

The doctor glanced at Crosby as if he held all the answers.

This time, maybe he did. "We'll work it out, Owen. You have my word."

Satisfied, the doctor said, "Why don't you help him dress? A nurse will be in shortly with his discharge papers."

As soon as he left the room, the officer stepped forward, hand extended. "Detective Albertson. We briefly met a few years back. Officer Larson."

"I remember." Crosby didn't correct him on the title. "Thank you for being here, Larson."

"He drove me here," Owen said, shooting the cop a look of gratitude.

"Not a problem. I had to take a report anyway."

Crosby appreciated that both the officer and the doctor had treated Owen with kid gloves. It was obvious he was on the ragged edge with worry.

"Unfortunately," Larson said, "Mr. Maclean didn't remember much."

"I was blindsided," Winton explained.

"And I was upstairs," Owen growled. "Dad was in the alley, hurt, and I had no idea—"

"No reason you should," Crosby said, cutting off whatever guilt-ridden admissions Owen might have made.

"I let you sleep in since you didn't have school today," Winton said. "In-service day," he explained to Crosby. "I had no reason to think there'd be trouble."

Because there never was—*until Burgess Crow.*

"He'd been out there forever before I found him," Owen whispered. "He didn't even have his coat."

"Fifteen minutes or so," Winton corrected, as if it were nothing.

Crosby put his arm around Owen's shoulders, hoping the human contact would help. "You did everything right, Owen, including calling 911. You acted fast and that's what matters."

The officer glanced at each of them. "I'll be on my way so you can have some privacy. A detective will be in touch, Mr. Maclean."

"Wait." Winton struggled to sit.

Both Crosby and Owen rushed to help him. Once he was upright on the side of the bed, left arm curved around his ribs, he offered his right hand. "Thank you, Officer. For everything."

Larson took Winton's hand in both of his. "Just part of the job, sir." As he started to leave, Crosby said to Winton, "Sit tight. Seriously, don't move. I'll be right back. I want a quick word with Larson."

He stepped out with the officer, moving a few feet from the door. "Could you have someone drive by his place for a few days?"

"Yeah," Larson said, very somber. "I already promised the kid we'd keep an eye out."

"I appreciate it." Crosby rubbed the knot of tension gathering in the back of his neck. "I'd like to talk him into closing down the store for a day or two but—"

"His boy already tried that. Mr. Maclean refused. I take it that's their livelihood and he doesn't want to confuse the clientele."

Crosby relayed the recent trouble with embezzlement, giving details Winton couldn't.

"I'll let the detective know, and we'll keep an eye on this."

"There's a chance it's related," Crosby said. "But I have my doubts."

"Something else I should know?"

"No." Nothing that Crosby could share. When he heard grumbling from the room, he thanked Larson again and hurried back in.

Owen stood in front of Winton, as if to bar him from standing. Fifteen and trying to be a man…it was a tough age.

Crosby stepped up beside him. "Can you tell me exactly what happened?"

Disgusted, Winton said, "He ambushed me after the delivery guy left." His gaze cut to Owen and he added, "I hadn't even finished my coffee yet, and Owen hasn't had anything to eat."

"Quit worrying about that." Owen ran a hand over his hair. "I'm not starving."

Taking that as his cue, Crosby fished out his wallet and handed money to Owen. "Well, I am. Why don't you head down to the cafeteria and grab us sandwiches or something that we can take with us? We can eat on the way home."

Before Owen could protest, Winton added, "Great idea. Get me a coffee, and maybe a pastry or cake or whatever. It's the damn truth, I need the caffeine and sugar right now."

Owen frowned. "You're sure I shouldn't—"

"He needs to eat," Crosby said low, hoping to convince Owen. "If he wants something sweet, then that's what he should get."

"Oh, right," Owen whispered back. "Well, if you're sure...?"

"I am. Get us whatever you want that we can eat in the SUV, okay? Thanks."

Moving with a purpose now, Owen headed out.

Crosby and Winton both waited. When they were sure he was out of range, Winton cursed and pushed to his feet with a grimace. "By the time I heard the guy coming, it was too late. I turned and he punched me. I didn't even have time to get a look at him."

Crosby locked his jaw.

"I'm not a slouch," Winton insisted, "but he took me off guard. Lost my balance, and when I fell, I cracked my head on the brick wall. The doc thinks that's how I bruised my hip and leg, too."

Seeing it in his mind amplified the rage churning through Crosby. "And your ribs?"

"Several well-placed kicks. Last thing I remember is turtling up to cover my head...and then Owen was there, scared out of his wits." More softly, Winton said, "There was enough blood that he thought I was dead. For that alone, I'd like to kill the punk who did this."

Christ, the shit was starting to add up. "Could I convince you to—"

"No, son. I appreciate it, I really do, but I'm going home. I'll have Owen spend the night with one of his friends. Since tomorrow is Saturday, he can hang out there. But I need to open my store as usual. It's bad enough that customers will wonder why I'm not there now."

With perfect timing, Crosby's phone buzzed. He checked the screen, saw the name of the caller, and answered. "Crosby here."

Cade said, "Place was locked up tight, so tell Owen he did a great job. A few people stopped by saying they'd seen the cops and ambulance. Instead of going into details, I told them he was mugged, but was okay. He is, isn't he?"

"He will be," Crosby vowed, then quickly updated Cade on Winton's condition.

Cade gave a low whistle. "I'm glad it's not worse."

Because they both knew Winton might have lost his life as a sacrifice, just so Crow could draw them out. "Me, too."

"Since I'm inside now, want me to put a sign in his front window? A lot of people are curious."

Crosby frowned. "I thought you said the place was locked."

"It was. It will be again."

Right. Locked doors didn't slow down McKenzies. "We should be leaving here in just a few. Winton insists on coming home—"

"Of course," Cade said. "I'd be the same, and so would you. Want me to stick around until then?"

He couldn't ask him to do that. "We'll be fine. Hang on a sec." Covering the phone, he asked Winton about the sign.

"He's inside now?"

"Long story, but yes. I promise he didn't break anything."

Winton managed a crooked smile. "That's some family you're getting involved with."

"I'm aware."

At that, Winton even chuckled, then had to hold his ribs again. "Tell him there's a sign in my back room hanging off a nail on the side of the top shelf, to the left of the doors. It says *Closed until...* He could write in *noon*."

"No," Crosby insisted. "Today you need to rest. How about tomorrow morning?"

"I'll be fine—"

"But Owen won't. Give him a break. You can handle one day of rest, right? For his sake?"

"Damn." Winton gave it quick thought, then nodded. "You're right. Ask Cade to write 9:00 a.m. tomorrow."

Crosby relayed the message.

"No problem. I'll take care of it. And Crosby? We're on it, okay? We'll figure out what's happening."

"We who?" If the McKenzies thought to take over—

"My family," Cade said simply, "and you."

They kept throwing him for a loop, offering so much backup. He rubbed a hand over his face, feeling like an ass now for jumping to the wrong conclusion. "Thanks."

"No problem. If you need anything else, let me know."

"There is one thing. I still haven't heard from Madison. Have you—"

"I talked to her twenty minutes ago. She was in the shower when you called. Sorry, dude, but she's on her way to you."

Taken aback by that statement, Crosby said, "She's coming here? To the hospital?" But...of course she was. Madison was an *act first, ask later* type of person. "We're ready to leave."

"No, she told me to let you know she'll meet you at Winton's place. She didn't call you because she figured you'd be with Winton and she didn't want to interrupt."

Or more likely, she didn't want to take the chance that he'd nix her plans. "I take it you didn't mind calling?"

"Since I'm not rushing over to hold your hand, calling seemed necessary."

Crosby smiled. Was that what Madison wanted to do? Hold his hand?

"Listen," Cade said. "Madison doesn't like to show her worry.

She thinks it makes her look weak or something, but she wants to be with you because she cares. Don't brush her off, okay?"

"I wouldn't." Aware of Winton watching him, taking it all in, Crosby said, "Seriously, thank you."

Cade fell silent a few seconds, then said, "It's what family does."

*Family.* Was he adding the McKenzie clan to his eclectic mix? Maybe.

After ending the call with Cade and putting his phone away, Crosby helped Winton dress. The slow process was an indignity no able-bodied man should have to suffer. Winton was proud, used to living his own life, running his store and raising his son alone while never complaining.

It pained Crosby, seeing a man who'd been like a father to him move with such obvious pain—the way his face went pale when he tugged up his pants and his inability to get on his socks and shoes.

Someone would pay, Crosby vowed, Burgess Crow and whatever pricks he'd hired to do this.

Crosby was in the middle of helping Winton to a chair when Owen returned, and right behind him, the nurse.

Within twenty minutes, they were heading out to the car, Winton in a wheelchair pushed by a nurse, Owen keeping stride beside him and Crosby scanning the parking lot. Something felt off, so he wouldn't let down his guard until he got both Winton and Owen safely inside their home.

And then he'd need to figure out how to keep them safe until he found and demolished all the threats.


After sending Cade on his way, Parrish walked throughout Winton's store, familiarizing himself with all the windows on the main floor, as well as the doors, as he checked the locks. Not bad. He'd be willing to bet most of the upgrades were thanks to Crosby.

Gary, the man he'd brought along to assist Winton, walked the outside perimeter, looking for any and all places for an ambush. Many of these old buildings had fire escapes, windows that were too warped to lock and sometimes security gates near the loading dock that could be forced open.

Wondering what was taking Gary so long, Parrish checked on him and saw that customers from the neighborhood continually stopped by, their expressions worried as they asked after Winton. Clearly Winton was well-liked and respected by those who knew him. Made sense. If he hadn't been a nice, stand-up guy, he wouldn't have had such an impact on Crosby.

Not everyone could help raise a man who'd be worthy of Madison.

Parrish finally got an accounting from Gary, and as he'd suspected, the fire escape was secured and all egresses were in good working order. Other than being caught outside by a thug, Winton's place of business was as protected as possible.

Going back inside and stripping off his coat, Parrish stepped behind the counter, sat on the stool and dialed Silver.

She sounded a touch anxious when she answered with, "Parrish? Is something wrong? Is Winton okay? What's happened?"

Crosby had said she was a worrier. Now he had the proof. "I'm at Winton's store. Crosby should be here any minute with Winton and Owen. While I waited I wanted to check on you."

"Never mind that. How's Winton? I've been worried to death."

Leaning back against the wall, his feet braced on the bottom rung of the stool, Parrish smiled. "My understanding is that he took a few hits but he'll be fine."

"Oh, thank God."

"What he shouldn't do," Parrish continued, "is overwork himself or suffer another threat. That's why I brought over one of my best men to keep an eye on things until Crosby and I can get the bas…" He amended that, removing *bastard* from the sentence. "…the man who's causing the problems."

"You think it's the same son of a bitch who shot at you and put out that bomb scare?"

His smile turned into a grin. So much for him censoring his language. "Yes, I do. Burgess Crow is trying to hurt Crosby and me by hurting those we care about." His voice naturally went a little huskier when he said, "That's why I'm concerned for you."

Rather than dwell on the meaning of his words, Silver laughed. "Y'all already locked my place up tight, remember? Now tell me about this man you're leavin' to babysit Winton."

The second she started shortening her words, Parrish knew her mind was running the same path as his own, so he ignored the question and instead asked, "When may I see you again, Silver?"

"Hmm…" She seemed to give it some thought. "I'm guessing Madison and Crosby will put off their date tonight, right?"

"Not at all. I plan to insist that they keep their plans."

"Insist, huh? Because?"

*Because the sooner they work out their issues, the sooner we can work out ours.* He shook his head. Now was definitely a time for diplomacy. "We have this in hand for now. No reason to let the cretin disrupt plans more than he already has." He was about to tell her that he needed to see her again, and soon, when Winton came in the door with Madison and Owen helping him. Interesting. "Sorry, but I need to go. I'll call you back when I can."

"Sure," she said, as if it didn't matter.

With his gaze never leaving the new arrivals, Parrish murmured, "Think of me, Silver, because I'll be thinking of you." He ended the call on her husky laugh.

Hurrying to Madison and Winton, Parrish said, "Here, let me help."

Madison said, "Thanks, Dad."

Winton gave him a quick glance.

"Upstairs?" Parrish asked. The man seriously needed to be in bed.

"Not yet." Winton accepted his help, but said, "Just get me to the counter. And Owen, stop worrying. It'll be fine."

Frowning over that, Parrish supported Winton as much as the battered man would allow. "Where's Crosby?"

"Taking care of trouble," Madison said, rushing around to get Winton's stool. "I got here right behind him, so I knew a white truck had been following. Apparently Crosby did, too. As soon as he parked, he ordered me—*me*, Dad—to help Winton inside, and then he took off to confront whoever was in the truck."

Interesting. Crosby's first instinct was to protect Winton and Owen, and whether Madison realized it or not, he'd relied on her to ensure that. "To confront them where?"

"They pulled into the lot across the street."

When she started to move away, Winton clasped her arm. "Now, honey, don't go off annoyed. Owen and I still need your help."

Appearing stressed, Owen asked, "What if they hurt Crosby? What if they come in here next?"

Seeing the boy's worry, Parrish naturally wanted to console him. "Madison will stay with you both, and I'll go oversee things with Crosby." He snagged up his coat and shrugged it on.

"And you are?" Winton asked, slouched on his stool, his face pale beneath the bruises.

Holding out his hand, he said, "Parrish McKenzie, Madison's father, Crosby's employer." Winton briefly clasped his hand, but he still had a firm grip. A good sign that.

"I'm Winton. Owen is my son."

"Nice to formally meet you both, though of course we could have had better circumstances." As Parrish buttoned up his coat, he said, "By the way, a friend of mine is out back. He might look scary, but he's here to help. Madison can bring him in to introduce him."

Owen blinked at that. "Okay."

To give each of them something to do, Parrish said to Winton, "I want you to wait ten minutes and then call the police. Say only that there appears to be some trouble outside, understand? Don't give any details or names." Crosby would need every second of those ten minutes to question the men. He'd have liked more time, but in this, with Crosby's family, he'd bend to his preferences. If Crosby wanted to get more involved, then he could. "Ten minutes, understand?"

Winton, who now appeared determined, nodded his head. "I'll see to it."

"Good man. We'll have you more comfortable soon." He turned to go.

Madison opened her mouth but Parrish gave one quick shake of his head. She knew when he was serious. This was one of those times.

After a reassuring pat to Owen's shoulder, Parrish headed out, did a quick search of the nearby businesses and immediately spotted Crosby across the street stalking toward a small parking lot. The white truck hadn't yet noticed him. They'd apparently pulled into the lot, then turned around so that the front of the truck faced Winton's store.

Crosby headed up the walkway in front of a tailor shop. He never slowed his step, but he did unzip his coat and shrug his shoulders to loosen them.

Clearly he intended to engage.

Feeling the familiar weight of his gun at his side, Parrish followed Crosby's path, his steps faster so he could catch up.

He didn't want to miss a single thing.

Crosby's fury ramped up with each measured step he took, but he didn't let it get in his way. Instead he planned his attack—and it would be an attack. An urge burned through his blood, the urge to lay hands on the cowardly fucks who'd dared to follow him with Winton and Owen in his car.

He knew now that this was the unease he'd felt leaving the hospital. It would have been simple for Crow to instruct goons to wait for him there. It didn't take a genius to know Winton would need a ride home.

All a setup, but he was nobody's dupe.

He'd been onto them before he'd left the hospital lot. How to handle it, that had been the foremost issue. Winton's and Owen's safety was the first priority.

It was sheer luck that Madison had shown up at the exact same time, leaving him free to take care of business. Or it could have been her knack for perfect timing. Either way, he wanted to kiss her for being there when he needed her.

Pausing at the corner of the building, Crosby remained out of sight while he listened, but he didn't hear anyone on foot. A motor idled, and he made the safe assumption that the goons would remain in their ride, at least for now.

More than ready to engage, he strode around the corner of the building, his intent gaze taking in everything. The driver of the truck put it in Park with a jerk.

Crosby didn't know if their intent was to trap him, or to hurt Winton again, or maybe just to report back to Burgess Crow. Didn't matter either. They'd overstepped and now they'd pay.

The two men were busy talking to each other and didn't notice Crosby until he was only a few yards away. When they did spot him, their expressions went from startled surprise to smug antagonism.

The big guy in the passenger seat got out and circled the hood of the aging truck. Adjusting a trucker cap, he sneered. "Dude, you want something?"

"Yes," Crosby said, still advancing. The guy looked about twenty-two or -three and more obnoxious than trained. "I want to know if either of you pricks touched the shop owner."

"Who?" the man asked with absurdly faked innocence.

"You're good at playing dumb, but then you're not really playing, are you?"

That put the idiot in an aggressive stance. "What the fuck did you say?"

"I said you're an idiot." Crosby was almost within reach of him. Luckily the guy came forward, stepping away from the truck, which made it easier for Crosby to keep an eye on the driver, too. "What I want to know is if you're the cowardly dick who sucker punched a man thirty years his senior."

*"Motherfucker."* Predictably, the idiot threw a wild haymaker. *Perfect.* Crosby ducked, at the same time countering with a powerful right hand to the man's chin. The blow sent the fool staggering back and his hat went flying.

Crosby heard a curse and the creak of the driver's door opening. Time was short.

While the hat wearer was off-balance, Crosby kicked his right knee, causing his leg to buckle in a truly horrific angle, then he landed a hard left to the bridge of his nose. Blood sprayed and the man crashed back against the truck, slowly sliding down to the bumper before dropping to the ground, mouth open and eyes rolled back, one leg awkwardly extended.

With that settled, Crosby turned to confront the driver a mere second before he was tackled to the ground. This guy was of a similar age but heavier, not all of it muscle.

Crosby was already rolling as they landed, shifting position so that the driver was mostly on the icy ground. They scrambled a few seconds while the guy tried to throw Crosby off. Being so close, Crosby didn't have a lot of room for an effective punch, but he landed an elbow that cracked against the man's cheek and eye, causing him to go slack.

It was all the advantage Crosby needed. He reared back for leverage and threw three quick punches—jaw, temple, jaw— then twisted his hand in the man's shirt and dragged his face closer. He didn't want to knock him out. He wanted answers. "Who sent you here?"

"Nobody," the guy whined, his words slurred, his left eye already swelling shut.

Crosby leaned into him even more. "Lie to me again," he dared. "Do it and see what happens."

The implicit threat did the trick. "Crow, but I don't know him, man. Someone else gave him my name and number." He went completely limp, all fight gone. "It's the truth. I'm just here cuz I was promised easy cash to find out where you live. Nothing personal, I swear."

Ice ran through Crosby's veins. "How were you going to get in touch with Crow?"

"He called me. I was gonna call him back."

Crosby hard-thumped the man's head to the frozen pavement once, then held out his hand. "Phone and wallet."

"Christ," he groaned, his eyes squinted shut.

Crosby waited.

"Yeah, sure, whatever. Hundred bucks ain't worth this shit." He levered up a hip, pulled a wallet from his back pocket, then a phone from his front right pocket.

Crosby took the wallet and found the man's ID. "Open the phone."

Grumbling, the man cleared the passcode, then handed it to Crosby.

That was almost too easy. Jerking the guy over to his stomach and putting a knee in his back, Crosby said, "Lock your hands behind your neck. That's it. Now don't move." After pocketing the ID and dropping the wallet, he scrolled through recent calls, found one without a name, and held the phone around for the man to see.

"No, stay flat so I can keep an eye on you."

"The ground is wet and—right, right." He went limp again.

"Is this him?" Crosby asked.

"Yeah."

Crosby tapped the number and immediately the call was answered with an anxious, "You got an address to share?"

"No, but I have a message for you. I'm going to cripple you, Burgess Crow. You miserable, stinking coward, I promise you, you're going to rot in jail for the rest of your life—*after* I'm done with you."

Stark silence lasted for three seconds. "Crosby Albertson, I assume."

"I know you, Crow. I know you're a chickenshit who sends out anonymous threats, a spineless excuse for a man who abuses women and a fuckup who sends hired lackeys to do his dirty work. I know how you think, and I know where you hide. Start looking for me now because it won't be long until I find you."

Without another word, Crow disconnected.

*Fuck.* Crosby had hoped the bastard would get angry in return, that his anger would cause carelessness and he'd give away a clue.

"I swear," the man on the ground said, "I don't know where to find him. Brick might know. He's the one who shared my deets, but I don't know where to find Brick these days either."

Using more pressure than necessary, Crosby stood.

Slowly, with a lot of caution, the guy turned and sat up. "Could I have my phone back?"

Crosby wanted to jam it down his throat, but he resisted the impulse.

"Ahem." Parrish leaned against the brick wall, arms folded, at his leisure. He gave a tip of his head meant to beckon Crosby over.

"Make a move," Crosby told the goon, "and I'll fucking shoot you."

"Right." He held up his hands. "Not moving."

Keeping his eyes on both punks, Crosby stepped over to Parrish. "What are you doing here?"

"Not a damn thing, apparently." He nodded at the phone. "Madison might be able to find something on it."

"Might?" Did Parrish think he was an idiot? Madison would find all kinds of things, but who knew if any of it would be useful. In that moment, he didn't care that Parrish was his boss and Madison's father. "Head back to the shop. I'll be there in a minute."

Parrish's brows went up, but he didn't appear offended by the order.

Crosby turned and went back to the first guy he'd roughed up, relieving him of his wallet and taking his ID, as well. He lifted them so the men could see. "I know who you are. I know how to find you. If you, or anyone I can trace to you, ever comes near this store again, I'll make sure you regret it in more ways than you can imagine."

The guy with the busted knee just groaned.

His buddy, still stretched out on the ground, nodded. "Got it."

"Spread the word. Make it clear that anyone working with or for Burgess Crow is on my list. You got that?"

They both nodded.

"Cops are on the way." Crosby could hear the distant sirens. "You want to stick around to talk to them?"

"Hell no," the driver said fast. He glanced at his buddy. "Not sure he can walk, though."

"Then I guess you better carry him." When neither man moved, Crosby growled, "Go *now*, before I change my mind."

Jumping up, the driver collected his friend and the two of them began limping to the truck.

Crosby stood there, waiting, until the truck reversed farther into the lot, made a sharp turn and went down a backstreet. Still rigid with too much anger coursing through him, Crosby flexed his knuckles.

He needed to find Crow. He had to protect Winton. And

he really should decide if he wanted to involve the cops in any of this.

So many decisions, all of them in conflict.

*Fuck it.* He jogged across the street to the store, in a hurry now to see to Winton… And more than ready to tell Madison how glad he was that she'd shown up when she had.

*"Son of a bitch."* Burgess violently hurled the phone, shattering the case against the side of the dresser. A cold sweat gathered at his temples and slid down his spine.

How had Crosby gotten to his men? Incompetents! In the old days, he would have had them disciplined for failing him. But now? He had Brick and the motel owner and his girls at the compound hidden in the mountains. Not exactly a reliable crew, ready and willing to be his muscle. To have that type of loyalty, he needed money.

*That cop sounded so fucking sinister. He was going to kill his lackeys. They'd had one job…*

The growled threat had been far too believable. If Crow gave him the chance, Crosby Albertson *would* demolish him.

Fear sent a shudder coursing through him. He didn't mind inflicting pain when necessary, but to receive it? His skin crawled with just the thought of punch after punishing punch striking his body. He'd seen plenty—broken bones, flattened noses…blood.

But not *his own.*

Shaking, he vowed to shut down Albertson—from a safe distance—before he could ever lay a hand on him.

Time for him to put a little space between himself and his quarry while he reformulated his plans. He'd go to Brick and force that son of a bitch to work a little overtime, to dig and dig until he found what Crow needed: Crosby's fucking home address.

Throwing clothes into a suitcase and grabbing a few toiletries, he took a last look around the room—and his gaze landed on the mirror.

Oh, God no. Inching closer, Crow stared at the terrible sight looking back. It wasn't him. *He* didn't look like that. Haunted.

Fearful.

It was as if he'd aged ten years and shrunk to half his size overnight.

*How dare that fucker do this to me?* He'd always looked boyish, always looked kind and innocent. But this? *This?*

Oh, Albertson would pay.

He'd pay with everything he owned.

And everyone he cared about.

# CHAPTER FOURTEEN

Crosby was no sooner in the door than Madison was confronting him. She'd had more than enough time to get Winton settled, to reassure Owen as much as she could and to stew.

Just as she reached Crosby, a stinging lecture at the ready, he pulled her close in a tight embrace and took her mouth in a warm, almost desperate kiss.

So yeah, of course she responded. Crosby's kisses were out-of-the-stratosphere *amazing*.

The second he let up, Crosby asked, "Where's Winton?"

If he hadn't looked so concerned, she might have blasted him before explaining. Instead she patted his chest. "Upstairs in his bed. Owen is sitting with him, refusing to budge."

Frowning, Crosby said, "I thought Winton was sending Owen to a friend's house."

"I know, but Dad brought backup, so that's not necessary now."

"Backup?" Crosby looked around. "Where is Parrish?"

"Oh, no you don't." Madison caught the front of his shirt as he started to turn away from her. "You and I have something to discuss."

His gaze searched hers, then he bent and kissed her again. "Can it wait for a bit? Right now I have a million things to do."

"Crosby," she growled, frustrated because she knew he was right and that she should be more understanding. But she needed to explain right now that certain things wouldn't fly. "You *sent* me inside."

"What?" Honest confusion brought his brows together. "What are you talking about?"

In a bid for patience, she drew a deep breath. "You ordered me to take Winton inside and for me to stay with him. You put me in a terrible position with Winton looking so injured. I had no choice but to do it, but damn it, I could have helped you out there—"

Sounding far too reasonable, he said, "I didn't need help."

No, from what her dad had said, he hadn't. "That's not the point!"

His mouth tipped up on one side. "So I should have helped Winton inside so you could confront the men who followed me?"

"Well…no." Damn it, he was making her feel bad.

"Owen couldn't have managed alone, not when he's so shaken." Crosby cupped her face, kissed her again, then once more. "You're misunderstanding, babe. I didn't *order* you to do anything, I *trusted* you to do it. To get Winton safely inside, to handle a second threat if there was one." Another kiss, this one lingering before he put his forehead to hers. "To do what I couldn't because I can't be in two places at once."

Her heart started tripping.

"I love Winton and Owen." He straightened, cupped a hand to her cheek and said, "Having you here when I needed you was a godsend."

Her gaze searched his and her frown lifted. "When you put it that way…"

"What did you think?" he asked softly. "That I was afraid you couldn't handle yourself? I've seen you in action, remember? I know better." He pulled her in against his chest, rocking her side to side. "I'm *glad* you're here, babe. Thank you."

Wow, way to pile on the guilt. She tucked her face against

his hard shoulder and filled herself with his scent. "What happened out there?"

"We got a phone off them," he said, with no explanation of how that had happened. He dug it from his pocket and handed it to her. "Let me know if you find anything useful."

Wow. Just like that, he'd hand over the phone, as if they were truly a team. Feeling hugely reassured with his trust, she promised, "I'll start working on it right away."

He nodded. "Parrish didn't leave, did he?"

God, Crosby looked gorgeous with his unshaven face and mussed hair. His clothes, damp from brawling in the snow, and his knuckles looking bruised—which gave her an idea of what had transpired—made her internal temperature rise. He was... so perfect. Kind and sexy, capable and strong, so very much her equal in every way that mattered. Yet it was more than that. He caused her system to riot in ways she'd never experienced before.

"What?" Crosby asked, his gaze warming and his smile lifting. "You're giving me the funniest look."

Very briefly, she let her palm rasp over his rough jaw. Here, in Winton's store, under these dire circumstances, was not the place for her to lose her head.

She couldn't explain all the ways he drew her, so instead she stepped to the door, locked it, and then returned to take his hand. "The back door is already secured. I was just waiting on you. Come on. Everyone is upstairs."

Madison had enjoyed exploring the living space above the shop. It was necessarily small, but laid out well. The door at the top of the stairs, which had a sturdy dead bolt to be used when necessary, like when Winton and Owen were sleeping, opened into a hallway. The kitchen was straight ahead.

Crosby glanced in, but no one was there.

She took him to the right down the hall, passing a vintage black-and-white-tiled bathroom on the same side as the kitchen, with the living room on the other.

Again Crosby paused, but no one was in the living room either.

"Down here," she said, leading him toward the low drone of conversation at the end of the house, where two bedrooms were situated at opposite sides of the hall. Owen's room was empty, but Winton's room was crowded with Owen standing at one side of the bed, Parrish in a chair on the other, and a gigantic man who looked like the clichéd villain from a superhero movie leaning a hip against the dresser.

Stalling in the doorway, Crosby's gaze swept the room, then settled on Winton, who now, thanks to Owen's help, wore a loose T-shirt with pull-on plaid pajama pants. A quilt covered him to midthigh. He was propped against the headboard, several pillows behind his back...and a smile on his battered face.

Madison thought he was the sweetest guy ever.

At fifty-three, her father was three years older than Winton, yet seemed much younger. Winton had a comfortable grandpa-vibe to his personality. She would assume he'd adopted that air for Hallie, except that it seemed to be a part of his persona, likely always there.

"Gary is the backup?" Crosby whispered to her.

She grinned. "Yup." Crosby probably recognized him as one of the employees from the task force.

Presently, Gary was in the middle of telling a horrific story about how he once smashed four grown men in a conflict. It was a colorful, grisly accounting of events and Owen looked suitably impressed.

"The point," Gary said, "is that I can handle any trouble that comes our way."

"I don't doubt it," Winton said, and honestly, he looked relieved. Understandable, since he'd also have to worry for his fifteen-year-old son.

"But," Gary said with dramatic effect, one finger in the air, "I'd also like to try my hand at other stuff while I'm here."

"What stuff?" Owen asked.

"Anything you do, I guess. Stock the shelves, tidy up, load or unload supplies."

Winton shook his head. "I can't ask you to—"

"You're not asking," Parrish assured him. "Gary is one of my most trusted men. He's also one of the hardest working."

Gary puffed up his already massive chest. "It's the truth. I don't do well with idle time. Since tomorrow is a Saturday, I take it the squirt can show me around?"

Judging by his grin, Owen didn't mind being called a squirt. Next to Gary, he was. "Be glad to." He said to Winton, "We'll have it covered, Dad. You just need to heal up."

"There," Parrish said. "It's all settled. Gary will set up his cot in the break room."

"There's a bathroom right there," Gary pointed out. "And I can empty my cooler into the break room fridge, so I'll be more than comfortable."

"We'll all rest easier knowing you're both safe." Parrish's gaze met Crosby's as he stood. "Could I have a word?"

Crosby nodded, but as Gary, Owen and Parrish left the room, he went to Winton.

Madison watched him stare down at the older man. The bruises on Winton's face had already darkened, turning puce in the center, spreading out to violet and plum, and in some places, black.

Crosby's hands curled tight but his voice remained soft. "How do you feel?"

"Pampered." Winton smiled toward Madison. "That one is a natural coddler."

Was she? She'd certainly enjoyed helping Winton as much as she could, especially now that she understood Crosby's reasons for asking her to stay with him. "It was my pleasure."

"She was riled," Winton said to Crosby. "Told her there wasn't any reason."

"No reason at all," Crosby agreed, but he didn't look away from Winton. "If you need anything—"

"I need you to get on to work. I've taken up enough of your day."

Seconds ticked by, then Crosby whispered, "I'm so damn sorry this happened to you."

In a tone meant to reassure, Winton promised, "I'm fine, son, really. Now that I've had my coffee and I'm off my feet, the aches and pains are letting up. I'm even thinking of taking a nap."

"That's exactly what you need," Madison said, stepping up beside Crosby, hugging one of his arms. "But you have both our numbers now, so if you think of anything, anything at all, please don't hesitate."

"You see?" Winton said. "She's special."

"Very," Crosby agreed as he slipped free of her hold, only to put his arm around her and hug her into his side.

A glow of contentment tried to warm Madison, but she found it impossible while looking at Winton's poor battered face. She leaned forward to press a careful kiss to his cheek. "We'll find the ones responsible."

"Madison," Crosby murmured, gently tugging her away.

Right. She shouldn't go making admissions about her or her family's participation with things like this. Then again, Winton probably had some serious assumptions right now, with her dad and Gary hanging around.

"Parrish is waiting for me." Crosby took Winton's hand. "I expect you to take it easy, okay?"

"Doesn't look like I have a choice." He smiled again, then closed his eyes. "Thank you both."

As they left the room together, Madison thought it was a shame that Crosby didn't like her family that much, because she certainly adored his.

Crosby found Parrish at the break room table with Owen and Gary.

"Winton is going to nap," he explained.

"My dad?" Owen said with surprise. "Napping?"

"He was half asleep before we left his room," Madison assured him. She headed to the little break room fridge and found a bottle of water.

Owen immediately stood. "I was going to play an online game with a friend. I'll do it upstairs so I'll hear Dad if he needs anything."

Gary warned, "Don't go out without telling me."

"I won't." He hesitated at the door. "Um…make yourselves at home?" Then he was gone.

Smiling, Crosby shook his head. "I doubt he'll go far from his dad's side for the rest of the day, maybe the entire weekend." He watched Madison sit, but he didn't take a chair for himself. Too many unanswered questions kept him from relaxing.

"I checked his injuries." Parrish pushed back his chair. "Winton may come off as a gentle soul, but he's solid. All that loading and unloading, working sunup to sundown, I suppose. His injuries are mostly superficial. He really will be fine."

It was nice having a physician…*in the family*? Crosby mentally shook his head. No, Parrish wasn't part of *his* family. Not yet anyway.

But did he want that? He glanced at Madison and everything inside him clenched. Sure felt like he did. He definitely wanted her… And she was a package deal.

To stay focused on immediate priorities, Crosby gave a nod at Gary and asked Parrish, "So you arranged this?"

Parrish gestured at the back door. "Let's talk outside."

Madison started to stand, but Parrish put a hand on her shoulder. "Give me a few minutes with him. I won't keep him long."

"Dad," she warned, her eyes narrowing.

"Do you want him free this evening or tied up with work?"

She tried scowling, but Parrish didn't budge, and finally she said, "Free, if that can be worked out. But I assumed—"

"Never make assumptions, honey." He patted her shoulder and walked away.

Their relationship continued to amaze Crosby. He had no idea what Parrish might need to say to him that Madison couldn't hear, but he kept pace with him anyway until they stood in the wide opening of the alley that delivery trucks used.

"Even before you spoke to Crow, I assumed this was related. Cade agrees. I'll feel better if you accept the protection I'm offering to Winton."

*He'd* feel better. Incredible. Crosby's life as a cop hadn't exposed him to people like this. Criminals, yes, both the evil kind, and those who were just desperate, or crushed by circumstances. There was a brotherhood in the police force and he'd both trusted and respected the men he'd worked with.

None of them had Parrish's money or power to throw around.

It wasn't what he'd known, and even now, he couldn't bring himself to easily accept it.

Uncomfortably humbled, Crosby rubbed the back of his neck. "You've done so much, Parrish. I don't even know what to say."

Parrish stared into his eyes. "Say that you agree innocent people should never suffer at the hands of soulless evil."

Why did he get the feeling Parrish was talking about more than the current situation? It seemed like there was some hidden message here, as if there was a specific answer he wanted.

Did the question pertain to more than the attack on Winton? Maybe. Did it matter? Right now, in this moment... No. "That's a given."

It was subtle, but he saw something close to satisfaction flicker over Parrish's face. It was there and gone too quickly for Crosby to understand. "Gary really is excellent at what he does. He's not privy to our private business but he's been with me long enough that I trust him completely for this."

"Damn." Crosby shook his head. "I work for you, but so far you're doing everything for me."

"That's not true. You're a conscientious worker. You've been a partner when I needed one, like during the bomb threat. And the truth is, your involvement with my daughter makes you more than an employee, so this goes well beyond work obligations."

"Because of Madison."

Parrish paused. "There's also Silver. If my daughter lost interest in you tomorrow—"

Crosby scowled at where this was going.

"—and even if you quit the job, you wouldn't be done seeing me."

"Because you're hung up on Silver?"

"Hung up?" The phrase appeared to amuse him. "I'm fascinated, charmed and more interested than I've been with a woman since Marian. It's something of an adjustment for me." He peered down the alley to the street. "When Silver shared her past, it was obvious she expected me to stop calling."

"Didn't have that effect, I take it."

"Not at all. I admire her courage." His probing gaze met Crosby's. "I'm glad it was you there that day. Most cops would have followed protocol and who knows where Silver might have landed, or if she'd even have survived. Worse, I might never have met her."

Crosby had often wondered the same thing. Usually he was a "by the book" officer of the law, but that day, he'd instead gone with his instincts, bypassing the playbook and investing personally. If he hadn't? The what-ifs were something that could drive a man insane. "You're wrong about one thing. Once Silver made up her mind, she would have found a way, with or without my help." Of that he was certain.

"You could be right." Shaking off the somber tone of confessions, Parrish scrutinized him anew. "What you did for her, what you continue to do, proves that you understand other forms of justice."

"Only on rare occasions," Crosby specified. They both knew

that overall he trusted the system to be the right answer, even when it sometimes failed him.

And yet today, when dealing with Crow's hired thugs, he'd bypassed police and handled things himself…as Parrish often did.

Maybe that made him the worst sort of hypocrite.

"Rare occasions," Parrish murmured in acknowledgment. "Yes, I'm aware. That's an issue that remains."

An issue? Parrish was being too damned cryptic today. "Listen, when it comes to Crow," Crosby assured him, "I'll handle it." In whatever way necessary.

Parrish's smile taunted. "Not if I handle it first."

Renewed tension gripped Crosby's shoulders and he took a step forward. "What the hell does that mean?"

"You already know the answer to that."

Parrish thought to take over? Oh, hell no. "Crow wants *me*. He used Winton to get to *me*. He paid goons to follow me so he could find out where *I* live."

Parrish stiffened with his own measure of determination. "And that puts Silver at risk."

"You think I don't know that? It puts my *daughter* at risk, too, damn you, and *I will handle it*."

"Through your slow legal channels?" Disdain burned in Parrish's eyes. "Before the law catches up to him, Crow could do a lot of damage."

Behind them, the door opened and Madison slipped out. She wore her coat but hadn't zipped it yet. Arms folded around herself, she said, "Boys, your voices are starting to carry. Gary's wondering what's going on."

Crosby didn't budge.

Parrish, being as cool and controlled as Cade, shifted his gaze to Madison. "Everything is fine. Just a small disagreement."

Obviously, she wasn't convinced. She looped her arm through Crosby's. To hold him back? Or to stand at his side against her father? Ha! As if she ever would. He knew only too well how the McKenzies stuck together.

It was probably just her way of inserting herself into the discussion. "It's under control, Madison. You can—"

Tucking in her chin, she eyed him. "I'd strongly advise you *not* to tell me to go back inside."

Even at the worst of times, she wrung a smile out of him. "Wouldn't dream of it. I was going to say you can relax."

"Oh. Well... Perfect." She smiled at each of them. "So what are we doing?"

Parrish said, "Just sorting out the best way to handle things." His gaze flicked to Madison. "Our way, or Crosby's way."

"Oh." Trying for a mild tone that didn't fool Crosby at all, she asked, "And what did we decide?"

"I decided that I'm getting back to work." Crosby knew he should have been on his way already, but his discussion with Parrish had gotten out of control.

"Right." With her attention bouncing back and forth between him and her father, Madison waffled. It was a very unfamiliar reaction for such a take-charge woman. "And tonight?"

"Tonight you two will have dinner." Parrish's smile was a little too tight. "As planned."

"I'll need to check on Winton," Crosby pointed out.

"Leave work early and do that." At his most autocratic, Parrish stated, "But understand that things have already been arranged."

Just what the hell did that mean? "What *things*?"

"Bernard is making fettuccini that he'll deliver here at six. He'll let me know how Winton is feeling."

"You know, you don't have to take over *everything*." But then, knowing Parrish, maybe he did. It came to him naturally.

Much as it did for Crosby.

So why was he being so ungrateful about it? Probably because he sensed that Parrish was up to something.

"I assume you'll have spoken to Winton by then." Parrish

lifted one shoulder, unconcerned with Crosby's ire. Yet his gaze was understanding when he said, "Winton and I got along extremely well, but I'm still a stranger. If he needs anything, I'm sure he'll contact you directly."

"I'll make sure he knows to do that."

"Besides," Parrish continued. "I have plans tonight."

"What plans?" Madison asked with suspicion.

Parrish said, "You and I can speak of it later. As Crosby said, he needs to get to work."

She blew out a breath. "If you two could stop posturing, maybe I could figure out if I still have a dinner date."

For once, Parrish held silent. In fact, after giving Crosby a long look, he went back inside.

Appreciating that, Crosby tipped up her chin and kissed her. "Promise me you'll be careful today."

"I'm always careful."

"Madison…"

She smiled. "I'll be *extra* careful. How's that?"

For her, it was a huge concession. "Thank you."

"I want the same promise from you," she said. "That's fair."

He smoothed a hand down her long silky hair, then lifted a handful to his face, breathing her in, imagining—*wanting*—so many things. "When I'm this close to finally being with you? I guarantee I won't get reckless."

Her beautiful hazel eyes went brighter. "Dinner?" she asked softly.

"At six, as long as nothing else happens. That should give me time to swing by here on my drive home." He kissed her once more. "What do you have on the agenda today?"

"The phone you took off the idiots tailing us will keep me busy for a little while."

He searched her expression, saw something that looked like a touch of guilt and knew there was more. "And?"

She didn't look away. Even when keeping secrets, that wasn't

Madison's style. "I may have an idea of Crow's general location." She raised her voice, overriding his immediate protest. "Nothing final yet. I'm still digging, and until I can nail it down, there's nothing you can do."

"Tell me—"

"Crosby." She touched her fingertips to his mouth. "We both have plenty of obligations today. I'm doing my best to find him, I swear. Can that be good enough for now?"

Seeing her, touching her, went a long way toward blunting the rage that continued to burn inside him. Damn it, he couldn't insist, not when she looked at him like that, with trust and so much more in her golden gaze.

Even tempered by Madison's presence, he knew the rage wasn't going anywhere. It'd be with him until he settled things with Crow, once and for all.

Maybe he wasn't so different from Parrish after all.

But by God, he'd be different in how he treated Madison. "I didn't mean to pressure you."

Relief took the strain from her expression. "Thank you." She gave him a kiss on the mouth, then his jaw and his throat. "Let's go before I get carried away and decide to eat you up in a freezing alley."

Wonder of wonders, he laughed.

And for that reason alone, he knew Madison was the one for him.

Crosby felt sure it was the longest day in history. There'd been glitch after glitch at work, with one guy calling off sick with the flu and another sustaining an injury while sledding with his kids the night before.

In and around sorting that out, and playing catch-up after getting to work late, Crosby had looked up the information from the driver's licenses he'd taken off the punks. So far nothing had popped but he had several leads he'd like to follow.

He'd gotten home with a mere fifteen minutes before Madison was due to arrive, barely enough time to shower, shave and change into casual clothes.

Then to top it off, dinner had seemed to take forever. Both he and Madison were anticipating the evening and were tense because of it. Luckily, thanks to their efforts to stay engaged with Hallie, his daughter hadn't suspected a thing. Madison had even taken the time to color with her while Crosby and Silver did the dishes.

Silver had been the one to call a halt to the evening. She decreed it was time for Hallie's bath so they could settle down for some serious girl time. She'd literally shooed Madison and Crosby on their way—and Hallie had helped. Apparently Silver had chosen a sparkly purple polish for Hallie's toes, and his daughter could barely wait.

In so many ways, Silver was a blessing.

Now, *finally*, he and Madison were alone in his kitchen. Crosby remained just inside the door, watching as she stripped off her boots and then her coat.

She glanced at him. "Is there a reason you're just standing there?"

"Enjoying the moment." His gaze caressed her as he removed his coat and hung it on a hook by the back door. "You are by far the most stunning woman I've ever known. If you want to continue taking things off, go right ahead. I left all the blinds closed this morning."

Her slow smile scorched him. "You want me naked right here in your kitchen?"

"You think there's any way in hell I'd say no?"

Madison laughed. "Well, too bad, because I'm heading to your bedroom. Once we're *both* naked, I want a nice comfy bed nearby." As she spoke, she began walking away.

She also peeled off her sweater.

Rigid with anticipation, Crosby fell into step behind her.

Just watching her walk was a turn-on. She put a little extra sass in her step, swaying her slim hips in a way guaranteed to make him hard. Once she entered the bedroom, she turned to face him and tossed her sweater to a chair. Next, she stripped off her socks and sent them toward the chair, too.

"Keep going."

"I plan to." Holding his gaze, she unsnapped and unzipped those body-hugging jeans, then hooked her thumbs in the denim at each side of her hips to push them down.

Crosby couldn't take his eyes off her. He closed the door and leaned back against it. Now that he knew how things would end, he found his patience—or at least a measure of it—enough that he could enjoy every second of her show.

The tight material bunched at her knees so she sat on the side of his bed and extended her right leg. "A little help?"

She didn't have a shy bone in her body, but in this, she wasn't necessarily bold either. She was just... Madison. Comfortable in all that she did, confident with good reason, open about what she wanted and willing to go after it without reserve.

It was sexy as hell, and again, it freed a part of him that he hadn't known was locked away. He didn't have to worry about moving too fast or too slow because he knew Madison would let him know if he did less or more than she wanted.

The second he clasped her ankle, she leaned back on her elbows and her eyes went heavy. Her hair slipped over her shoulders, leaving her bra-encased breasts on full display.

And what a bra it was. Sheer with edges of lace in a color very close to her skin. Her panties matched, but were a little more opaque, like a teaser for things to come.

When he easily worked the snug denim over her slender foot, Madison lifted a brow. "Had some practice with skinny jeans?"

He wouldn't tell her that his daughter often wore them, but unlike Madison, Hallie didn't help by pointing her toes. Instead, he lowered her leg to the floor—situating it a little wider than before—and accepted her other ankle to repeat the process. The sight of her on his bed, all but bare, her legs parted and her breasts rising and falling with deepened breaths was enough to incinerate him.

Without looking away from her body, he dropped her jeans. One hand on each of her knees, he opened her legs more and stepped forward.

Breathless, Madison said, "Wait. I want to see you, too. Take off your clothes."

He trailed the fingers of both hands up and down her inner thighs. "Let's finish with you first. I think that'll be safer."

"Finish with me?"

Ah, for a take-control woman, she didn't sound all that certain at the moment. He loved it. Loved the idea that he rocked her foundation. Loved that she was different with him.

Loved…everything about her.

Crosby lowered himself over her, mindful that his belt wouldn't abrade the tender skin of her stomach. He cupped a hand to the back of her head and took her mouth in a kiss that went continually deeper, hotter. He wanted her on the ragged edge.

God knew he was already there.

Sliding a hand over her left breast, he fondled her, feeling the heaviness of her flesh, the strain of her stiffened nipple.

The front catch of her bra opened with ease. He brushed the material aside and rasped his palm over her.

Gripping him more tightly, her tongue dueled feverishly with his. She lifted one long leg alongside his hip. He rocked against her twice, three times, heard her groan and knew he had to get a grip. Otherwise, it'd all be over far too soon.

Dragging his mouth from hers, he kissed the warm length of her throat, the silky skin of her shoulder, all while strumming her nipple with his thumb. He nibbled his way down her chest to the sensitive curve of her breast.

Going perfectly still, Madison held her breath while her heart thundered.

She smelled so good he couldn't resist nuzzling his nose against her plump breast, closer and closer to her nipple.

Her breathing raced in excitement.

Feeling her tension grow, Crosby took his time. He knew what she wanted, but he also knew the buildup would maximize her pleasure.

Tunneling her fingers into his hair, she tried to hurry him along.

He smiled against her…and circled her nipple with his tongue.

"Crosby," she rasped in demand.

He closed his mouth over her nipple and gently sucked.

That caused an immediate reaction; she arched her body, her strong legs locking around his hips, her fingers clenching in his hair.

With his free hand, he stroked her other breast, lightly pinched her nipple, tugged and rolled.

"Oh, God."

"Easy." He carefully untangled her fingers and pressed her hands beside her head. Her eyes were half-closed, her lips swollen and damp. "Let me," he whispered. "Let me enjoy you. Let me make you feel good."

*Let me make you mine.*

Her delicate nostrils flared on a deeply indrawn breath. She licked her lips and finally nodded. No questions asked.

"You'll relax?"

"No." As if to anchor herself, her hands gripped the comforter beneath her. "But I'll stay put."

Always so honest. "Good enough." He took her mouth for a brief, hard kiss, testing her, but she only tightened her grip.

He wondered if she might rip the bedding. That'd be interesting.

Moving slightly to her side, Crosby returned to her breasts, licking each nipple, nipping with his teeth, tugging again, and then sucking—until Madison tipped her head back, eyes squeezed shut and hips twisting.

Crosby flattened his hand on her stomach, loving the slight curve of her belly, the toned muscles, the dip of her waist. He drew one nipple deep, sucking strongly at the same time he slid his hand into her miniscule panties.

He thought she was going to come off the bed, her reaction was so strong. He loved that, too, the way she so completely let herself go, no reserve and no holding back.

She was already silky wet, his fingers gliding easily over her heated flesh. When he cupped her in his palm, he felt her pulsing.

His lust burned even hotter. Yet it wasn't only lust. He'd felt that before, and this, with Madison, was as different as a sprinkling rain compared to a tornado.

Taking a soft love bite of her ribs, he pressed one finger into her. As if to keep him right there, her sleek feminine muscles clenched around him.

Moving that single finger in a prelude to sex, he encouraged her. When he felt her trembling, he added a second finger.

They were at the end of the bed, which gave him leverage, until Madison managed to brace one foot on the floor and lifted her hips against him.

He pressed against her, taking her flat again.

"More," she whispered.

Yes, he definitely planned to give her more. A lot more. But first… Taking his fingers from her, he shifted lower, easing off the end of the mattress and stripping away her panties.

With her now completely bare, he positioned himself between her long, open thighs.

She bit her lip, her gaze fixed on the ceiling while she labored for each breath.

Yes, he loved her like this.

Watching her, he lifted her legs over his shoulders and pressed forward. She was wide-open this way, but he wouldn't call her vulnerable. Not his Madison. The lady had more ability than three average men combined.

She was here now, with him, because that's where she wanted to be.

The significance of that wasn't lost on him.

Lightly he blew on her damp flesh and heard the catch in her breath. He traced his fingertips over her, parting her sleek lips, and then pressing back in again. He turned his hand as he withdrew, turning it again as he sank back in. Over and over, he worked her until his fingers were drenched.

Her beautiful neck arched, her nipples flushed and tight.

He watched the movement of his fingers, seeing her sex all pink and wet, and he couldn't wait a second more. He licked over her clitoris, then around his buried fingers, tasting her, breathing her in.

Madison gave a deep, harsh moan, her hands fisted fiercely in the bedding.

Such a perfect reaction. He used his tongue on her again, this time with more finesse, stroking repeatedly over her clitoris, rubbing it, teasing.

Her legs squeezed his shoulders and her scent intensified.

He looked up the length of her tensed body. "I want you to come now."

Breath left her in a vibrating groan. "Yes, please."

With his own heart hammering, Crosby closed his mouth over her, oh-so-gently sucking, working her with his tongue. He kept two fingers buried inside her, curled to reach just the right spot.

She tasted like heaven and he could have eaten her for an hour, but Madison had other plans. Far too soon, she gave a throaty cry, her body convulsing.

He didn't let up, not yet. He stayed with her, keeping her at the peak until she gave a broken sob of completion.

Breathing hard and fast, Crosby untangled her legs from his shoulders and stood over her. She looked boneless—and ready to slide off the end of the bed.

Amazing that he could be rigid with need, and also tenderly amused.

"Let's get you more comfortable."

She murmured something, but he didn't hear what.

Sliding his arms under her, he lifted her up to the top of the bed, then stepped back. Seeing her there looked incredibly right.

He wouldn't mind seeing her like this every morning and every night, maybe for the rest of his life.

She opened drowsy eyes and sighed. "I need a second to recoup."

"Are you sure about that?" He toed off his shoes, stripped away his socks and walked them over to the closet. Her clothes, however, were all over the room.

He turned back to find Madison now propped up on stiffened arms. She nodded at his body. "Go ahead."

"You perked up awfully fast."

"Hello. You're removing clothes. Did you think I'd sleep through it?"

Her current pose, hands braced behind her, one leg bent, kept his cock throbbing.

"Well?" she said. "Go on."

"You're so good at stripping off clothes, why don't you do it for me?"

The challenge put a sparkle in her eyes and slowly curved her lush mouth with an eager smile. "Oh, I'd like that. Good idea."

God. Crosby wondered if he'd just made a tactical error.

# CHAPTER FIFTEEN

Crosby didn't move as Madison sat on the side of the bed, looking at him with decisive intent. Her gaze traveled all over him in a heated sweep, lingering on his shoulders and chest, then his thighs, and finally on the fly of his jeans.

His brain told him to keep it together, but his dick wasn't listening.

When she stood and came toward him, all lethal grace and sensual promise, he knew it was going to be a rush to the finish line. Hell, he'd known it all along, which was why he'd wanted to ensure her pleasure first. All the waiting, the buildup and the uniqueness that was Madison, obliterated any claim he had on control.

Without a word her hands pressed to his chest, coasted up and over his shoulders, feeling him, exploring. Then, fingers spread, she brought them down his sides and to his abdomen. "You stay in incredible shape."

Nope, he couldn't carry on a casual conversation with her while she did this. It was her way of taking control, and sure, she could have a turn at that.

Next time.

"You don't need to tease, Madison. You know I'm on the ragged edge. Either you want my clothes off or you don't."

"I do." Those soft hands went under the hem of his shirt, molded to the oblique muscles along his sides and then moved over his lust-tightened abdomen. She trailed them back up again, pushing his shirt to his shoulders. "Raise your arms."

Not a problem. He lifted them, and also bent forward a bit to make it easier on her.

She went on tiptoe to pull the shirt off over his head. Holding it to her bare breasts, she asked, "Do I have to hang it in the closet?"

Like he gave a shit about his shirt right now? As an answer, he took it from her and pitched it across the room.

Smiling, she kissed his throat, her sharp little teeth grazing his skin as she opened her hands over his pecs. "I've wanted to touch you like this from the day I met you. And after seeing you in swim trunks? I go to sleep every night thinking about your very fine body—against *my* body."

"You're not alone in that, babe." He tangled a hand in her hair and tugged, lifting her face. "I think about you all the damn time." Even when he shouldn't.

"Good," she whispered, at the same time that she opened his belt.

Their gazes held.

The hiss of his zipper being drawn down ratcheted up his tension—and then her hand was there, reaching into his boxers and closing around his cock.

Crosby concentrated on breathing.

She squeezed and he locked his jaw.

She stroked from the base up to the head and oxygen left his lungs.

"I was going to tease," she said. "After all, turnabout is fair play and all that. But I don't think I can. Now that I'm touching you, I want you, all of you this time, right now." Her hands slid over his ass, shoving down his pants and boxers until they were low enough for him to kick free. She stepped back to look at him, her attention locked on his erection.

Knowing his own limits, Crosby caught her shoulders and turned her. "In the bed, babe." He went to the closet and got out the new box of condoms he'd picked up.

Madison quickly yanked away the spread from his bed before hustling into the middle of the mattress. She flipped back her hair, hugged his pillow and waited.

Madison McKenzie, naked in his bed, waiting for him.

Didn't get much better than that.

Crosby ripped open a condom packet and rolled it on in record time. He'd gotten only one knee on the mattress and Madison was already kissing him, pulling him down to her in a heated rush.

It was all a frenzy from there. Mouths fusing together, hands touching everywhere, tongues exploring and bodies pressing. He stopped trying to think of control, and he was pretty sure Madison did, too.

They moved on instinct, guided by need. And maybe something more.

Madison straddled him. He caught her waist and turned so she was under him, her legs already around his hips. She didn't seem to mind, not with the way she kept kissing his chest and his shoulders.

Reaching between them, he opened her, positioned himself and sank in.

He felt her teeth on his shoulder, her heels pressing into the small of his back.

Breathing hard, he asked, "Okay?"

She held him too tightly for him to see her face, but she nodded.

Shifting, he went deeper.

She gasped, and then tilted up to take even more of him.

They fell into a steadily building rhythm of advance and retreat, each thrust harder, faster until Crosby felt the surge of release.

Thankfully, seconds before he lost it, she cried out with a second powerful climax that bowed her entire body and squeezed his cock tight in a rush of wet heat.

Yeah, if he hadn't already been on the verge of coming, that would have done it. He pressed his face to her neck and let himself go.

A few hours and a third orgasm later, Madison felt vindicated. She'd known all along just how it would be with Crosby. Now at least he understood why she hadn't given up on him, even when he'd turned her away.

Getting her liquefied muscles to move, she shifted from her sprawled position on her back to her side so she could see him. Eyes closed, sandy hair badly mussed, gorgeous bod on full display, Crosby looked down for the count.

"Are you asleep?" she whispered.

"Probably dead," he replied. When she laughed, he cocked one eye open to see her. "Hey. You're too far away."

"Mmm." She snuggled closer, loving the way his arm went around her, how she fit so perfectly against him. "You have to be exhausted." God knew he'd had a trying day that had started far too early.

His chest hair drew her, so she lightly stroked her palm over him. Crosby had a stellar chest with well-defined pecs framed by wide, hard shoulders. His biceps were a thing of beauty. And his flat abs...

He kissed the top of her head. "Why would I be exhausted but you wouldn't?"

"You started running before sunup and haven't had a chance to slow down. Plus, I know from experience that worrying about someone you love can take it out of you." She worried about her brothers and father all the time, but she couldn't tell them so. They'd take it as an insult to their expertise.

Now there was Crosby, too. She loved him so much, everything about him—including the way he made love and how wild he made her feel. She knew he'd be added to her reasons for worry, especially with Crow out there, trying to cause trouble.

"It was a busy day," Crosby agreed. "But Winton will be okay, and with your dad's help, he'll be safe." He was quiet a moment, then he tugged her up and over him, both of his arms loosely wound around her waist. "What are you thinking?"

"That being with you was every bit as awesome as I expected." Because *he* was awesome.

Lazily, he trailed his fingertips up and down her spine. "You weren't wrong." His fingers continued on until he cupped one cheek of her behind. "You blow my mind, Madison. You always have. Before meeting you, I couldn't have imagined getting involved with anyone. Between raising Hallie, my unconventional setup with Silver and work, there never seemed to be enough time to date, much less have a relationship."

She hugged him. "I'm very, very glad you made time for me."

"I've never discussed my arrangements with anyone. People see Silver and they tend to misunderstand, but you didn't."

She reared back to see him. "You're not the type of man who would take advantage of a woman."

His smile was slow and smug. "I like how you always assume the best of me."

"No assumption. You're an incredible man. I didn't have to know you long to see it. Dad, Cade and Reyes see it, too."

"Your dad," he said, "has the hots for Silver. That could slant his view."

Sharing his grin, Madison hugged him again. "It's true, but that has nothing to do with his opinion of you. Like me, Dad is a great judge of character."

Dismissing that, Crosby glanced at the clock. "What do you have planned tomorrow?"

Inwardly, Madison grimaced. She knew she had to tell him, but she didn't want to give up the cozy afterglow of sex just yet. To buy herself some time, she said, "You first."

His big hand continued to cuddle her backside, his thumb sweeping lazy circles over her skin. "Let's see. First I'll check on Winton in the morning, make sure Owen is holding up okay."

Folding her arms on his chest and looking into his dark eyes was something she wanted to do for the rest of her life. With Crosby, she felt entirely connected. Could he possibly feel the same? "And after that?"

His gaze held hers. "I plan to start digging for more info on Crow."

Uh-oh. Her thoughts scrambled over several scenarios, none of them good. "How, exactly, do you plan to do that?"

"I spent years as a cop, babe. I have my ways."

She didn't doubt it, but the vagueness of his answer left open too many possibilities. They should be sharing information and plans... Yet she hadn't. Crosby was astute enough to pick up on that. Was that causing him to hold back, too? If so, she had no one but herself to blame.

Tentatively, trying to ease into things, she said, "You know, it could be risky if our efforts...overlapped." Or worse, if he and her family went snooping in the same place. "You wouldn't want to give us away, and vice versa."

"I'll be careful not to tip my hand." As if waiting for something, he continued to study her. "I know you will, too."

He appeared so watchful, she accepted that her time was up.

Frustration warred with dread. She'd wanted tonight to cement her relationship with him, and instead she felt cornered. Well, she never ducked trouble. As a McKenzie, she faced it head-on.

On a sigh, she said, "Please don't be mad."

This time his smile didn't reach his eyes. "Going to tell me you were disappointed?" His fingertips glided over her hair, gently tucking it behind her ear.

"Don't be dumb, Crosby. Of course I wasn't." And he knew it, which meant he also knew she was hiding something. That would explain his restrained air.

"Then explain to me why I'd be mad." His hand dropped to her shoulder and his gaze held hers.

She drew in a deep, bracing breath. "Remember I told you I had a general idea of where to find Crow? I spotted him on one of the traffic cams so I was able to narrow it down."

Though he didn't move, his expression changed. Gone was the warmth. Even the intimacy seemed to have faded.

Madison forged on anyway. "Tomorrow morning, we—my family and I—are going to scope out the area and see if we can pinpoint his exact location."

He was so still, he could have been carved from stone. His ebony eyes narrowed and a muscle ticked in his jaw. "When was that decision made?"

"Last night." Seeing the bloom of his ire, she hurried to finish her explanation. "We would have checked the location this morning, but there were road crews working nearby and that made it dicey. I'd planned to put it off, then everything happened with Winton and—"

"Fuck," he muttered low, clasping both her shoulders to shift her to the side.

*Because he wanted to leave her.*

"I'm sorry!" Madison wrapped herself around him, making it impossible for him to leave the bed without hurting her, which she knew he'd never do.

He stilled again, his body utterly rigid. "Let. Go."

"No." She squeezed tighter and though she might be slim, she wasn't a weakling. "I don't want you to let go either."

"What the hell is that supposed to mean?" And then in the

next breath, "How could you keep that from me?" He dropped his head back. "You know he's threatening my family. You know *my daughter* could be in danger, yet you didn't see fit to share?" His laugh held no humor. "Great fucking partnership we have."

As awful as those words were, she welcomed them. She'd much rather he rage at her than walk away. "I'm stuck, damn it!" When her voice shook, it infuriated her. She never, ever showed such a weakness. "You think I wanted to be in the middle between you and my dad? Well, I *don't*." With her knees on either side of his hips, she sat up on his abs and scowled at him. "The McKenzies have their own way of doing things."

Crosby remained coldly furious, yet his tone sounded moderate when he said, "Your way includes lying to me? Cutting me out?"

"That wasn't my idea."

"But you went along with it," he accused.

"Hello." Throwing out her arms, she said, "I'm here right now, trying to explain." And once he knew, her dad would be pissed.

"Yeah, I notice you waited until after you got what you wanted."

Oh, now that infuriated her. "If you mean you, yes, I wanted you. I've been ridiculously obvious, right?"

Crosby ran a hand over his face. "So what now? Does Parrish plan to make Crow disappear?" His brows gathered together. "Would that have been kept from me, too?"

Even knowing he spoke from anger, she snapped, "You see? It's that attitude that made Dad cautious."

"Parrish put *me* in charge of dealing with Crow."

"Before he knew it was Crow. Before he knew it was personal. When he thought he was the only target." She softened her tone, desperate for him to understand. "Everything is different now."

His gaze cut over her. "Yeah, it is." Again, he tried to lever her away.

She braced her hands on his shoulders, resisting. "Dad is just concerned that you'll try to do things by the book and then Crow could get away."

"Right." He glared at her with bitterness. "Because I'm so fucking inept, I couldn't manage to nail the bastard." His jaw flexed. "You only told me now because you don't want me getting in your way. How did you put it? You don't want me overlapping your operation, maybe giving you away."

Damn him, why did he have to be so stubborn? "I didn't mean that exactly."

"Don't worry, Madison." With a lot of derision, he said, "I understand how the McKenzies operate."

That made *her* even madder. "Like hell you do! You've studied us, and judged us, but damn you, Crosby, you haven't been there!" Resentment churned, not all of it aimed at him, and acknowledging that brought her voice lower, to an agonized whisper. "You haven't witnessed anything firsthand."

Catching her shoulders, Crosby turned and pressed her to her back.

Since she was tired of fighting already, she let him.

Holding her like that, partially pinned beneath him, his gaze moved over her face, scrutinizing her. Whatever he saw, it softened his frown.

"No," she strangled. "Don't you dare go all sweet and understanding just because I'm..."

"Because you're what?" He cupped the side of her face. "Human?"

"Female!"

As if that took care of the last of his anger, his mouth twitched. "News flash, babe. I've known you were female for a while now."

"You know what I mean. Just because I'm a woman, you think I'm...overwhelmed by stuff or something."

"Everyone gets overwhelmed sometimes, men and women alike."

Not in her family.

"There's no reason for you to be so frustrated."

Frustration was only part of what she felt. "Fine. Then admit you wanted me too."

"That can't be in question."

"You brought it up, accusing me of waiting until I got what I wanted, but—"

"I'm sorry." Now with both hands, he framed her face. "You threw me for a loop."

"I know. I'm sorry, too."

Accepting that with a nod, he said, "So tell me. Have the McKenzies already made up their minds to murder Crow?"

"*What?* No!" She shoved against him, he didn't budge and naturally she didn't want to hurt him either.

Honestly, it relieved her to know she couldn't storm away.

Disgruntled, she grumbled, "Clearly, you don't know as much about us as you think you do."

"Ditto." He searched her eyes. "You can always share with me."

That didn't exactly sound like he planned to end things. Hopeful, she nodded. "Okay, fine." If he could be so blasé about her excess of emotion, she could, too.

After watching her a second more, he sat up at the side of the bed and braced his hands on his knees.

Madison stared at his back, at the deep furrow of his spine and the muscles over his shoulders and ribs.

*Mine.*

Crosby could bluster and grouse and he could get as mad as he wanted, but the truth remained. He was hers and she wasn't about to let him go.

Trying to be inconspicuous, she took a few deep breaths and considered what she should say next.

"I have the driver's licenses of the punks who followed me

to Winton's store." Crosby didn't look at her as he spoke. "I'll start with that."

"What?" He'd thrown that out there so casually, she couldn't quite process it. Could that be his idea of an olive branch?

He didn't repeat himself, saying instead, "One of them mentioned a guy with a unique name. I know enough snitches off the street that I should be able to figure out who that is."

Gasping, she levered up to her elbows. "You didn't tell me any of this!"

He glanced back at her—then all over her. "Guess we were both holding back."

That look about did her in. Yes, he was still angry, but the ice had left his expression. Softer, she whispered, "I wanted to tell you everything. Dad is…cautious. This has become personal for him, and he wants, maybe needs, to ensure that Crow won't pose a future problem." When Crosby said nothing, she added, "I think he wanted to tell you. In fact, I'm pretty sure he would have." Eventually.

Frustration emanated from him…then he ran a hand through his hair. "Fuck," he said again, this time without the edge of anger.

"I know." She really did. *Please don't let this become a problem for us.*

Taking her by surprise, Crosby turned and stretched out beside her, his head propped on his hand. "I don't want there to be secrets between us."

"I don't either. It's just…it wasn't my decision."

He pressed a finger to her lips to silence her. "I get it. Your family is doing their own thing. I see now how that could be a problem for you."

*Hmm.* He was suddenly so understanding she wasn't sure where this was going. "I didn't want to be in the middle, but—"

He shook his head. "The thing is, it's a two-way street. If you don't confide in me, I can't confide in you."

*No.* She knew something like this was bound to happen, but it'd be a backward step when she only wanted to move forward with Crosby. "I've been thinking about a lot things."

"I assumed." His fingertip traced around her lips, leaving them tingling. "I doubt that sexy brain of yours gets much rest."

Sexy brain? Wow, what a nice compliment. It signified respect, right? At least that's how she took it. It warmed her and gave her hope that they might be able to work through the difficulties.

Madison cleared her throat. "Well, my sexy brain wanted tonight with you—you were right about that. I figured if I'd told you sooner, it might have soured things—"

Amused, indulgent, he murmured, "And you wouldn't have had those three big Os."

Her smile twitched. "Well, there is that." Needing to touch him, she scooted closer. She couldn't keep her gaze off his body. They were both still naked, and they still had time before she'd have to head home. "It's not just that, though. This was a big step for us. I hope a step in the right direction?"

"I think so."

He *thought* so? She frowned. When she said, "I want more nights like this," it came out sounding like an order.

"Same."

Madison pushed him to his back and straddled him again. "You're killing me with these too-simple answers."

Holding her waist, he asked, "What type of answer do you want?"

"The truth!"

"Fine." He pulled her down to kiss her hard. "Playing second fiddle to your family is never going to work for me, not for the long haul. I know myself and I understand my own shortcomings. I'm not a man who could accept secrets, regardless of the reason."

Her heart skipped several beats.

Crosby kissed her again. "For now, it's fine. Period of adjustment and all that. But if this is going to last—"

"I want it to," she whispered. *I want that so much.*

"—then you need to trust me, all the time, every time, whether Parrish does or not." All too seriously, his intense, dark gaze scrutinized her. "If you can't do that, I'll need to rethink things."

It took her only a second to realize he was right. She was an equal partner with her brothers, and that meant she had to stand up for what she believed and what she wanted. Namely, Crosby. "I do trust you. Completely."

His fierce expression eased. "I trust you, too. Just as much."

Madison knew what she had to do, but she'd need to do it her own way. "Tomorrow…"

"It's okay, babe. I meant it when I said I understand. We both have to figure out a few things."

Her eyes flared. What did *he* have to figure out? "Crosby—"

"Tomorrow, you do your thing, I'll do mine and we'll talk early evening. Okay?"

No, it wasn't okay. He'd be out there, exposed to Crow and his ilk, and she wouldn't be there to cover him. He needed her. He needed her whole family.

"It's getting late." He cupped her breast and bent to nibble on her throat. "Let's make the most of the time we have left."

They'd have their whole lives left, if she had anything to say about it, but yes, with his mouth teasing her sensitive skin, his warm hand already busy on her breast, she decided she could make her points tomorrow.

Tonight was for this. Tonight was for *them.*

Tomorrow she'd work out the rest.

Madison grumbled as they pulled into the motel lot. Already the morning had gotten away from her, and going another night without enough sleep made her cranky.

Then she'd think of Crosby and all the amazing ways he made her feel and she'd almost smile.

She held that back, though, because all the McKenzie men were giving her looks, as if they knew what she'd done last night and weren't sure how they felt about it.

Well, too bad for them. She knew how she felt, and it was so spectacular she wanted to embrace it forever.

A life with Crosby.

*I deserve that, don't I?*

"She's checked out again," Cade muttered.

Reyes, who was driving, glanced at her in the rearview mirror. "Makes me want to go pound on Crosby."

Cade snorted. "You're the one who told her to go for it."

"Yeah, well, saying it and seeing it are two different things."

Madison kicked the back of his seat. "You didn't *see* anything, you ass."

"Please don't abuse my car," Parrish murmured beside her as he peered through the tinted windows at the beige stucco structure. It was one long line of window-door combinations, each unit separated by a skinny, apple green wrought iron trellis that matched the color of the gutters. An office entry sheltered by a torn canopy marked the middle of the line. A brown shingled roof and salt-covered walkway finished the ramshackle look. "This is it," he said. "I know it."

"You sense it," Cade corrected. "Not at all the same thing."

Reyes chimed in with, "You're too personally involved, Dad. It's why you should have sat this one out."

"It's because I'm involved that I'm here."

Playing mediator, Madison said, "I wish I could have gotten some good intel off the cell phone Crosby gave me." She'd looked through texts for drug deals, hookups and friendly banter. Nothing that indicted Crow. The calls, both sent and received, were short, all but for a few calls from Crow. The number Crow had used hadn't led her anywhere at all.

"We'll know more once we check out the place," Cade said.

Madison balanced her laptop on her knees, already missing Crosby and wondering what he might be doing. "Sucks that they don't seem to have security cameras. Even the biggest dives have them now." She could have looked for Crow in the feeds.

Reyes nodded at the glass office doors, opaque with built-up condensation between the panes. A dismantled camera hung overhead. "Used to have them," he said. "Maybe someone wanted them turned off."

"Crow," she whispered. Yes, that'd make sense. When you spent your time making bomb threats at popular hotels and shooting at wealthy businessmen on public roads, you wouldn't want video proof of your whereabouts.

"I'm more laid-back than Cade," Reyes announced. "I'll go inside and see what I can find out."

"Be careful," Madison warned automatically and got a look from both brothers.

Her father seemed intent on staring at the building.

Fifteen minutes later, Reyes returned. "Unfortunately, the desk manager is skittish as shit. He claimed he didn't know Crow, hasn't seen anyone matching the description, and if I'd pressed him, I swear, he might've pissed himself."

"Huh." Madison typed away on the laptop.

"What is it?" Cade asked. "You get something?"

"Yup. I have access to the computer files. Just found the registry and… Bingo. What do you want to bet John Smith, who checked in three weeks ago, is actually Burgess Crow? We can verify by going to room number ten."

Cade frowned. "I only see eight units, four on each side of the manager's office."

"Probably around back, too, right?" She bent to see out her father's window. "The parking lot wraps around, so it makes sense there would be rooms back there, too. Not like they'd need all that parking space for only eight rooms."

"Drive off," Parrish said. "We'll park a short distance away and walk back in."

Madison lifted her brows. "You want to go in number ten right now?"

No one answered at first. Cade and Reyes seemed to be as alert as she felt. It wasn't like her dad to rush a setup. He was a detail person, wanting everything arranged in advance... That is, unless someone was in imminent danger.

"Dad?" Her worry for Crosby mushroomed fast.

He turned to her. "Change of plans. We'll take you back to your car first."

"No, I—"

"I want you to go to Silver. Stay with her and Hallie until we wrap this up."

His alarm became her own. "If you're that concerned, I need to tell Crosby." She'd be firm on this. With or without her dad's agreement, she would keep Crosby apprised of everything.

He surprised her by saying, "I agree. You can call him on your way, but we need to go now."

As Reyes backed out of the space, Cade turned to look over the seat at Parrish. "What do you know that you're not telling us?"

He drew a deep breath. "Nothing. No facts of any kind. It's just a feeling. My instincts are screaming that something is off. It's been that way since I woke this morning, but the feeling is getting stronger."

"I should have stayed behind," Cade said. "I could be in his room right now, finding a clue."

"Or it could be booby-trapped," Reyes reminded him. It was a situation he'd once run into himself.

"Like you, I'd have scoped it out first, checked through windows and figured out what I was dealing with."

"I don't want either of you alone," Parrish said. "You'll go into the room together and I'll wait in the car so I can keep watch for any trouble."

Tension showed in the set of his shoulders, the angle of his jaw. Madison reached over to touch his forearm. "Dad, what if Silver isn't home?"

"She is. I spoke with her before we left."

Her eyes flared. "You told her what we were doing?" *And she wasn't supposed to tell Crosby?*

"No, we just…chatted. She mentioned that they'd be staying home today so I saw no reason to frighten her."

Madison wondered how Silver would feel about that once she knew. "I see."

"The house is as safe as we could make it," Cade pointed out. "The monitor will alert her to anyone approaching from any angle."

"She's smart," Reyes added. "She won't take chances."

But they all knew you couldn't be sufficiently careful when someone was patient enough. One mistake, one moment of inattention and disaster could strike.

Madison didn't say anything else. Instead, she concentrated on what she'd do—like confess to Crosby that she loved him and explain to her family that he was now a part of things, or she wouldn't be.

And if it came down to it, she'd protect Silver and Hallie with her life.

Finding Brick was easier than Crosby had expected. Hopefully he could wrap this up, get the answers he needed and return back home to Hallie. She wasn't used to him taking off on Saturdays anymore.

Before coming here, he'd stopped by to see Winton. The bruising was really bad today, and Winton moved like an eighty-year-old instead of a man of fifty, but he was in good spirits.

He hadn't yet navigated the stairs, but between Owen and

Gary, he'd had plenty of company, and he'd especially loved his time with Bernard last night.

"He's downright entertaining," Winton had said. "Made me laugh a few times, then apologized all over himself for it when I winced. I swear, that made me laugh even more."

Winton had praised the food, too, and Bernard had promised to visit again.

There were things about Madison's family that Crosby might never be able to accept, but there was so much good, too. Such caring and generosity convinced him that he was getting the better end of the deal.

What would Madison get? Just him—and his daughter. His wonderful mix of family.

His loyalty for life.

By God, he'd stop pointing out the ways he disagreed with her family's methods and start concentrating on all the remarkable things they did for society instead.

And that made, what? The hundredth time his mind had wandered to Madison? She entered his thoughts every other minute.

Parked at the curb in front of the apartment building, Crosby gave it a quick survey. A great many people knew Brick's reputation, and several people he'd talked to had met the man, but few knew where to find him. No wonder, since he lived in a different part of town, in a nicer neighborhood than where he did business.

Crosby had used his own way of ferreting out information via street snitches to track Brick to this address. At first he hadn't had any luck, but all scumbags had their friends, and Crosby had finally uncovered the information he needed from a dealer.

Dressed in one of his oldest sweatshirts with jeans so faded he hadn't worn them in two years, he did his best to look like the *opposite* of a cop. After silencing his phone, he pulled his knit hat down to cover his ears. His coat concealed the Glock in the holster at his side. Given Brick's lifestyle, he might get shot on sight if anyone mistook him for the law.

Now would have been a good time to have Cade or Reyes at his back, but he'd kept them out of the loop. Parrish had already put Madison in the middle. Crosby didn't want to do the same. They'd work out their issues together, and hopefully both of them would learn to give ground.

Once inside the building, he paused to listen, to let his senses grow alert to any misgivings. Something was off, but he wasn't yet sure what it might be.

Going up the stairs to the second floor, he continued to glance around. When he reached Brick's apartment, he withdrew his gun but kept it at his side and knocked.

A muffled, "Who the fuck is it?" came through the door.

Remembering the dealer, Crosby said, "A message from Wayne."

Locks clicked open, a chain dropped and a rheumy-eyed dude with a greasy man bun peered out. Startled, he stared at Crosby, slack-jawed, before finally sputtering, "What?"

Sour breath made Crosby want to step back, and only sheer force of will kept him close enough to block the door if Brick tried to close it. "Wayne said you owe him."

He blinked, nervously looked past Crosby, then shook his head. "The fuck I do. I pay when he delivers."

*I bet you do, because Wayne would have already sliced out your liver.* Why was Brick so nervous? A bead of sweat trickled down his temple and he started breathing a little faster.

Rolling a shoulder as if it didn't matter to him, Crosby leaned against the door frame. It gave him a better view inside, but he didn't see anyone else. "Says you shorted him a ten-spot."

Indecision held Brick in place for a moment, then he grumbled, "Fine, whatever." He licked his lips. "Wait here." He started to close the door.

Crosby put his foot in the way. "Planning to slip out some-how?"

"What?" Brick's laugh was a pitch too high to be natural. "You think I'd risk my neck going out a window over ten bucks?"

Resolute, Crosby held his gaze. Alarm bells were clanging, impossible to ignore. He needed in the apartment now, before it was too late.

"Fine. Suit yourself." Brick left the door ajar and backed away a few feet before turning and hurrying his pace.

Crosby watched as he went through the cluttered living room and down a hallway. A quick glance behind him verified he was still alone. He stepped inside and silently secured the door.

Brick was hiding something. Crosby needed to know what.

The apartment was a mess with dishes on most surfaces, clothes draping furniture, and there on a desk, an open computer.

His heart stalled when he saw an image of his own house on the screen. *Brick knows who I am, and he knows where I live.*

*Who else has he told?*

Gun drawn, Crosby called out, "Brick?"

No answer, but he heard a door close and then the sound of it being locked.

Son of a bitch! The idiot was really going to try a window.

Using care, Crosby went down the hall, taking a quick peek in the bathroom and the hall linen closet. He found both empty. He could see into the kitchen and there was no place to hide in the room he'd just left.

If Brick got away, he'd lose his chance for answers.

It took one good kick and the locked door gave way. There across the room, Brick was trying to squeeze his alcohol-bloated body through a too-small window.

Crosby cleared the room in a glance, saw no one else and reached Brick with three long strides. Grabbing his shoulder, he brutally yanked him back. Flailing, Brick crashed onto the floor. A .38 special fell from his waistband.

After kicking the gun across the room, Crosby holstered his weapon, jerked Brick up by his shirtfront and slammed a fist into his jaw. He was so angry that he hit him two more times just to make sure he had his attention. When he released him, Brick collapsed to the floor.

The man who was feared by many now looked dazed and afraid.

Aiming his Glock, Crosby growled, "Who else was here?"

"No one." He spit blood to the side and started to sit up. "I swear."

Crosby kicked him in the chest, sending him sprawling again.

"Motherfucker!" Hand flat to his sternum, Brick struggled for air.

Crosby aimed at his knee. "Answer me before I shoot out your kneecap. If that doesn't work, I'll keep shooting and we'll go from there."

Grimacing with every move, Brick rose to his elbow. "No one is here…now."

"Who *was* here?"

He swiped messy hair away from his face. His bun was now more loose than contained. "Look, I didn't want to tell him, okay? I don't even like the little prick. He blackmails everyone."

"*Who?*"

"Burgess Crow."

A red haze of fury clouded Crosby's eyes. Through clenched teeth, he growled, "Crow was here?"

"He hates you, man," Brick said with a grisly smile, blood framing each of his yellowed teeth. "I gave him your name when he said I had to, but I didn't tell him anything else. I don't fuck with cops—or even ex-cops. But then Crow showed up here today and he threatened me. Not like you're doing. Hell, I could wipe the floor with him."

"He has something else on you? He blackmailed you?"

Brick shrugged. "I'm not keen on going to prison, so I gave him what he needed."

"My home address?"

"It came down to me or you. I chose me."

"When was this?" The urge to shoot Brick was strong. "When did he leave here?"

"It's probably been an hour or more now."

Dear God. Crosby didn't even think it through, he just sent his foot into Brick's face, sending two teeth flying. Brick went down without a sound.

In that moment, Crosby didn't care if the fucker lived or died, but if he came to, he didn't want him reaching out to Crow. Jerking a power cord from the wall by the bed, Crosby tied Brick's hands behind him. Rushing, he jerked open the closet to find something to bind his feet, and found a nightmare of bondage devices.

Sick fuck. Grabbing a whip, he used it to hog-tie Brick, securing his bound hands and feet to the bed frame. The prick wouldn't be going anywhere anytime soon.

Crosby rushed from the room, snagging the laptop on his way.

Outside, he did a quick look around, saw it appeared clear and jogged to his SUV. Tossing the laptop on the passenger seat, he sped away.

While driving, he pulled out his silenced phone and saw two missed calls from Madison. *Shit.*

His return calls went unanswered.

Reaching out to the cops was the logical answer, but with no time to think, he instead went with his gut.

He called Parrish.

# CHAPTER SIXTEEN

*Damn it, Crosby, why don't you answer?* An anomalous sense of panic had a death grip on Madison as she drew nearer to Crosby's home. She wouldn't rest easy until she ensured Hallie and Silver were safely locked inside, and until she laid eyes on Crosby and her family.

Was this what love did to people? Made them fretful about everything, sending thoughts of worst-case scenarios to plague their brains? She hated it.

But she loved Crosby, so she supposed she'd have to get used to it.

As soon as she saw Silver and Hallie building an igloo in the front yard, she let out a breath. One worry down, only a gazillion more to go.

Silver shaded her eyes against the sunlight reflecting off the snow. When she realized it was Madison, she said something to Hallie and the little girl cheered.

Emotions danced over her heart, making it pump faster. Yup, she loved Hallie, too. And Silver, the woman who'd apparently snagged her dad's heart. How could she not love Silver?

She pulled into the driveway and stopped near the garage.

Madison hated to spoil their fun, but she needed them inside, behind locked doors, before she could let down her guard.

The second she reached the yard, Hallie started talking a mile a minute in her high-pitched voice about what they were doing and how much fun it was. Despite her worries, Madison laughed and lifted the little girl for a long hug.

"We weren't expecting you," Silver said without accusation as she dusted snow off her gloves.

"I know and I'm sorry. Dad sent me."

Silver tucked in her chin. "What do you mean, Parrish sent you? Why?"

Hallie bounced in her arms. "You can help us with our igloo. It has to be big enough for Dad!"

How precious. Even now, Hallie was thinking of Crosby. "It's a fine igloo, and I'd say it's already big enough."

Hallie laughed. "Huh-uh. Dad is really big, almost as big as Kenzie. Grandma says Kenzie might get in the igloo with us, too. It's got to be bigger."

Silver gave a sheepish grin. "Parrish would do whatever Hallie asked. Guess I couldn't resist the idea of him crawling in the snow."

"I'm sure he'd love it." When Hallie wiggled to get down, Madison set her on her feet, but kept hold of her hand.

She *really* hated to spoil things, but with a quick look at Silver, Madison said, "Why don't we go inside for hot chocolate first?"

"But we're almost done," Hallie complained.

Picking up on Madison's unease, Silver nervously scanned the area. "I've kept the phone on me." She lifted it from her pocket to show that the security app was open on the screen. "The only alert was when you got close."

"I'm glad you're being so careful." Madison didn't want to scare either of them; she just wanted to get them inside. To accomplish that, she started for the walkway.

Insistent on getting her way, Hallie pulled in the opposite direction.

Silver's now-anxious gaze darted everywhere. And suddenly the phone in her hand emitted a series of beeps. She froze.

Quickly, Madison pulled Silver forward. She'd drag them both if she had to—but no, they were already out of time.

There across the street, still a good distance away, Crow stepped out from behind the trees.

He had a gun aimed at them as he came forward. "This is perfect," he called out, his attention on Madison. "I had no idea my luck was finally turning, yet here you are, with—I presume—Albertson's family? Lovely. Just lovely." He spoke congenially while threatening with the gun. His tone didn't even change when he smiled and said, "Move, and I'll kill you all."

Those worst-case scenarios were now going berserk in her brain. *Did I lead him here?*

She'd been extremely cautious, but how else would he have found them?

The panic surged…until she ruthlessly suppressed it.

Crow was here—that's what mattered. She couldn't, wouldn't, let him hurt Hallie or Silver.

So she did the only thing she could think of.

She stepped in front of them, saying low to Silver, "Hold on to Hallie and stay behind me. If you get a chance, run for the back door." If she tried for the front, she'd be too much of a target. "Do you understand?"

"Yes." Face pale, Silver tucked Hallie behind her.

Crow, the miserable bastard, grinned. "Ah, the little warrior, still offering protection. You're good, bitch, I'll give you that."

Madison said nothing. She just stared at him. The alert from the system had already gone out to Crosby, her father and brothers. Not the police, because they'd never gotten around to working that out with Crosby.

Now she sort of wished they had. A cruiser would probably

get to them faster. That is, unless Crosby was already aware of the situation?

But he hadn't answered her calls, and... Dear God, *what if Crow had hurt him?*

He mistook her sudden intake of breath. "Yes," he said gleefully. "I heard all about your antics at that quaint store. You helped the cop fend off three men, isn't that right?"

If he kept talking, that would help buy her time. "Tell me, Crow, are you the cowardly dick who blindsided Winton?" She wouldn't ask about Crosby. At the moment, she wasn't sure she could handle the answer and she couldn't afford any distractions. "If so, I might have to dismantle you."

Laughing, he moved the barrel of his gun slightly, as if visually circling her heart. "I heard you were impressive, but you can't dodge a bullet, now, can you?"

Very true. And once he shot her, what would happen to Silver and Hallie? She couldn't think about that either. She needed Crow to get closer so she'd at least have a fighting chance. Cocking out a hip, she smirked at him. "Shoot that gun out here and cops will be on their way."

He pretended to consider that. "Pop." He went on tiptoe, as if that allowed him to see Silver and Hallie. "Pop, pop." With a shrug, he said, "Done, and I'm out of here. What a surprise that would be for the cop."

Whatever it took, she'd keep that from happening. "You actually think you'd get away?"

"Of course."

"My father would never stop until he found you. Do you know what he does to men like you, Crow? It's not nice. He has a...particular *dislike* for your ilk." She took a cautious but casual step forward. "He would enjoy your suffering."

"Shut up." His grin long gone, Crow stomped forward two steps. Madison came forward again, too, willing to meet him, but he halted, blinking fast over her audacity. "Don't move."

Knowing he wouldn't like it, she smirked again. "Afraid of me? That's amusing." With any luck, Crosby and her family had already seen the feed and were on their way. Maybe they were already here.

His lips quivered and his breathing labored. "You can't goad me into giving up the advantage!"

Wow, he'd lost his nerve fast. That could be a good thing, but might also make him reckless enough to just start shooting.

Keeping her gaze locked on Crow, she turned her head slightly to whisper to Silver, "You need to start backing away, very slowly, toward my car. Use it as cover when you run to the back."

"Shut up!" Crow yelled. "No talking or I'll shoot you right now."

"Will you?" she asked, mocking him. "And then what?" As if she pitied him, she shook her head. "Escape for you is already impossible."

"*Bullshit.*"

"Backup is here, Crow. You feel it, don't you? My father, my brothers, Crosby—one of them already has you in his sights. You're dead meat."

He took a hasty glance around before glaring at her. "I don't believe you."

Was it true? Madison honestly didn't know, and yet, *she* suddenly felt it. Hopefully it wasn't an illusion from desperation. "No instincts, huh? Wonder how you've survived so long."

"I have instincts, bitch." A dark flush colored his pale, rounded cheeks. "How do you think I escaped Detective Albertson two years ago?"

"I'm guessing dumb luck."

"No!" His mouth pinched and the hand holding the gun trembled. "I knew something was going down and I hightailed it out of there."

"Scurried away, huh? And since then you've been living in shitty little motels? Yeah, that sounds like you escaped—barely."

His eyes flared.

"Yes, Crow," she taunted, "we found your pathetic little room. We found *you*. Do you really think you made it here without being followed?"

Madison sensed more than saw that Silver had retreated while staying behind her. She was still too far from the house, but at least she was no longer paralyzed with fear.

Hallie, bless her heart, hadn't made a single sound. The poor girl had to be petrified.

In that moment, Madison reminded herself that she was her father's daughter.

Crow was a trafficker. He was likely responsible for the death of many women. He might have had a hand in the abominable treatment Hallie had suffered as a baby.

He didn't deserve justice.

He deserved a very painful death—and she wanted to be the one to deliver it.

Making certain Crow's attention stayed on her, Madison came forward another step. "Your only hope of getting out of this would be to take me as a hostage." She pretended to give that some thought. "Yes, that might do it." If she could convince him, at least he'd be away from Silver and Hallie. She'd call that a win regardless of how it lowered her odds of survival.

Though of course, she had a lot of faith in her own ability. Given any opportunity, she'd put Crow down without a second of remorse.

"Madison," Silver whispered, frantic. "Please don't."

Because it was necessary, Madison tuned out her plea and prayed that Silver would keep backing away. "What do you say, Crow? Want to try a daring getaway with me?"

"Maybe," he said, his brow scrunched as he pretended to consider it. "I'd have to shoot you first."

Well, that could prove problematic. "Shooting me would defeat the purpose, right? Who cares about a dead hostage?"

"I didn't say I'd kill you." Trying to cover his fear with brass, he asked, "Where do you want it, bitch? Shoulder, leg? Maybe in your gut?" He took aim.

"You keep calling me bitch, and I'm getting real sick and tired of it."

He ignored that. "The only way I'll be in a car with you is if you're bleeding out so you can't cause me any trouble."

"How good of a shot are you?" She started advancing again. "Because I have a serious urge to kick your ass, and wounding me is only going to piss me off more."

Crow stumbled back a step—and chaos erupted.

Too far away. Crosby knew he needed to get closer, but if Madison kept pushing Crow, he just might snap.

Through his earpiece, Cade asked, "Why are you hesitating? Take the shot."

"Take the fucking shot," Reyes agreed.

They could all hear the conversation through the security apps. Madison seemed hell-bent on bringing Crow's wrath down on her own head... And he knew it was all in an effort to give Silver and Hallie a chance.

"Shut up," Crosby whispered to her brothers, easing around a tree to find a better shot.

"What's the holdup?" Fear made Cade's voice unnaturally sharp. Of course, it was his sister in the crosshairs, so that made sense.

"Madison stepped in front of Hallie and Silver," Crosby explained in a harsh whisper. "If I shoot him, I might hit her."

"Crow's definitely going to hit her," Cade said, sounding a little sick. "He's close enough that he can't miss."

"You have to try," Reyes barked.

"No *try* to it," Crosby assured them both. "I'm going to kill the fucker." Silver had now backed up until she was almost to

Madison's car. Every time she moved, Madison did, too, making sure she had cover.

It struck Crosby that Madison was sacrificing herself, and he couldn't bear it.

"I need silence," Crosby said. The brothers' instructions, as well as their worry, was only a distraction—one he couldn't afford. He pulled away the earpiece and dropped it in his pocket.

Where the hell was Parrish? When Crosby had called him, he'd discovered that Parrish, Cade and Reyes were all together. They'd made plans on the fly while they all headed to his home.

Parrish was supposed to circle around the back and go into Crosby's house for a better view of Crow. From the garage window, he could probably take a clean shot.

Naturally, Crosby had gotten to the house first, but Cade claimed that Parrish was already closing in on foot while he and Reyes came in behind Crosby.

They were all on the scene, all close…but close enough to prevent a catastrophe?

Careful not to break a twig or in any way alert Crow to his presence, Crosby stepped from tree to tree. When he was fifteen yards away, he took aim and willed Madison to move.

Instead, she began boldly striding toward Crow. *What the hell?*

Crow didn't like that move either.

Everything happened at once.

Shouting at Madison to stop, Crow stumbled back.

Silver scooped up Hallie and took off in a high-stepping run through the snow.

Crow pivoted to shoot at her instead.

And Crosby squeezed the trigger.

At the same time, Madison gave a feral yell and leaped at him.

For a single frozen moment in time, Crosby's heart completely stalled.

Then the bullet struck Crow high on the left side of his back, propelling him forward and, thankfully, throwing off his aim.

Madison landed against him, already throwing punches. She and Crow sprawled sideways in the blood-splattered snow.

As he broke into a run, Crosby automatically noted details, like the way Crow's gun fell from his limp hand to sink in the snow, how Madison reared back in perfect form, fist cocked for yet another punishing blow...

How she then slowly lowered her hand to feel Crow's neck instead. Cursing, she scrambled off him to retrieve his weapon.

Crosby could hear Hallie wailing, saw Parrish come charging around the house. And he saw Madison, standing tall, her long hair lifted by the winter wind.

Staring at him.

Crosby was already halfway to her, his heart now thundering.

"He's dead," she called out, as if that should calm him. Of course it didn't. He needed to touch her, hold her—she shocked him by turning away and heading for Silver and Hallie.

Before she'd taken three steps, Parrish was there, grabbing her into his arms, running a hand over her hair, her cheek. He kissed her forehead, saying something low and moved to check on Crow.

When Parrish stood, and they both walked away from the downed man, Crosby knew for a fact that Crow was no longer a problem. Holstering his gun, he refocused on the rest of the scene.

Madison appeared fine, but Silver lay on her side in the snow. Hallie was next to her, loudly sobbing.

His daughter was understandably upset, but thanks to Madison, very much alive.

When Crosby reached her, he lightly touched her hair. "Hallie?"

"Daddy!" She scrambled away from Silver, arms up and cries renewed.

Lifting her, Crosby crushed her to his chest. "You're okay, baby. Shh, you're okay now." *Thanks to Madison.* "I'm here."

Her little arms held him as fiercely as she could. "It's okay now. I've got you." Finally she quieted, but Crosby could still feel her trembling.

Madison looked at him with misery in her eyes. "I'm so sorry."

With her words barely registering, Crosby pulled her close, too. Crow's vile blood stained her neck and the front of her puffer coat. "You're okay?"

She nodded fast. "I tried to protect them…"

"You *did* protect them. Thank you." He kissed her temple, words catching in his throat. *He could have lost her.* He could have lost all of them. "Silver?"

Kneeling in the snow, Parrish finished checking her over.

"I'm fine." She pushed away his hands. "I just twisted my stupid ankle, that's all."

"It's not *all*," Parrish said, his voice firm and calm as he clasped her shoulders. "Your face is almost as white as the snow."

"Because I'm *freezing*." She struggled to sit up.

"Hold on to me," Parrish insisted, already sliding his arms under her. "I'm going to carry you inside."

"Bossy, that's what you are," Silver said, but she didn't fight him.

"Grandma?" Hallie whimpered.

"We're both fine now, baby," she promised Hallie. "Madison made sure of it."

Suddenly Madison took a step away from him. Arms straight at her sides, hands fisted, she stood alone.

"Babe?"

"He must have followed me here," she whispered in an agonized confession. "I swear I was careful but…" She swallowed heavily. "This is my fault."

"No, honey, it's not."

She shook her head. "Then how did he…?"

"You're a tech whiz, Madison. You already know how."

Needing her close, he hauled her in to his side and kept her there. "Come on. I'll explain everything once I've seen to Hallie."

Before they could get too far, Reyes and Cade arrived. As if they'd already expected Crow to be dead, they merely stepped around him in a beeline for Madison. Reyes reached her first, snatching her from Crosby and crushing her close.

Cade stole her away, his touch gentler as he smoothed her hair and examined the blood on her. "Not yours?"

She shook her head. "Crow's. I was…close to him when Crosby shot."

Reyes looked back at the dead man. "I want to kill him all over again."

Even now, after everything she'd just gone through, Madison was keenly aware of his daughter. She nudged Reyes hard, then nodded at Hallie, who kept her face tucked into Crosby's neck as he repeatedly stroked her back.

Acknowledging that, Cade said, "You can all go inside. Reyes and I will handle this."

Crosby didn't ask how. He didn't care how. "Thanks." Hugging Hallie close and enfolding Madison's hand in his own, he started them moving.

Once inside, he got Hallie changed out of her snow-covered clothes, grabbed a blanket off her bed and sat on the couch with her in his lap. She continued to hiccup every so often, but she wasn't crying now.

Finally she whispered, "I was so scared, Dad."

"Me, too," Crosby said, kissing the top of her head and squeezing her again. "I've never been more afraid."

"That man sounded so mean."

"I know, but Madison didn't let him hurt you."

Madison, who'd been pacing around the living room, glanced at him with red eyes, then away again. She seemed so distant. And she still seemed pained.

He needed to get her alone, to tell her how much he loved her, but they'd have to settle everything else first.

Cade came in. "Where's Dad?"

"In Silver's room with her."

Nodding, Cade was about to walk that way when Parrish came out, carrying Silver again. He deposited her oh-so-gently on the couch with Crosby, then pulled over the padded stool and a pillow, and propped up her foot.

"I don't think anything is broken," Parrish remarked to Crosby, "but when we finish up here, we'll take her home so I can do an X-ray."

It still amazed Crosby that Parrish had so much medical equipment at his home, but given how they lived their lives, it made sense.

He noticed that Silver's clothes were different now. Huh. Apparently Parrish had helped her with that.

He glanced at her, one brow raised.

She blushed and muttered, "Hush."

Reaching over, Crosby playfully tugged on a hank of her hair—his way of letting her know he wasn't judging. "How do you feel?"

"Like an idiot." She gave a crooked smile. "Madison handled everything. She was so ferocious. My only job was to run, and I mucked that up by falling."

"Running in snow isn't easy," Madison said, still pacing.

Crosby didn't know if it was the adrenaline keeping her on her feet, guilt because she still felt she was responsible or just the antsy aftereffects of a dangerous situation.

He would have loved to have her on his other side, snuggled close, but she kept her distance.

Hallie sleepily climbed over Crosby, stretching out so that her head rested on his thigh and her feet touched Silver. After a shaky yawn, she closed her eyes.

"Poor baby," Silver crooned, stroking her hip and leg. "You just rest now, sugar. Everything is okay."

Crosby covered Hallie with the quilt again.

Now that his daughter was giving in to exhaustion, everyone lowered their voices.

Parrish went first, saying, "I can handle this if you let me."

Crosby didn't doubt it, but he asked, "Handle it how? Understand, Parrish, I'm not questioning your methods, but I assume we need to get our stories straight."

Startled by that, Madison's head came up and she stared at him.

He tried giving her a reassuring smile, but given the worry in her eyes, it didn't help. He needed to hold her. He needed to tell her how much he loved her.

Cade interrupted those turbulent thoughts. "When you called, you said Brick is the one who spilled the plans?"

Oh, shit. He'd forgotten all about Brick. During that initial call, he'd been told they'd found Crow's motel room, too.

Not that it mattered now, but they'd taken several things from the room that linked Crow to different associates. They probably would have ended up at Brick's apartment, too.

Crosby gave a quick glance at Hallie, saw she was out, and very quietly explained how he'd found Brick, what he'd uncovered, and how he'd left Brick in his apartment.

"Dead or alive?" Parrish asked softly, as if it didn't matter to him.

It definitely didn't matter to Crosby. "All I know for sure is that he isn't going anywhere." He'd bound him tight enough that, if he wasn't dead, he had to be in agony.

"So here's what we'll do." Parrish sat on the arm of the couch by Silver. "I'll call the police and let them handle most of it. We can say we got the alerts on our phones and that's why we're here. It hasn't been that long and there was a lot of confusion, so that shouldn't be a problem."

"You can say I was hysterical," Silver said, "if that'll help."

Parrish smiled at her. "No one would ever believe it."

She muttered, "It's not far from the truth."

"We won't mention Brick," Parrish decided. "Cade can check on him now, and if he's dead, they can think that Crow got to him first."

"If he's not?" Reyes asked. "Want me to—"

With a glance at Crosby, Parrish shook his head. "If he's not, just leave without anyone seeing you. We'll ensure his misdeeds are discovered and that'll take care of him. If he suffers in the meantime, it's no more than he deserves."

Silver put her hand on Parrish's thigh. "I like that plan. It sounds tidy."

Wow. Silver had gotten on board a lot faster than Crosby had. Now, however, he no longer felt like objecting to their methods. Aware of Madison watching him, Crosby said, "If you're involving the cops for me, it's not necessary."

That lifted Parrish's brows. "It's expedient." Lower, he said, "This time."

"Fine by me." Glad to have that handled, Crosby asked, "So… is Crow still in my driveway?"

"I put a tarp over him," Cade said, "then I pulled my truck in at an angle so if anyone comes by, they won't see him."

They literally had everything covered. "Thanks."

Everything except his relationship with Madison.

Parrish bent to brush a soft kiss over Silver's mouth. "Sit tight. I'm going into the kitchen to make the call."

Cade and Reyes followed him. Less than a minute later, the brothers left.

Silver rested her hand on Hallie. "Go on," she said, with a meaningful glance at Madison. "Work it out before the police get here. I'll be with the squirt in case she wakes."

Grateful for Silver's help, Crosby nodded. He carefully wedged a pillow under Hallie's head then went to Madison. Staring out the front window, she seemed very lost in thought, mired in her worry and unnecessary guilt—until he took her hand.

Her gaze lifted to his. "Crosby, I—"

"Hold that thought." Loving her, wanting her to understand, he led her down the hallway to Hallie's room and closed the door behind them.

Knowing she needed to hear it, he got right to the facts. "The man whose name was distinct is Brick. I tracked him down to his apartment and went to see him in hopes he had information about Crow."

"Crosby," she complained, "you should have had backup!"

*This.* This was one of the things that made Madison so special. Despite the gut-wrenching fear he hadn't yet shaken off, she made his heart happy just by being herself. "Brick found my address and he gave it to Crow. When you called, I had my phone on silent because I was going into his apartment."

She covered her mouth with a hand.

"You said you were careful, and I'm sure you were. I *know* you would never lead trouble to Hallie or Silver, because I know you. I know how incredibly good you are. I would never doubt you, honey."

A sob escaped her. "You're sure it wasn't me?"

"Madison." Stepping away from the door, he reached for her, tugging her against his chest, against his heart. "I went through ten different hells when I saw you standing up to Crow."

She rested her hands on his shoulders. "I had to. I know how much you love Hallie and Silver. I couldn't let anything happen to them."

"I love you, too, babe. So damn much." Seeing the surprise in her amazing hazel eyes, he cupped her face. "You can't know what it was like, hearing you taunt that bastard. I wanted to blow his brains out, but my angle was all wrong and I was afraid he'd hurt you before I could—"

She touched her fingers to his mouth. "When you didn't answer, and then Crow showed up, I thought maybe he'd hurt you…" Tears welled in her eyes and she swallowed hard. "I wanted to fall apart but I couldn't."

He smiled at that. "You're too well trained to fall apart."

"Hallie and Silver needed me."

"*I* need you. So damned much." He kissed her, a gentle touch full of choking emotion. "I don't care what Parrish does or doesn't do. I don't care about a few secrets. I love you, Madison McKenzie."

She flung her arms around his neck, and unlike his daughter, she had bruising strength. "I love you, too." Immediately she pushed back. "I'd already decided that I would never again keep anything from you. I swear it, but you have to swear, too. You can't take chances like you did today, okay? You're with us and we work as a team, so I want us to share everything."

That suited him. "Perfect."

She caught her breath. "And Hallie…will she mind me being a part of your life?" Then she frowned. "We are getting married, right?"

His heart expanded, filling him up. Biting back a smile, he said, "Madison, I love you. Will you marry me?"

More tears fell as she nodded. "Yes." She glanced around the room. "I'll have to add an addition to your house, okay? I'll need my own office and—"

Laughing, Crosby kissed her again, then used his thumbs to wipe away her tears. "I hear sirens. I think the police are here."

"You know what?" She rubbed her eyes, smudging her mascara in the process. "You can say I was the hysterical one. My acting skills are adequate, and the way I look right now, no one will doubt it."

A month later, Crosby parked outside Madison's one-car garage—which would eventually become a three-car space—and then he entered the code on the biometric lock to open her front door. He stepped inside, not surprised to see her at her desk, immersed in research, a cup of hot tea beside her.

At least Bobcat greeted him, twining around his legs and purring loudly. Lifting the cat, Crosby said, "You're looking forward to our visit with everyone, aren't you, bud?" They'd have dinner tonight with Parrish, Madison's brothers and their wives, Silver and Hallie.

As Crosby approached, Madison held up one finger, so he paused.

If he interrupted her, she wouldn't lose her place. Madison was too sharp for that, but they were gradually falling into a pattern that worked for both of them.

She was used to uninterrupted time to work, and he didn't want to intrude on that. She valued the time they had together and always wrapped up business soon after he got home.

On her small dining table, he saw the plans for the addition.

Parrish had at first announced that he'd be expanding her house as a wedding gift, but when Silver had elbowed him, he'd quickly amended that he'd love to do it—with their permission, of course.

No getting around it, Madison came from money. The house, as it was currently laid out, didn't really suit them, so Crosby had agreed. Anything to be with Madison, now and always.

He was even getting used to Parrish's generosity. It was as much a part of the man as his unrelenting pursuit to save trafficked victims.

Her house would quadruple in size, so it'd take a while, but so far they'd managed just fine.

Parrish hadn't surprised anyone when he married Silver two weeks ago. After that mess with Crow, he'd brought Silver home and there she'd stayed. Other than a week for a honeymoon to a private island in the Maldives, Silver had remained Hallie's babysitter. While Silver was gone, the brothers had gladly picked up time with Hallie, already considering her a niece though he and Madison wouldn't marry for another month.

Bernard was over the moon, doting on Hallie to the point that Crosby had to pull him aside and remind him—several times—not to spoil her so much or she'd no longer be the "delightful, adorable, charming" child that Bernard liked to praise with numerous adjectives.

He and Hallie both loved the mountain, but Hallie was especially partial to the creek cutting through Madison's property. Overall, she remained a happy and secure child, despite the occasional memory of Crow and all his threats.

After a little more typing, Madison closed her laptop and beamed at him. "Hey." Already leaving her chair, she strode toward him with that *I want you* look that he loved so much.

Crosby waited, letting her thoroughly kiss him without taking over. It took a lot of concentration on his part. For both of them, taking over came naturally.

Bobcat decided he had better things to do than be stuck between two humans, so he jumped down, walking away with his tail in the air.

"We have half an hour before dinner," Madison said. "Want to fool around?"

"Your brothers are already at your dad's. They pulled in ahead of me."

"So? They can wait on us." She started unbuttoning his shirt. "There are a lot of things we can do in thirty minutes."

He didn't need to be convinced.

On the way to the bedroom, she said, "I need you to look at the new layout for the addition. I want Hallie's bedroom to be just right. Silver was helping me with it, too. We have some awesome ideas."

Madison changed the plans often, but she'd soon lock them down. Honestly, he was fine with whatever as long as he had his loved ones together. "Okay."

He closed the bedroom door behind them and pinned Madison against it. Taking his turn at the lead, he kissed her until they were both frenzied with need.

She grabbed his hand to drag him to the bed. "My wedding dress is ready. I go for the final fitting tomorrow."

"I'm sure it'll be perfect." Because Madison was perfect.

And as he'd predicted, they were absolutely perfect...together.

★ ★ ★ ★ ★